. . . . eautifully evokes the Northern California setting. A wonderfully satisfying read." —Mary Jo Putney, *New York Times* bestselling author of *Uncommon Vows*

"Dempsey delivers another enticing read, complete with a captivating mystery and spicy, sexy romance."
—*Booklist*

"Skillfully plotted and filled with realistic detail, this fast-paced story deftly interweaves romance, murder, and ambition with issues of social status and trust."
—*Library Journal*

"Jolly good fun. . . . I look forward to reading more from this talented author. *Catch the Moon* is a suspense novel of the highest order and is a must buy."
—Romance Reviews Today

"Wow! In *Catch the Moon*, Ms. Dempsey's talent shines with vibrant characters . . . a compelling read. . . . Readers will find themselves delightfully consumed by the passion and drama, which feels so realistic, it could have come straight out of the headlines!"
—The Romance Readers Connection

continued . . .

Too Close
to the Sun

———

Diana Dempsey

AN ONYX BOOK

ONYX
Published by New American Library, a division of
Penguin Group (USA) Inc., 375 Hudson Street,
New York, New York 10014, U.S.A.
Penguin Books Ltd, 80 Strand,
London WC2R 0RL, England
Penguin Books Australia Ltd, 250 Camberwell Road,
Camberwell, Victoria 3124, Australia
Penguin Books Canada Ltd, 10 Alcorn Avenue,
Toronto, Ontario, Canada M4V 3B2
Penguin Books (NZ), cnr Airborne and Rosedale Roads,
Albany, Auckland 1310, New Zealand

Penguin Books Ltd, Registered Offices:
80 Strand, London WC2R 0RL, England

First published by Onyx, an imprint of New American Library,
a division of Penguin Group (USA) Inc.

First Printing, August 2004
10 9 8 7 6 5 4 3 2 1

To my mother, with love

Chapter 1

Gabriella DeLuca stood alone at dawn among the grapevines. To her east, beyond a stand of towering oak and eucalyptus, the sun poked above Napa's Howell Mountains, struggling to banish the fog that on this June morning hung heavy on the valley floor. Within hours the sun would win the battle, bathing the earth in hot light and pushing the grapes, olives, prunes, and walnuts toward harvest.

She stared at the small blaze she'd carefully set beside the steepest hillside vineyard owned by her employer, Suncrest Vineyards. In one hand she clutched a photo, in the other a bouquet of long-stemmed red roses Vittorio had given her, in another country, in another life. The roses were dry now with age, and brittle to the touch. Without allowing herself another thought—for already she had given this thought enough—she tossed the desiccated blooms into the fire.

Whoosh! The flames shot high into the air as they greedily consumed their prize. Gabby watched the last petals fall into ash.

"Vittorio Mantucci," she whispered, *"arrivederci. . . ."* She closed her eyes, mentally saying good-bye to the only man she had ever loved. Whom she'd also lost, unfortunately, meaning she had a grim record of oh-for-one in the *amore* department. But this morning— one year to the day after Vittorio had pulled the heart out of her chest and stomped on it with his Gucci loafer—wasn't about heartache or fury or regret. The last 364 had been about those. This morning was about ending it, for now and forever.

Gabby lowered her gaze to the glossy five-by-seven Kodachrome in her left hand. It showed her and the former love of her life in brilliant Chianti sunshine, grinning idiotically, him dark and gorgeous, her blond and unbelievably happy, vineyards and olive trees and promise all around them.

She remembered that day clearly. They had had a picnic. They had sparred over the relative merits of Tuscany versus Lombardy, never agreeing whether his family province won out over her ancestral home. They had made hasty but wonderful love on a ging-ham blanket, then thrown on their clothes so Vittorio could snap a photo, setting his self-timed camera on a tree stump before scampering back toward her to get in place on time.

It took great force of will for Gabby to toss the photo on the conflagration. But toss it she did—then she watched it disappear, edges first, till finally Vittor-io's face caved in on itself and melted away. She stared at the space where it had been for some time, then threw in a whole packet of photos. Those took longer to be annihilated but eventually they were. That seemed to prove something.

"How's that for an Italian exorcism?" she mur-mured, then had to laugh, choking on her tears, both regretting the past and not regretting it, wondering if ever again she could think the name Vittorio Mantucci without a fresh gash in her heart.

So she'd traded Italy's wine country for California's.

Tuscany for Napa Valley. Not such a bad deal, really. It was home, she loved it, her whole family was nearby. What did she have to complain about? And she'd traded Vittorio for—who? *Someone wonderful*, she told herself. Someone American like her, who she'd understand through and through. Someone who'd stick by her even if everybody in his family howled objections.

Or—and this poked a hole rather quickly in her romantic bravado—maybe she'd traded Vittorio for *nobody*.

Oh, and don't forget. She hadn't traded Vittorio. He'd traded *her*.

Gabby flopped down onto the vineyard dirt and eyed what remained of her exorcism stash. All of it reminded her in one way or another of her three years interning for the Mantucci family winery. There was the one-pound box of fettuccine, Vittorio's most admired noodle, and a box of wine. Yes, a *box* of wine, because Gabby knew there was no greater insult to her former lover's memory than wine so cheap it was packaged like fruit punch.

She was just feeding a fistful of fettuccine into the fire when she heard a shocked male voice call out behind her.

"Gabby, what in God's name are you doing?"

It was Felix Rodríguez. He walked toward her, a heavyset mustachioed man who'd been vineyard manager at Suncrest as long as her father had been winemaker, meaning ever since Gabby was five years old. Like her, Felix wore jeans and work boots. Unlike her, he sported a helmet similar to the kind coal miners wear, with a sort of flashlight mounted on the forehead. Perfect for keeping one's hands free while traipsing around vineyards. To put out rogue fires, for example.

"It's not in God's name, Felix," Gabby told him. "It's in Vittorio Mantucci's."

Felix's eyes flew open at the accursed name, which all DeLucas, and Felix by extension, were banned from uttering. Then he looked at her stash, and his eyes widened further. "You're barbecuing *spaghetti*?"

"It's pasta, Felix, pasta. And I'm not barbecuing it. I'm just burning it." She sighed. This was a hard ritual to explain.

No doubt Felix would lump in this lunacy with her other inexplicable behavior. Like renting a house far up-valley and a difficult half-mile drive up an unlit, unpaved road. It screamed isolation, and she knew what every-body thought about that. *She wants to be alone because of that Italian boy who broke her heart.* The heads shook; the tongues clucked. Sometimes it seemed that the old families like hers majored in grapes and minored in gos-sip. *She should have known he'd marry one of his own.*

She sort of had known, but had ignored it. And she rented the house not only because nobody lived nearby but also because it allowed her to live right next to vineyards. Which unlike Italian lovers had a certain predictable, soothing rhythm to them.

Felix harrumphed. "You shouldn't have come in so early today. You should be home sleeping so you're not tired for Mrs. Winsted's party tonight."

"God, Felix, don't remind me!" She tossed in the rest of the fettuccine, box and all. "Why *anyone* would celebrate Max Winsted coming back to Napa Valley is beyond me."

"She's his mother."

"All I can say is, Ava Winsted proves that a moth-er's love is blind." It wasn't often that Mrs. W drove Gabby crazy, but she was doing so now. Hand over Suncrest to that nincompoop son of hers? "What is she thinking, Felix? He's going to kill this place. He's going to come in here and run it in whatever asinine way he wants to, and he's going to kill it."

Felix wouldn't respond to that. He would keep his

mouth shut and his head down and not risk his job, which was probably what Gabby should do, too.

She shook her head. That was the problem with working for a family-owned winery. If the family ran out of sensible people to run the place, the winery got screwed. And all the employees along with it.

"Maybe Max learned something in France," Felix offered.

"All Max Winsted learned in France is how to say *'Voulez-vous coucher avec moi ce soir?'* in three different levels of politeness," she shot back. But Felix didn't seem to get the reference.

Gabby poked a stick at her fire. It was all so frustrating. And scary. She'd come back to California to pick up the threads of her life, grow into the winemaker she knew she could be, maybe even recover enough to love again. After losing Vittorio, all she wanted was the bulwark stability of her family and of Suncrest, both steady, unchanging, the Rocks of Gibraltar of her emotional landscape. The DeLucas were fine, thank God, but the winery? With Max Winsted taking over, all bets were off.

She'd known him since she was five years old and he was a newborn, and pretty much from the day he was out of diapers he was a jerk. He got more smug and self-satisfied every year. And the biggest irony of all was that even though he was born to Suncrest and the employees only worked there, sometimes she wondered if he loved it as much as they did.

He sure didn't act like it.

Gabby felt Felix's eyes on her, and she forced a smile. "I'm sorry, Felix, I shouldn't be so negative." She knew she shouldn't, since as assistant winemaker she was fairly high up in the management ranks and should be rallying the other employees around their new boss. "It's just hard for me to imagine working for that . . . *buffoon.*"

He stifled a smile, then his face turned somber. "I know you love this place, Gabby."

She stared at him. "You do, too, Felix."

He sighed, his eyes skidding to the fire. "We all do."

A wind came through, riffling the flames. Gabby shivered, half wishing the sun would halt its rise, the day would never dawn, the homecoming party would never happen. But she'd learned the hard way that wishing didn't always make things so.

Will Henley Jr. was proud of himself. He'd positively blasted through his morning ritual. Once the alarm at his San Francisco bedside blared at the usual 4:30 A.M., he did a killer half hour on the rowing machine—a holdover from his years as stroke for Dartmouth's lightweight crew—then noted the workout's intensity and duration on a chart. He scarfed a few bowls of whole-grain cereal, showered, shaved, and selected a pin-striped suit and lightly starched French-cuff dress shirt from his custom collection. Then he sped his silver BMW Z8 the two fog-bound miles from his Pacific Heights Victorian to his corner office in a refurbished redbrick warehouse on the Embarcadero.

That put him at his mahogany desk at 5:45 A.M., a ball-busting early arrival even by the type A standards of Will's employer, the private-equity firm General Pacific Group, known among the business and financial cognoscenti as GPG.

Will settled in to sip the low-fat latte he'd had sent over from the building's dining room. Strewn across his desk and file cabinets and handcrafted bookshelves were dozens of Lucite cubes, each representing a GPG deal he'd helped transact. On the north wall hung a flat-panel screen flashing real-time stock quotes from Europe and the closing numbers from Asia. Wall Street wouldn't begin trading for nearly another hour.

But Will's first task that morning had nothing to do with financial markets or private-equity transactions. He lifted his phone and punched in a Denver number he knew by heart. And even though a voice-mail announcement came on saying Rocky Mountain Flowers wasn't yet open for business, Will began speaking at the tone.

"Hey, Benny, pick up." He waited a beat. "Pick up, Benny. I know you're there. It's Will Henley in San—"

"Hello." The voice was slightly out of breath.

"Hey! Thanks, guy. Did I catch you sweeping?"

"First thing every a.m."

"Sorry to interrupt."

"No problem." Benny clattered around a bit. "So what is it this time, Will? Anniversary? Birthday?"

"Birthday. Beth's."

"Roses or tulips? Or I could do some sort of combo for you—"

"Do a combo." Will squinted, thinking. "Pink and yellow—she'd like that. And send it to the office, not the house."

Benny laughed. "So everybody can ooh and aah over it. The usual message?"

"Please." Will smiled. It was a good message. It made her happy every year.

"You got it, sir."

"Put 'em in a vase rather than a box, please, Benny, and try to deliver them early in the day, okay?" Will glanced up to see Simon LaRue, one of GPG's general partners and hence a truly big dog, hovering at his door. He waved him in. "Very good," he said into the phone. "Thanks, my man."

Will hung up while LaRue halted in front of his desk, six feet two inches of perfectly groomed American male in a three-thousand-dollar handmade suit.

Simon LaRue might be dark-haired, but he was a golden boy, just like Will, just like all the partners at GPG.

He arched a brow. "Sending some lucky lady flowers, Henley? Anybody we should know about?"

Will laughed and tried to look enigmatic. Given his perennial bachelor status, which at age thirty-four was rapidly becoming a point of fascination not only within his family but also among his conservative colleagues, he didn't want to admit the bouquet was for his sister.

Nor did he want to admit, even to himself, one tiny part of his motivation for the gift-giving. It was residual guilt, even after all these years, for leaving Beth in Denver to run Henley Sand and Gravel while he traipsed off to chase his dreams. As the elder child and only male, custom demanded that he follow his father at the helm of the family business. But Will had wanted a bigger stage. And by God, had he gotten it.

LaRue smiled. "Ah, those were the days. Bachelorhood with all its infinite pleasures and variety." His slim, manicured fingers lifted a Lucite cube from Will's desk. "So you gonna make lots of money for us in Napa Valley?"

Will settled back in his chair and linked his hands behind his head in a deliberate gesture of confidence, though that was hardly what he felt in this regard. "Don't I always?"

"There's no such thing as always." LaRue toyed with the cube, his dark eyes focused on it as if mesmerized. "There's only your last deal."

That was one of the machismo-laden truisms GPG partners bandied about. There were others, even less clever, all of which basically boiled down to *What have you done for me lately?*

Will laughed again. "Hey, my last deal made us ten times our money!"

"And is still in business. These days that's a stun-

ning success. But from you we'd expect no less."
LaRue replaced the cube, next fingering a framed
photo of Beth, posed in Aspen alongside her husband
and twin sons and an assortment of skis and poles.
All four sported matching sweaters, Will's own Scan-
dinavian coloring, and the goggle-eyed sunburn produced by a Rocky Mountain ski vacation. LaRue's
brow arched. "You ever heli-skied, Henley?"

That was the sort of testosterone-driven extreme
sport of which LaRue—and all right-minded GPG
partners—would approve. "Do you mean was I ever
dropped from a chopper in a remote location to ski
solo down a kick-ass pristine mountain with no one
around to save me if I screw up?"

LaRue nodded.

"Nope. But it sounds like good old-fashioned fun."

LaRue laughed out loud this time, the desired response. He set down the photo, focused briefly on its
mate—a fortieth-anniversary shot of Will's parents—
then sauntered back toward Will's door. "Give my
regards to the lovely Ava," he threw over his shoulder, and then he walked out.

Will sighed and unlinked his hands, then leaned forward to rest his elbows on his desk and sip his cooling
latte. The last thing Ava Winsted wanted from Will
Henley—or from anybody else at GPG—was regards.
She'd much rather the entire firm disappear from her
life and that Will Henley in particular stop making
offers to buy her winery. She'd told him no, and apparently she'd meant it.

But that didn't mean Will Henley would give up.
He hadn't gotten where he was by caving.

He grimaced, imagining the look on Ava Winsted's
Hollywood-perfect features when he crashed her son's
homecoming party. Not crash, *exactly*—he had finagled
his way in as an invitee's date—but barging in where he
wasn't wanted was not among Will's favorite activities.

Still, he had to go. As far as he could make out,
Suncrest was his key to making money in Napa Valley.
And he had to make as much money as possible to
satisfy GPG's general partners and investors, whose
lust for huge returns was unquenchable.

Will drained the last of his latte. Yup, he'd gotten
that bigger stage, all right.

Ever the actress, Ava Winsted forced herself to
laugh—to sound positively gay—as she turned from
the French doors in her casually elegant, light-filled
living room to face Jean-Luc Boursault, the Paris-
based screenwriter she hoped would pen a new, post-
Suncrest chapter for her already storied life.

"I'm just thrilled to see Max take over," she lied.
"He learned so much in France, he'll bring an entirely
new perspective to Suncrest. Who knows? He might
even end up a better vintner than his father."

Ava watched Jean-Luc decide—wisely, she thought—
not to challenge that fantastic pronouncement. From
his perch on a cheerful blue-and-yellow Cottage Victorian armchair, he merely took another sip of his Suncrest sauvignon blanc, which Ava considered a
delightful late-morning libation. Slight of build, with
thick graying hair and eyebrows that threatened to run
one into the other, Jean-Luc looked bohemian, affluent, and intellectual, much as he had when she'd met
him fifteen years before. "Porter Winsted," he offered
mildly, "is a difficult act to follow."

Who knew that better than Ava? Her late husband
had been a man among men, the scion of a Newport,
Rhode Island, family who'd built two stunning careers—
in commercial real estate and winemaking—yet remained to the end hardworking, self-effacing, and
kindhearted.

Ava's eyes misted. She turned her back on Jean-
Luc to gaze out the French doors, the familiar pan-

orama of vineyards and olive and eucalyptus trees blurring into indistinct masses of green and gold under the valley's unremitting midday sun.

She felt Jean-Luc's hand soft on the small of her back. "You miss him still."

Still. Two years only he'd been gone. Two years already he'd been gone. Sometimes when she awoke, Ava forgot Porter was dead, and reached out across the cold, cold sheets only to remember. The stab of pain that followed was astonishingly raw, every time. But it happened less and less often now, which in its own way saddened her. She was growing used to him being gone.

"I will always miss him," she told Jean-Luc. *But I'm only fifty-five and I still feel alive, most days anyway.* She turned her head to meet her friend's eyes. They crinkled with a smile, and she was reminded again that Jean-Luc was in love with her, and had been for some time, and would wait however long it took for her to be ready for him.

Which might not be that long anymore.

"Will you miss running the winery when Max takes over?" he asked her.

At that, Ava had to laugh, but didn't have to lie. "Not in the least. You know me, Jean-Luc. I am many things, but a businesswoman is not among them." She turned from the view to wipe nonexistent dust from a round glass-topped table crowded with art books and photo frames. "I had to run Suncrest after Porter died. And I think I managed it reasonably well."

"Better than that, Ava."

She shook her head. "My heart was never really in it, not the way Porter's was." She cast her mind back to those long-ago years when she'd resented Porter's passion for Suncrest. Perhaps *obsession* was a better word. No woman could be as demanding a mistress as a fledgling winery, and it had caused their young marriage real distress. But they had emerged intact, and the winery prospered beyond anything they'd imagined. "Porter loved Suncrest, Jean-Luc. It is his legacy."

But it is not mine. Hers was as an actress.

Hollywood would have no room for her, Ava knew. She might have assiduously protected her blond, Breck-girl looks, and no one could deny that she had some impressive credits to her name, but she was still a fifty-something has-been. Fortunately Europe was more willing to embrace women *d'un certain age* who still knew how to light up a screen. Screenwriters like Jean-Luc Boursault even wrote parts for them.

Ava's mouth pursed in wry humor. Imagine that.

Jean-Luc returned to his armchair, his wineglass refreshed. "And you are certain Max can manage as well as you?"

"Oh, of course." On went Ava's megawatt smile, for even with a friend as dear as Jean-Luc she felt compelled to maintain the fiction that she had complete confidence in her son. What she'd learned in Hollywood was equally true in Napa Valley: Image was everything. She would not derail what chance of success Max had by appearing to doubt him from the start. "He grew up in the wine business. And now he's had this apprenticeship in France. He's far more knowledgeable than I ever was."

And far more reckless. And far less disciplined. And so stunningly oblivious of his own limitations.

Ava sipped from her wineglass, thinking back to those painful weeks before Max had decamped to France. The whole episode was so unseemly and embarrassing, and she hated even to think of it. Such a classic tale: a young lady, the daughter of a small Sonoma vintner, who, the morning after, regretted what she had done. Started to think it hadn't been her choice at all. Ugly accusations flew from her father, and veiled threats, and Ava hastily cobbled together a face-saving solution. She wrote a massive check to charity in the family's name and packed Max off to the Haut-Médoc, claiming a long-planned apprenticeship.

She shut her eyes. Why was there so little of the father in the son? Where was Porter's caution, his thoughtfulness, his good sense? True, Max had many natural gifts. He was intelligent and nice-looking and didn't lack for confidence or charm. But there was a wildness to him that frightened Ava and made her worry for the future.

And now of course there was the problem of Suncrest. She knew that the most prudent course would be for her to continue to run the winery. Yet, though it made her feel horribly guilty to admit it, she was done with it—*done*. She'd had enough of marketing strategies and distribution agreements and P&L statements. She could play the vintner no longer. It was a role she was handed against her will, and she'd hated it from the moment she walked onstage.

Of course, the other option was to sell it to Will Henley and GPG. Suncrest would survive if she did, though probably not in a form which Porter would have approved. Those buyout firms changed businesses—she was a savvy enough businesswoman to understand that. But sometimes it was hard to believe Suncrest would fare any better in Max's hands.

Ava abruptly set down her glass. "Shall we have lunch?" she asked, and swept toward the sun-drenched terrace beyond the French doors without waiting for Jean-Luc's answer. "I've asked Mrs. Finchley to lay a table for us in the pergola."

Jean-Luc looked confused. "Didn't Max's flight land two hours ago? Shouldn't we wait for him to get here to eat?"

"Oh no, let's not." Ava knew her son well enough to know it was unwise to wait for him for anything.

* * *

Ninety miles south of his mother's intimate lunch with Jean-Luc Boursault, Maximilian Winsted was doing some entertaining of his own. He stood at the foot of a San Francisco Airport Marriott queen-size bed, puffing on a Gauloises cigarette and eyeing Ariane, Air France flight attendant, First Class. Her bodacious Parisian self was draped across the bed, the top half of her uniform strewn all over the industrial-strength blue carpet alongside her bra and pumps and pantyhose. She was giggling so much, she kept spilling her champagne on her breasts, where it ran across her nipples and only made her laugh harder. At this rate, Max didn't think it'd be a huge challenge getting off the bottom half of her uniform, too.

Vive la France!

He chuckled, took a last gulp of his own bubbly and stubbed out his cigarette. Bet Rory never got a stewardess into bed, or Bucky either, that tool. They didn't have anywhere near his charm. Sure, he'd had to spend most of the ten-hour flight from Paris standing at the rear of the cabin flirting and telling stories, but now he was going to get his reward: Ariane's full roster of private First Class favors.

I can still top them, he told himself. So what if Rory was graduating from Yale Law and Bucky was in med school? Max Winsted was still the biggest stud from Napa High, class of '97, and he was about to get even bigger.

"Viens!" The arm holding the champagne glass motioned him to come closer. Her bright red lipsticked mouth smiled, her big dark eyes teased. *"Viens jouer, Max!"*

"Let me just shut the drapes." After eighteen months of French food and French pastries and French wine, Max suspected he'd look better in the dark.

Since his shirt was already off, he sucked in his

stomach before he walked to the windows, double-thick to keep out the roar of the 101 freeway six stories below. He was surprised to see how much traffic there was even at noon. He had plenty of time, though, since the party didn't start till seven and from here the drive home took only an hour and a half.

Besides, he'd get there when he got there. The party was more for his mother than for him, anyway. The important business started the next day, when he got down to running Suncrest.

He tugged on the drape cord to shut out the view. "Your winery is how big?" Ariane was behind him all of a sudden, pushing her boobs into his back and reaching around his belly.

"Big." Max turned to face her. "More than a hundred thousand cases a year." At least that would be true once *he* was in charge.

Ariane grabbed him lower, holding his gaze. Her eyes sparkled. *"C'est très, très grand."*

He harrumphed. "No kidding."

"You're very rich?" She pronounced it *reech,* but he got the point.

"Très," he told her. *And just wait to see how much richer I'll be this time next year.*

Oh, he had plans. Big plans. Suncrest would really be on the map once Max Winsted was at the helm. No more treading water like it had been under his mother's management. Of course, what else could you expect from her? She didn't have a practical bone in her body. And while his father had been an excellent businessman in his day, he'd been old-style. Too cautious. Too plodding.

"What types of wine"—Ariane was kissing his neck now, her left hand still working its magic south of the equator—"do you make?"

"You know what?" He wasn't interested in wine talk at the moment. "Let's go over there."

He pushed her back toward the bed, where she didn't need one single *s'il vous plaît, mademoiselle* to whip off her skirt and lean back giggling against the pillows, five feet six inches of living, breathing, willing French female. Who, thanks to Max Winsted, was about to have the best time of her entire life.

Chapter 2

The sun was setting as Max Winsted's homecoming party began. Gabby took up a position on the pebbled path that curved in front of Suncrest's rustic sandstone winery building and did her best to play hostess. She'd never been too keen on the social aspects of the wine business, but having to pretend to be enthusiastic— when secretly dying inside—was a new exercise in painful.

"Rosemary, Joel, wonderful to see you." She grasped the hands of the newest arrivals and puckered up to repeat the air kisses she'd spent the last half hour producing.

"You must be so pleased Max is taking over." Rosemary Jepson, with her husband a longtime Calistoga vintner, was a rail-thin bottle-blonde who rivaled Ava Winsted for Most Glamorous in the Over Fifty category. "If he's half the vintner his father was, he'll really give us a run for our money."

Not much chance of that, Gabby thought, but she forced a smile and tossed out her line for the evening. "It certainly marks a new era for Suncrest. We're so happy you can celebrate it with us."

"Where is the guest of honor, anyway?" Rosemary

Jepson's blue eyes pierced the crowd with the laser focus of a party expert. "I don't see him."

"He got caught up in a meeting in the city that ran long." Gabby hated to lie, but that was the excuse Mrs. W had ordered her to deliver, as none of them actually knew where Max was. "Something important came up suddenly, and Mrs. Winsted asked Max to handle it. We expect him to arrive shortly."

The older woman's brows arched, as if she were deeply impressed. "How very ambitious of him," she purred, "to handle important business his very first day back." Then she abandoned Gabby to follow her husband into the crush of the party.

The chattery, wine-sipping throng was grouped around two soaring date palms, their trunks wrapped for the occasion with tiny white lights. Between them hung a banner spelling out BIENVENU, MAX! in red, white, and blue, colors as patriotic in France as they were in America. To the west, the sun hung low over the Mayacamas Mountains, burnishing the sandstone winery a honey gold and kissing the dark green canopy of the grapevines that covered the gentle slope down to the road. The Winsted residence—an exquisite contemporary home complete with pool and pergola—lay slightly east of the winery proper, separated by grapevines and gardens and olive trees. Banks of fog huddled in the distance, as if politely holding back their arrival until the guests repaired inside for dinner.

Gabby watched Ava Winsted flutter among her guests and concluded she must have been—must *still* be—a very good actress. She appeared completely unruffled despite the fact that her son, her guest of honor, the whole raison d'être of this party, had failed to show up. She was a vision in white silk, her peroxide blond hair pulled tight into a chignon and a Queen of England diamond necklace at her throat. She wove expertly in and out of groups, never spending more than a few minutes with anyone yet managing to leave everyone charmed and entertained and not in the least slighted. Like many wives of Napa vintners, Ava Winsted had been Suncrest's "cultural affairs" director, until that role of social secretary and PR head became more work than she wanted. Porter Winsted had serious trouble filling the post, for the simple fact that no one was as good at it as his wife.

Gabby sighed. She'd envisioned such a role for herself in years past, when she dreamed of being Signora Mantucci. Maybe sheer love for Vittorio would have made her more of a social animal. As it was, she much preferred the solitary pursuits of winemaking. Nurturing the fruit, tracking its progress in the oak, blending the varietals just so, all to help her father create wines they could both be proud of. Wines that carried the Suncrest label but that privately she felt were as much her family's creations as those of the Winsted's.

Her father sidled up alongside her. "You look wonderful tonight, sweetie."

She did like the slinky violet sheath she'd bought in San Francisco for the occasion, though neither it nor the matching pashmina did much to ward off the evening's chill. "So do you, Daddy." She reached up to tweak his bow tie, though it was ramrod straight. With his deeply tanned skin and thatch of dark hair streaked with gray, Cosimo DeLuca was a handsome man. Like his oldest daughter, he preferred kneeling among the grapevines to hobnobbing with the valley's smart set. But he cleaned up beautifully, and in a tux looked positively debonair.

"Any sign of the prodigal son yet?" he asked.

"Not a one. Maybe he decided to stay in France." *That would be a blessing,* she added silently, watching her father drain his sauvignon blanc. She knew he wished Max Winsted would fall off the face of the earth even more than she did, though unlike his daughter, he was too well-mannered ever to say it.

She shut her eyes. Twenty-five years her father had worked at Suncrest. *Twenty-five years.* His heart was breaking, Gabby knew. He was so stressed about Max taking over. She knew that some days he feared he'd lose his job, and others he worried that he'd hate it under Max's stewardship. But what could she do about it? What could any of them do?

She nudged him gently. "Don't worry, Daddy. It'll be fine even when Max takes over."

Her words, which she couldn't even make herself believe, hung between them. Her father was silent, then turned to her, his eyes devoid of their usual sparkle. "You should get a job at another winery, Gabby. You know enough now to be head winemaker. You shouldn't be assisting me anymore, and you shouldn't stay here with Max taking over."

"No." The idea made her heart pound, like a horror about to happen. Abandon Suncrest? Abandon her father? That's not why she'd come home to California. "I'm not going anywhere. We're going to make it work, even with Max coming. Besides . . ."

She stopped. She shouldn't say, especially here and now, what she secretly hoped for. That if Max managed to show up, he'd tire fast of the hard work of running the winery. That he'd step aside for someone else to take over. Her father, for example. Then she *could* become head winemaker. Maybe her sister Camella, the middle of the three DeLuca girls, could get promoted from the reception desk. Suncrest would run like a dream.

And it would be almost as if the DeLucas owned the place.

Gabby watched Camella approach bearing a lipstick-stained wineglass. Where Gabby had inherited her mother's Northern Italian blond hair and hazel eyes, Cam got the more stereotypical olive skin and black eyes and hair. With her plump figure, round face, and forever unruly dark locks, she looked as if she'd been plucked from an Italian village. That night she wore a bright red peasant-style dress that only heightened the effect.

She arranged herself next to Gabby, narrowing her eyes at the crowd. "There isn't a single good one here," she whispered.

"There never is," Gabby whispered back, having already arrived at the same grim conclusion.

She downed the rest of her wine. Dress up, make up, do your hair, go to a party—sometimes she wondered why she even bothered. Of course, tonight's bash was work, but every party seemed to remind her of the sad truth she didn't let herself dwell upon too often. That the valley might be great for growing grapes, but it didn't produce much in the way of desirable single men.

Will picked up his date to the Suncrest party at the lush St. Helena estate her family called home. The forty-acre property boasted vineyards—naturally—an enormous Mission-style winery, and a matching ten-thousand-square-foot home complete with red-tile roof and campanile. It went well with the other manses in the neighborhood, a faux French château here, a Victorian pile there.

Stella Monaco pulled open her massive oak front door even before Will's convertible rolled to a halt on the sweep of graveled driveway, a brunette nymph in a turquoise halter sundress that Will guessed retailed for a thousand dollars at Neiman Marcus. She bounded toward the car like a puppy, hair flowing, feet bare, strappy sandals clutched in her hand. She was a free and daring spirit thanks to the enormous celebrity and wealth her father had accrued as an international hotelier. He'd become a vintner, of course, the mega-successful man's top choice for second career.

She threw herself into the passenger seat and then turned to smile at Will. She was lovely, and stylish enough to understand the great attraction—to men at least—of minimal fuss over hair and makeup.

He smiled back at her. "Hope I haven't kept you waiting."

"No." She tossed her sandals in the footwell. "My parents left already, though, so we'll meet them there."

He put the car in gear, "On our way, then," and after a few turns got back on Highway 29, the main artery—all of two lanes in most stretches—that bisected the valley.

Once he was truly on his way to Suncrest, Will began to wish the drive were longer. Not only did he dread Ava Winsted's first glimpse of him at her party—opportunistic financier, interloper, uninvited guest, she'd think all of that and more—he wasn't clear on how he was going to make money for GPG in the wine business. It was easier said than done. Many of these wineries—gorgeous as they were—ranged from breakeven to money pit. Suncrest had real possibilities, though, because it was a well-respected brand whose operations could be ramped up and made much more profitable.

But that was true only if the Winsteds sold to GPG. Ava had made it clear she'd have none of it. She had to "preserve Porter's legacy," she told him, and he hadn't come close to convincing her that selling to GPG would achieve that goal. Now that her son was coming into the picture, it was Will's job to find out if he might be more amenable.

Fortunately, Will didn't need to force conversation with Stella, whose chatter flowed as freely as her dress.

He'd met her weeks before at the annual Napa Valley Wine Auction, where a three-liter bottle of her father's first vintage took top honors by fetching sixteen thousand dollars for charity. She was entertaining and attractive but, he was discovering, a bit scattered. For example, there was her current indecision over career options, which ran the widest gamut he'd ever heard of. Should she go to Oxford, she wondered, like Chelsea Clinton had? Or become a movie director like Sofia Coppola? Or maybe launch a clothing line like Stella McCartney?

She sounded genuinely perplexed. "But that might be too confusing because my name is Stella, too?"

"Probably would be," Will allowed, figuring this was the sort of conundrum faced by a modern-day American princess. He slowed to a crawl when they hit the stretch of 29 that was St. Helena's Main Street, on this June evening jammed with tourists trying to park near the tony eateries where they had reservations for dinner.

Stella gazed out the window, twisting an auburn lock around her index finger. Round and round and round. "My father says he'll support whatever I do."

That's handy, Will thought, but merely made an approving noise and nosed his car around a parallel-parking Jeep which clearly belonged to a local. LIFE IS A CABERNET declared its license-plate frame, and for the valley's moneyed residents, it certainly was.

Stella twisted toward him suddenly. "Do you want to buy my dad's winery?"

That question was a surprise. "Hadn't really thought about it," he said carefully. In truth, he hadn't. Robert Monaco was a canny businessman and already ran his operation at full throttle. That wasn't what GPG was looking for.

"Because he won't sell, you know." Stella turned

back toward the passenger-side window. "He's had offers, but he always says no. Gallo offered him forty-five million."

Will accelerated as they cleared St. Helena's downtown. "That's a nice chunk of change."

Stella shrugged, clearly unimpressed by eight-digit numbers. "Maybe. But what would he do if he sold?" She sounded baffled again. "He's sick of owning hotels. Plus he loves the lifestyle here. So does my mom. It's so much more"—she groped for the word—"*natural.*"

That was it in a nutshell for the newbie vintners whose previous lives had had nothing to do with wine-making. Will made a left onto Zinfandel Lane, a narrow, tree-lined road that would shoot them to the Silverado Trail and Suncrest, confident he understood men like Robert Monaco.

They'd already done the grubby, unglamorous work of amassing piles of money. They'd done it in hotels and commercial real estate and oil and technology and consulting. Now they wanted the *natural* work of wine-making, living among rolling vineyards near towns with romantic names like Rutherford and Yountville. And if they lost money, as so many did, so what? There was more where that came from.

Another turn and they were on the Trail, heading south. Valuable as Napa Valley farmland was—in fact, the most valuable in the nation—this so-called Rutherford Bench was the primest cut of all. Somehow the mix of soil, rainfall, fog, and sunshine combined to create a veritable Eden for grape-growing, particularly of the cabernet sauvignon variety for which the valley was most famous.

And in the midst of those blessed acres lay Suncrest. Will drove through its stately bronze gates onto the long, imposing drive that led to the winery, a pile of roughhewn wheat-colored stones shimmering in the sun's waning light. Stella reached down into the foot-well to strap up her sandals.

"Napa is getting a little small-town for me," she declared, which seemed to Will an odd observation when here they were in one of the most affluent, glamorous, self-indulgent spots the world had to offer. He rolled the car to a stop behind another guest's navy Mercedes sedan, a white-jacketed valet scampering toward him to relieve him of the burden of parking.

Stella, now shod, stepped out of the car and tossed her auburn hair over her shoulder. "I'm ready for L.A. or New York or London," she announced, and apparently so dazzled the valet that he promptly dropped Will's car keys in the dust. She giggled and sashayed toward the party, clearly conscious of both men's attention and ready to have a good time, small town or not.

Will followed, grimly determined to mimic her enthusiasm.

Ava was just wondering how to escape a particularly long-winded foursome—all of whom were making good use of the open bar—when she felt a gentle touch on her left arm. Her savior was Mrs. Finchley, her long-time English housekeeper, who wore a meaningful expression in her light blue eyes.

"Excuse me," Ava murmured, and let herself be led to the edge of the festivities. She and Mrs. Finchley leaned their heads in close.

"It's Maximilian, madam," the older woman said.

Before she caught herself, Ava's hand flew to her throat in a rush of relief. But all she said was, "Good, he's arrived. He's changing?"

"No, actually—" The older woman paused, her expression pained. "He's not here just yet. He phoned to say he's on his way."

Ava was silent for a moment, conscious of trying very hard not to become very angry. "On his way from where, exactly?"

"From a hotel near the airport."

The revelation hit Ava like a slap. Knowing her son, it was pointless wondering why Max was in such a place, and whether he had been for the entire nine hours since his flight landed, and why he'd waited until now to inform his mother that he would be seriously late for the gala party she was throwing in his honor. He was simply doing what he wanted to do—what else was new?—without thinking about anybody else.

It was quite clear that after eighteen months of supposed apprenticeship in France, her son was as cavalier and self-absorbed as ever.

She gathered herself, acutely conscious of the vulturelike eyes of her guests and of the much more kind and sympathetic gaze of Mrs. Finchley. Ava knew her housekeeper truly felt for her employer being burdened with such an incorrigible son. Whom she still loved, and always would. A fact Ava feared Max made good use of.

She fixed her eyes on Mrs. Finchley. "How soon did he say he would get here?"

"About an hour and a half, madam."

Meaning he had just left that damned airport hotel. Fine. "I don't care to hold dinner," Ava said.

"Very good."

Ava consulted the diamond-encircled face of her watch. "Let's serve as planned in fifteen minutes." Max would miss his own welcome-home meal. Fine. He could stop at McDonald's or some such place on the drive up. "Please rearrange the seating cards so Max is not at my left hand." Where, she did not spell it out, his absence would be screamingly obvious throughout the entire five-course meal.

"Very good, madam," and Mrs. Finchley moved off

to make everything right, the stalwart, capable soul that she had always been.

Jean-Luc materialized at Ava's side. He wore his tuxedo Hollywood-style, his dress shirt open at the neck and not a stud or cummerbund in sight. "Max has arrived?"

Ava forced a smile onto her face. "Not yet. His meeting in the city ran long," she heard herself say, "and he lost track of the time." Jean-Luc's eyebrows shot up as if to say *Max lost track of nine hours?* but Ava scanned the crowd behind him for a distraction and just kept talking. "See that pretty brunette? Stella Monaco. Let's go say hello," and she took hold of Jean-Luc's arm to steer him toward the new arrival.

Then she saw the man in Stella's wake and stopped cold.

"Ava, what is it?" Jean-Luc laid a hand over Ava's fingers, which, she realized, were clenching his arm.

I cannot believe that man had the gall to come here tonight. Though no one would believe him an interloper. Will Henley looked more CEO than pariah. In black tie, with his blond all-American looks, he looked like a top get for any A-list party.

But Ava knew better. He was persona non grata here. He was the one celebrant at this fete who wanted Maximilian Winsted *not* to inherit his legacy but to have it sold out from underneath him. So that he and his partners could profit from Porter's decades of hard work.

How many times had she told him that no, she would not sell? Two? Three? Yet here he was, yet again, and with Stella Monaco—of all people!—whom clearly he had used to gain entrée. This posed a serious danger, for the last thing Ava wanted was for this gossipy young girl to spread the rumor that Suncrest was on the block. It didn't matter that it wasn't true; any hint that Ava would consider selling just as Max was taking over would undermine him from the first.

A mother's love, she thought. *It's almost idiotic.* Despite how dismissive her son was of her that night, she was still hell-bent on shoring him up. Of course, she wanted him to succeed for her own reasons, as well—to free her to begin a new life, away from the burden of the winery.

"Is it him?" Apparently Jean-Luc had followed the line of Ava's eyes, for now he was staring at Will Henley, too. "Should I ask him to leave?"

Ava merely shook her head and resumed walking, her equilibrium partly restored as a plan brewed in her mind. Jean-Luc fell into step beside her.

If Will Henley wanted to sniff around Max to see what he could find out about, let him sniff away. It wouldn't do him a damn bit of good anyway, unless his nostrils could pick up a scent from sixty miles downwind.

Ava released Jean-Luc and held out both hands to Stella. "You look lovely, dear," she murmured, which prompted the obligatory round of air kisses and returned compliments. Maintaining her brilliant smile, Ava extended her right hand to Will. "And who is your handsome friend?"

The girl's eyes danced. Ava knew there were few bigger feathers in a twenty-year-old female's cap than dating a good-looking, wealthy man ten years her senior. "Ava, this is Will Henley, from San Francisco. And Will, this is Ava Winsted, the—"

"Esteemed owner of Suncrest," Will cut in. He grasped her hand. "Congratulations on your son completing his apprenticeship in France. You must be very proud."

Ava eyed this dashing interloper and found herself admiring him. To please her, he would maintain the pretense that they didn't know one another. Surely he didn't want to rile her up any more than he already had by crashing her party. After all, he wanted her to sell him her winery.

"I am very proud," she told him, each word a stone forced between her smiling lips. Then she spied Gabby DeLuca a few yards away and decided she would suit Ava's scheme just fine. "May I borrow your Mr. Henley?" she asked Stella sweetly, a rhetorical question if ever there was one, because she immediately took hold of Will's arm and steered him away from Stella before the younger woman could utter a word.

"Gabby," Ava said, and deposited Will Henley in front of her, "I'd like you to meet this interesting fellow. I'm sure you'll enjoy chatting with him." Then she moved off to locate Mrs. Finchley, her mind on damage control. Her first task was to redo the seating arrangements at dinner so that Mr. Will Henley would find himself quite surrounded by loyal Suncrest employees and hence properly contained.

This guy is not from the valley, Gabby thought, her breath catching in her throat. *There is no way he could live here without me noticing.*

He towered over her, six feet who-knew-how-many inches of blond, broad-shouldered American male. He had the look of success about him, and it wasn't just from the tux. It was the fighter-pilot square jaw, the nononsense directness of the gaze, the confidence of the smile, the powerful aura he emanated without saying a word.

She found her voice and extended her hand. "Gabby DeLuca."

"Will Henley." His fingers closed around hers, his hand big and warm and enveloping. All too soon he released her and looked off into the distance, squinting his blue, blue eyes, which produced a fan of tiny lines on his lightly tanned skin. "DeLuca. Isn't Cosimo DeLuca the winemaker here?"

"That's my father." Who had disappeared in the last few seconds, and taken Cam with him. "Are you in the wine business?"

He skated past that. "Wasn't he just named one of the top five Napa winemakers by the *Chronicle*?"

"He was! But he should've been number one on the list."

"Spoken like a loyal daughter."

"No, I just know good winemaking when I see it."

He chuckled. "You must see it pretty often here in Napa Valley."

"Well, I see it in my father." She trotted out a rusty old flirtatious glance then, and it seemed to still work, because something in Will Henley's keen gaze told her she had his full attention. "And I see it in me."

He laughed out loud. "Plenty of self-confidence you've got there. I like it! And where do you make your wine?"

"Here." *I like it!* rattled in her brain. "I'm my father's assistant."

"Ah. I'm a fan of Suncrest wines myself. So you *are* good at what you do," and he cocked his head as he looked at her, as if he were trying to puzzle something out.

They lapsed into silence while the party pulsed on around them. *Now what?* She was flustered. She used to be a good flirt—a natural, in fact. Her parents laughed to this day over the smiles and winks and sideways glances she'd perfected by age four. They got pretty worried about it when she hit fourteen. But now she was so out of practice, she could barely get past the introductions.

At least not with this heartthrob. Out of the social black hole of Max's homecoming fete—where she knew everyone and everyone knew her and there wasn't a romantic possibility in the bunch—had emerged this guy, a rare specimen indeed. Almost the last of a dying breed, as far as she could tell. Will Henley was the diametric opposite of grunge, which was so popular among the women she knew but which had never appealed to her much. This guy looked traditional in the best, most gracious all-American way—like Cary Grant come back to life blond and young.

But not *too* young. That was another good thing, too.

"So you read the *Chronicle*," she said. "Does that mean you live in San Francisco?"

"Pacific Heights."

"Do you work in the city?"

"I do."

Silence. She watched his gaze skitter away. This might be the first guy she'd ever met who didn't want to talk about his job. Could he be unemployed? That didn't seem possible. Yet lots of brainiac tech types in the city were out of jobs since the Internet bubble burst. "Do you work for the CIA or something? You don't seem to like to talk about it."

He shook his head, smiling. "Nothing so mysterious. Or glamorous. I'm in finance."

"What area of finance?"

"Investments. So tell me, Gabby," and his eyes came back to her face, "do you ever give personal wine-country tours?"

She felt a little flutter of excitement. *Is he asking what I think he's asking?* "Do you mean, for example, to men who work in investments and live in Pacific Heights?"

"I have to say that's a category I'm particularly interested in."

"Well, you know, it's funny you should ask. Because

just this morning I was thinking of having business cards printed up that say 'Gabby DeLuca, winemaker and part-time investment-guy tour guide.' "

He threw back his head and laughed. She watched him, grinning herself. Maybe the exorcism that morning had actually worked, because here she was with the incipient hots for a man other than Vittorio. Will didn't even *look* like Vittorio, which seemed a victory of sorts, too. But he did have that same straightforward quality, like he was somebody with backbone.

Of course, look at all the backbone Vittorio had. He went spineless when his parents told him to dump me for the vintner's daughter next door.

A waiter swept past with a tray full of fresh wineglasses. Will swiped two, handed one to Gabby, and raised his as if in toast. "To your tour business," he said, "and its first, very lucky, customer."

They touched their glasses together, their gazes locked. Gabby sipped, a giddy feeling washing over her, as if her sauvignon blanc were really sparkling wine and its bubbles were flooding her veins with good feeling. Then the bubbles crashed together and exploded, for who sashayed up and wrapped her arms around Will Henley's waist but that party-girl bombshell, Stella Monaco.

"Having a good time chatting up the cellar workers?" she asked him. Then she turned to Gabby, her lips smiling but her eyes stone cold. "Thanks so much, Gabby, for keeping my date amused."

Ouch. But then Will Henley made Gabby like him even more than she already did.

"Yes, thank you, Gabby." He gave her a smile that somehow made the girl clinging to his waist fade right into the background. "You can be sure I'll book that tour."

When Gabby tried later to reconstruct the rest of the evening, she found that she could summon few of

the details. Stella succeeded in spiriting Will away, but
not for long; because once all the guests were funneled
into dinner, Gabby noticed that he had been seated
between her father and Cam, and Stella was way at
the other end of the room, squeezed between Felix
Rodríguez and Bucky Forrester, a high-school friend
of Max's.

Who was still nowhere to be seen. The second great
astonishment of the evening.

Gabby thought that Ava—always an inventive
hostess—had been truly inspired when she decided to
serve dinner in the tiny building that housed the
French oak barrels where Suncrest's famed vintages of
cabernet sauvignon were aged. Built in the nineteenth
century of the same hand-cut sandstone as the land-
mark winery building, it nestled in its shadow—a cozy
refuge that smelled of old wood and fermenting wine
and the dust of two centuries. The forty diners found
themselves seated at a long, narrow table draped with
white Egyptian cotton, wine barrels stacked ceiling-
high all around them. Flickering candlelight from eight
wrought-iron candelabra provided the room's only illumination, while baskets of white, yellow, and pink
roses were a gorgeous complement to Ava's delicate
Worcester china and glittering Venetian crystal. Three
violinists at one end of the room sprang into musical
action once everyone was seated, a welcome distraction for those awkward silences that invariably descended from time to time during a five-course meal.

But nothing could disturb Gabby that night—not
the wine writer to her left she usually found too snob-
bish for words, or Stella's father Robert Monaco to
her right, who didn't bother to look in her direction
the entire evening.

What made the evening magic was Will Henley
seated half a table away. Will Henley catching her eye,
or raising his wineglass to her at a toast. Her keen

awareness that he was watching her during those moments when she refrained from watching him.

They arrived at dessert. White-jacketed waiters laid down plates of plum clafouti adorned with little puffs of whipped cream, and poured coffee, tea, grappa, and port. Mrs. W rose to speak, and all at once Gabby was reminded of the extraordinary fact that Max had never shown up to his own homecoming gala—*he'd never shown up!*—and the evening was almost over.

Yet Ava Winsted stood at the head of the long table looking unperturbed, smiling, winking at this guest and then that. Gabby realized anew that this was a woman with incredible self-possession. She appeared so at ease, so composed—yet had to be churning inside. What public humiliation her son heaped on her, and on Suncrest. What disrespect.

When the room had fallen silent, she spoke. "I am so very proud of my son this evening. I certainly wish he were here with us, but when I asked him yesterday, while he was still in France, to handle an important meeting in San Francisco this afternoon, he didn't hesitate for a second. He wanted to plunge right into business. He is truly his father's son."

Applause followed that line, and Gabby dutifully clapped along. She tried to catch her father's eye down the long table, but he had his head bent and was mopping his forehead with a handkerchief. Gabby's heart ached for him. At least she had Will Henley to distract her from the sickening truth that Max Winsted, no-show or not, was taking over Suncrest. Her father had nothing else to focus on. On either side of him sat Will and Camella, both of whom had their gazes trained on their hostess.

"When tomorrow dawns," Mrs. W continued, "Max will be here at Suncrest, bursting with ideas and excitement. I only wish his father were here to witness his enthusiasm, for it was Porter's fondest hope that his son take over the winery and continue to lavish it with the loving care that has made it the success we enjoy tonight."

Clapping followed that line, too, along with a few *bravos,* and a man far down the table to Gabby's right called out a hearty *Hear! Hear!* Gabby was just about to raise her grappa to her lips for a sustaining sip when all of a sudden she glimpsed a movement far up and across the table, not far from where Mrs. W stood. Then, almost disbelieving, she realized that the motion had come from her father, who was half rising from his chair with a stricken look on his face and both hands clutching his chest.

Then he toppled to the floor, slamming into Will Henley on the way down.

She heard a woman cry *"My God!"* then understood with some shock that the words had erupted from her own mouth. She was out of her chair then—in fact, she realized it had toppled backwards behind her—and was scrambling around the table toward her father. She was vaguely aware of men and women rising to their feet, their voices raised in confusion. Thunder pounded in her own ears and two childish syllables beat in her head. *Daddy. Daddy.*

He was on the ground, panting for breath, Will crouched next to him, trying to loosen the collar of his dress shirt, leaning his ear close to her father's chest.

"Does anybody have an aspirin?" he yelled out. "You . . ." and he pointed to a man next to him. "Call 911 and run down to the gate to tell the paramedics where to come."

Somebody found an aspirin, somebody else a glass of water. Motion, bustle—to Gabby all of it was a blur. She saw only one thing in that horrible pandemonium: her father on the stone cold cellar floor, a grotesquely weak reflection of the man she'd always known him to be.

Chapter 3

Will stood outside the emergency room of St. Helena Hospital with Gabby and her mother and sisters knotted all around him. They made an incongruous group, he knew, he and Gabby and Cam in black tie and cocktail dresses, clearly ripped from a gala and thrust into this antiseptic, fluorescent-lit corridor where people hungered for news they often didn't really want to hear.

Will feared this news wouldn't be good. When Cosimo DeLuca had been strapped onto the gurney and rolled toward the ambulance, its strobe lights painting red stripes on his face, he had looked ravaged, a shadow of the hale and tanned figure he'd been earlier in the evening.

Now, an hour later, Will tried to keep his own manner quietly confident, tried not to let his worry channel into Gabby's makeup-smudged, fearful eyes. But it was difficult. Her gaze seemed to bore into him, to demand answers to questions he hoped she wouldn't actually ask. *How is he doing? Why is it taking so long to hear something?* And, when her eyes were most frightened, *Is he still alive?*

Oh, those eyes. Hazel, long-lashed, wide—very wide.

Eyes a man could drown in. Set in a lovely tanned face. Her hair was wavy and the color of wheat, and was tied in a knot that was getting looser every hour.

He tore his eyes away from her, with some effort. He was about to give her body an even more in-depth analysis than he'd already conducted, and this was hardly the appropriate hour for such a perusal. He forced himself to stare instead at the swinging doors of the ER, and eventually he saw a doctor emerge.

He was black and maybe thirty—a little young for comfort in a situation like this one—but fast moving and clear eyed and somehow reassuring. He spied their little group even before Will could signal him, as though in residency he'd trained in how to match patient and family with no wasted motion. He held out his hand to Will. "Dr. John Hearst. Are you the son-in-law?"

The words tripped off Will's tongue. "Friend of the family."

Dr. Hearst switched his gaze to Sofia DeLuca, a small, plump brunette who from the moment she arrived at the hospital had looked every frightened inch the wife of the patient. "Mr. DeLuca is having a large heart attack," he told her, and Will's own heart clenched as he watched Gabby's face crumple and her arm tighten around her mother's shoulders. "We're doing everything we can to stabilize him."

Gabby spoke, her voice almost inaudible under the sudden blare of the PA system calling some other hapless family member to the nurse's station. "Is he going to make it?"

The doctor seemed to dodge that. "Everything we know about a heart attack like this one tells us that his best chance of survival is if we can get the blocked artery in his heart open. What we'd like to do is give him phrombolitic therapy."

"What is that?" Gabby asked.

"Essentially it's a clot-buster drug. We would ad-

minister it through an IV." The doctor turned again
to Sofia DeLuca. "Let me add that normally we would
seek the patient's consent. But though your husband
is conscious, Mrs. DeLuca, he's groggy, and I'm not
convinced that he's competent right now to make an
informed decision."

"So you need my mother to give that consent,"
Gabby said. "Is that right?"

Dr. Hearst nodded. "Yes, it is."

This part of the drama Will understood. This was
the cold, hard, make-a-tough-decision part. "What are
the risks of this therapy?" he asked.

"It's a powerful medication. There are potentially
serious side effects." Dr. Hearst turned his gaze to
Gabby. "For example, serious internal bleeding. A
fatal bleeding. Or a bleeding stroke."

In other words, Will thought, *he could die.*

Clearly Gabby also understood the implications. She
blanched, though she made no move and no sound.
Her mother whimpered the word *stroke* and shuddered. One of the two sisters—Will had forgotten her
name—started crying in earnest, sobbing and choking
and clutching her mother's hand.

"We want to administer the drug sooner rather than
later," the doctor added.

So there was time pressure, too. Of course. Emergencies didn't allow the luxury of considering life-and-
death questions from every angle.

Will watched Gabby murmur to her mother and sisters, the four of them a tableau of a family in trauma.
He couldn't make out her words, but it was obvious
that she was discussing the drug. Or *trying* to discuss
it, because it was just as obvious that no one else was
saying a thing. Her mother and sisters all seemed in
too much of a state to weigh in.

*She's going to have to push her mom to give the go-
ahead*, he realized, and his heart went out to her. She

would have to take responsibility for the decision that could save, or end, her father's life.

He could see the weight of that burden etched on her face. He shook his head, his worry now tinged with frustration. He'd come to the hospital to help this woman and her father, yet was stymied at her moment of greatest need. It would be presumptuous of him, essentially a stranger here, to declare what the right course of action was, though it seemed fairly clear. Then again, right and wrong were easy for him in this situation, he knew. It wasn't his father behind those swinging doors.

"Dr. Hearst, what are the risks if you don't give Mr. DeLuca the drug?" he asked.

The answer was immediate. "The risks of doing nothing are much greater. At best Mr. DeLuca will be left with a severely weakened heart. At worst we won't be able to stabilize him at all."

"And if his heart is weakened," Will said, "there's a greater danger of more of these episodes down the road?"

"Absolutely. And the next episode may be even more serious than this one."

In other words, the next heart attack might well kill him. If this one doesn't.

Gabby bent her head toward her mother. "Mom?"

Silence. No one spoke. No other DeLuca seemed to have what it took to say yes or no.

"Mom, we've got to do this," Gabby said. "You've got to give the doctor your consent. I really think it's the right thing to do."

Finally, her mother gave a barely perceptible nod. That was all it took. "We'll know more within the hour," Dr. Hearst said, and he went back the way he had come, the emergency room's swinging doors slapping back and forth behind him.

Good for you, Gabby, Will thought. He watched

her lead her mother to a wooden bench against the wall, beneath a poster with pastel flowers that tried to strike a cheerful note in this otherwise grim setting. The sisters followed, then sat on either side of their mother and leaned in close. It looked as if they were setting up a human cordon around her, though the sad fact was that the danger they all feared couldn't be guarded against. It would appear silently, suddenly, as a shadow in Dr. Hearst's eyes, or in a grim set of his mouth, when next he emerged from the ER to hunt down the DeLuca family.

Gabby broke away from her family and approached him, high heels clicking on the highly polished linoleum floor. Funny how affecting he found this woman. And it wasn't just the sex appeal. In this short while, he felt he'd learned a fair amount about her character. And found it damned impressive.

She halted in front of him. "I really appreciate your coming to the hospital and staying all this time, Will, but you should go. It's getting so late, and we don't know how long it'll be before we hear something more. And besides . . ." She stopped.

Will finished her sentence. "You feel weird about my being here when I really don't know your family."

She seemed relieved that he'd gone ahead and said it. "I feel like I'm imposing."

"You're not imposing. I'm here because I want to be." He realized he must truly be exhausted, because he was saying what popped into his head without thinking it through first. He tried another tack. "I just want to help if I can." *Even though you don't know me from Adam. Even though we just met.* "I don't know, call me a Boy Scout."

That brought a smile, wan and weak but a smile nonetheless. "Don't you have to work tomorrow?"

God, yes. He had back-to-back meetings, starting with a breakfast—seventy miles south in San Francisco—at 7:00 A.M. He had two sets of deal papers to redline, and a dozen phone calls he had to make. And about a dozen more he really *should* make.

Including one to Stella Monaco, who probably didn't understand why Cosimo DeLuca's cardiac arrest had taken precedence over her party plans.

"It's manageable," he told Gabby, then tried to gauge what he read in those eyes of hers. "Would you rather I went?" He felt compelled to ask the question, though he wanted only one answer. "I would understand if you wanted to be alone with your family. But I'd rather stay. . . ." His words petered out. "Help if I can."

What he didn't say hung in the air. He could almost see it under the too-bright hospital lights, like the words in a bubble in a strip cartoon. *I want to make sure your dad's okay. Be here if the clot-busting drug doesn't work. Be here if he starts bleeding, like the doctor warned us. Be here if . . .*

Gabby looked at him, and he could see those same doomsday scenarios spin out in her mind. Watching her, scared and sad and worried, a good part of him wanted to bundle her body into his arms, make his own strong, even heartbeat convince her that she'd done the right thing, the brave thing, for her father.

"All right," she said. "Please stay."

Gabby watched Will and wondered what to make of him. His behavior went well beyond Boy Scout, to a level of gentlemanliness she hadn't thought existed anymore.

"How about," he said, "we go down to the Starbucks on the first floor and get everybody coffee? It seems to be open all night. It was open when we got here."

She shook her head. "I don't think I should go anywhere."

"We won't be gone long." He cocked his chin at

her family. "And I think at this point everybody could use a pick-me-up."

"That's probably true." And it did sound good, doing something normal and everyday, something not filled with life-and-death questions.

Her feet led her back to her family. "Will and I are going down to the Starbucks. Does anybody want anything? Mom?" She realized she didn't ask, *Does anybody want to come with us?*

And no one did, mercifully, not Cam or her youngest sister Lucia or her mom. Gabby took their orders, then she and Will headed for the elevators. When they arrived at the first floor, he directed her toward a short hallway to the right.

"It's next to the Burger King," he said, then chuckled.

"Can you believe they have fast food in hospitals?"

"Too bad the gift shop's closed. We could see if they sell cigarettes."

"They probably do."

Amazingly at this hour, Starbucks had a line. Gabby wrapped her pashmina a little tighter around her naked shoulders.

"Cold?"

"I'm okay."

A beat of silence. Then, "Really?"

She turned to look at him. He stared back at her, unblinking, as steady and silent as a buddha. She had the sudden thought that she could tell him anything and he wouldn't be shocked. "No, I'm not all right." She was almost surprised to hear herself say it. Goodbye, social facade. Hello, reality. "It really upset me to have to push my mom to give the go-ahead for that drug."

He seemed unfazed. "I can understand that."

"I wish one of my sisters had said something to

back me up. I'm scared that giving it to him was the wrong thing to do."

He shook his head. "It was the right thing to do, Gabby. And for what it's worth, I think you were brave to make the decision."

She wished she felt brave. That would be a lot better than petrified. "But he could have a stroke from it." She almost couldn't speak the words. "He could even die." *And then it would be all on me. How could I live with that?*

"There are risks on both sides. The bottom line is how strong his heart is going forward."

It almost made her angry, him being so cool and logical and sure. "How do you know?" Her voice came out snappish, loud. "Don't try to tell me what the 'bottom line' is. Even Dr. Hearst admitted it's risky."

Immediately she felt guilty. Here Will was being more considerate than God, and she was berating him for trying to reassure her. He looked away and said nothing. The line inched forward. They were next, after a dark-haired man in a droopy sweater carrying a sleeping toddler on his shoulder. The child was only inches from Gabby's face, his thumb planted firmly in his mouth. She focused on his dewy skin, his soft little baby snore, the long, long lashes draped on his sleep-flushed cheeks.

Once, many years ago, she had been a child like that, and the man lying upstairs fighting for his life had held her on his shoulder in exactly that way.

Tears stung her eyes, for reasons she couldn't name. Fear. Exhaustion. Anger, at her family and at God and at who else she wasn't sure. She had an enormous desire to be shot back in time to before this nightmare had begun, so she could have spirited her father away to some refuge where he would have been safe, though she wasn't sure anymore that such a place existed. She castigated herself for missing Vittorio, for loving him, for giving a damn about him at all. What was losing him compared to this? It was nothing. Nothing.

The man with the child moved forward to the counter and ordered. Gabby bit her lip, hung her head, caught the sob that rose in her throat. Will was silent, but she could sense his gaze on her face, could almost hear the gears of his mind turning.

Then she felt the gentle pressure of his hand on her back, moving her up to the counter. But she didn't want to raise her head, she couldn't make herself speak, her tears were a hairbreadth away. After a moment she heard Will start to order, what he wanted, what everybody in her family wanted, getting it all right when she hadn't even known he'd been listening, then throwing in a cappuccino and a brownie for her.

He pressed a few paper napkins in her hand. "Go sit down," he murmured when the clerk had moved off. But by now she knew she couldn't check her tears; she could no longer hold them back. She backed away from him and pitched blindly past the people behind her in the line, her pashmina flying off her shoulders to land somewhere on the coffee-stained floor. Then out into the corridor, where she pushed open the first escape hatch she could find, a metal exit door which led into a stairwell where finally she could let the agony flow.

Her body was racked with sobs, which came thick and fast and loud, echoing in the chilly industrial stairwell. Some caught in her throat, some shrieked to the upper floors of the hospital, some choked in little gasps that tore at her soul. She collapsed onto a stair, deathly cold through the thin fabric of her dress, and rubbed her hands down her naked legs, shod in

strappy little silver slingbacks that looked obscenely
out of place on the concrete floor, another sour note
in a thankless night.

Minutes later the door opened. Will stood outlined
in its rectangular frame, concern grafted onto his all-
American face. Behind him and across the corridor
she glimpsed yet another ragtag crew of strangers
lined up for Starbucks coffee. The door clanged shut,
and he came to sit beside her on the stair, which required her to shuffle toward the railing to make room.
He leaned forward, linked his hands, and let them rest
between his knees.

No platitudes or baseless reassurances came out of
him, no *Are you okay?* or *Everything will be fine.* He
said not a word, just sat and studied his fingers.
Around them fluorescent lights buzzed. People got
into the stairwell floors above, went up or down a
level, chatting and laughing, then exiting with a metal-
lic finality. Neither of them moved or spoke. She
started to calm down. Somehow Will's stalwartness,
his silent comfort was an enormous counterweight to
the freakishness of the occasion.

She stopped crying, and realized that she had crumpled paper napkins in her hand that she could use as
makeshift tissues. She flattened one out and blew her
nose into it and was about to wipe her cheeks with
another when Will took it out of her hand.

"Here," he said, and pivoted toward her. He went
to work mopping her cheeks, his own face as serious
as if he were piloting a fighter jet or doing laser
surgery. She had a fleeting vision of him as a little
boy, all white-blond hair and blue eyes and sun-
burned nose, brow furrowed and tongue wedged between teeth as he painstakingly filled in his coloring
book or glued together his balsa-wood model air-
plane.

Then, "I think I got everything," and he handed her a napkin mottled with beige, pink, and black gobs of color.

Even in the midst of all of this, she had to chuckle. "I think that was every bit of makeup I had on."

"I'm extremely thorough." But he didn't laugh; he looked as serious as ever. Then he abruptly stood up, grasped her by the arms, drew her to her feet, and after gazing into her eyes for a moment, kissed her.

She could have stopped him. It was hugely inappropriate—it was the wrong place, wrong time. All of that occurred to her, but none of it seemed to much matter. She simply let herself sink into an attractive man, realizing with some surprise that it just so happened she very much liked how this particular man smelled and felt and tasted.

Especially when he backed into the wall and took her with him, pulling her tight against his body, giving her a tutorial in how good she could feel. He abandoned her mouth to kiss the skin along her neck, leaving a trail of pleasure behind him, then moved on down her shoulder. Her left spaghetti strap fell—or was pushed, she wasn't quite sure—and her fingers dug into his hair while heat built deep, low, in her body.

It was suddenly too much. She pulled back, heard his ragged breathing, tried to slow the rampaging of her heart. Their eyes met.

"I'm sorry, Gabby." He gave her a sheepish smile. "I got a little carried away there."

"You weren't the only one."

They smiled at each other for a moment longer. Then, "Shall we have our coffee?" he asked.

"We should probably take it upstairs."

"You're right," he said, and led her—after a pause for dress and hair smoothing—to a table for two where her pashmina and their order sat waiting.

They started back toward the elevator. "My turn to apologize," she said. "I'm sorry for yelling at you before."

"Don't worry about it." He smiled at her again.

She sipped her cappuccino while they waited for an elevator. It was true—she did feel better. And, oddly, not at all awkward. She felt no need to bring up their kiss in the stairwell, and no worry about it, either. An unending stream of people moved past them to get into the Starbucks line, get served, move on, and be replaced by still more. "Where are they all coming from?"

"What amazes me is that there are always people in hospitals, at all hours, worried about somebody. When you're working or sleeping or doing whatever. It's like a whole other world that you just don't think about." He tipped back his head and drank from his cardboard coffee cup.

She watched his throat work as he swallowed. "At least until you're there yourself."

He met her eyes. "Then what's going on in the hospital is the most important thing in the world."

"It sounds like you've been through this yourself."

An elevator appeared. They got inside, and the doors closed them in. Will nodded as if casting his mind back in time. "Three years ago, my mom had an emergency triple bypass."

Gabby took that in. "Is she okay?"

"Better than ever."

"Where does she live?"

"Denver. Where everybody in my family lives."

"But you're in California."

"Have you lived anywhere else?"

"One other place. Castelnuovo."

His brows flew up. "Italy?"

"Tuscany. The Chianti region, to be precise."

"To study winemaking, I bet."

But that's not all I learned. In fact, that's not the half of it.

He narrowed his eyes at her. "I'd also bet there's a story there."

"An epic."

He smiled. "Then perhaps we should leave it for another night."

I hope there is such a night. A normal night, when her father was fine and tucked into his bed at home. When the biggest thing she had to worry about was how to look pretty for a man she found attractive. Such simple things, yet at this moment they sounded like nirvana.

They had just emerged from the elevator when Camella came flying toward them down the corridor. Gabby's heart picked up a staccato rhythm. Then she saw that her sister was smiling. Tears were drying on her cheeks, but she was smiling.

She grabbed Gabby's arms. "Daddy's okay. They're taking him to ICU. The doctor said his EKG is better."

Thank God. Thank God. "So the drug is working?"

"The doctor thinks so. Daddy squeezed his hand. That's a really good sign," Cam started to say—then she choked on her words and couldn't say more.

Neither could Gabby. They clutched each other, both sobbing, and through the relief that coursed through her body, Gabby was conscious of Will stepping away, giving them space. "Can we see him?"

"Yes, on the way to ICU."

"You go on," Will said from where he stood, "I'll wait for you here, and I'll also call Ava to let her know what's going on."

"Thank you," Gabby began, but already Cam was pulling her away, toward her father. Before she disappeared around the corner, she saw him in the hallway, his jacket on his arm, standing and watching her, as if he had nothing more important in the world to do.

"I am truly sorry for missing the party," Max told his mother, turning her Mercedes sedan into the parking lot that fronted St. Helena Hospital. "I know it meant a lot to you, and I really dropped the ball by showing up so late. Believe me, I'll make it up to you. I promise."

Massive silence yawned from the passenger seat. His mother was mad at him, so mad she was barely speaking, but he didn't doubt he could get her past it. A little mea culpa, a little charm, a little attention, and she would forgive him. He had a way with women, always had, and his mother was no exception.

He nosed the Mercedes into a parking space and killed the engine. "I'm glad you let me drive you to the hospital," he told her. "I am seriously jet-lagged but I appreciate that you let me do this for you."

"Maximilian Winsted, do not say another word to me," and all of a sudden his mother's hand gripped his thigh with a force that made him wince. "I am neither as stupid nor as gullible as you seem to think."

He pried her fingers off his thigh. Geez, had she been lifting weights or what? "Mom, you're the smartest woman I know. I have the utmost respect for you."

"I cannot take any more of your bullshit," she declared, then climbed out of the car, slammed the door, and headed for the hospital entrance without him.

Max sat still, shocked. His mother never swore. The worst that ever came out of her was *Damn!* or some variation thereof. For a second he considered just waiting for her in the car, then thought better of it.

No, he had to get back on her good side. The last thing he wanted was to be living with *and* working alongside a moody female, though that pretty much defined the breed. Life would be a great deal more pleasant if she wasn't down his throat constantly.

He sighed, then heaved himself out of the car and went after her. How she could make a federal case out of his failure to appear at her party was beyond him. Then again, she'd always been obsessed with trivialities: clothes, decor, the finer points of etiquette. He could never make her understand that the party hadn't really been for *him*, anyway. It had been for *her*—her opportunity to show off, to play the lady of the manor. *He* was just the excuse. But he'd never known her to exhibit that degree of self-awareness.

Max forced himself through the sliding glass doors and into the reception area. He hated hospitals. They stank, they were depressing, and they reminded him of when his dad was sick after the stroke. When that was going on, Max felt like he lived in the hospital. This very one, actually. And once he didn't have to go to the hospital anymore—well, that wasn't good, either.

He found the intensive care unit. A tall blond guy in a tux whom Max didn't recognize was standing outside the door looking through its narrow rectangular window.

"Hello," Max said, guessing from the black tie that this was someone from the party. The guy spun around, and Max held out his hand. "Max Winsted. Are you here for Cosimo DeLuca, too?"

"Yes, I am." They shook. "Will Henley. Good to meet you."

Max didn't know the name. He started to reach for the door handle, but Henley stopped him.

"You can't go in there right now. They're letting in only two at a time, and your mother's in with Gabby DeLuca."

"Right." The winemaker's daughter. Always had been kind of a babe. Max stepped back from the door.

"What have you been told about Mr. DeLuca's prognosis?"

Henley stared at him for a moment, as if he was trying to decide how much to divulge. "Well," he said eventually, "the doctors gave him a clot-dissolving drug, and the early indications are that it's working. But he's not out of the woods yet. The first twenty-four hours will be critical."

Max nodded. Truth be told, he wasn't all that interested in the medical details. Then another thought struck him. "Are you the person who called my mother a while back to say it was a heart attack?"

"Yes, I am."

Who was this Will Henley? Max wondered. Was he new to the valley? Something about him made Max think he had his shit in gear. Max was about to ask a few probing questions when his mother emerged from ICU, pulling a doctor mask down from her face. Right behind her came Gabby DeLuca, doing the same thing.

Max didn't know what it was—Gabby's slinky purple party dress or her hair piled up on her head or something—but it immediately struck him that here was a woman who was actually looking better with age. She'd stayed thin, she had a good tan, and he'd forgotten how killer her hazel eyes were. Hadn't his mother told him about a year ago that she'd become assistant winemaker, helping her dad? The thought marched across Max's brain that Gabby DeLuca just might become one of his favorite employees.

But she didn't even seem to notice him. Instead she looked right at Henley. "Dr. Hearst says he's stabilizing. The drug really seems to be working."

"That is great news, Gabby." Henley smiled and rubbed her arm. She looked like she might burst into tears at any moment. "He'll get through this, you'll see."

"I'm sure he will," Max said, and then Gabby turned toward him.

"You finally got here," she said, which immediately ticked him off. Here he was—just off a transoceanic flight, going out of his way to check on her father's condition—and the first words out of her mouth were accusatory.

He was about to deliver a pithy retort when his mother cut him off by stepping in front of him and grabbing both of Gabby's hands. "As I said before, Gabriella, please let me know if there's anything at all I can do. I would be more than willing to bring in a specialist from out of town, for example."

"Thank you, Mrs. Winsted, I really appreciate that."

"Your father is very dear to all of us at Suncrest."

Gabby nodded. Again she looked like she might start crying. "I have to say that at this point I am pretty satisfied with the quality of care here."

Good, Max thought. In his opinion, his mother had been too quick with that offer. He knew only too well who would end up paying for any out-of-town cardiologists.

"Please keep it in mind," his mother insisted. Then she turned to Henley and took his hands. "You've been extremely helpful, Will. I truly appreciate what you've done tonight."

He just nodded and looked heroic. Then again, Max thought, who didn't in a tuxedo? He looked down at his own T-shirt and wrinkled cargo pants, which he'd been wearing for twenty-four hours plus, and shook his head, more anxious to leave by the second.

"I'll call you in the morning to see how he's doing," his mother told Gabby, "and don't you spend a minute worrying about anything else." Then she nodded at Henley and that was finally it. She turned and walked away, leaving Max to make his own good-byes and trail after her like a pet dog.

When they arrived at the elevators, he jabbed the DOWN button. "So Mr. DeLuca will make it?"

"It appears he will. Thank God." Her voice was clipped.

I hope they don't sue us, he thought. The valley was full of hotshot lawyers who'd love nothing better than to go after the Winsted family. An elevator opened up, and he and his mother got in. He decided to continue his PR campaign. "It was really clever of you to offer to bring in a specialist."

But his mother shook her head as if she were disgusted. "I didn't do it to be clever. I did it because Cosimo DeLuca has been a valuable employee for as long as you've been alive."

Man. She made it sound like she cared more about DeLuca than she did about her own son. Max shook his head. She could be *cold*.

The elevator stopped, and more people got in. Max didn't speak again until he and his mother walked out on the first floor. Then, "I suppose this means he could be out of commission for a while."

"I would imagine at least through midsummer. I intend to ask Gabby to take over as lead winemaker while he convalesces," his mother informed him, which stopped Max dead in his tracks on the hospital's shiny green linoleum floor. Nearby at reception, a woman giggled at a security guard leaning toward her over the counter.

"Don't you think that's *my* decision to make? After all, I'm running Suncrest now."

He found his mother right in front of his nose almost before he saw her turn around. "What makes you think that?" Her voice was low and cold and unlike anything Max had ever heard out of her before. "You will run Suncrest when *I* say you will run Suncrest. Your behavior tonight has been beyond abominable. I have half a mind to go right back upstairs and tell Will Henley I've decided to sell."

She stopped then, and Max had to say he was glad she did, because he couldn't believe what he had just heard. "*Sell?* Who the hell is this Will Henley, anyway?"

"He's an investor from San Francisco. With a firm called GPG. And I have to tell you that I am a lot higher on him right now than I am on you."

Then she turned her back on him and walked out. Max watched the big sliding doors part and her sweep through, a group of orderlies splitting in two to get out of her way. It was like watching Moses part the Red Sea.

What did she mean, *sell?* Didn't she understand that it was his *right* to run Suncrest? To inherit it and to run it? He was the only heir, for Christ's sake!

Max imagined a world in which his mother sold Suncrest. It made him feel as marooned as if the 747 that had flown him home from Paris had crash-landed on a desert island and left him as the only survivor. His heart began to pound, and for a moment he felt like *he* was the one suffering cardiac arrest. He was hot, and scared, and wanted only to sit down and catch his breath.

But that was the last thing he could do. Because if he wanted any chance of bringing his mother back around, he'd better not leave her standing outside in the cold.

Chapter 4

Saturday, midmorning. Gabby stood in Suncrest's Rosemede vineyard, holding a walkie-talkie in one hand and a cell phone in the other, its caller on hold. Fog lingered here on the valley floor, enveloping her in a chill gauzy mist. She lifted the walkie-talkie to her mouth and pressed TALK.

"Felix, I'm halfway down row sixteen in Rosemede, and I don't see anything." No mildew on the vines, no rot, no parasites. One of the field-workers thought he'd seen evidence of a pest, but apparently he hadn't. "Anything in Calhoun?"

A beat later Felix's voice blared back, rough with static. "I think we're gonna have to spray here. We got some sort of mite. Not too bad, though."

She shook her head. The vines were so at the mercy of Mother Nature, which meant Gabby was, as well. A winemaker lived and died by the quality of her fruit. But the threats were many and varied. If it wasn't insects or cutworms, it was gophers or rabbits or deer. A virus or a fungal disease. A killing frost in spring, or a heat spike in summer, or a too heavy rain. Or, God forbid, flooding.

This time of year, the grapes were the size of peppercorns and as hard as bullets. Soon they would begin to swell and soften and color. Their sugar level would rise, and birds would become the next threat.

Gabby's scientist's soul loved the year in–year out tending of the grapevines. The routine, the order, the predictability. Yet every year was *slightly* different from the year before: no two were exactly alike. They were the same enough that she knew what she was getting, different enough that it stayed interesting.

"You want me to come help?" she asked Felix.

"I got Pepe with me. You go have your talk with Mrs. Winsted."

I'd rather spray the fields. But "Ten-four," she said, then switched the walkie-talkie for the cell and pushed HOLD. "You still there, Cam?"

She waited. Nothing. Her sister had hung up. And there was no way to reach her, as she'd been using a pay phone at the hospital. Gabby stowed her cell and headed for the Jeep she'd abandoned at the vineyard's edge.

What a difference thirty-six hours made. How light her heart now felt. After those first horrible hours, the news about her father had all been good. *He's responding to commands,* Dr. Hearst said. *He's breathing fine, we can take out the tube.* Most likely her father would be moved out of ICU that very night, to something called the telemetry unit. She wasn't sure what that was, but she knew the relocation was a good sign.

With Cam at the hospital with Lucia and their mom, Gabby was free to spend some time at Suncrest. Where she was doing two jobs—her own and her father's.

She hopped into her little ragtop Jeep—impossibly dirty as always, as it spent most of its time on mud-packed roads—and started the half-mile return trek to the winery. She wished she could put off going to see Mrs. W. What could she want? To bring in a new winemaker to replace her father? Or was it something about Max?

Gabby bumped the Jeep slowly along, worried what Ava Winsted might have up her cashmere sleeve. But those ruminations didn't prevent her mind from soon spinning in a different direction.

Would Will Henley call again? The other night after Mrs. W and Max had left the hospital, Will had also said his good nights. But he'd taken her cell number and actually called it later that very day. He'd asked after her father and wanted to hear all the medical details. Then . . . that was it.

What? What did she expect? For him to call every day?

Gabby stowed the Jeep in the employee lot to the rear of the winery. It was quite possible that Will Henley was just very polite and gentlemanly, and that she'd been wrong to read a more personal interest into his behavior. He'd described himself as a Boy Scout, hadn't he? Maybe her family's medical crisis was just the emergency equivalent of helping an old lady across a street or coaxing a cat down from a tree.

And the kiss? Well, maybe it was just lust—hot and fleeting—getting the better of him. Or maybe he'd been so exhausted he wasn't thinking straight. Or maybe he'd liked her that night but had already thought better of it. Any of the above multiple-choice answers could well be correct.

She entered the main winery building through the rear door, next to the barrels of vineyard nutrients and weed killer. She planned to make a pit stop to wash up but was accosted by Mrs. W, who naturally looked stunning in sleek black pants and soft white sweater. Gabby sported shorts, dirt-caked running shoes, a baseball cap, and a polo shirt under a fleece vest. With streaks of dust on her legs from the vineyard.

Gabby watched Mrs. W take in her smeared condition in a glance. "With no one around today," the older woman suggested, "let's talk in the break room."

She doesn't want me to get her upholstery dirty. But really, who could blame her? Mrs. W worked out of her husband's old office, the most elegant room in the winery.

They arranged themselves on bright orange plastic chairs around a scratched Formica table. Fluorescent lights buzzed overhead, while the concession machines made their usual low chugging sounds. The whole room gave off a strong Lysol smell, like the cleaning crew had gone haywire the night before.

"I spoke with your mother this morning, and she told me your father continues to improve," Mrs. W said. "I am so glad to hear that."

"He gave us all quite a scare."

"He certainly did. And I imagine his recuperation will take some time."

Now was the moment to sound as reassuring as possible. The last thing Gabby wanted was for Mrs. W to bring in a winemaker on top of her, or to hire consultants who might muck up the process she and her father had created.

"The doctors say he'll have to take it easy for six weeks or so, but after that I'm sure he'll be back to normal. And in the meanwhile, I will be more than happy to take up the slack, Mrs. Winsted. I've worked at my father's side for years and completely understand how he does things. You don't have a thing to worry about."

Mrs. W gave Gabby one of her trademark penetrating stares. "Do you enjoy the work, Gabriella? Are you sure it's what you want to do?"

"I love it! I love everything about it." Gabby thought Mrs. W didn't look entirely convinced, though she found it easy to imagine that the former actress would find the often hot, dusty, grubby labor of wine-making extremely unappealing. "I studied enology in college—it's what I've wanted to do all my life. I love the farming aspect, too, and the science—I studied chemistry, too—and of course there's art in wine-making, as well."

"Yes, there is, isn't there?" Mrs. W continued to eye her narrowly. Gabby found herself wondering why Max wasn't participating in this little tête-à-tête. If he was taking over, wouldn't he have something to say about Suncrest's lead winemaker, arguably its most important position?

But Mrs. W broke into her thoughts by clearing her throat suddenly, as if she'd made a decision. "Well, Gabriella, I do believe you can handle the extra load. So I will leave it to you to oversee the winemaking during your father's convalescence. But"—and she raised a warning finger—"if he is not able to come back to work by harvest, I will need to make other arrangements."

That gives me two months. The rush of relief Gabby felt was tinged by anxiety. It was all up to her now, and it never had been before. "Thank you so much, Mrs. Winsted. I appreciate your confidence." *I hope some of it rubs off on me.*

Mrs. W stood up. "Certainly," she said, then bestowed a cool smile and sailed off, her business done.

Gabby's was just beginning.

Ava had one last hill to climb to finish her four-mile run. She consulted her sport watch, squared her shoulders, and forced her Nike-shod feet to keep pounding the narrow dirt road that wound through Suncrest's vineyards. Napa's withering midday sun beat on her fair skin, taunting her resolve. A less will-ful woman might have judged this final incline insur-mountable and taken an easier route home, but Ava was enough of a headbanger to keep going.

Running was one of the few things she did without an audience, never straying from her own property. She didn't care for panting and sweating in public, or for showing off the cherry-red flush that blotched her cheeks when she exerted herself. True, she sometimes ran across field-workers, all Hispanic men, only a few whose names she knew. She didn't enjoy their watch-ful eyes, but with them she didn't feel much need to maintain appearances. She might pretend to share the bold earthiness of Ava Gardner—whose name the teenaged Anna Schroeder appropriated when she first arrived in Hollywood—but in truth she was shy and a little prissy and cared a great deal about the opinions of others.

At length she crested the hill, her chest heaving in a delicious agony of pain and triumph, and was re-warded with a mind-boggling view of vineyards falling away from her in every direction, a thick canopy of dark green leaves hiding the grape clusters that dan-gled beneath. By late June the vines had stopped their frenetic growing and were turning their energy into ripening the fruit. In two months, harvest would begin.

Ava caught her breath and scanned her acres, and wondered whether she would be present to see the grapes cut from the vines.

Just that morning, Jean-Luc had bounded out of the guest room to tell her that his screenplay had sold. His agent had called his mobile, he told her, his face flushed with excitement. This was the very screenplay that boasted a role for her, a comeback role, an I'll-show-you-I've-still-got-it role. She knew she did, Jean-Luc believed it, and he would return to Paris to find out if France's film moguls agreed and would give her the part.

If only it were that easy.

She began the downhill trot, keeping an eye out for ankle-spraining rocks. She wanted to go to Paris. She wanted to leave Suncrest in Max's hands. But how could she without some confidence that he wouldn't destroy it while she wasn't looking?

Yet a scheme had begun to take shape in her mind. Will Henley played a part in it, and he would come onstage that very afternoon.

She picked up her pace, both anticipating that scene and eager to reach her home, which she now spied a quarter-mile ahead, nestled among olive trees and grapevines. It was a 1960s ranch house just east of the winery proper that could not have been more plebeian until she and Porter took it over. They transformed it into a light-filled oasis, airy and elegant and yet supremely comfortable. And it was very California, with skylights and huge windows and French doors in nearly every room, so the gardens and terraces were always mere steps away.

She was just loping around the side of the house toward the pool and the pergola—where Mrs. Finchley always had waiting for her a chilled post-run sport drink—when a shiny red Mercedes convertible careened noisily onto the driveway behind her and sent up a spray of pebbles, several of which struck her naked legs.

Max beamed at her from the driver's seat. "Like it?"

She was so taken aback, it took her a moment to approach the car. It was a sleek conveyance, indeed. She eyed her son. "Did you purchase this vehicle?"

His face was aglow. "I most certainly did."

"Is buying this supposed to convince me you're ready to run Suncrest?"

"What does this have to do with Suncrest?" He laughed, his smile open and wide, his dark eyes dancing, and for a moment her heart clenched. She remembered the little boy he had been—cheerful, rambunctious, and unscathed. Nothing had ever gone wrong, and it seemed that nothing ever could.

In those golden years, she believed she'd been a good mother. It hadn't been so much of a burden then, like it was when he was a baby and it was again when he was a teenager. During those tumultuous phases it was either more drudgery than she could take, or more angst—more fights, more disappointments, more sulks.

She hadn't enjoyed it. She got into a cycle she wasn't proud of. Pushing Max onto nannies and into boarding schools, then feeling guilty and going hugely overboard in the opposite direction, buying him extravagances, taking him on trips. When he behaved like any spoiled boy would, how could she be surprised or angry?

It was what she had trained him to be.

She shook her head, suddenly bone tired. "I just want to know what spending an exorbitant amount of money on a sports car has to do with Suncrest."

He shook his head, still smiling, then got out of the car and approached her across the pebbled drive. "It doesn't have anything to do with Suncrest." Then he held out the key. "It has to do with you."

She frowned. "What?"

"I bought the car for *you.*" He came closer and pressed the key into her hand. "Come on, give her a spin."

It was as though the synapses weren't firing in her brain. "Max . . ."

"Mom." His gaze was steady. "I noticed when I was driving your car the other night that it's getting old. I wanted to do something to make up a little bit for the other night, and I thought of this."

"But it's too much! It's . . ." Her voice failed her. *It misses the point,* she wanted to say, *it's too much, it's not what I need. It's not what I need to see from* you.

But he wouldn't be dissuaded. "Look, now that I'm back, we need a second set of wheels anyway. I thought I'd use your car and you can tool around in this. Don't look so stunned!" He laughed again and lowered his voice. "It's just you and me now, Mom. I want us to stick together—I want us to be on the same page. I know I've screwed up a lot in the past, but I want you to believe that I'm going to try harder. Say you'll take it, as a token of goodwill if nothing else."

She looked for deception in his eyes and found none. She wanted to believe him, she wanted to! Nothing would give her more relief or satisfaction.

Ava eyed the car warily, like it might explode, or take off suddenly on its own. It *was* beautiful—sleek and sexy and cherry red, much flashier than anything she'd pick out for herself. But who wouldn't agree that Ava Winsted was due for a bit of fun?

"Come on." Max cocked his head at the car, grinning.

"But I'm so dirty, I'll make a mess."

"You won't make a mess," and he nudged her toward the driver's door.

It drove like a dream. She loved the wind blowing through her hair, and it was such fun to blare the radio while screaming down the Trail, feeling twenty-one again and like a Hollywood starlet, racing around L.A.'s canyons dreaming of how rich and famous she would someday be. She and Max even raced up an isolated mountain road to Max's favorite overlook, then barreled back down again at a marvelously in-sane speed.

She had such a good time, she forgot to tell Max who was coming to visit them at Suncrest that very afternoon.

Will arrived at the winery for his meeting smack on time at four o'clock, dressed for the occasion in khakis, dress shirt, and navy sport coat. He didn't mind working on a Saturday—his wasn't the sort of job that hewed to nine to five—and besides, he was damn curious why Ava had scheduled this little get-together.

It seemed too much to hope for that she'd done an about-face and was now considering selling Suncrest to GPG. But what else could it be? Their other meetings had all been at his behest, Will Henley a flannel-suited beggar offering her millions on bended knee. Was it possible that her son's absence at his own homecoming party was less noble than Ava had made it out to be? Maybe now she didn't want to hand him control of the winery? That was plausible.

It would save his own ass nicely, too. For Will had pinned all his hopes on Suncrest. He knew that if he could get his hands on that winery, with its unique attributes of brand name and prime vineyard property, he could expand it and earn GPG's investors the millions they were expecting from a Napa Valley acquisition. Suncrest was such an attractive prospect that Will had cast his net no wider—a risky strategy if ever there was one.

If it paid off, LaRue and everybody else at GPG would brand him a hero. But if not . . .

Will refused even to consider that possibility. He cooled his heels on the curvy path in front of the winery. The building was locked, and he saw no one around, though on this sunny June weekend many of Napa's other wineries were buzzing with tourists. Suncrest was elite enough that it didn't do visitor tours except by appointment.

Gabby might be around though, right? he wondered. No doubt she was putting in extra hours filling in for her father. Then again, she could just as easily be at the hospital. The idea of running into her—here, now—made him jittery. He was anxious to see her—beyond anxious, really—but didn't want to have to explain his business at Suncrest. In fact, his professional code barred him from doing so. Loose lips killed deals. But if he wanted to get to know this woman, as he most assuredly did, the nature of his employment at least couldn't remain a mystery for long. He found, though, he wasn't looking forward to getting into that, either.

He shook his head, irritated with himself. What was he, embarrassed about his work? That was nonsensical. GPG was a prestigious organization, filled with high-caliber individuals who did valuable work, resuscitating companies that might well have gone under otherwise. True, those restructurings always came at some cost, but what change didn't? GPG was a bastion of free enterprise, in which he ardently believed. His fervor was almost patriotic.

Yet . . . Gabby might not share his view. Many of the people who worked for the companies that GPG acquired didn't grasp the bigger economic picture, particularly if the change in ownership landed them on the unemployment line. He thought it was highly unlikely that would happen to Gabby, though. In fact, if GPG acquired Suncrest and ramped up its operations, her fortunes might well improve. No doubt she'd make more wine, lead an expanded staff, earn more money.

"Will," Ava called, sailing toward him on the winery path, a vision in a peach-colored sweater set and slim white pants. She looked as cool and elegant as a parfait. Max followed in her wake, freshly shaved this time, in much the same outfit as Will, minus the blazer. He looked considerably more presentable than he had at the hospital, where indeed his garb had belied the notion that he'd spent the afternoon in a business meeting in the city. Knowing a bit about Max's history, Will hadn't quite bought into that line, but couldn't fathom another explanation for his extraordinary absence.

So, Will wondered, *could it be Max who wanted this meeting?*

Ava poked a key in the winery's big oak door, which groaned open as if it were the entry to a medieval castle. "I thought we'd talk in my office," she murmured, then led them through the somnolent tank room—filled with enormous stainless steel tanks that would be abuzz with fermenting activity in the fall—and up some stairs to an office that Ava called her own but that clearly had not been redone since her husband's day.

It had the feel of a club room, Will thought, and could not be more masculine. It was paneled in cherrywood, with built-in shelves of the same rich material loaded with sports trophies, framed photographs, and leather-bound volumes. An imposing mahogany desk marred by only a few neat stacks of paperwork sat atop an Oriental carpet, while two tartan sofas ate up much of the remaining floor space. Roman shades half-drawn on the large windows blocked the intense afternoon sun.

The office said more eloquently than Ava Winsted ever could that she did not intend to continue running Suncrest. She had made no mark on her late husband's professional domain, either because she couldn't bear to or because she didn't expect to be around long enough to make it worthwhile.

The housekeeper Will recognized from the party bustled in with tea and scones, which she arranged on the low table between the tartan sofas. All three sat while she poured. She had barely exited before Ava got down to business.

"I asked you here, Will, because I'd like you to bring Max up to speed on our discussions regarding Suncrest." Her gaze was steady. "I told him that your firm has made an offer to buy the winery."

"I'm certainly interested in hearing what you have to say." Max smiled broadly. "But I have to tell you that I agree with my mother on this. I have no interest in selling."

Will tried to get a read on Max. He seemed intelligent and charming enough, and certainly looked the part of the well-bred heir. That didn't jibe, though, with Will's research, which had produced a different picture—that of a restless, self-indulgent youth who'd never shown more than mediocre ability in the classroom or on the athletic field. He'd gotten into some scrapes both in high school and at USC, where apparently he'd majored in parties and minored in women.

That wasn't indicative of much, though. Will had always been straitlaced but many solid, highly successful people had wild college careers on their résumés.

Will launched into his spiel. "I must compliment both of you on Suncrest," he told them. "It's in an enviable position. The label is well-known and synonymous with high-quality, high-end wines."

Ava nodded. "That was always the niche Porter envisioned for Suncrest."

"And he made that vision a reality. It is quite impressive to have remained competitive in that category for so long." Will turned to Max, confident that for all his apprenticing in France, Ava's son had only a rudimentary understanding of the wine business. "My firm is interested in the wine sector for a variety of reasons. As you well know, wine sales have grown at double the rate of the economy since the 1980s."

Max nodded sagely. "That's certainly true."

"In addition, the demographic trends are very positive for premium wines. Ten thousand baby boomers turn fifty every day, and that will be true for the next dozen years. In short, we view the wine business as an attractive area for investment."

"So do we!" Max laughed again. "That's why we don't want to sell."

Will leaned forward and set his elbows on his knees, gearing up for the core of his pitch. "Your family has built a tremendously successful winery, thanks to enormous effort, persistence, and skill." He raised his head to catch Ava's eye. "Yet I can imagine that you might be in a chapter of your life when you want to move in a different direction, be free of a winery's constant demands. Enjoy the fruits of all that labor."

"You make a good point," Ava murmured.

Will almost fell out of his chair. That was the most receptive comment Ava had ever made to him on this subject. Then he had a revelation.

She was using him to frighten Max. She had no more intention of selling Suncrest to GPG than she ever had. But she wanted Max to *believe* she might sell.

Ever the actress, Ava Winsted was playing a part, for an audience of one. And Will was, for lack of a better term, her prop.

Fine. He was unfazed. She had given him the opportunity to repeat his case to her, and to make it for the first time to Max. These transactions were never sealed on the initial meetings, anyway. They were based on trust, earned over time. Emotions, ego, ambition invariably played a role. The human factor was huge.

Will continued. "GPG is prepared to invest in Suncrest and assume control of the winery, leaving you with cash and a substantial stake in the upside. Or"—

and he leaned closer to Max for the kill—"we could take Suncrest entirely off your hands. Free you up. Provide to you, in cash, the substantial value of your holdings." He paused for dramatic effect. "For thirty million dollars."

Will watched Max's pupils dilate. He'd seen that before, too.

"Thirty million dollars," Ava repeated softly. "You see, Max, why I find Will's offer so compelling."

This time, Max made no kneejerk comment about "no interest in selling." He was notably silent and contemplative.

"This is a lot for you to digest," Will told Max, "especially as you've just come home to California. Here." He handed Max a business card. "Call me anytime to talk further. I know that once you start to chew on this, you'll have all kinds of questions."

Ava rose to shake his hand, an unmistakable gleam of satisfaction in her light blue eyes. "You certainly have given us food for thought today, Will. Thank you again for coming all this way." Then she led him and her son out the way they had come.

Gabby had just reached the main winery building when she ran right into Will, standing next to Max. She spied Mrs. W some distance away, walking along the path toward her house.

"Will!" Flummoxed, Gabby tore the ratty baseball cap off her head, the first thing she could think of doing to improve her appearance. It was woefully inadequate, she knew. In the ninety-degree heat, after four hours of helping Felix and Pepe spray three mite-infested vineyards, she was sweat-stained, dirt-smeared, and stank to high heaven of pesticides. "What brings you back to Napa?"

One look and she realized that though she was thrilled to see him, he wasn't in the least excited to see her. Quite the opposite, in fact. He wore a wide-eyed stare, like the Ghost of Christmas Past had just appeared on his doorstep.

That's it, she thought, and her heart plummeted. It was over before it had even started. She'd misread him, misread feeling in tune with him. Those shivers had only been going up *her* spine, because now he made her feel about as desirable as a social disease. Then again, who could get jazzed about a woman who smelled like one part lime-sulfur to two parts methyl bromide?

He jerked his thumb back to indicate the winery building behind him. "I just had a chat with Ava and Max."

"More than a chat." Max laughed. "FYI, Gabby, Will here made an offer to buy Suncrest."

Immediately Will piped up. "I'd rather not get into that, Max."

Gabby frowned. "Made an offer to do *what*?"

"Oh, I understand." Max shook Will's hand. "We'll talk soon," he said, then nodded at Gabby with a weird smile and took off after his mother at a half jog.

Will turned toward her. "So how's your father?"

What did Max mean, Will made an offer to buy Suncrest? "He's better all the time." She gave him a brief rundown, concluding with the mysterious move to the telemetry unit. "I guess that's good, but I don't really know what it means."

"Telemetry means being measured from a distance. They'll put lots of sensors on him so they can track any changes to heartbeat and intercede immediately if they have to. Of course, that's what they do in ICU, too, but this allows them to staff at a lower level."

She took that in. He sounded cool, businesslike—not warm and easy like the Will from the other night. *What happened? And what is this business about Sun-*

crest? "What did Max mean, you made an offer to buy Suncrest?"

He stared at her with a funny expression, as if she'd caught him with his hand in the cookie jar. Then, "I really can't talk about it, Gabby."

"Does that mean it's true?"

He said nothing, just looked at her like all he wanted in the world was to get away. But no way she would let that happen. Not after this bombshell.

"Before you said you were in investments. But what you actually do is buy companies? I don't understand."

Was this guy a liar? Was he some kind of corporate raider? Was he not at all what he seemed to be?

Was he another Vittorio?

Will rubbed his forehead, hard, looking away from her at the long drive that sloped down to Suncrest's bronze gates on the Silverado Trail. Then once again his eyes met hers, and her breath caught as she read the truth in their blue depths. "Do you have time to take a walk?" he asked her.

She most certainly did, so they set off. Silence ballooned between them, broken only by the crunch of their shoes on the gravel that bordered the drive.

Finally, he spoke. "This is confidential information, Gabby, and I really should not be discussing it with you. But I will tell you if you promise to keep it to yourself. It is very important that you tell no one."

She didn't like the sound of any of that but by this point would rather hear it than not. "I won't say a word."

They walked farther. She heard him take a deep breath, and steeled herself. Then, "It's true. I'm a partner with a firm called GPG, and we've made an offer to buy Suncrest."

There it was, out. It was true, as she had known it

would be from the moment Max had spilled the beans.
She said the first thing that came into her head. "But
Suncrest has always been in the Winsted family."

He said nothing to that.

"Did Mrs. Winsted approach you?"

"No, I approached her."

"Does she want to sell?"

He shook his head. "She says no."

"But you don't believe her?"

"I'm hoping I can persuade her to change her
mind."

"Is this the first conversation you've had with her
about it?"

He hesitated on that one. Then, "No. I've had several meetings with Ava. This is my first with Max."

Things were starting to click into place in her mind,
building a jigsaw whose picture she wasn't at all sure
she liked. "Mrs. Winsted doesn't want to sell, but
you're hoping Max will convince her to go along."

He didn't seem to like that line of reasoning.
"We've made a proposal that we believe both of them
should find very attractive."

"Who's this *we* you're talking about?"

"As I said, I'm a member of a partnership. General
Pacific Group."

She thought maybe she'd heard of them, though
she'd never been much for the financial pages. "Why
couldn't you tell me this before?"

"Because it's the first commandment of my job not
to discuss the offers we make. It's highly confidential,
Gabby. I shouldn't be telling you any of this."

Am I supposed to be flattered? She wasn't. Mostly
she felt that he'd misled her somehow, if he hadn't
actually lied. At the party he'd dodged her questions
about what he did—very deftly, too. Now she knew
why.

Thoughts bobbed and weaved in Gabby's mind like

the birds that cavorted in the cloudless sky above. Acres of Suncrest vineyards lay on either side of them, the vines heavy with grapes, getting sweeter every second under the heat of the sun. On the Trail twenty yards ahead, perpendicular to the drive, cars sped past at high speed, going sixty, seventy miles an hour, as fast as they could get away with.

They halted at the winery's bronze gates. She turned to face him. The late afternoon sun glinted on his blond head, caused his blue eyes to squint. She noticed for the first time how long his lashes were, and how fine the bones of his nose. He looked the same as ever—intelligent, steady, honorable. Vittorio had appeared to be all those things, too. In fact, in many ways he had been. But not in all.

"You didn't want to run into me today," she said, "because you didn't want to have to tell me what you were doing here."

He met her eyes. "That's true."

"You knew I wouldn't like it."

He said nothing.

"Well, you were right."

She turned away from him. Ahead of her rose the Mayacamas range; beyond her sight, miles away, roared the Pacific. Purple mountain majesty, above the fruited plain.

"Do you know what those mountains are called?" she asked him.

Silence. Then, "I know the ones behind us are the Howells."

"These are the Mayacamas. Do you know what the tallest mountain around here is?"

"Are you having fun quizzing me, Gabby?"

"Yes, I am. Do you want to answer?"

"I can't."

"I didn't think so. It's Mount St. Helena to the north, forty-three hundred and forty-three feet." She shook her head, anger starting to build in her chest. Mixed with fear, spiced with disappointment. "You don't know anything about this place. You don't care about it. You're like those huge liquor companies that come in here and buy up the wineries. All they care about is making as much money as possible, as fast as possible. To hell with the rest of us."

"Look, Gabby." He tugged on her arm, forced her to abandon the view to look at him. "I'm not ashamed of what I do. I work for a reputable organization with lots of good people in it that's helped many struggling companies survive."

"But Suncrest isn't struggling! We're doing just fine, thank you. And I don't care how so-called *reputable* your company is." She forced herself to take a breath, though it didn't calm her in the least. "You just don't get it! The whole valley is changing. It's not the way it used to be, the way it was when I was growing up."

He threw out his hands. "What *is* the same?"

"I am!" She pointed at her chest, heard the frustration in her own voice, though she knew it was unfair to blame him and him alone for the world shifting around her. "I'm the same as I always was, and so is my family. So is my father, who makes wine the old-fashioned way. That's the way I want to make it, too, one bottle at a time, not off some assembly line like it's Coca-Cola."

He shook his head. "That's not going to happen."

"Oh, no? How can you be so sure?"

He hesitated. Then, "It's true that some of the employees of the companies we acquire—"

"Lose their jobs." She didn't usually interrupt, but she didn't want him to get away with some euphemism. "They get canned. They get fired. They lose their pensions and their health care."

"Very often a lot *more* of them would've gotten

fired without us, because their company would've gone
entirely out of business."

"You know what's going out of business? The
family-owned wineries. Pretty soon they're all gonna
be *gone*, like the mom-and-pop hardware stores.
There's going to be the Wal-Mart of wineries and
that's it."

He shook his head. Maybe he was getting angry,
too. "I don't feel too sorry for those families, Gabby.
They walk away with a great deal of money. They're
hardly taken advantage of."

Gabby wanted to cry. There was no way Max
wouldn't want "a great deal of money." He'd looked
so cocky standing there next to Will, spouting off
about the offer. And then what would happen to Suncrest? She knew what a sea change occurred when a
winery changed hands, especially when the new owner
was an outsider. It would go all corporate. Suncrest
would be so different, she wouldn't even recognize
it anymore.

And her father. What would happen to her father?
Maybe it was good she couldn't tell him about this.
The stress might make him have another attack. Then
again, she might explode from having to pretend she
didn't know.

All she knew at that moment was that she wanted
to get away from Will Henley. How ironic, because
right then he was saying the very words that ten minutes earlier she'd been dying to hear.

"Gabby, I don't want this to make a difference between us. I'm really glad I met you the other night,
and I want to get to know you better."

"Well, it does make a difference." She backed away
from him. Why did everything have to go wrong? First
Vittorio. Then her father getting sick. And Suncrest
would never be the same whether Max ran it or Will

bought it. She'd come back to California hoping some things at least would be the same as they always were. What a pipe dream that had been.

And Will! She'd just met him, she shouldn't give a damn, but still she felt a crushing disappointment. He was a big corporate raider guy, which was about as different from her as a man could get. They didn't see the world the same way at all. Somehow she'd gotten the idea they did. Apparently she hadn't learned a single thing from the catastrophe with Vittorio. She'd been blind or a fool or both. Again.

"Gabby . . ."

"No." She turned away from him and went back the way she'd come, up the drive toward the old stone winery, which looked so vulnerable, so honey-gold and luscious in June's clear light, so ripe for the picking. It was getting hard for her to see it, though, it was getting blurry, and she knew her tears were mixing with the dust on her face to make her look like the lost soul she felt herself to be.

"Wait, Gabby, stop . . ."

He was behind her, calling, but she just shook her head and sped up, started running, then heard the muffled ring of the cell phone in her shorts pocket. *Damn!*—but she had to answer, it might be somebody from the hospital.

But it wasn't. She knew that instantly. She recognized the voice in less than a heartbeat. Maybe she'd recognized the breathing.

"Gabriella," the caller said. "It's Vittorio."

Chapter 5

Early Tuesday evening, with the sun still shining in the June sky, Max stood in his father's old office with a pretty young thing who worked for St. Helena's best stationery store. "I don't think you get it," he told her. "I need the invitations done in forty-eight hours, not ten days. You told me you have an in-house calligrapher, right?"

She nodded, tendrils of blond hair bobbing around her little heart-shaped face. "We do, but—"

"Then what's the problem?"

She seemed scared to say it. Her voice got all breathy, which Max quite liked. "But she's got other projects ahead of yours. And June's one of our busiest times."

Very gently, Max put his arm around her shoulders and gazed into her eyes. He watched her catch her breath. Very sweet. "Amy, that's your name, right? Amy?"

She nodded, mute.

"Amy, what I want you to do is put this project *ahead* of everybody else's. First in the line. Top of the pile. And to make that easier for you, I'll offer to pay a little extra. Say"—and he cocked his head, very much enjoying the feel of her eyes on his face—"five percent." He arched his brows. "Wouldn't you say that's generous of me?"

"Well . . ." She seemed confused. "Can I ask my boss?"

"Yes, you may. And you tell her"—he knew it was a woman; no man would be caught dead working in Primrose Paperie—"that Suncrest will keep using your store if you'll do us this one little favor this one little time." He smiled and lowered his voice. "Now that I'm back in California, we're going to be doing a lot of entertaining here at the winery. And I would really like to work with you again, Amy."

Her blue eyes got even wider, and Max felt that old familiar tightening in the groin. All that white skin, all that curly shining blond hair, that pert little tipped-up nose: he couldn't help but wonder how much of little Amy was exactly what shades of blond and pink. Maybe someday he'd find out. She might be a bit low wattage, but who said he had to talk to her for longer than the duration of one meal?

"Now you run along," and he helped her gather up her bulky stationery binders. "First thing tomorrow morning my assistant will fax over what you need to know. And she'll pick everything up late Thursday."

The moment the girl scuttled away, Max slammed the door after her and pulled out a cigarette from his trouser pocket. He felt like a model using nicotine as a weight-control device. Yet he wanted to lose the France avoirdupois but quick. And his favorite French Gauloises cigarettes were helping.

He raised a Roman shade and cranked open a window, then leaned out to encourage as much smoke as possible to flow away from the office. His mother hated the smell of tobacco. And these days, what his mother hated, Max too abhorred. He was a perfect son—considerate, somber, attentive—all to encourage her to go wheels-up for Paris and leave him free to run Suncrest as he desired.

The little junket he and Miss Amy were planning was a step in that direction.

Max half shut his eyes, watching his cigarette smoke curl into Napa's aqua blue sky. What a perfect scheme he had hatched. An overnight in Pebble Beach for a handful of important men, complete with golf at Cypress Point—of course that exclusive club counted Max as a member—exquisite lodgings, and a fabulous meal served alongside Suncrest's most cherished vintages. And on the guest list? Orwell Hampton from *The Wine Watcher* and Joseph Wagner from *Wine World,* two men whose wine scores translated into prestige and best-seller status for those few labels it ranked most highly. Two men whose favor his father had been above coddling, because his father believed the wine alone should be judged. As if *that* worked in the real world.

Max felt a surge of anger, which he tamped down with a second cigarette. He would not allow either parent to upset him—either the dead one or the live one. Though he had a gripe with both. It annoyed him that his father had not made more of Suncrest, made it into a bigger and more profitable enterprise. No, Porter Winsted had left that to his son to do. And his mother! She had truly pissed him off, not once but twice—by not handing him control of Suncrest right after his father died and then repeating the insult when Max came back from France.

Of course, those weren't the only things she'd done to him. Somehow, even when he was a kid, she'd made him feel like he was a huge burden to her. He remembered back to his tenth birthday. Apparently it'd been too much trouble for her to give him a party. So she made Mrs. Finchley do the entire thing, from the invitations to the cake to the band to the magicians. She hadn't even stayed home for it! The other kids noticed she was nowhere around. He'd been so embarrassed.

Max inhaled a huge hit of nicotine. *Man.* And now the huge irony was that he could relieve her of the winery, and she wouldn't let him do it! Of course he'd seen through that little charade with Will Henley; he knew she wanted him to believe she'd seriously consider selling. But if that were true, wouldn't she have done it already?

The good news was that this humiliating limbo—Is Max running Suncrest? Is he not?—would end soon. He could tell that his mother's anger was dissipating. That was the thing with actresses, of course: they never stayed with one emotion for long. Chances were good that before long she'd jet off to Paris, no doubt to get a good thumping from that Jean-Luc of hers. Actually, it might be just what she needed.

Max stubbed out his cigarette on the exterior stone windowsill, then stashed both butts in an envelope which he would hand-carry downstairs to dispose of in the break room trash. He sat down at his father's old desk, where a small brass clock informed him that it was already half past six, meaning official business hours were long over. Was it too late to make the day's most important call?

No, he decided, and picked up the phone. Will Henley didn't keep banker's hours. And Max wanted to get this over with.

He would inform Will Henley that Max and Ava Winsted did not want to sell Suncrest Vineyards, though thank you very kindly for your interest. Max had lined up a few reasons to feed the good investor, though none of them touched on the truth.

Max Winsted had big plans for Suncrest that made Will Henley's offer a hopelessly pathetic lowball.

* * *

It was just after seven when Will put down the phone from his call with Max Winsted. Immediately his intercom buzzed. "Your sister is here," his assistant murmured.

Good. He was curious to hear what had brought her in from Denver on such short notice. He touched the intercom button. "Please show her in, Janine, thanks."

He rose from his tufted leather chair to approach the huge paned windows across from his desk, which provided a sweeping view of San Francisco's Embarcadero. Chichi restaurants vied with hulking warehouses for waterfront position, both hiding the piers that jutted into the choppy waters of the bay. Joggers, dog walkers, and businesspeople—locals all—made up only a small fraction of the foot traffic. Most of the pedestrians could be easily identified as tourists by their shorts and spanking-new FISHERMAN'S WHARF or ALCATRAZ sweatshirts. Like most nonlocals, they had naively believed that San Francisco—being in California—would be warm in June, and had gotten a chilly surprise. In the distance, commuter traffic rumbled across the Bay Bridge, a feat of design and construction that never lost its marvel status in Will's mind despite how often he stared at it, his brain finessing the details of whatever deal was top-drawer at the moment.

One deal that had slid a bit from that vaunted position was the acquisition of Suncrest Vineyards. Max Winsted had given Will the official brush-off. What Max didn't understand was that Will Henley was not deterred so easily.

No, the Winsteds weren't ready to sell Suncrest yet. But that didn't mean they would never be. In fact, Max's call hadn't put Will off in the slightest. He remained as convinced as ever that one day, one day *soon*, the Winsteds would cave.

Will lifted a blue Lucite cube from atop the low coffee table in front of his sofa and twisted it this way and that. Suncrest was a winery in transition, a winery in flux. He respected Ava Winsted—he judged her to be a fairly canny operator—but he found it hard to believe that at this stage of her life she wanted to pour her energy into Suncrest. And Max? Max was a lightweight. Will calculated that the young heir, who'd never really had to do a day's work in his life, would tire of running Suncrest once he got a whiff of just how unglamorous the day-to-day gig could be.

Fine. Will would remain at the ready to relieve both Winsteds of their burdens. And he would prove—to himself and everyone else at GPG—that his strategy of focusing on Suncrest and Suncrest alone had been correct.

And in the meanwhile, perhaps he could focus on another quarter? He smiled and bent to return the Lucite cube to the table. Some things required more effort than others, but then some things—or people—were worth it.

An image of Gabby DeLuca rose in his mind. Passionate, sexy, strong-willed Gabby DeLuca. A highly attractive woman who also showed a lot of backbone.

For example, take how she felt about Suncrest. Clearly it was a huge part of her life and of her father's. The fact that she loved it as she did, though she didn't own a piece of it, spoke well of her—of her passion for her work, her loyalty, her good heart. It was understandable that she'd gotten so upset on learning of his desire to acquire it.

So maybe she was a little naïve about business. So what? He wasn't hiring her to run one of GPG's companies. In fact, one of the things he liked about her was how different she was from him, how refreshingly noncorporate.

"Will?" His sister stepped inside his office.

"Beth, you famous CEO, you." He enfolded her in a hug, then frowned and pulled back. "Is it my imagination or have you lost weight?" That wasn't all that had changed in the two months since he'd last seen her. She'd cut her hair fashionably short and streaked it, and was wearing more makeup than usual. Her sleek navy-blue suit was also a departure from her former preference for spring-bright colors. "You look great," he told her, though he wasn't fully convinced he liked this chic new version of his only sibling.

"Ah, I was getting sick of the same old, same old." She pulled away. "How are you? You look a little tired."

"No more than usual. Sit down." He waved her toward his cocoa-colored leather sofa. "Do you have business in town?"

They both sat. "A few meetings," she said. "I had some this afternoon, and I've got a few more tomorrow morning. Then I head back."

"Quick trip."

"Hm." Her gaze skittered away.

He regarded her. Something else was different, beyond her appearance. Was the workload getting to her? Well established as Henley Sand and Gravel might be—their grandfather had founded it sixty years before—running a sizable construction-supplies business was no cakewalk. Especially not while raising two boys, aged seven and five, though her husband, Bob, more than pitched in with the childrearing.

"Are you hungry?" he asked her.

"I could eat."

Will chatted about this and that on their ten-minute walk along the Embarcadero, Beth remaining uncharacteristically quiet. Once they arrived at the waterfront restaurant where he'd booked a table—which

boasted killer bay views and even better seafood—
"You order," she told him, without even glancing at
the menu.

This was not Beth's style, either. Will set his own
menu aside and leaned close across the linen-draped
table. "What's wrong?"

She hesitated.

"Come on, Beth. I can see something's bothering
you."

"All right. This is why I really came out here, anyway." She threw up her hands. "It's Bob. He wants
to move back to Philadelphia."

Will frowned. "That's where his family's from,
right?"

"And now his father's got some health problems.
They're getting older, but aren't we all?" She shook
her head. "He says that after nine years of doing what
I want, we should do what he wants for a change."

"I didn't realize he *wasn't* doing what he wanted
in Denver."

"It was news to me, too."

Will was silent for a moment, pained by the hurt in
his sister's carefully mascaraed blue eyes. "Is he
serious?"

"Very." She gave a short, harsh laugh, with no hint
of humor in it. "He already sent out résumés. He
wants to make the move this summer, before the new
school year."

"Do the boys know?"

"No. I'm praying it just goes away. I'm actually hoping the economy stays sucky so maybe he won't get
any offers." Her eyes teared up then. She made a
choking sound and tried to hide her face with her
hand. "And I'm afraid that if he does get an offer,
he'll go without us."

"Oh, Beth, he wouldn't do that." Will reached a

consoling hand across the table, but his sister just
shook her head and dug in her handbag for a tissue.

So this was why Beth had come into town—to tell
him this. It must be serious. Yet if a tornado had cut
a swath from Kansas to San Francisco, Will couldn't
have been more surprised. Beth and Bob's marriage
had always seemed rock solid to him, like his parents'.
From the moment Bob had appeared on the scene
Beth's senior year in college at Boulder, he and Beth
had seemed made for each other. Both engineers.
Both skiers. Both kid-lovers and eager to start a family. They even looked the same, like brother and sister,
blond and athletic and outdoorsy. When the boys
came, the picture was complete. Both had everything
they'd ever wanted.

A waiter swept past and laid a basket of bread on
their table. Beyond the windows, the bay waters did
their ceaseless dance. Puffy clouds scudded across the
twilit sky, while white lights began to shiver on the opposite shore as Berkeley's bohemian night came alive.

Will watched Beth stare out the windows with blank
eyes. This explained the weight loss, the new look.
She was doing what she could to entice, to hold on.
If Bob were there, Will knew he would have wanted
to throttle him. Though he probably would have been
wise to wait for Bob's side of the story.

Which Will could easily imagine. Beth always saw
her family and Bob never saw his. When he went out
to Colorado for college, he didn't necessarily intend
to stay forever. Henley Sand and Gravel had become
a bigger part of his life than he'd ever imagined. His
wife was tied to Henley S and G's CEO job.

And Will knew why. Because it wasn't good enough
for that damn brother of hers. It was too pedestrian,
too humdrum, too small a stage for a Harvard Business School graduate.

Will hung his head, guilt rising in his throat. Once in his life—*once*—the Golden Boy had rebelled. One of his greatest fears had always been that someday it would come back to bite him.

"You know, Beth . . ." He didn't quite know how to say it. He knew that was because he didn't say it nearly enough. "I hope you understand how much it means to me that you stepped in to run Henley S and G. I wouldn't be able to do what I'm doing if you hadn't. And it's probably not how you imagined your life, being tied to it, and to Denver."

She shook her head. "Look, Will, Denver is my home. And I'm tied to that company because I want to be." She leaned forward to force him to meet her eyes. Her voice was low and passionate. "So what if when we were growing up we always thought you'd run it? Times change!" She gave a little snort. "It's not like Japan, where the emperor's got to be male."

He pinched the skin between his eyes. "But sometimes I still feel like a shirker."

"Working eighty hours a week? I don't think so." She made a scoffing sound. "Anyway, what do you think I should do?"

"About Bob? I'm kind of out of my depth giving marital advice."

"Take a stab at it."

The devil sat on his shoulder and whispered. *Tell her that whatever Bob does, she should stay in Denver.* He tried to shake Beelzebub off, though it wasn't easy.

"I don't know," he said. "It sounds like a midlife crisis to me."

"At thirty-two?"

"You guys started young."

"That's true."

"I'd try to ride it out. I think there's a good chance he'll give up the idea. He may even go back to Philly to interview and realize he's not that crazy about it.

He may realize he doesn't really want to live that close to his family again. You don't know. Maybe he's just trying to make a point."

"Well, he's certainly done that."

They sat silently for a time, then again Beth spoke. "Maybe you're right." Her expression grew more hopeful. "I hope so." She sighed and took one last swipe across her nose with a tissue before stuffing it back in her handbag. "Okay, I'm officially ready to talk about something else." She tried to put a smile on her face, but only partly succeeded. "Let's dissect *your* love life."

Gabby DeLuca. He had to admit it was a stretch at the moment to link her name with that phrase, yet if hope was on the menu, she was the woman who came to mind.

"I did meet somebody who's pretty interesting," he told his sister.

"Good!" She narrowed her eyes at him. "So why do I get the idea there's a problem?"

"Well, for one, I'm trying to buy the winery she works for."

"For one? There's more?"

He sipped from his water before speaking. "She thinks I'm a capitalist pig."

Beth arched her brows and reached for her menu. "She reads you like a book. I like her already."

When Tuesday night finally rolled around, Gabby cursed herself for having agreed to meet Vittorio. When he'd called out of the blue on Saturday to announce that he was in Napa Valley and wanted to see her, why had she agreed? she asked herself. What had she been thinking?

She hadn't been thinking about *not* seeing him. That rebel idea had been shot down instantly, like an enemy aircraft. She knew she ran a high risk of heartbreak. She feared her recovery would be seriously set back. Yet she also knew she could not pass up the chance to see Vittorio for the first time since she'd left Castelnuovo. Maybe, she told herself, seeing him might actually help her. Maybe he'd changed in some horrible way that would make her wonder how on God's earth she'd ever fallen in love with him. Maybe he'd gotten grotesquely fat or gone bald or sprouted nose hairs.

Or maybe she was trying to rationalize what she was about to do, which on some level she was ashamed of. Going out of her way to see Vittorio after what he'd put her through made her either a fool or a glutton for punishment. Or both. She noticed she told no one about her intention to meet him—not Cam, not Lucia, not her mother, not her father. No one. Because she knew they'd try to talk her out of it, or insist on going along, and she knew she wanted to be alone with him.

For in a tiny, mischievous part of her brain, where naughty ideas lurked and pranced, she wondered if maybe Vittorio hadn't gotten married after all. Maybe he'd pulled out at the last minute, so overwhelmed by his love for Gabriella DeLuca that he couldn't possibly wed another. Maybe he'd succeeded in bringing his parents around. Maybe the senior Mantuccis were willing to accept her now, seeing how their beloved Vittorio was still—one year later—so desperately in love with the pretty American.

Who was, after all, of Italian descent.

She arrived at Bistro Jeanty slightly late so as not to appear overanxious. That had required sitting in her car for ten minutes, which had required parking on a side street so Vittorio wouldn't happen to see her when he himself arrived. She had deliberately chosen a restaurant as the place to meet in the hope that being in a public place would keep her from screaming or throwing things or maybe even crying. And she'd dressed down—black slacks and sweater, minimal jewelry, subtle makeup—both because she didn't want him to think she'd gotten all dolled up just for him and because she knew he liked her best this way.

She ordered herself to be strong, exited her car, marched into the tiny restaurant—cozy and chic and French—and felt something akin to a heart spasm when she spied him at a table in the rear, looking as handsome and sweet and wonderful as ever. Lovable, loving, warmhearted Vittorio.

Wearing a wedding ring.

"Gabriella." He rose from his chair and grasped both her hands, then kissed her cheeks, Italian-style. His dark eyes were alight with the fire she remembered; his features were as straight and Roman; he was as tall and lanky and well dressed in the casual but expensive clothes he purchased twice yearly in Milan.

Damn.

"You look beautiful," he murmured.

So do you, she almost said, their little private joke, though it didn't seem all that funny anymore. "I'm sorry I kept you waiting," she said instead, which wasn't even true.

They sat. The business of fine French dining buzzed on around them. People chattered and clinked glasses, and oohed and ahhed over their selections. One thought chanted nonstop in her brain: *It's Vittorio. Vittorio. Vittorio.*

"What brings you to the valley?" she asked him.

"Business. You know, it's gorgeous here. As lovely as you told me."

He had never come home with her while they were dating. When she returned to California to visit, which she did twice, she traveled alone. It was one of the few points of contention between them. It was also an omen, she realized later, that she had failed to heed. There had been a reason he didn't want to meet her family or to see where she came from. On some primal level, he must have known he wouldn't do right by her.

A waiter came by. They ordered sparkling water—his preference—and French wine—hers. A bit of a slap at him. Small-minded, she knew, but nastily satisfying.

"How is your family?" he asked.

"A week ago I would've said fine. But then my father had a heart attack."

"Oh, no." Vittorio's features twisted in what looked like genuine concern. "Gabriella, I'm sorry. How is he?"

"He's still in the hospital. Better, but weak. His heart is pumping at only half the strength of before." That was a malady she understood, as a matter of fact. It took a long time for a battered heart to get back to full strength. If it ever did.

"And your family?" she asked in turn, just to be polite, because she hadn't been too keen on Signor and Signora Mantucci. And they had never been other than chilly to her, at least once her romance with their son began to blossom.

Vittorio began to recite the latest Mantucci doings. Food was ordered and presented and cleared; their superficial chatter continued. After a time they moved on to what was new with his family's winery, which she was curious about. She learned that he was assuming more responsibilities as his father aged. As was right and proper for the eldest son, who was now settled. Now married.

Around them the crowd ebbed and flowed, the ebbing never lasting long because this was a popular eatery with delectable fare. Darkness fell beyond the small curtained windows, the deep velvet darkness of the valley, where city lights couldn't dim the firmament's sparkle.

Interestingly, the name of one person never passed

Vittorio's lips, one person who certainly loomed large in his life. For a very long time, in fact, she'd loomed large even in Gabby's, though the two women had never met.

Their entrées had just been cleared when Gabby popped the question. "How's your wife?"

Vittorio nodded as if he'd known this would come up. He leaned his elbows on their small table and linked his long fingers, studying them with apparent fascination. His wedding band glowed in the candlelight.

He raised his head to meet her eyes. "Chiara is pregnant."

Gabby understood of course that Vittorio had sex with his wife. She'd forced herself to understand that it had even happened more than once. Certainly it hadn't been as frequent or as wonderful as their own lovemaking—surely it was more pro forma than that—but she'd inured herself to the fact that it had happened, was happening, would continue to happen.

She hadn't forced herself to consider the likelihood of a child.

Or to fully comprehend that she would not bear the tender little creature who would inherit Vittorio's dark long-lashed eyes or ready smile, or the soft, soft hair that stayed curly even when it was sopping wet. But that sad truth was stampeding across her brain now. Chiara would bear that child.

"When is she due?"

"August."

And she would bear it soon.

Gabriella didn't allow herself the indignity of counting backwards to calculate exactly when the dastardly impregnation had happened. It had happened—that was all that mattered.

Vittorio was talking. "Gabriella, there's something I want to say to you."

She looked away from him and tried to steel herself anew. This, too, had the sound of something real, and she was rapidly hitting her limit of real for the evening.

"I am so sorry for how I hurt you," he told her. "Not a day goes by when I don't think of you or feel so bad for what I did to you."

He paused for a response. She stared at their tablecloth, stained now, not perfect and white as it had been before.

He went on. "I should never have let it go so far."

That hurt. She raised her eyes. "Are you telling me you would prefer that it had never happened, Vittorio? You'd rather take it back?" She'd never wanted that, not once. She wouldn't give up a single morning of waking beside him, a single thrill of seeing him after an absence, a single walk through the vineyards holding hands. One of her self-help books told her that meant she was truly living. She'd thrown it against the wall.

He shook his head. He looked tired—exhausted, really—and older than he'd looked just the year before. "I don't really want to take it back, Gabriella. But I knew there would be problems with my parents, and I didn't do anything about it. I was too happy, I guess. I didn't want it to stop."

Their gazes locked. She saw the pain in his eyes, mirroring her own, and for that moment was thrown back to that savage day when she first lost him, when amid the brutal destruction of her own world her heart had broken all over again for *him*, for his rage and pain and frustration. She had, in some ways, suffered for two. She had understood that he had counted on his parents to bestow their blessing, even though he had to have known they wouldn't. She had understood how deeply their refusal had hurt him. She had understood how their edict that he live his life on their terms—or else—had disillusioned him, robbed him of the last of his youthful innocence. Maybe, if he'd been a different man, their stubbornness would have given him the strength to marry her.

But was that a matter of strength? She wasn't sure. Vittorio was the man she loved precisely because he *couldn't* walk away from his family. The love and loyalty that infused his soul were what made him so dear.

"When my parents told me they wouldn't accept you, Gabriella, you have to understand, it was like they were saying, Vittorio, you have a choice. You can cut off your arm or you can cut off your leg." He leaned closer, a plea in his voice. "Do you understand?"

She hesitated. Then, "I understand you chose them over me."

"I had to! I couldn't choose you and keep them. And if I couldn't keep them, then you and I would never be happy."

"Are you happy now?"

He fell back against the spine of his chair. *No,* his silence screamed. *Not really,* his dark eyes repeated. And there her heart went all over again, there came the tears to her eyes, there came the fragile, beautiful wish in her soul that even without her, he would be happy.

I must love him still, she thought, *because no matter what, I want the best for him. Even if it doesn't include me.*

"I want you to be happy, Gabriella. I want you to find a man who loves you with all his heart. Who can do better than me." His voice broke. "When you find him, maybe I can forgive myself."

She rose from her chair then, unable to speak for the tears in her throat, for the new gash across her healing heart. She hoped that in her eyes he could read the words that shouted in her head. *Vittorio, Vittorio, you're already forgiven.*

He seemed to understand, because he nodded, and didn't try to stop her when she walked out the door, for the first time in her life leaving him behind to watch her go.

Chapter 6

"Can you believe this?" Max asked, grinning.

Ava had to smile as she watched her son. Dressed in his makeshift pajamas of sweatpants and T-shirt, his mussed dark hair haloed by the morning rays streaming through the kitchen windows, he wore a look of satisfaction few *Wine World* reviews had ever provided any Winsted.

"The 1999 Suncrest Cabernet Sauvignon," he read, "serves up dazzling layers of tightly focused currant, anise, and blackberry. Excellent structure, remarkable focus, richly elegant. An extraordinary effort." Max slapped the magazine and let out a whoop. "You can say that again!"

Ava arched a brow, leaning her robed back against the long granite-topped center island. "Are you taking credit for the winemaking now?"

"Nope. But I am taking credit for this review." And he gave her that lopsided grin again, like a mischievous imp daring her to contradict him.

But she couldn't. Not this time. Ava's slippered feet padded over to the stovetop as the teakettle began to whistle. How could Max's "schmoozing"—as he put it—not be credited for this best-ever *Wine World* review? A ninety-four, Joseph Wagner had given the 1999 cab. In Porter's day, J. W. had never rated a Suncrest vintage above ninety. Was it coincidence that this A+ score followed Max's hosting of the Pebble Beach jaunt? Who could be so naïve?

Perhaps it was true that Max would never be the vintner his father was. Still, he might be effective in his own way. And wasn't that as much as she could hope for?

Ava poured boiling water into her tempered-glass coffeepot from France, freshly ground Sumatran beans already inside. She didn't like electric coffeepots— they were gauche somehow, besides which they cluttered the counter. European-style coffeemaking better suited her sensibilities, as did the high-tech German oven and the handcrafted white cabinetry it had taken a team of woodworkers two months to complete.

"You know, Mom, I've been tossing around another idea I'd like to run past you." Max hoisted himself atop a black leather-covered stool at the island's curved far end. "I'm thinking of hiring consultants. Just to get another perspective on where Suncrest is and where it's going. I could use a thought partner on some marketing ideas I've been playing with, for example."

Ava laid a sourdough loaf on the wooden cutting board and sliced off a few pieces, then poked them into the toaster. This was both to speed breakfast and to give her time to think.

How sage he sounds, she thought, *how very sensible! Another "perspective"? A "thought partner"? And he actually wanted to run these notions past her first?* This was certainly a change. Max's traditional mode of operation was to go off half-cocked. It had been some time since Ava had enjoyed a swell of maternal pride, but she was starting to feel positively buoyant now.

She pulled a few jars of fruit preserves from the

Sub-Zero. "That's an expensive proposition, though, isn't it?"

Max abandoned his stool to fetch plates, knives, and napkins, another departure from the *I'll sit here, you serve me* Max of old. "It is, but it can more than pay for itself. And I'm not planning on using them long." He pulled two Italian ceramic mugs from the glass-fronted cabinets. "I won't do it unless you're in favor, Mom. I know we need to keep costs in check."

"I'm not against it," she heard herself say.

"Good." He bussed her on the cheek, smiling, then proceeded to boil more water for oatmeal and to chop dried cherries to mix in. By himself. Briefly Ava thought that another mother might have been more gratified if her offspring had begun to perform these tasks at age twelve, but she was thrilled to witness them even at twenty-five. There had been many a day when the teenaged Max had made such heavy use of Mrs. Finchley that Ava had feared the housekeeper would flee in high dudgeon to her native Bristol.

Max flipped on the TV—but not before a "Do you mind?"—and ate his breakfast alongside Ava without once swearing at the news anchors. Then he carried every single plate, mug, and piece of cutlery to the sink—hers included. He didn't actually load them into the dishwasher, but he did rinse them, then straightened the dishtowel that hung from a hook near the oven.

Then, "I'm going to shower," he declared, and half jogged out of the kitchen as if the day's business were too important to delay. Ava watched, wondering if it was all an act and fearing it might well be.

But perhaps it wasn't. She felt an uncharacteristic wash of hope where her son was concerned. For a moment she could actually envision a sparkling future in which Max was a reliable and considerate son who managed Suncrest with an able hand. Then she could enjoy life with an unencumbered heart. True, without Porter. But perhaps with Jean-Luc.

Thinking of him made her smile. Maybe she *could* swing a quick trip to Paris. Jean-Luc had been virtually begging. And though she hated Paris in summer— it was crawling with tourists and the heat positively radiated—he had suggested they decamp to the countryside, where, it was true, the high temperature was far more tolerable.

Amid those pleasant thoughts, Ava was about to embark on her daily run when she saw Gabriella's mud-caked Jeep pull into the small parking lot behind the barrel-aging building. Ava waved a hand in the air to motion the girl closer.

She arrived at a trot, dirt-smeared as usual. "Good morning, Mrs. W."

"Good morning, Gabriella. Have you seen the *Wine World* review?"

"I did!" The brows behind the trendy violet-lensed sunglasses shot up in obvious surprise. "I'm going to show it to my father. He'll be thrilled."

"Good, that's what I wanted to make sure of." Though privately Ava believed Max had much more to do with the review than Cosimo DeLuca—winemaker though he might be—she had learned in her Hollywood days that a wise woman shared credit. "How is your father doing at home?"

"Champing at the bit."

"Well, you can tell him that I believe Suncrest's future has never been brighter. Exciting new things are in store for this winery. He has that to look forward to."

"Excuse me?" Suddenly Gabriella was leaning forward, all intensity. "What exciting new things? Is something happening to Suncrest?"

Ava frowned. "Whatever do you mean?"

She looked flustered. "I mean . . ." Her mouth

slammed shut. Then, tentatively, "Are there any changes in the offing that perhaps I should know about?"

What is this girl going on about? Then Ava had a revelation, one she found quite disturbing. *Could Will Henley have told Gabriella about the offer?* Of course Ava had taken note of the attraction between those two at the hospital—it was almost embarrassingly palpable—but she'd never imagined that a man in his position would divulge such sensitive confidential information. Certainly not to a woman in whom his interest could only be sexual.

Ava gave her voice an intensity of its own. "Despite what anyone else may have told you, Gabriella, I can assure you that the only change on the horizon is Max's management of the winery. This is the beginning of a thrilling new era for Suncrest, one that my husband and I looked forward to for years."

Ava watched the girl's eyes go wide behind her sunglasses. "Yes, Mrs. Winsted," she said.

"I trust you're as enthusiastic about this transition as I am? Because it is crucial that Max be surrounded by loyal employees. I will not have him undermined by his own staff."

"I understand. And let me assure you, I am excited." She paused, then, "I'd like nothing better right now than to see your son take over Suncrest."

"All right, then." Frowning, and silently cursing one Will Henley, Ava waved off her young employee.

Gabby hurtled her Jeep south along Highway 29, heading for the town of Napa and her parents' house. Here, around Yountville, the valley was wide around her, with gently mounded foothills rising to the east and west. Elsewhere in California, their green lushness might well be hidden beneath tract housing. But the restrictive zoning in this part of the valley kept them closer to a natural state.

Will would probably disapprove. Gabby snorted quietly. *Too bad.* He was out of luck these days, at least with regard to Suncrest. It was fantastic news that he hadn't been able to persuade Mrs. W to sell. There was still the open question of how Max would run the place, but just maybe he wouldn't do anything idiotic.

Perhaps she'd luck out and things in her life would stay pretty much the same. That's what she hoped for, deep down, though it made her feel boring and unadventurous to admit it. From when she was a girl, she'd liked habits and routine, order and predictability. She used to make daily agendas for herself. *Up at 7 A.M. Shower/breakfast till 7:30. To school by 7:45. Class till 11:15* . . . On and on, for the whole day. It gave her profound satisfaction to cross through each checkpoint on time, *X* each item off the list. It gave her a sense of control and forward motion.

But falling in love with Vittorio shredded her lists like confetti and tossed them out the window to blow away. Life became a free-for-all. And a delicious one, which surprised her. Things happened when they happened, and the wonder of it was, she didn't mind. Lovemaking in the middle of the day. Bathing at four in the afternoon. Walks at all hours. Lunch at three, with maybe a nap after. Working till nine to catch up, then wine and pasta and bed, with Vittorio, always with Vittorio.

Until the day always ended.

Highway 29 widened to two lanes, a signal that she had arrived in the more heavily trafficked southern end of the valley. Gabby maneuvered around a slow-moving flatbed truck and wondered if Vittorio was still in Napa. He felt gone, somehow. Yet he'd felt gone the moment she'd walked out on him at Bistro Jeanty. She knew it was good that the ache that followed was dull, not searing, that she felt hollow, but not lost. It meant she was getting over him, for real this time.

A few minutes later she hit Trancas Street and turned left. This area, nearer to San Francisco, was a lot less glamorous than the bucolic towns farther north. The snobbiest folks from up-valley would drive through as fast as possible, turning their noses up at what was basically generic commercial suburbia. Four-lane thoroughfares and strip malls and fast-food chains held sway. Unfortunately, all the concrete meant you could easily forget you were in one of the most naturally beautiful spots on earth.

After a few zigzag turns, Gabby found herself on the cul-de-sac of her childhood. Her parents' home was one among a series of California bungalows: all small and tidy and differentiated by how well their owners tended their particular square of lawn. The DeLucas benefited from both Cosimo and Sofia being neat freaks.

Gabby pushed open the unlocked front door to find her father in the living room, wearing pajamas and watching a raunchy TV talk show. He punched OFF on the remote control the second he saw her, a sheepish expression spreading over his unshaven face.

She had to laugh. "I caught you!"

He threw up his hands. "How am I going to do this for six weeks?"

"You have to take it *this* easy for only the next few weeks." She kissed his cheek, then perched on the brown corduroy couch next to his easy chair. "How're you feeling?"

His face twisted into a *not bad* expression. Even though he was convalescing, Gabby was shocked to see her father's life reduced to daytime TV and too much free time. A musty smell lingered about him, as of clothes too long worn or a bath too hastily taken.

The colorful afghan she and Cam had crocheted as
teenagers draped over his legs, as if he were an invalid
in a wheelchair. A small tray cluttered with pill bottles
rested on the side table next to the cheesy Leaning
Tower of Pisa coasters she'd brought back as a gag
souvenir from Tuscany. She pivoted a few of the bottles to face her. Toprol. Zocor. Bayer aspirin.

"I think I'm due to take one of those," he said,
cocking his chin at the aspirin.

"I'll get you some water."

It was in the kitchen that she noticed the flowers. A
showy assortment of white roses, orange lilies, and yellow oncidium orchids, delivered in the sort of vase that
Gabby's mother would save rather than recycle. There
was only one person they could have come from.

Will Henley hadn't disappeared from her mind, despite his ongoing silence, which now had persisted for
nearly three weeks. Still he lingered at the edge of her
consciousness, occasionally giving her pause to wonder.

Why hadn't she heard from him? Did she want to?
Had he been interested in her only when it was possible he might acquire Suncrest, in which case he would
have wanted her support, and both DeLucas' winemaking expertise? Could he be that cynical?

Gabby returned to the living room and handed her
father the glass of water, trying to keep her tone light.
"That bouquet in the kitchen is really beautiful."

Her father tipped back his head and swallowed the
aspirin with an H_2O chaser. "You know it's from that
Will Henley fellow, right?"

*Was it her imagination or did he sound fake casual,
too?* "I know he sent some flowers to the hospital."

"And sent this bunch here. I remember liking him,
when I was talking to him during that dinner." Her
father's tone turned wry. "Though I have to say the
rest of the evening is kind of a blur."

"He was very helpful," she heard herself say. "He

really took charge when you had the heart attack, then he came to the hospital and stayed till past two."

"Did he really?" His brows arched as if that tidbit gave him something new to think about. "I liked him," he repeated; then his eyes strayed to the blank TV screen. Gabby had the funny feeling he was waiting for her to say something confidential, something girly and private that didn't pass often enough between fathers and their grown-up daughters.

She was quiet for a time, then, "I like him, too." It hung in the air, an admission of truth swinging back and forth in the breeze billowing inside through the open front window. "But I think I gave him the impression I didn't. I think I may have overreacted to something he told me."

Her father's gaze snapped back to her. "How so?"

Gabby crossed her arms and stared out the window. Some neighborhood ten-year-olds were using the cul-de-sac the way it was meant to be used: as an asphalt baseball diamond. All that was different from her day was that a good number of the players were girls.

There were things she couldn't tell her father about Will Henley. That he'd tried to buy Suncrest, for example. That news flash was strictly verboten, not to mention that her father would find it highly upsetting.

"He's in business," she began. "In the city. With some hotshot company that does investments." She paused, then, "It makes me think he sees the world very differently from how I do."

"You're in business, Gabby. Suncrest is a commercial enterprise."

"It's not the same thing. You and I don't spend our time worrying about whether Suncrest makes money. We just try to make the best wine we can."

He laughed. "Well, it's good *somebody's* worrying about it! Otherwise Suncrest wouldn't have lasted for long."

She reclaimed her seat on the couch. "Don't you ever think the valley's changing too much? That it's a lot more about making money than it used to be?"

"Oh, sure. For lots of folks, money's all they're interested in." He paused and looked away from her, his dark eyes taking on a faraway gleam as if he were thinking about other times, times she'd never known. "But that's not true for everybody. Never has been." He frowned and moved his eyes back to her. Narrowed. Penetrating. "Are you worried that's what this Will is like?"

She shrugged, feeling slightly embarrassed and very cornered. "A little."

"Just because of the outfit he works for, the kind of work he does? Do you even really understand what that is?"

She heard the incredulity in her father's voice. She met his gaze and scrunched her nose. "You're thinking maybe I judged him too fast?"

"Well, it certainly seems to me that he's been very nice to us. And he didn't have to be. It's not like the DeLucas can boost him up the corporate ladder." He shook his head, his mind clearly made up. "Nope, he didn't strike me as the sort of man who cares only about money."

A tiny hope leaped in Gabby's heart as she listened to her father. *Maybe he's right. All I've seen Will be is considerate and helpful. I wonder if it's me who's been the jerk here?*

It was ironic. She hated when people judged her on the basis of snippets of information. She was her father's assistant winemaker, so they assumed she got her job not because she was good but because of that inside connection. She was nearing thirty and never married, so they thought she was too uppity or picky or careerist to get a man. Now she'd gone and made slapdash judgments about Will, relying almost entirely on her own biases.

Great work, Gabby.

Her father continued, but now he had a sparkle in his eyes. "You know, I noticed him staring at you all during that dinner."

"You did?"

"Yes, I did." He paused. "And I liked him."

She didn't know quite why, but tears pricked behind her eyes. "Oh, Daddy," she managed, then she had her arm around his neck and her head against his shoulder, and it was as if all the fear and heartache of the past days fell away like a winter cloak shed in the first warmth of spring. Her father's heart was beating a steady rhythm, for the first time in years her life didn't begin and end with Vittorio Mantucci, and an American man named Will Henley had sent her father flowers—twice—and stared at her all through dinner.

She raised her head to see that her father's dark eyes were moist, too. "You know," he said, "if you made a mistake, you can always apologize."

She could. And she realized she wanted to. "Do you—?" she started to say, but she didn't even need to finish.

Her father patted her knee. "Just come back later, honey."

She kissed him and then was off, in the Jeep, on 29 back to the winery, not sure what she was going to do about Will Henley but knowing it was going to be something.

It turned out he beat her to it.

"You got a package," Cam chirped from the reception desk when Gabby burst into the winery, hell-bent for who knew what. "I put it on your desk."

It was a small box wrapped in string and brown paper, like an old-fashioned delivery. She knew it was from Will even before she opened it, though a big clue was that the return address read SAN FRANCISCO. She tore into it with excited fingers.

Inside was a white box tied with light blue ribbon. Then tissue paper, then something cool and roundish and ceramic. Carefully she pulled it out.

It was a pig. Pink and cheerful-looking. With a big round rump and a squiggly tail and perky pig ears above an enormous snout.

There was a note attached. Which read, *Dinner Saturday over July 4th weekend? Please say yes. Give your favorite capitalist something to look forward to . . . Will.*

Will always thought that GPG's Monday partners' meeting was like a grown-up version of Show and Tell. For the junior partners like him—who were intent on currying the favor of the senior partners like Simon LaRue—they generated a fair amount of performance anxiety. You had to describe your deals-in-progress in realistic terms yet still project supreme confidence about them. If the partnership got any whiff of doubt, it would be a deal-killer. And while you benefited from their best thinking, you might also get creamed by their analysis.

This group didn't miss much.

Will sat at his usual place at the conference table, its mahogany expanse littered with folders, documents, charts, and the occasional laptop computer. Lunch had been cleared, but the coffee and water services remained. Modern art of the multimillion-dollar variety hung on the pristine white walls, while perfectly tended phalaenopsis orchids in blue-and-white Japanese pots perched on the two side tables. For this session, three of the usual attendees were missing—two away on business and one on a long weekend. At midafternoon, seven pairs of challenging eyes turned toward Will.

Simon LaRue spoke from the head of the table. He was allowed to play pasha when managing partner Hank Faskewicz was out of town, and clearly lived for the role. "What do you have for us, Will?"

Will rattled off the latest on his telecom and publishing deals, generating the usual aggressive backflow of questions and comments. He finished with, "We've got a term sheet with Internco, and I anticipate we'll be finalizing that deal by the end of the month," which generated nods all around.

He took a deep breath. *Now for the hard part.*

"With regard to our acquisition plans in Napa Valley, the Winsted family of Suncrest Vineyards has passed on our initial offer. However, as we've discussed here before, the winery is in transition. The only heir, Max Winsted, who's twenty-five years old, is just back from France to manage the operation. I remain confident that in the short to medium term he'll find running Suncrest sufficiently challenging that the situation will play out in our favor."

He leaned back in his chair. *The End,* he hoped, but it was not to be.

Directly across from him, fellow junior partner Susan Amos Jones frowned. She was African-American, a Rhodes Scholar, and married to a director of the biggest consulting firm in town. "Are you looking only at Suncrest or are you considering other opportunities in Napa?" she asked him. "Aren't there more than two hundred fifty wineries there?"

"Suncrest offers a distinctive value proposition, Susan." Will leaned forward and steepled his fingers. "The brand is well known but underutilized. It's focused exclusively on cabernet sauvignon and sauvignon blanc but could be applied to a broader range of varietals targeting the same customer base. In addition, the winery owns significant property in the so-called Rutherford Bench, which produces superior cabernet sauvignon grapes. It's extremely difficult to acquire vineyards in that area, and this acreage has not been fully planted because the owners have been content to run a smaller operation. And as I've said before, I believe the family situation is such that given a bit more time, the Winsteds will be primed to sell."

Omar El-Farouk piped up, from Will's right hand. Stanford B-School, fabulous New York connections, national amateur cycling trophy. He was the third young partner, meaning he and Susan and Will were competing for the one senior position that might open up over time. "You *are* looking at other options, correct?"

Will turned cool eyes in his direction. "Of course." Looking? Sure. Doing more than that? No. Feeling a bit queasy about that strategy at the moment?

Yes.

At the head of the conference table, Simon LaRue cleared his throat. "I believe there's fairly significant time pressure here. I understand that both Diamond Capital and the Richmond Group are going to try to buy Napa wineries to bundle them into real-estate investment trusts and take them public. And I know of more than one European winery investigating Napa acquisitions."

Unfortuately for Will, LaRue was attuned to valley gossip. He and his third wife owned several acres of prime vineyard in Sonoma Valley, where LaRue played vintner in his spare time. He fancied himself deeply plugged in to California's wine country, though Will suspected his most intimate connections were with his fellow vintners' wives.

LaRue focused his hawklike eyes on Will. "What's your timetable, Henley?"

Getting tighter by the second. "We'll have a deal by the end of September," he pronounced, though this was the first time he'd given himself that deadline.

LaRue put a thoughtful expression on his face, doing a nice imitation of the firm's absent graybeard, Hank Faskewicz. "Late September may be fine," he intoned, as if it were solely up to him and not the firm's entire senior partnership. "But I'd rather we step up the pace. Once other firms recognize the Napa opportunity, we'll be looking at auctions. And nobody makes money when everybody chases the same deal."

Will nodded. Despite his discomfort at the not-so-veiled pressure, he knew LaRue was right. He also knew LaRue believed Will shouldn't be putting all his eggs in the Suncrest basket.

The meeting ended shortly thereafter. Will beat a hasty return to his office, feeling an urgent need to get an enormous amount of work done. He found waiting for him eleven phone messages, twenty-three e-mails, and one festive red gift bag with white tissue paper poking from the top.

He smiled as he picked up the bag. He knew who he wanted it to be from. He was almost reluctant to delve into it for fear he might be disappointed.

He reached inside. First he encountered a small parchment envelope, unmarked, which he set aside. On his next foray his fingers closed around a box that just fit in the palm of his hand. He pulled it out. It was white, with a small gold-and-red sticker on it proclaiming the name of the St. Helena store where the item had been purchased. His heart began to beat just a bit faster.

Carefully he opened the box. Nestled within a tissue-paper bed was a glass heart the color of the deepest burgundy. It felt cool and weighty in his hand. He peered at it closely, puzzled by its unorthodox design. For the heart was meant to appear broken. The glass was split down the middle, almost but not quite to the base, with each half sporting a beautifully rendered jagged edge.

He frowned, slightly worried. Surely the heart in question wasn't already broken?

He opened the parchment envelope and scanned the note inside, written in a curlicue feminine hand: *Dinner accepted, with pleasure and anticipation. From your favorite bleeding heart . . . Gabby*

Ah. He chuckled. He understood. Will Henley stood in his office on that workaday Monday afternoon, and for a short, happy time Simon LaRue and tricky acquisitions and impossible deadlines all seemed just a bit less important.

Chapter 7

Max had just stashed his mother's bright red convertible on the pebbled driveway behind the house when he spied Gabby DeLuca in the employee parking lot a hundred yards away, getting out of her Jeep and heading for the main winery building. She strode at a rapid clip across the asphalt, from which he could see the heat rise in shimmering waves. She wore khaki shorts and a white U-necked T-shirt and a blue-and-white bandanna that held her hair back from her forehead. He positioned his hand above his eyes to shield them from the midday sun and just watched her.

She is a babe, he concluded. *Look at those legs.* Long, tanned, and thin, but with enough muscle to prove she worked out. He let his eyes rove farther up her body, and a smile he wasn't even aware of curved his lips.

Max could use a piece of that. It'd been a while. And wasn't it ironic that the female who inspired his ardor just so happened to be the person he most needed to see at that very moment?

He called out her name, and she spun to face him. He approached her, helping to close the distance between them, knowing he needed to exhibit supreme charm to accomplish both items on his agenda.

He halted a few paces away from her, but close enough to smell the Coppertone she used to protect that pretty skin of hers from Napa's scalding summer sun. It was a favorite of his, reminding him as it did of the bikinied girls of his youth. He smiled at her, widely, invitingly. "How you doing, Gabby?"

"Just fine, Max, how are you?"

"Never better." He smiled at her again. She didn't exactly smile back, but Max didn't mind having to work it. "You know, you're just the woman I want to see."

"Really? Why's that?"

"A little something's come up I want to talk to you about." *A big something's come up, too, but we'll save that for later.* He jerked his thumb back behind him. "Why don't we talk up at the pool? I'll get us some fresh lemonade."

She seemed surprised but then shrugged. "Sure. Sounds good."

Max allowed her to lead them along the narrow path back toward the house, which also allowed him to assess her posterior from closer range. In his opinion, it bore up well under this closer scrutiny. "I just dropped my mom off at SFO," he told her.

She half turned as she kept walking. "You drove all that way just to drop her off at the airport?"

"Oh, it's not that far." He tried to sound as though to Thoughtful Son Max, it was nothing to go a bit out of his way for Dear Old Mom. Actually it was a 150 fucking miles round-trip, but he couldn't risk her having a last-minute change of heart. "She's going to Paris for a few weeks." Even saying it made him grin. It'd taken some expert maneuvering to get her to go, but he'd succeeded. Clearly he was on an upswing.

Gabby laughed. "You Winsteds must love France. One gets back and another one goes."

"Well, she's been doing so much around here lately, she really deserves a break." *See how considerate I am? Can you imagine just how nice I'd be to you?* "Don't you like France, Gabby?"

"I do, but I'm more of an Italy person."

"Ah." He paused, then, *"La dolce vita per la bella ragazza."*

She just laughed, but he felt sure his compliment hit its mark.

They arrived at the house, and he led her around the side path to the interior yard, where the pool, lawn, and pergola baked in the heat. Just beyond a low mesh fence, vineyards stretched as far as the eye could see, hemmed in by mountains faded to a dull purple by the sun's white-hot light. He could almost smell the grapes ripening.

"I'll be right back," he said, and returned a few minutes later to find Gabby relaxing on a white wicker rocking chair in the pergola's cool shade. Her long naked legs were crossed and her head was thrown back against the neck rest. She lifted it when he handed her a tall glass of lemonade and raised his own in toast. *"Salute!"*

They clinked glasses and then both downed a good bit of the lemonade. He prided himself on having had the presence of mind to bring out the whole pitcher. He refreshed her glass. "You did an apprenticeship in Italy, right?"

"I did. You know what, Max?" She set down her glass, ice cubes clinking. "I don't mean to be rude, but I've got tons to do today. What was it you wanted to talk to me about?"

So she wasn't much for foreplay. Fine. "Well," he started, "I've been talking to some marketing consultants, very highly regarded folks, and we've come up with an exciting plan for this year's sauvignon blanc."

"Great." She waited. "What is it?"

"You know those hot new French bottles? Bordeaux style but twice the weight? Very in these days, the newest thing. Sell like hotcakes."

She said nothing, just watched him. A little frown appeared between her eyes.

Here goes nothing, he told himself. "We're going to use those bottles for the sauvignon blanc."

"Oh!" She paused. "You mean for next year's."

That's what the consultants had suggested, but no, that's not what he meant. Why wait? The time to move was now. "No, I mean for this year's."

Silence. A bee buzzed nearby. Gabby leaned forward so that her wicker rocking chair tipped frontways as far as it would go. "For this year's? You're joking, right?"

He laughed. It sounded funny, oddly fake, in the thick air. "I'm serious, Gabby! The rebottling will make some extra work for you, sure, but it'll be so worth it. The sauvignon blanc will jump off the shelves. We'll break sales—"

"Max." Her tone irked him. It sounded like his mother's most of the time. "This doesn't make sense. The wine was bottled back in March. The release date is ten days away. It's warehoused. It's ready to go. The bottles are fine. If you want to switch for next year, that's something to think about. But—"

"Gabby." It was not for her to tell him how the bottles were. "I understand your concern, I understand it'll make more work for you to rebottle this vintage. But this is a marketing decision, and I don't think you are in any position to make marketing decisions for this winery."

Apparently she didn't agree. "Have you considered the implications? The potential damage, for example?

A million things can go wrong during rebottling, and any one of them could hurt the wine. Particularly a delicate white like a sauvignon blanc."

He had to bite his tongue. Of course he'd thought about that! Sure, he'd heard horror stories about decanting, but like all horror stories, they were exaggerated, overblown. And who was Gabby DeLuca to wonder—out loud—if Max Winsted knew what he was doing?

But she kept going. "I just want to protect the wine. That's priority number one. And we charge a lot for our sauvignon blanc—it's very dangerous to risk a degradation in quality. Especially when we don't have to."

Max started to get seriously irritated. He slapped at a mosquito squatting on his forearm. Its corpse left a bright red blotch of blood on his skin. "There is a very good reason why I want to do this, Gabby, and I'm taking the time to explain it to you. Which I certainly don't need to do."

"Have you considered how much this will cost? And what are you gonna do with the old bottles? Just throw them out?"

No, he wanted to scream, *I'm going to use them for the new rosé Suncrest will be making next year!* But he didn't want to get into the topic of adding varietals with this woman, who no doubt wouldn't cotton on to that idea, either.

"I have to say, Max, I don't like this." She stood up and set her hands on her hips. She sort of loomed over him, even though she wasn't that tall. Truth be told, he wasn't finding her all that attractive anymore. "If it gets out that we rebottled, everyone will assume there's something wrong with the wine." She paused, then, "And why wouldn't they? No winery would decant unless it had to!"

In other words, you're an idiot, Max. All of a sudden

he stood up, too, and she backed away a step. If she were a man, he might have punched her, for by now he was pretty damn pissed off. Particularly because he realized he hadn't thought about the PR implications of rebottling.

But he wanted those French bottles. He knew—he *knew*—the wine would sell faster. It would be yet more proof that Max Winsted knew what he was doing. And weren't his instincts spot on? Hadn't he been right about the wine reviews?

She spoke again, and this time her tone was big-time accusing. "Does your mother know about this?"

That's it. He'd had enough—of her tone, her complaints, her arrogance. And all because she didn't want to go to the trouble of rebottling! Sure, she said all she cared about was the wine. But he knew that was just an excuse. "I'm doing this, Gabby. With or without you. Now are you in or not?"

"So you don't care that the wine could be hurt?"

"It's your job to make sure it isn't. So I repeat, are you in or not?"

She threw out her hands. "I have to be in, if only to try to keep the wine from being ruined! So I don't really have a choice, do I, Max?"

The threat was unspoken but as loud as a fighter jet directly overhead. *No*, Max thought, *not if you want to keep working here. Or if your father does. Remember that health coverage he's depending on right about now? Who do you think pays for that?*

"Another thing," he said. "I don't want to miss the release date so—"

"What?"

"You heard me." He couldn't miss the date, because then everyone would think something *was* wrong. Not to mention that Suncrest would lose shelf space if the new sauvignon blanc wasn't out on time.

"It's Tuesday today. You've got till a week from Friday. That's plenty enough time."

"But we're talking about twenty thousand cases! And it's July Fourth weekend coming up. Everybody's off for three days. By the time we get the bottles back from the warehouse and get a decanting truck in here and reprocess the wine and rebottle it, we'll never make the release date!"

He moved a step closer to her and stared right into her eyes. He watched her stiffen. "You are going to make that date." He kept his voice low. "I don't care how you do it. Make people work the weekend. I'll pay overtime. Just do it."

"This is insane."

"Just do it."

He would have liked her to look away before he did, but it didn't happen. She just narrowed her eyes at him and then stalked off. He watched her go.

Does your mother know about this? she'd asked him. As if the decision weren't his to make. He pulled his cigarettes out of his shorts pocket and lit one. Of course his mother didn't know about it. Hell, she hadn't even known when he'd hired the consultants. He'd only told her he needed her approval to make her happy. He'd hired them days before.

The nicotine didn't calm him like it usually did. Somewhere in the back of his mind a doubt rose and flew, dipped and buzzed, like those damn mosquitoes. He tossed the half-finished cigarette on the lawn.

Women. Stubborn. Set in their ways. Think they know best when they don't know a damn thing.

It took him a second to smell the smoke, another three or four to stamp out the tiny blaze his cigarette had ignited on the sunburnt lawn. He stared at the miniature charred circle, amazed by how fast the fire had started, thinking he'd better remember to make the gardener patch the area before his mother got home from Paris.

Three thirty Saturday afternoon found Gabby at Suncrest. Near the bottling line but not on it, because the equipment had broken down.

Cam came to sit next to her on the idled forklift, her round cheeks flushed, dark hair pulled back into a haphazard ponytail from which numerous curly strands had escaped. Like Gabby, she wore beat-up jeans, work boots, and a T-shirt. None too glamorous but right for eight hours on an assembly line. "When did Felix say he'd get back?"

"He should be back by four."

"I hope he gets the part we need."

"You're not kidding."

They lapsed into silence, though mariachi music blared through the high-ceilinged warehouselike room where the mechanized bottling line hulked silently, like a wounded beast. Six of their fellow bottlers lounged on various stools and crates and boxes. Gabby knew none of them was as anxiety-ridden as she was. Sure, people griped about having to work the entire July Fourth weekend. But double overtime eased that pain. And nobody but Gabby DeLuca had to worry about how well the finished product turned out, or whether they'd still make the release date.

Cam spoke. "I can't believe Max is making us do this."

Gabby shook her head. She'd toyed with the idea of trying to reach Mrs. W in France, even quizzed Mrs. Finchley about her boss's whereabouts. But she'd come up empty. The veteran housekeeper was too loyal and well trained to divulge any personal information to a mere Suncrest employee.

"This was exactly what I was afraid of when Max took over," Gabby said. "That he'd make a bunch of asinine decisions. But even I never imagined he'd come up with anything this stupid."

"Mom almost had to tie Daddy down to keep him from coming in here today."

"His reputation's really on the line. More than mine."

Since they were rebottling on the q.t., everybody would blame any deficiency in Suncrest's 2003 Sauvignon Blanc directly on the winemaker. Surprisingly poor winemaking for Cosimo, they'd say. Wonder if it had anything to do with his daughter helping him for the first time? Her first vintage as assistant winemaker—and thanks to Max Winsted, it might taste like swill.

It was so frustrating. A classic no-win. If the rebottling went well, all she'd have accomplished was to help Max achieve his French-bottle coup. But if it went poorly, the blame was on her and her father, who was laid up trying to recover from a heart attack Gabby was convinced Max Winsted had brought on!

And where was the man of the hour? Nowhere in sight, though maybe it was better that way. When the leased decanting truck had rolled in Thursday—to uncork the old bottles and decant the contents back into the stainless-steel tanks where the wine had aged till March—Max had been around. Strutting like a peacock, asking idiotic questions, basically getting in the way. He'd been around Friday, too, when Gabby had spent the day carefully feeding nitrogen into the tanks to displace the oxygen the decanting had introduced. Now it was the three-day weekend—at least for those people who didn't have massive work crises—and she didn't see hide nor hair of Max. Nor did she expect to until the holiday was over. Let the peons do the work—that was his attitude through and through.

"Your dress for tonight is gorgeous," Cam said. "Will's going to love you in it."

Gabby had to smile. Little sleeveless wrap dress, soft and swirly with a deep V neck, in a black-and-rust pattern that went really well with her hair and skin. It was hanging in Suncrest's women's lockers because she'd known she wouldn't have time to get home to shower and change. "You don't think it's too much?"

"No." Cam vigorously shook her head. "It's perfect. Just sexy enough but not over the top. With those strappy black sandals of yours, it'll be great. Where are you guys going?"

"Bistro Don Giovanni."

"Fabulous. I'm so jealous."

Gabby glanced at her watch. A bubble of nervousness pulsed through her veins. Felix better get back soon with that corker jaw. If the line was operational again by four thirty, she could bottle for two hours, hop in the shower, and be ready for Will by seven. Felix could oversee the last ninety minutes of production. She wouldn't be too nervous letting him handle that much.

They had to finish the shift, because they had to bottle four thousand cases a day. Otherwise they wouldn't get the twenty thousand done in five days. And they'd miss the release date.

4:15 rolled around. Still no Felix. Gabby walked outside to stare down the drive to the Trail. For some reason that didn't make Felix reappear.

4:30. She called Leo Gordon, the bottling-line manufacturer's rep. He'd promised Felix he had the right corker jaw for their line. His cell phone went directly to voice mail.

4:45. Gabby went in search of Cam and found her in the break room. She looked up from her paperback and frowned. "Still nothing?"

"This is getting serious."

"You are not going to cancel dinner."

"Cam, we have three and a half hours of bottling to do."

"So? We can do it without you."

Maybe they could. No part of her wanted to blow Will off. But so much could go wrong with the rebottling, and it was up to her to make sure that it worked. And what could she even use for an excuse with him? She couldn't tell him the truth. As it was, she'd have to pretend they were bottling the sauvignon blanc the first time around. *Oh, there's so much demand, we want to release a little earlier than we'd intended!*

The capitalist pig he'd sent her had fast become one of her most precious tokens. She'd named it Warren for Warren Buffett—one famed investor whose business values she'd long admired—and set it atop her nightstand between her alarm clock and current stack of paperbacks.

Every time she saw Warren, she thought of Will. And was reminded anew that he didn't take himself too seriously. And that he had a sense of humor. And that he cared enough about her to go out of his way to make this little private joke between them.

It was highly endearing.

At ten past five, Felix burst into the bottling area. "I didn't get it."

That blow nearly knocked Gabby to the concrete floor. "What?"

"Leo got the part numbers mixed up. He thought he had the right one, but he didn't." From a small plastic bag, Felix shook onto his weathered palm three variations of a corker jaw, used to compress corks before insertion into bottles. "I took these with me in case we could rejigger one to fit. If that doesn't work, Leo said we could try to borrow from Indigo Hill or Tulip Mountain. They've both got the same bottling line we do. Otherwise he'll get one for us Tuesday."

Tuesday! The next regular business day. Meaning

they'd lose two and a half bottling days. Meaning they'd never make the release date.

Gabby's mind raced. But borrowing would require telling rival wineries that Suncrest was bottling the Saturday evening of July Fourth weekend. How weird would that look?

She made an instant decision. "Felix, you try to make one of those fit. I'll make some phone calls."

Forty minutes and five delicately worded phone calls later, she succeeded in convincing Mirador Winery in Sonoma Valley to lend her what she needed. She sent Felix to get it—as none of the rejiggering had come even close to working—sent Pepe to get pizza for the crew, and stared at the big, round, white-faced clock that hung in the break room.

5:50. We can't start bottling till seven at the earliest. So we won't be done till 10:30. What do I do?

"You go on your date," Cam declared. "Felix can manage the line. Don't worry."

How can I not worry? But how can I cancel on Will?

At seven o'clock on Saturday night, Will stood outside the big oak door of Suncrest's main winery building. He wiped his palms down his trouser legs. Again.

So much for his usual sangfroid. The Will Henley who brokered deals with big-name CEOs and extracted concessions from hard-ass bankers was disconcerted to find himself more than a little undone by the prospect of an evening with a five-foot-six-inch blonde with hazel eyes, a ski-jump nose, and a fascination with crushing grapes into wine. It occurred to him that maybe he should have shown up with a wrist corsage. He was about as nervous as he'd been on prom night.

He took a breath, pushed open the door, and walked into the winery. His feet led him toward surprisingly loud clanging noises directly ahead, which competed for aural dominance against ear-splitting Mexican music. He stepped into an open warehouse-like space where a half-dozen people were spread out around some kind of assembly line. It took him a few seconds to recognize what they were doing.

A forklift carted a massive stack of cardboard wine cases—all labeled SUNCREST SAUVIGNON BLANC 2003 and bound together with shrink wrap—out big rear doors to a Mack truck. Dozens more cases waited for attention, some filled and some empty. Pizza boxes, soda cans, paper napkins, and plastic cutlery littered a metal table set up against the north wall.

He frowned. They were bottling on Saturday night? Over July Fourth weekend? And they must've been at it all day, too. He was pondering that mystery when he caught sight of Gabby approaching him across the expanse of concrete floor, and all of a sudden couldn't care less what her crazy colleagues were up to.

He got an eyeful of long bare legs in high-heeled sandals and long bare arms swinging at her sides and long-lashed eyes the color of honey. She moved with an easy grace, like an athlete or a dancer, hips undulating in a mesmerizing rhythm beneath the thin fabric of her summer dress. He swallowed, his throat suddenly dry, remembering the feel of that warm supple body pressed against his, the baby-velvet softness of her skin, the sweet demands of those full coral-colored lips.

She stopped a few feet away, and his nostrils filled with the same musky perfume she'd worn the night they met. "Hi," she said.

"Hi."

"You're right on time."

"And you're gorgeous."

The smile, which had seemed a bit tentative at first, widened. Out of the corner of his eye, Will saw two Hispanic women on the assembly line exchange a glance, smile, then refocus on the bottles whizzing past.

"You must be a real slave driver," he told Gabby, "bottling on Saturday night!"

"Oh . . ." She waved a hand in the air, causing the silver bangles on her forearm to crash together in a tinny collision. "Last year's sauvignon blanc sold out so fast, our distributor wants the new shipment earlier than we expected. So we've got to bottle all weekend."

He nodded, his businessman's mind immediately dismissing that explanation. Given what he'd learned about the wine industry, it made no sense. Sauvignon blanc was bottled in the early spring. Plus, all the overtime—probably double?—made it too expensive to be plausible. Maybe he could get Gabby to confess what was really going on over dinner.

"Shall we?" He crooked an arm toward her.

"Sure," her lips said, but she didn't move an inch. Instead her gaze fluttered toward the assembly line. Then, "Just a sec," and she ran off to huddle with what looked to be the senior man on the line. A half-minute later she hurried back. "Okay."

"Is everything all right?"

"Fine!"

But her voice was unnaturally chirpy, and there was something jittery about her movements. Still, she grabbed a small black handbag from atop a crate and accepted his arm. They had made it nearly to the big oak door before a cacophony rang out behind them. Two women shouted "Stop the line!" equipment clanged, a bottle broke, then another. Finally a loud male voice called out "Shit! Stop!" and a prolonged mechanical groaning rent the air. Followed by silence.

Gabby halted in her tracks. Will looked down to see her features twist in a grim mask of indecision and worry. "What is going on?" he asked her.

She hesitated, then, "We're having a little trouble with the bottling."

Unfortunately, that much was becoming clear. So was the fact that it was her responsibility. Holiday weekend or no holiday weekend. Date or no date.

He watched her and saw a woman aquiver with tension. Brow furrowed, lip clenched between her teeth. Her reluctance to leave radiated like a force field.

It was admirable, he had to admit, though his own competing desires roared through his head. He saw the evening he'd been anticipating for days slip away like a party balloon in a summer sky. His heart sank as he envisioned a long disappointed drive back to the city, hungry, alone, frustrated, Gabby-less. He steeled himself. "You're not okay with going out to dinner, are you?"

She said nothing, just drew in a breath through her teeth. Then what to do hit him, and he smiled. Like all good solutions, it was obvious and made perfect sense. "How about," he said, "we stay here and I help you guys bottle?"

Her head swung back toward him, her eyes wide. "What?"

"I don't know, it might be fun!" He laughed. Actually, it might be. He hadn't done anything remotely resembling physical labor since the days of his youth, when he'd routinely pitched in to help with the grunt work at Henley Sand and Gravel. In some ways that had been more satisfying than a lot of what he did now.

"But Will . . ." Gabby's voice faltered. "You don't really want to bottle. It's assembly-line work, it's tedious, you're all dressed up, and besides, you couldn't help anyway because of insurance problems. You're not a Suncrest employee."

"Hire me as a consultant. Just for tonight." He was Mr. Problem Solver now, a guise as comfortable for him as old jeans.

She shook her head, disbelief still evident in her voice. "But aren't you hungry? Don't you want to go out to dinner?"

"Gabby." He took her hands. Small, cool to the touch, wonderfully delicate. "We could go out to dinner or not. It doesn't really matter." He stopped himself from voicing the next unrehearsed line that sprang to his lips. *I just want to be with you. It's kind of all the same to me what we do.*

But he might as well have said it for the smile that came to her lips. Something passed between them then, something more than a look and less than an electric charge, though Will could swear he felt the air around them still, enveloping them in a bubble of their own creation. He had the same sensation he'd had at the hospital: *I can't believe I just met this woman. I feel like I've known her all my life.*

She cocked her head, teasingly. "I bet there's some pizza left."

And there was. They ate their impromptu dinner sitting on crates, knees almost touching, occasionally leaning their heads in close to talk, because once the assembly line got moving again, the noise was deafening. Between bites of black olive and pepperoni, Gabby explained how bottling worked—the orbiter that jetted air into the bottles to rid them of debris, the filler function, the corker. Soda cans in hand, they strolled to the capsuler, where the metal casing was put on the bottles, followed by the spinner, which tightened the casing. Labels went on last.

They halted at packing, where two people worked at a breakneck pace to put twelve bottles into each case. "You might be able to handle this," she told him, her breath a tingling kiss on his ear. "But I'm not sure you're up to it." He pulled away to see her eyes sparkle with a mischievous light.

"Or maybe you could do this." She stopped at flap-gluing and box-flipping. A woman slapped preprinted labels on each case, detailing the winery name and wine type, plus the date and time of bottling and UPC code.

"What's your job?" he asked her.

She tossed her soda can into the trash with apparent nonchalance. "I'm the boss."

He smiled. He'd figured.

Gabby ended up assigning him a brute force task—stacking the labeled cases. After that they were shrink-wrapped and carted away by the forklift. Will rolled up his sleeves and was about to get started when she reappeared at his side, by now out of her little black dress and into jeans and a hot pink T-shirt. She looked pretty darn good that way, too.

"There's something I didn't tell you," she said, and handed him ear plugs and plastic safety glasses.

"What's that?"

She winked. "Your shift won't be over till after ten," she said, then sashayed away, distracting him for some time from his carrying and stacking duties. But once those got under way in earnest, he had a lot less leisure than he would have liked for eyeballing the boss. The cases came fast and got heavier and heavier, though he felt compelled to keep moving them along just as fast. Muscles he rarely gave much thought to began to ache in earnest.

He noted that Gabby herself was in constant motion, pitching in at various stops around the line, relieving people when they slowed or needed a break. Every once in a while she halted near him and caught his eye through her safety glasses and his. A smile—an *Are you okay?*—and she moved on. Once she relieved him briefly, and he was mightily impressed by her hauling and stacking abilities.

It was strenuous. It was dusty. His hands blackened with dirt; his muscles rebelled. This was so far from how he'd imagined this Saturday night when he'd sent

Gabby the capitalist pig. Yet music blared. People laughed. Dancing broke out, usually by Gabby's sister Cam and the label-slapping woman he learned was named Zenobia. Once Cam and Gabby danced together, and once he and Zenobia did. There wasn't a Winsted in sight, and not once did he miss them.

When ten minutes past ten rolled around and the line clanged to a halt, he was almost disappointed. Until people started washing their hands and stamping their time cards and filtering out into the night, when it occurred to him that he might finally get Gabby alone.

She tore her safety glasses off her head and approached him. Her hair was matted, most of her makeup was sweated off, and her T-shirt sported a lightning streak of grime down the front. But she lit up that warehouse like a klieg light.

"Good job!" She high-fived him. "Thanks to you, we met our goal of four thousand cases for the day. We might use you again if you can keep up that pace."

He wouldn't tell her he'd be sore for days. Instead he said, "You hungry?"

"I'm starving."

"Any place still open at this hour?"

"Little place called DeLuca's."

It took him a second to comprehend. When he did, his smile widened. "What's their specialty?"

Gabby grinned back. "PB and J. Served alongside a nice chardonnay."

There was that electric charge again. It pulsed through Napa's night air—blessedly cool now—all the while Gabby closed down the winery for the night. And all the while his Z8 trailed her Jeep along the narrow moonlit roads that led to her home.

Chapter 8

In Gabby's estimation, Crystal Mountain Road lived up to the latter half of its name. Narrow, twisted, and steep, it snaked uphill from Highway 29 through a forest of oak and eucalyptus—the sort of road where one vehicle had to pull over to the dirt-packed shoulder to let oncoming traffic pass. During daylight hours, the higher elevations revealed stunning mountain and meadow and vineyard panoramas. At night, with no streetlights for miles and a leafy canopy obscuring the moonlight, all Gabby could make out was the strip of asphalt illuminated by her high beams, and occasionally the yellow-eyed stare of a startled feral cat whose nocturnal wanderings she'd interrupted.

Behind her she could hear the guttural growl of Will's automobile. She smiled. So much for its city-clean chassis. It would get baptized by Napa dust tonight.

She flipped on her left directional to alert Will, then made a sharp turn onto the even narrower dirt drive that climbed farther uphill to her house. Her Jeep rocked on the rutted surface, while branches reached out from the surrounding woods to slap the vehicle's sides. She halted on the small pebbled clearing in front

of the house, and Will parked behind her. Engine
sounds died away, replaced by the wind's whisper
through the treetops. On this foggy night, so rare in
the valley's summer, stars winked against their black
velvet backdrop, peering down with curiosity on the
man and woman who stood in awkward poses on the
earth below.

Gabby was nervous suddenly. Was it a huge mistake
to bring Will here? What would they talk about? What
did she want?

*For the night to go on. Not to have to say good-bye
too soon. Another chance to get back into that bubble
with him, that bubble where the rest of the world falls
away.*

He came to stand beside her. "This could safely be
described as remote."

She laughed, though she was embarrassed by the
observation. "I guess I have a little hermit in me."

"Does your family live nearby?"

She heard the puzzlement in his voice, the words
he didn't say. *What are you doing living up here on
this mountain all alone?* But she didn't want to answer
that question. Not yet anyway.

She made her voice light. "No, they live down in
Napa," and began walking toward the house. "Come
on, I'll show you around."

She fumbled with the house key, her fingers clumsy
and uncooperative, her every sense vibrating with the
awareness of Will hovering behind her. She wished
she'd disposed of the recycling piled by the stoop,
hosed down the canvas barbecue cover, visibly grimy
even in the dark. Finally she pushed open the door
and hurried inside to turn on a few lights.

Her house showed best at night, she knew, when
soft lamplight smoothed its rough edges. Worn turned
into cozy, frayed into charming. Her furnishings were

a hodgepodge of heirlooms, hand-me-downs, and flea-market finds. Grandma Laura's sideboard, shipped a decade before from Milan. Her mother's cedar hope chest, draped with the white runner the young Sofia had handstitched in high school. The rustic pine dining-room set Gabby's father had restored. The iron fireplace pokers Gabby had picked up in Castelnuovo, now ensconced beside the stone fireplace.

That night, a ceramic pitcher of yellow and orange zinnias graced the low pine coffee table and filmy white curtains at the paned windows danced in the night breeze. Gabby thought the effect was delightful, but that was no surprise. This was her oasis, her refuge, the place where she both escaped the world and readied herself for it. But she knew how shoddy and unsophisticated it might appear to Will. She didn't know much about him but could guess that country casual wasn't his style.

He stood in the doorway as imposing as a Viking, tall and broad shouldered, sleeves rolled up to reveal well-muscled forearms covered with light blond hair. Gabby realized with a start that he was the first male who wasn't a relative who'd ever visited her home.

He stepped farther inside. "This is great! When was it built? Was it a house originally or something else?"

Either that's real enthusiasm in his voice or he's a fabulous actor. "It was a barn first, built in the late 1800s. I know it went through several renovations. These fir floors were put in fifty or sixty years ago. And I'd bet the skylights are a seventies addition."

He grinned. "That sounds about right," and shook his head. "So this was built before Napa was real wine country."

"Not true! There were tons of wineries here in the late nineteenth century. But then came Prohibition."

He stood across her living room. Watching her.

Smiling. All of a sudden, she didn't know what to do with her hands. Her mouth kept moving as if it had a will of its own.

"It got really crazy during Prohibition. There's a story that the Foppiano family was forced to dump ninety thousand gallons of red wine into the Russian River."

He moved a step closer. "What a waste."

"Not really. Lots of folks came out to the riverbank to drink."

He laughed, then stepped even closer until he was breathtakingly near. She was forced to tilt her head back to look into his eyes. His voice softened as his blue gaze held her hazel one captive. "So, Gabby De-Luca, you're a local historian as well as a winemaker."

She found herself unable to break his stare. "I'd better be, given that I'm an investment-guy tour guide."

"Ah, that's right!" A light twinkled in his eyes, a faraway star. "How's the tour business?"

"Improving."

"When does your first client get his first outing?"

"I'd say he's getting it tonight." They gazed at each other for a moment longer; then she backed away from him, undone. His nearness, his maleness, the unmistakable undercurrent of attraction that pulsed between them roiled her senses and tipped the safe world she'd created into something she'd long ago forgotten. She'd felt nothing like this since Vittorio, and even with him she'd settled fast into a comfortable domesticity. What she felt now—this hyperawareness, this ubersensitivity—was strange to her, and not entirely welcome.

She headed for the kitchen, eager for escape. "I'll open some wine," she called over her shoulder, and unearthed a Sonoma Valley chardonnay. But seconds later he was beside her again, appropriating the bottle, pulling out the cork, telling her a funny story about his Aunt Mina, who insisted on serving Mateus Rosé—over crushed ice—on every major holiday.

Gabby was laughing and, she realized, comfortable again. They touched their wineglasses together.

"To your bottling effort," he said. "May it get done on time."

Amen. She sipped, squashing a compulsion to confess what they'd really been up to that night. She might be trusting Will more—a *lot* more—but as far as she knew, that old adage about loose lips remained as true as ever. "So," she heard herself say instead, "are you still interested in the house specialty?"

His brows arched. "You mean the PB and J?"

"Yup."

"I'm game," he said, which set off a flurry of searching for bread and jars and spreading knives. Will held up the peanut butter and peered at the label. "Well, I'd say this product confirms the conclusions I've drawn so far about you, Gabby."

"Have you been holding me under a microscope?"

"Metaphorically, of course. Though I wouldn't object to a real-life close-up inspection." He paused. She felt his eyes on her profile and busied herself with scraping the last bits of raspberry jam from the jar, which all at once seemed of paramount importance.

He went on. "For example, I deduce not only from this all-natural peanut butter but from the rest of your home that you're a believer in simple, high-quality materials. You choose honest, true things and let them speak for themselves. You're straightforward, not fussy. You're substance over style."

Her hands stilled, her knife poking uselessly into the empty jam jar. She felt herself being lulled into a delicious torpor hearing him speak of her like this. It was as sweet as a caress, and somehow just as intimate.

"I see it, too, in how you dress." His voice was low,

soothing. "I see it in how little makeup you wear, how you leave your hair free." She heard him set the peanut-butter jar down on the tiled countertop. Then he was right beside her, leaning against the counter. She stared unseeing at the white tile backsplash, keenly aware that his gaze was riveted on her face. "You're a woman who's so comfortable in your own skin that you don't need any pretense."

Silence. *He's going to kiss me again. If I let him.* Her heartbeat got away from her, and her memory flew back to that hospital stairwell. How he'd felt. How she'd felt. *Oh, God. And he hasn't even touched me yet . . .*

But then her hands took over, smashing the two slices of wheat bread together in a haphazard sandwich that she held out in his direction. "Eat," she said, sounding like her mother, cursing her nervousness, wondering how on earth she could be so attracted to a man yet so fearful of his touch.

You're afraid what it could lead to.

And what heartache could follow.

He cooperated. He laughed and let the moment slip, and allowed the two of them to down their midnight snack while chatting about nothing in particular. Then he roamed, wineglass in hand, examining the family photos plastered on the fridge with kitschy little magnets, the black and red rooster tiles that showed up intermittently among their all-white brethren, the Tuscan plates arranged on stands on the countertops. When he fingered the kitchen curtain aside, his voice grew curious. "Is that a hot tub I see out there?"

"Sure is. It was probably put in when the skylights were."

"Care for a dip, Ms. DeLuca? Given how much abuse our muscles took tonight?"

That was an idea. She'd used it the night before, and it'd been heaven. She cocked her head, some of her girlhood flirting ability bubbling to the surface. "You trying to get me in my bikini, Mr. Henley?" Actually, she realized, she wouldn't mind seeing him in a more dressed-down state.

"I was thinking we might skinny-dip." He winked. "After all, I hardly came equipped with trunks tonight."

"Ah, but unfortunately for you I can solve that problem." She set down her sandwich. "Back in a sec."

She returned bearing a pair of grotesquely garish red-and-yellow plaid trunks. "Now before you say anything, you should know these belonged to my father. He should've thrown them out twenty years ago, but I finally got him to donate them to my going-to-Goodwill stash. I just haven't made it there yet."

"Lucky for me." His tone was wry. He accepted the trunks with about as much enthusiasm as if she'd handed him a soiled diaper.

Gabby abandoned him to get into her favorite bikini—hot pink and push-up. She grabbed towels, wrapped one around herself, and hightailed it out the kitchen door to find Will already in the tub, both wineglasses beside him on the warped redwood deck, broad shoulders glistening from the water, hair wet and slicked back.

His eyes never left her. She didn't think she imagined the gleam in their blue depths as he watched her shed the towel and slide into the water. She threw her head back to wet her hair then settled across from him, bobbing slightly as a strong jet of water massaged her back. She tried not to be too obvious as she assessed the hunk of near-naked maleness a few feet away from her, looking impossibly strong and handsome.

Around them, the valley slept. A crescent moon hung high, a lone cloud scudding across its silver surface. Far away a coyote howled, a plaintive and lonely sound that on other, solitary nights had echoed in her own soul.

Gabby felt herself being lulled into somnolence by the water's warmth and rhythmic churning. She sipped the last of her wine and watched the tub's steam writhe into the night sky, feeling no need to say a word. How wonderful that was. How rare.

It was Will who broke their silence. "I can see why you like it here. It makes the real world feel very far away."

"I feel that way sometimes. But then I remember this world is real, too."

"You grew up in Napa?"

"And then went to college in Davis. About an hour away."

"What did you study?"

"Enology. With a double minor in viticulture and chemistry."

"Tell me about the time you lived in Italy."

The question startled her. She would have preferred to delve into safer topics, like his schooling. *What can I tell him about Castelnuovo? I fell in love, and it was magic. Then I lost my love and it became a nightmare.*

She thought for a moment. "I worked in a winery in Tuscany, and it was a lot like working in Napa and yet different in interesting ways. People were very friendly"—*except for Vittorio's parents*—"and I learned a lot about my own heritage." She paused, then, "It was a very special time."

"How long ago was this?"

"I got back a year ago."

"How long were you there?"

"About three years."

She noticed he was eyeing her in that way he had, that way that analyzed and penetrated, with an intense concentration that made her feel he missed nothing and grasped far more than she actually said. Then he simply looked away and nodded, as if he were filing information away for future study.

"You're smarter than I am," he told her. "While you were in Tuscany, I was killing myself in San Francisco. Eighty-hour weeks, one deal after the next, one trip after another, juggling a bunch of negotiations at the same time." He shook his head, then laughed. "Don't get me wrong. I like what I do. But sometimes I have to wonder. . ." He stopped.

"If it's all worth it?"

"Something like that."

The revelation pleased her, made him seem less of a businessman and more of a kindred soul. She decided to venture onto forbidden territory. "You must be really sorry you're not going to be able to buy Suncrest."

His brows flew up. "You heard about that?"

"Not directly. But Mrs. Winsted made a point of telling me how Max was taking over and how thrilled she was and how she and her husband had looked forward to that for years. She said enough that I drew my own conclusions."

He looked away. "Max did reject the offer."

"Are you very disappointed?"

He said nothing for a time. She had the idea he was choosing his words carefully. Then, "I am. But there's more than one winery in Napa."

"That's certainly true."

"You must be relieved."

"Well, you know where I stand on that." She swirled the wine in her glass, then heard herself say, "You know, part of me wondered if you were only interested in me because you might buy the winery. And then you'd want my support, and my father's."

Instantly he moved across the tub to within inches of her, half kneeling so their eyes remained level. "It's never been that at all, Gabby. Sure, I would want your expertise if the deal went through, but you've got to know my interest in you doesn't have anything to do with your ability to make wine."

His eyes were very serious. Then they dropped to her mouth and lingered there, before he raised them again with apparent reluctance. It was as if she asked, *Why? Why are you interested in me?* because a second later he answered that question.

"I don't care what work you do, Gabby. I care that you're beautiful and smart, and have a good heart." He looked away from her and squinted into the dark, as if he'd find the explanation there. "When I'm around you, I like how I feel. I haven't felt that way in a long time."

You and me both, Gabby thought. They stared at each other. She realized that for good or ill, she believed him. And that she'd gotten the bubble she wanted at the start of the evening, the bubble where she and Will were the only two people in the world.

All at once his hand reached out to find the nape of her neck and lingered there, soft and titillating. Before she could resist the movement he pulled her toward him and claimed her mouth. She felt his other hand encircle her waist and pull her tight against the length of him, crushing her breasts against him, allowing no whisper of space to separate their bodies. Somewhere in her dizzy delight she parted her lips for his inspection, wanting more as he deepened the kiss, needing more in the marrow of her soul, wondering how she had ever been crazy enough to think she could do without his kissing her again. Her own hands reached around his head, toyed with his short wet spiky hair, clutched the strong slippery breadth of his shoulders, reveled in the wonderful manly feel of him, different from Vittorio yet so shockingly right.

He grasped her hips, his hands greedy on her naked

flesh, and pressed her hard against him. She thrilled at his arousal, so frank, so unabashed, so male. The idea of giving him what he wanted, what *she* wanted, allowing him to do what he would with his hands, with his mouth . . .

Perhaps the same vision accosted him, for he ended the kiss, though he continued to hold her. His heart was a hammer against her distended nipples, his breath a groan of sweet suffering in her ear. "You're killing me, Gabby," he whispered. "But I don't want to take it too fast with you. I want to do this right."

She knew what he meant. Maybe in a saner moment she would have wanted the same thing. But in that instant she knew where she would go if only he would take her, though it was so unwise. How willful, how foolhardy to care only for the union her body screamed for and not one whit for restraint or logic.

But Will had enough of both, and on this night Gabby wasn't sure if she loved or hated him for it.

He pulled away from her, and a chill washed over the skin that had been so warm a moment before. "Do you mind if I stay the night on your couch?"

"Not at all."

"I don't want to drive back to the city."

"I don't want you to, either."

"I don't want to leave you tonight."

His words hung in the night air, as frank and true as the stars in the sky.

She found a spare blanket and pillow and helped him set up a makeshift bed on her couch. It took every ounce of her will to leave him there and retreat alone to her solitary bedroom, where cold sheets awaited her, and restless dreams, and a night that took forever to become morning.

Will woke before dawn but did not allow himself to rise from Gabby's living-room couch until sunlight streaked across the skylights above his head. Then, pulling on his trousers, he padded to the front windows to inspect the view. It didn't take him long to step outside, barefoot, because it seemed nonsensical to allow glass to separate him from the beauties that lay beyond.

It was a stunning vista, lovelier than he'd imagined in the dark. He hadn't realized that vineyards were so close at hand—mere yards, not even a fence away. In the shade of century-old oak trees, terra-cotta planters burst with flowers, from delicate pink anemones to violet morning glories to deep purple lobelia. Against the house, rose vines heavy with white and pink blossoms climbed a rickety trellis. Gabby had a little vegetable patch going, as well: tomatoes, baby lettuces, beets.

Truth be told, the house in the midst of this natural wonder looked a bit the worse for wear—all brown shingle and chipped white window frames and slightly crooked stone chimney. It was vintage, to put it nicely. Run-down, to be frank.

Will didn't want to leave it. He didn't want to leave the woman who called it home. He didn't want to do what he had to do that day: drive away from Gabby, pack for a week in New York, board the red-eye that night, refocus his mind on his telecom deal. What he wanted to do was go back inside that ramshackle former barn and take Gabby DeLuca to bed—all morning, all afternoon, and preferably well into the evening. Maybe—*maybe*—he would allow food breaks, but that was hardly a given.

He could have taken her to bed the prior night, he knew. He'd felt her want—Christ, he'd tasted it, seen it, smelled it. Maybe he'd been a fool. He knew there was no perfect time for these things; there was no crucial moment. Yet some instinct had told him it was too soon, too fast, that he shouldn't rush it. There was a skittishness about her, a wariness. It made him think she was getting over someone, or didn't fully trust him yet. Maybe Suncrest was still in the way.

He grimaced. He hadn't *lied* about that, exactly, but he'd certainly committed a sin of omission. *No, Gabby, I'm not disappointed about Suncrest. I still believe I'll be able to acquire it!* But he would've landed right back in the doghouse if he'd told her that. And the bottom line was, he didn't want to muck things up with this woman. There could be something real with her.

Damned if you do. Damned if you don't.

Damn. Will threw back his head and stared at the morning sky, trying to convince himself that he would be able to manage the situation. No, he told himself, he wouldn't have to choose between Gabby and GPG. If he got to the point of acquiring Suncrest—which he'd better, since he had to make a Napa deal happen and this was the only winery he'd bet on—he would simply have to bring Gabby around to his point of view: Suncrest was better off in GPG's hands than in the Winsted's.

In the meanwhile, he couldn't lie to her. He *wouldn't* lie to her. But he would have to keep his mouth shut about a possible deal. Professional ethics demanded it.

He ambled back into the house to find the makings of coffee. The simple actions of opening and closing cabinets, foraging for coffee beans, a measuring spoon, a filter, centered and contented him. Eventually the aroma of coffee brewing prodded his brain cells, made other questions rise in his mind.

Why in the world did Gabby live alone on a mountaintop? Okay, she was a bit of a hermit. That jibed with her being a scientist and a nature girl. But she was young and single. That *didn't* jibe. He would've expected her to rent a bungalow in downtown St. Helena, near restaurants and bars and something resembling civilization.

Yet her reclusiveness attracted him. Clearly she wasn't on the prowl to snare a man. Nor was she afraid to break the mold. She did what suited her whether it was standard operating procedure or not.

He poured himself a mug of coffee and warmed his hands through the ceramic. *You got it bad, Henley. There's nothing about her you don't like.*

True, frightening but true. Gabriella DeLuca was exciting and comfortable all at the same time, at once a mystery and a mystery solved. He couldn't remember the last time a woman had exerted this kind of pull on him.

Maybe because none ever had.

He loped back outside to inhale more of the view, halting on the vineyard's edge to listen to a mourning dove, its lulling song absent from his city life. A few minutes later he heard Gabby call out behind him.

"Careful! Watch out for rattlesnakes."

He heard the teasing note in her voice but still had to stop himself from doing a fast-step pirouette away from the grapevines. He turned to face her. "Isn't it too hot for them to be out?"

"Not this early."

She was smiling, and looked sweet and sleep-tousled. She, too, held a mug, and wore a red plaid flannel robe that looked as if it got a lot of use. A crease was pressed into the soft skin of her cheek from the bedclothes. He felt another rush of desire for her and wondered how he would keep himself from tearing off that robe and taking her right here in the dirt.

She came to stand beside him, looking small without heels on. "Did you sleep well?"

"Like a baby," he said, then added, "Once I fell asleep." The conspiratorial light in her eyes told him she'd endured some sleeplessness, as well. *We're co-*

sufferers of the same disease, he thought. *My damn common sense.*

"I have some bad news," she said.

"I don't like the sound of that."

"I have to be back at Suncrest for bottling in a little over an hour."

"Mind if I join you?"

She laughed, a surprised happy sound light as a bird call. "You want to do that *again*?"

"Yes, I do." *I want as much time with you as I can get.* Already he had a crushing sense of how hard it was going to be to see her. He lived seventy miles away and had a killer job with frequent travel. He'd be lucky to get up to Napa some weekends. And she wasn't exactly sitting on her hands, either. "I have to catch a flight later but I'd love to help out this morning. If that'll work for you."

She was silent. He could almost hear the gears of her mind turning. Then, "You know those professional ethics you told me about before? The ones where you have to keep all kinds of confidential information to yourself?"

He looked away. "Sure."

"If you promise to honor that code for me, I'll tell you something."

Part of him wanted to scream *Stop! Don't tell me!* But something—curiosity? opportunism?—kept his lips from mouthing that warning. Instead he repeated, "Sure," one noncommittal syllable he hoped would keep her talking.

She regarded him solemnly, sipped from her mug, then spoke. "We're actually *rebottling* the sauvignon blanc. That's why there's so much time pressure to get it done. Max came up with this cockamamie idea of using these new French bottles. . . ."

She explained, and Will listened, and the more he heard, the more jumbled his feelings became. On one hand, this was an asinine management decision on Max's part. Meaning he was screwing up faster than Will had anticipated. Meaning there might be upheaval soon at the winery and an early opening for Will and GPG to step in and save the day.

Yet . . . this was clearly bad news for Gabby. She was Max's employee. She had to implement whatever strategies he came up with, sensible or not. That bothered him in a way it hadn't before.

Her eyes were on his face, squinting slightly as the sun gathered force in the sky. He understood the trust she put in him to confide in him like this. He knew she wouldn't have said word one if she knew he still considered Suncrest fair game. He regarded himself as a highly trustworthy individual but suddenly had to wonder if he was betraying her with his agenda regarding her employer.

Yet what could he disclose? He couldn't tell her that in his mind, Suncrest was still in play. Besides, he told himself, it might not be. He'd built his whole Napa Valley strategy around Suncrest, but the deal might truly be dead, the way she thought it was. Yet any intimation to the contrary would put her off him.

He couldn't risk it. He didn't want to. He tamped down his discomfort and just listened, saying nothing to encourage her but nothing to stop her, either.

Finally she wound to a close. "So if you're still game to bottle this morning—"

"Absolutely."

"—we could pick up some muffins at Dean and DeLuca first, then head over to the winery."

"Any relation?"

"I wish." She was edging away from him, smiling, her voice teasing, her hips swaying beneath the red plaid flannel.

Half an hour later, showered but back in the clothes he'd worn the night before, Will discovered that the

Napa Valley outpost of Dean and DeLuca was just as grand as its flagship Manhattan store. It was the sort of high-end specialty shop that catered to people who demanded six types of goat cheese—pardon, chèvre—and nine varieties of dried mushrooms. Of course, many of Napa's residents, particularly up-valley, were as pampered as their big-city counterparts. The valley might have begun as an agricultural backwater, but it was glossy now, and had the estates and restaurants and boutiques to prove it.

Will reached inside a woven basket and plucked two warm apricot muffins for himself, a cranberry for Gabby, and an assortment for the troops assembling at Suncrest. He was returning his change to his wallet when he heard a sharp intake of breath behind him, coming from Gabby. He pivoted to find a tall, swarthy man about his own age standing beside her.

"Vittorio," Gabby breathed, "you're back."

But this Vittorio fellow wasn't looking at Gabby, Will noticed, though he himself was acutely aware of her paralyzed state. The guy was eyeing him, with a narrowed gaze that said, *What are you doing with her at seven o'clock on Sunday morning?* Then, *I know what you're doing. And I don't like it.*

Vittorio lowered his gaze to Gabby, grasped her hands and kissed her cheeks, one after the other, European-style. "It's good to see you, Gabriella." His voice was accented—*Italian,* Will concluded—and undeniably affectionate.

Will's mind raced. You're back, she'd said to him. *So she's seen him recently.*

Again Vittorio fixed his eyes on Will, though he addressed Gabby. "And who is your friend?"

Will watched Gabby turn to face him, her eyes wide, her skin flushed, her movements jerky. Shock, confusion, uneasiness were written all over her. "Vittorio, this is Will Henley. Will, Vittorio Mantucci."

Will reached out to shake hands. "Pleasure to meet you, Vittorio. Are you visiting us from out of town?" *You heard me say* us? *That's her and me, Vittorio. Us.*

Vittorio's grasp was somewhat firmer than it needed to be. "From Chianti, actually."

Let me guess. Castelnuovo. "Are you also in the wine business?"

"Yes. And you?"

"No." Will smiled, refrained from saying more. *I'll let you wonder what I do. And I'll let you worry how well I know the woman you call Gabriella. . . .*

Though how well these two knew each other could not have been more painfully obvious. Will watched Gabby struggle not to stare at Vittorio; he saw the darting of her eyes to the far corners of the store, as if the July Fourth picnic displays had suddenly taken on enormous interest. For machismo reasons alone, Will wished he'd taken her to bed the prior night, just so he wouldn't be one down to this man who clearly had been Gabby's lover, the man who had made living in Tuscany "a very special time," the man who now had her locked in a queer sort of suspended animation.

She was in love with him. Maybe she still is.

Probably this explained her strange reticence when he'd asked her about Italy. At the hospital she'd promised him an epic. What he'd gotten out of her in the hot tub was barely a paragraph. And Will felt sure that the reason was six feet two and standing right in front of him.

The stab of jealousy that assailed him was embarrassing. He had no claim to her, no right to feel possessive. It was also absurd to think that a woman of her age, with her looks, her sweetness, her allure, wouldn't have a romantic history. Yet it chafed at him.

Vittorio ran a hand through his hair, and Will suffered a second shock. *The guy's wearing a wedding ring! Was this jerk married? Was Gabby his mistress?* Will felt a surge of dislike for old European marital customs. And clearly Gabby had seen Vittorio recently. *Is she still his mistress?*

But it didn't seem so, not from the stiffness between them. That was some relief at least. "Are you back here on business?" she was asking him.

"Yes. Some projects I'm working on are going faster than I'd thought."

What projects? Will's mind clicked into another gear. He filed Vittorio Mantucci's name into his mental Rolodex, determined to get the lowdown on this guy and whatever wine-industry business he was conducting in Napa Valley.

Gabby glanced at Will, and he read in her eyes that she wanted to leave. He himself was more than ready to get out of there. He made his voice all hearty friendliness. "Good to meet you, Vittorio." He slapped the guy's back as he moved past, a little too hard but he couldn't help himself. He then claimed Gabby's hand and pulled her toward the exit. "Enjoy your stay."

She was silent as they walked to their cars, then released his hand wordlessly and got into her Jeep. He trailed her to Suncrest, trying to ascertain how she felt from how she drove. Did that quick lane change mean she was upset? Was that swipe at her nose an indication she was crying? Was that a tissue she dug out of her purse?

He consoled himself with the fact that he couldn't have imagined her attraction to him the night before. He told himself it didn't matter that she considered him an outsider while Vittorio was a sort of wine soul mate, someone who understood what she loved because he loved it, too. He told himself that those two had parted for a reason, whatever it was, and that it needn't impede Will's future with her at all.

He didn't let himself dwell on how he himself was treating her, the little nagging worry that he wasn't being entirely on the up-and-up, that he had an agenda she didn't know about, and that if she did, he might be part of her history, too.

When they'd parked side by side in Suncrest's employee lot and emerged from their respective vehicles, he judged her skin a little blotched and her eyes a little puffy. But she produced a smile. Will knew good sense dictated that he not quiz her on their interaction with Vittorio, though he was dying to. This was another case where he thought restraint was the better part of valor.

They worked the bottling line for four hours. They shared lunch—hamburgers and salad—with their fellow assembly-linesmen. They chatted and smiled, and spoke of everything but the man they'd run into that morning.

When it came time for him to leave, Gabby walked Will out to his car. He leaned against its silver sun-warmed chassis and pulled her toward him so that her body settled gently against his. "Do you know what a wonderful time I had with you?" he asked her.

She smiled. There was sadness in her eyes, but a light, too. "Tell me," she said.

"So wonderful that I don't know how I'm going to make it till the next time I see you." He brushed her lips with his own. "How about next weekend? Friday night? I'll drive up after my flight gets in from Kennedy."

"You'll be exhausted."

"Is that a yes or a no?"

She hesitated only a second. "It's a yes."

He knew Vittorio was on her mind. He knew she

was conscious of her coworkers mere yards away, conspicuously not watching. So he tried to say what he felt in a short kiss and a long glance.

He drove away very much hoping she'd heard him.

Chapter 9

Driver in hand, Max stood on the eighth tee of the Sonoma Mission Inn golf course and prepared to launch his golf ball a Tiger Woods–like distance down the center of the straight-as-an-arrow fairway.

Rory stood a few yards behind him, awaiting his turn. "At least this hole doesn't have a water hazard," he said to Bucky, loud enough for Max to hear. "But that out-of-bounds all down the left side is something to watch out for."

"The right's no bargain, either, with those bunkers," Bucky murmured in that same fake-quiet voice. "Better go long and straight on this hole, Maxie boy."

Max shook his head. "Shut up," he said, then gave it one more waggle and let 'er rip.

All three watched the ball curve through the air on a rightish trajectory, then drop into the rough about twenty yards shy of the nearest bunker.

"It plays long from there," Bucky opined, walking forward while bopping the enormous steel head of his driver into the earth to locate a suitably firm spot into which to plunge his tee. "But maybe the rough is short enough that you can play driver again."

Rory chuckled. "Advance the ball another one-eighty up the fairway."

Max knew this was just more of the good-natured joshing he'd been taking since high school from these two, but still he was irked. He didn't like any intimation that he was in any way one down to them. "I don't see either of you joining the pro tour."

"True." Bucky took another flawless practice swing, his gaze locked onto the fairway. "Even though there's no way it could suck as much as med school."

Then he hit, and Max watched Bucky's drive cream his own by a good seventy yards. He was pleased that it, too, found the rough. "Maybe the wind took it," Max said. He didn't bother to keep the snideness out of his voice.

Bucky shook his head. "Gotta work on that high fade. Didn't hurt Jack Nicklaus, though."

Nicklaus, my ass. The only relief was that Bucky just said "med school" that time and not "Johns Hopkins Medical School," because it seemed like he couldn't stop bragging about his postgraduate education.

I'm enrolled in the school of hard knocks, Max told himself, *otherwise known as the real world. And I'm blowing its doors off.*

It had been a stellar week since he'd delivered his mother to her Air France flight. He'd spoken with her by phone every day since, both to keep up the pretense that he was the most dutiful son in California and to reassure her about Suncrest. He hadn't breathed a word about the ongoing rebottling, figuring he'd ease into that discussion once she returned to Terra Americana. His most fervent wish was that that day be pushed far into the future. At the moment she was still planning to fly home in a week, but he knew that if any woman was prone to last-minute itinerary changes, it was her.

Since Rory had already hit, all three hoisted their golf bags onto their shoulders and set off down the fairway. Max's bag banged rhythmically into his back, clubs clattering with every step. He'd felt forced to walk the course rather than use a golf cart, though at his current weight—in this heat—he would have much preferred the latter. Already, at eleven in the morning, it was above eighty degrees. The summer smell of newly mown grass filled his nostrils, reminding him of good times, being a kid, having tons of free hours and doing only what he wanted with them. Now he looked forward to a barbecued hot dog at the turn, and a cold beer to go with it, and going home after the round to nap on the hammock by the pool.

"So you're in town all summer?" he asked Rory.

"Yup. Don't start the job till after Labor Day. Just hope I passed the bar."

No way Rory didn't pass the bar. "The job's with a law firm in D.C., you said?"

Rory nodded. He was Max's height—that is to say, five ten—and about as sturdily built. His brown hair was thinning by the minute, and his wardrobe remained as uninspired preppy as ever. In other words, Rory looked human—unlike Bucky, who even after years of slaving away at pre-med and then med school still looked perfect. So much so, in fact, that he'd scored a date with Stella Monaco, a babe of major proportions who'd turned Max down twice. Max thought Rory should give up medicine and become a soap star. After all, what with the whole HMO thing, being a doctor wasn't the plush gig it used to be.

Then again, being a corporate lawyer didn't sound that entertaining, either. Max felt a rush of superiority that his own life was on such a splendid course. Running Suncrest, living in the valley, making scads of money without breaking a sweat.

He was the smart one, he told himself, he was the

one who had his shit in gear. Every once in a while Max worried that Rory or Bucky was making more of himself than he was—moving to the East Coast, joining some hotshot organization, working his way up to being hot shit himself. But that was stupid. Who was living better? Answer that.

And any joker who thought Max had everything handed to him on a silver platter could just guess again. It was tough following in a father's footsteps, especially one as successful as Porter Winsted. Max had to prove himself every day of the week, and that was some heavy burden to carry.

"So how's Suncrest?" Bucky asked.

"Fantastic." That was Max's standard response to that question. "I'm loving running it. Once we get through harvest, I'm going to focus on adding more varietals. I have some new marketing strategies up my sleeve, too."

That wasn't entirely accurate, but Max didn't want to get into the unglamorous arena of cost-cutting. Truth be told, the number-crunching was less than appealing. No matter how long he wrestled with some of those digits, they still kept insisting on coming out red.

He'd found out when he ran the numbers that the rebottling was a tad pricier than he'd anticipated. So what? Any good businessman knew you had to spend money to make money. Besides, he had plenty of ways to trim the winery's fat.

All three halted as they reached Max's ball, which poked halfheartedly out of the rough's long grass.

"Unfortunate lie," Bucky remarked, then waited till Max was lined up over his shot before he fired his next salvo. "It's good you're working on some marketing strategies, buddy, 'cause I'd say Suncrest could use 'em. I've been to a few of the hot restaurants in the city lately, and none of them had it on their wine list."

Max pretended to be unfazed by that revelation. He

stepped back from his shot and took a few more practice swings. "Like where?"

"Chez Spencer. Jeanty at Jack's."

Rory piped up. "It's not at Rubicon, either. I was just there the other night."

"Or at Boulevard," Bucky added.

Max stepped back up to his ball, his mind working. Well, well. It looked like his buds had just handed him a new marketing project. He sighed, imagining the tough work that lay ahead. That winery was just damn lucky he was back to run it. It needed his visionary management something fierce.

He hit. The ball launched beautifully into the cloudless blue sky, drew slightly, then plopped onto the fairway and rolled an additional twenty yards, putting Max in perfect position for a pitching wedge into the green.

"Center cut," Bucky said.

"Nice shot, Max," Rory echoed.

Max returned his seven iron to his bag and wordlessly accepted his friends' plaudits, not in the least surprised to be receiving them.

"Gabby, wait up, will you?" At twilight Cam's breathless voice rang out over Suncrest's Morydale vineyard, set on a west-facing slope to catch the afternoon sun and given a natural windbreak on three sides by walls of forest. By this late hour the sun had already dipped below the jagged crest of the Mayacamas, throwing the vines into shadow and allowing the grapes to relax after the day's frenetic sweetening.

Gabby was panting herself from hurrying along the hilly rows of vines. She halted at a waist-high wooden post both to allow her sister to catch up and to retie a piece of reflective aluminum tape that had come loose. Crows cawed overhead, as if taunting her efforts to frighten them away from the ripening fruit below.

"Damn birds," she muttered. They looked like a biker gang riding wings instead of Harleys across the dusky sky. She let her gaze drop to her sister's approaching form, encased in a gray sweatsuit Gabby thought should immediately go to the rag bag. "Hurry up, Cam," she whispered. She illuminated the dial on her digital watch and read its glowing turquoise verdict: 8:52. So much for getting home early.

Monday night her phone had rung around nine thirty. It had been Will, calling from Manhattan. They'd nattered on about his business trip, her rebottling, everything and nothing. Since then—two nights of zippo. She knew because, pathetically enough, she'd made sure to be home.

Okay, he was busy. So was she. But zippo?

It was hard to get a read on him. Maybe he was as careful about phone calls as he seemed to be about everything else—sex included. She had to admire him for that; it was quite a departure from how most men behaved. And it was true they hadn't known each other long. Not long enough to justify how intense it felt whenever she was with him.

She toyed with a piece of green Mylar tape that tied a vine onto a trellising wire. The scary truth was that part of her wanted to talk with him every day. And part of her hoped he'd go away and never come back. *You might be better off alone.* Safer, anyway, in her scientist's routine, where she could keep everything just the way she wanted it. Men had a way of mucking that up. They got in your hair, they got in your body, they got in your house, they got under your skin, and before you knew it, you weren't controlling anything anymore.

That's certainly what Vittorio had done. It had been wonderful and terrible both.

Cam reached her, seriously out of breath, wild dark hair bursting from beneath her black-and-orange Giants baseball cap. "Can you go any faster?"

"Sorry."

"This vineyard's really hilly, you know." She took a few restorative gulps of air. "Why are we here anyway?"

"To see if it's too dry." Which, in Gabby's estimation, it was. She squatted down to grab another handful of soil, which ran through her fingers like sand. Lots of winemakers believed that grapes, like artists, needed to struggle to achieve greatness, that rich, complex flavors grew out of difficult conditions. She believed that, too, to a point. "We haven't been using the drip irrigation lately, but I think we need to get back to it. I'm not sure there's enough groundwater here." She made a mental note to tell Felix in the morning, then rose and rubbed her hands together to get rid of the loose dirt. "Thanks for coming with me, by the way."

"No problem, I needed the exercise." She chuckled. "I didn't think I'd get this much of it, though."

Gabby nodded. Sometimes she forgot that other people didn't tromp the vineyards like she did, weren't used to the long exploratory hikes that gave her a feel for how the crop was progressing. Did they need to prune the foliage so the fruit got more sun? Were the vines getting enough nutrients?

She was especially eager to continue those walks now. Max had decided, in his infinite lack of wisdom, to fire some field-workers. *We don't need them*, he told her. *When we do for harvest, we'll bring them back.*

Yeah, right. Gabby knew what he was up to. The rebottling cost so much he needed to cut somewhere else. So, like the idiot owner he was, he took it out of the place that mattered to the wine the most, but to him the least. The vineyard.

Silence lengthened between the sisters, broken only by the distant drone of a small plane's engine and the nearby chatter of little birds who'd convened on the telephone wires to report to each other on the day's activities. The sky was an explosion of pink and orange hues, streaked with purple, as if the angels had run amok with their celestial crayons. Gabby loved this twilight hour, when her work was done, her muscles were pleasantly sore, and dinner, a bath, and bed awaited.

Out of the quiet, Cam spoke. "Has Will called?"

"Yup. From New York." Somehow it felt like a badge of honor to be able to say that. "He'll be back in San Francisco tomorrow and is driving right up."

"Wow." Cam shook her head, clearly impressed. "I need one like that."

Cam didn't enjoy massive success in the man department, though Gabby thought no one deserved a good one more than her sister did. "Come on," Gabby said, "it's getting dark. Let's walk back to the car," and turned to head for the Jeep, waiting half a mile downhill.

They had just arrived when Cam piped up again. "You know, I've seen Vittorio."

Gabby stopped cold, her fingers frozen on the Jeep's door handle. "What?"

"He's here! I mean, I'm not sure he's here this *second,* but he's been around. Everybody's seen him. I saw him at Gillwood's. Lucia saw him, too." She was their other sister, the youngest, whom old-timers usually referred to as "the married one." "The weird thing is, he came into her office."

"He wants to buy *real estate?*"

"Apparently he's interested in that land off 29 that's been for sale forever. You know, between Rutherford and St. Helena?"

Oh, God. Vittorio wants to buy vineyards in Napa.

That was too weird for words. Was the Mantucci family planning to expand into Napa Valley? They were a little small to do that—they ran a midsize winery, about the same volume as Suncrest—but maybe they'd joined forces with some bigger money, like a European beverage company or something.

The idea of Vittorio setting up operations in Napa Valley angered her. It wasn't enough that he ran roughshod over her heart? Now he wanted to invade her territory, the one sacrosanct thing she had left?

"Don't tell me Lucia's his broker," Gabby said.

"No." Cam shook her head. "Somebody else in the office. I'm almost afraid to ask, but did you run into him, too?"

"At Dean and DeLuca." Gabby didn't want to face the ire that would ensue if she told Cam she'd actually had dinner with him.

"How was it?"

She hesitated. "Odd. I was shocked, first. Then sad. A little angry, too, like I still can't believe what he did to me." Cam's gaze was steady on her face. Somehow Gabby wanted to downplay the emotions that had coursed through her, left her wobbly for days. "It's weird to see him wear a wedding ring. And his wife's pregnant now, too."

A train whistle sounded far away, its last notes vanishing into the gloaming sky. "Do you feel like you're over him?"

"Mostly."

Sometimes she worried she was to blame for the hold he still had on her. Long ago she'd come to believe that she and Vittorio had a great tragic love affair, one doomed by the gods. It imbued their love with a grand romantic quality. In some ways that conviction was one of her most cherished beliefs.

Yet was she clinging to an illusion? How great a love affair could theirs have been if Vittorio had been willing to set her aside? Wouldn't a great romantic hero fight against all odds to keep his love at his side?

Wouldn't he at least fight his parents?

"Well," Cam said, walking around the rear of the Jeep, "I wish you hadn't had to see him, but I'm glad he didn't call you." She hoisted herself onto the passenger seat. "That would've really pissed me off."

Gabby got into the car herself and carefully inserted the key into the ignition. "What would've been so bad about him calling?" She tried to keep her voice casual. "I mean, what if he had something to tell me?"

Cam didn't hesitate. "He's already told you plenty."

Will was driving to Napa as fast as the law would allow. Faster, actually. The desire that had clawed at him all week in New York now kept his foot pressed hard on the accelerator. He'd been fantasizing relentlessly about Gabby, in heart-stopping detail, and now she was waiting for him at her mountaintop retreat. He couldn't get there fast enough.

When they'd spoken on the phone, she'd been playful. He'd gotten no hint of the hurt and distraction he'd seen at Dean and DeLuca. Her mood had allowed him to push Vittorio Mantucci into the recesses of his mind, like an old attic box that didn't need to be sorted just yet.

You could fall in love with this woman. That knowledge hovered in the back of his brain, daring contradiction. None came. He was old enough to know what he liked and what he didn't. He knew he was a pretty traditional guy. He actually *wanted* to settle down. He gave more than a passing thought to kids. He wanted what his parents had, what his sister had. He was, as women's magazines portentously put it, *ready to commit.*

All he was waiting for was the right woman, a woman he could truly imagine sharing the rest of his life with. He hadn't known Gabby long, but by age thirty-two his ability to give thumbs-up or thumbs-down to a particular female was honed damn near to perfection. Some judgments took less than a minute. And with her, he experienced something truly exceptional. Every time he saw her or spoke to her—every single time—he liked her more. Found more to enjoy, more to admire.

If that keeps happening, he told himself, *this is it.*

Only one obstacle stood between them.

He pushed Suncrest from his mind as he made his way through St. Helena's Main Street—traffic stop-and-go on a Friday at dinner hour as tourists and locals alike crowded the chic little eateries. Finally Highway 29 again opened up before him, and Gabby's house lay only a few miles ahead. As his anticipation mounted, his cell phone rang.

He glanced at the readout of the incoming number and frowned—9 P.M. on a Friday, Denver time, wasn't a standard hour for his sister to call. He pushed the connect button. "Hey, Beth."

"Hey, yourself. You sound like you're in the car."

"You'll be happy to hear I'm heading up to see that woman I told you about."

"The one who thinks you're a capitalist pig?"

"Apparently I've convinced her I'm not that bad."

"Well, good for you."

She fell silent. Or, rather, stopped speaking, because Will heard sounds coming from her end, but they couldn't be described as speech. "Beth?" He paused. "Are you crying, sweetie?"

Full-out sob, followed by a loud sniffle. "Yes."

"What's wrong?"

"It's Bob."

Damn. "Is it the Philadelphia thing again?"

"He's there now. Interviewing. He just called. He

had dinner with people from some company that he says is thinking of hiring him."

"Did you fight over the phone?"

"No. Because I hung up."

More sobbing, so gut-wrenching that Will wished he could beam himself right over to Denver to console his sister, tell her it was all right, that somehow it would all work out in the end. "So he's still serious about this?"

"He wants me to put the house on the market."

Will did not like the sound of that. "What did you tell him?"

"That I wouldn't do anything irreversible until he had an actual offer. And then we'd talk about it. Hold on, it's call-waiting. It might be him."

Beth clicked off. Will shook his head. So this problem wasn't going away, as he had hoped it would. What if Bob actually accepted an offer? Beth would have to move to Philly then, wouldn't she? And what would that mean for Henley Sand and Gravel?

She came back on. "It is him. He's waiting." She sniffled. "I think he wants to apologize."

Good. "Call me if you need to talk." He hoped she didn't, for all sorts of reasons.

"I will. Have a good time tonight. Have a better time than I'm having." Then she was gone, off to try to keep her marriage on track, a marriage Will had never expected would be in trouble.

He made the sharp left turn onto Crystal Mountain Road. Apparently none of this was easy. Not the part about finding the right woman, not the part about keeping her. It got all mixed up with the chaotic rest of life. It was a wonder people ever stayed together.

But they did. His parents had. So had Gabby's.

He arrived at her house, and since he didn't have a timid cell in his body that night—he wouldn't make *that* mistake again—he called out her name and pushed open her front door and found her in the kitchen. She was wearing a long flowing skirt and a sort of blouson top that drooped off her shoulders in a way that said *Take me off. Take me off.*

His pulse quickened. He kissed her, and her lips were as soft as his feverish dreams had remembered them.

"Did you have a good week?" she asked him.

"Very good." He nipped at her mouth, swayed her in his arms.

She smiled, cocked her head to the side. "Did you miss me?"

"You don't know the half of it."

She slipped away from him, called back over her shoulder. "We finished the rebottling. I tell you, Max is such an idiot that sometimes I think Suncrest *would* be better off if you bought it."

He wanted no dash of cold water on this night. He went into the kitchen after her, came up from behind to nuzzle her neck. "Let's not talk about Suncrest."

She twirled to face him, her expression teasing. "You don't want to talk business tonight?"

"No, I do not."

"What do you want to talk about?"

"I don't want to talk at all." *I want to take you to bed and do terrible things to you. Repeatedly.*

He might as well have just said that right out loud, for the idea seemed to hover in the air between them like spoken words. Will watched Gabby still and catch her breath.

He didn't want to think and didn't want her to, either. He sensed that her need ran as deep as his, even if it was hidden under a thicker veneer of control.

He wanted the control gone.

On impulse he picked her up and threw her over his shoulder as if he were a firefighter rescuing her from a burning building. Funny, because he was the one ablaze. He made for the front door and on the way out grabbed the ratty old blanket she kept on the back of the couch.

In a few steps he reached the edge of the vineyard, over which the sun was beginning to set. He tossed the blanket on the ground and took a stab at flattening it out with his foot. He did a makeshift job then laid her on top, like the prize catch she was.

For a moment he stood and just stared at her. She lay on that rust-colored wool blanket staring back, her skin flushed and her lips parted and her skirt bunched around her hips. Her man-killer legs were slightly spread, and what he was dying to explore was cast in shadow. He was half-delirious as he dropped to his knees, bent over, and wrenched the tantalizing blouson top from her shoulders.

"You're not wearing anything underneath." He managed to get out that observation as he watched her nipples harden in the cool air. *Or maybe*, he thought, taking one in his mouth, *it isn't the air that's doing it.*

"Oh, God," Gabby said. She plucked at the buttons of his shirt, succeeded at getting most of them undone. Her breathing was ragged. "What in the world made me think you were a conservative businessman?"

"I have no idea."

He levered himself up to take off his shirt. He flung it, and it landed on top of the nearby row of grape-vines.

"Let's try not to disrupt the vines," she said.

"God, Gabby." He tasted her mouth again. Sweet, like wine and summer. Of this woman he'd expect no less. "Don't tell me you're thinking about the grapes now."

"It's not what you think."

He used his tongue on her nipples again, made her

arch against him in a way that nearly drove him mad. "What is it then?"

She pulled up his head so their eyes met. "Rattlers. At Suncrest we dislodge them by flinging dirt on the vines." A smile, a tease of a smile, spread over that gorgeous tanned face of hers. "Don't worry, they're shy."

"For all I care right now, they can come on out and watch the fun."

She threw back her head and laughed, a throaty roar that fired his imagination. He bunched the skirt up around her hips and got another surprise. "You're not wearing anything underneath this, either." He squeezed the flesh of her buttocks, deliciously firm and tight from all the tromping through the vineyards. He kept his eyes on her face and explored further, into the hidden parts of her, wet and ready.

She moaned. He bent his head down to her flesh. "Oh, God, Will."

"Tell me you want it."

"I do."

"Tell me you want it."

"I want it so bad, Will."

He offered himself to her in every way he knew how, in every way that would tell her how much she meant to him. She was bawdy and sweet, a temptress and an angel, a wonder he would never forget, never get over, and never get enough of.

He pulled her into the bedroom when the sun had fully set. Though his fever had abated, he wasn't sated yet: he was still as thirsty as a vine seeking water at the end of a hot summer day. The fresh sheets were cool against his skin, the air blowing through the window redolent with the scent of grapes heavy with sweetness.

Hours later, after food and wine and talk and still more love, Will was exhausted, in the best possible way. Gabby was nestled against him, his left arm stretched beneath her neck, his right cradling her soft naked warmth. Her hair, tickling his nose, smelled faintly of vanilla. Here in her mountaintop house, no city sounds assailed his ears—no sirens or car alarms, or maniacs taking advantage of Pacific Heights's abandoned midnight streets to hot-rod it from stop sign to stop sign.

Her voice, drowsy, wafted toward him. "Will?"

"Mmm?"

"Is it still possible you might buy Suncrest?"

That jolted him awake. "Why are you thinking about Suncrest now?"

"I don't know." She twisted to face him, and he relaxed, a bit. He saw joy in her eyes, and trust. "It's just on my mind, after we talked about it before."

I wish it wasn't. He tried to chuckle it away. "I don't want to talk about business now."

She half rose on her elbow and rested her head on her hand. She looked deliciously sweet and tousled, and the last thing she made him want to think about was work. "Are you saying it is possible?"

That was easy enough to answer. "Anything's possible."

"So you might still buy it," she murmured. Then she frowned slightly, and her voice grew more serious. "If you do, will you promise to try to keep it the same?"

"Gabby . . ." *What?* Those wide hazel eyes of hers were looking more worried now, more discerning. About all he was sure of was that he wouldn't lie to those eyes. "I can't really promise, no. If GPG ever does get to acquire Suncrest, I don't know what the deal will look like. It's not entirely up to me. You understand I'm a junior partner, right? I don't get to decide everything myself."

"But you'll try?"

Somewhere the old house groaned. *How many midnight promises were made here?* he wondered suddenly. In this old house, born a barn. In beds all over creation.

"I'll try," he said finally, which was true, and which seemed to satisfy her. She smiled and returned her head to her pillow, and drifted away.

He stared at her face for some time, then twisted onto his back to stare at the ceiling, unfortunately a little more awake now.

He would try, though he seriously doubted that would be enough.

Chapter 10

Five o'clock on a sweltering Saint-Tropez summer afternoon. Ava stood alone on the narrow balcony of her hotel suite, her eyes scanning the view for something new of interest. Beyond the centuries-old houses that covered the slope down to the harbor, the French Riviera sun glinted off the Mediterranean. Yachts bobbed in the water or plied its expanse, their decks covered by topless sunbathers supine on colorful rectangles of towel.

With a sniff, Ava drained her second *limonata*. She was no prude but no layabout, either, and disapproved of daytime nappers she strongly suspected were sleeping off one night's indulgences just so they could indulge in the next.

Refusing to think about her son—who no doubt would melt right into that indolent circle—she pushed the white-blond hair back from her forehead, which was damp with perspiration. Maybe a walk would calm her nerves. Jean-Luc's flight wouldn't land at Toulon for a half hour, after which he'd have to make his way east along the coast road, which had been known to take forever. She had plenty of time, far more than she needed.

Funny how she still had the sensation time was slipping away.

In white linen capris and matching sleeveless top, black-lensed movie-star sunglasses on the sweat-slick perch of her nose, she slipped the cell phone Jean-Luc had lent her into her handbag and set off for the shadowy cobblestone streets that zigzagged downhill to the harbor.

Saint-Tropez had begun life as a sleepy fishing village and centuries later played host to Impressionist painters drawn by the Côte d'Azur's crystalline light. But it was director Roger Vadim who put the hamlet on the jet set's radar screen when he cast wife and fledgling actress Brigitte Bardot in his scandalous 1956 film *And God Created Woman*.

Ava—who considered herself as much God's gift as La Bardot—strolled past a red-awninged café where lunch was just getting started. Tourists noshed on oysters and seafood salad and steamed artichokes, washed down with wine and Perrier. Given Saint-Tropez's rigorous nightclubbing, meals occurred at what Ava considered highly irregular hours—breakfast at noon, lunch at six, dinner at midnight. Though she felt terrifically unchic to admit it, her habits were far too American for that schedule. She and Jean-Luc dined at eight and bypassed the clubs, Ava secretly relieved not to have to compete with the hoi polloi for entry to an ill-lit cave where her eardrums would only split from the racket.

She meandered right at the next corner, past a used bookstore whose yellowing wares cascaded onto the street, and a charcuterie where sausages hung in links over a white-tile delicatessen counter stuffed with pâtés and *jambons*. She passed two aged men hunched over a chessboard and a group of boys who'd commandeered an alley for soccer. No one from either extreme of the age spectrum bothered to turn his head to give her the eye.

Ava was painfully reminded, yet again, that she was too old for the lascivious leer. The raw truth of it made her feel as dull and passed-over as the decaying volumes at the secondhand bookstore. Apparently the only man whose lust she could inspire was Jean-Luc, and she feared he was as washed up as she was terrified of becoming.

Jean-Luc. She passed through an opening in a shoulder-high stone wall to find herself at the harbor, remembering what he'd told her about his impromptu overnighter in Paris. It was to solidify the movie project, he said. The deal was struck, script revisions would ensue, casting would begin.

Yet she couldn't get past the idea that Jean-Luc was deluding himself. Ava settled on a bench to eye the goings-on in the harbor, most of which involved fishermen bringing in their hauls for the day. She knew enough French to understand the negative phrases that peppered Jean-Luc's phone conversations with his agent. She needed no dictionary to decipher his slumping body language. Though she didn't want to believe it, it seemed to her that his much-ballyhooed movie deal was as close to dead as the halibut twitching on the pier thirty yards away.

That Jean-Luc was out of France's cinematic loop had become painfully clear once she arrived at his Paris apartment. This was a man whose phone did not ring. Who took few meetings. Whose scripts were returned by the French equivalent of parcel post. Certainly he'd written—and sold—important screenplays in the past. But that was it: they were *in the past*.

Even his suggesting they repair to Saint-Tropez was another clue that his best days were behind him. Everyone knew the most fashionable destinations were seventy miles east, between Cannes and Monte Carlo. To holiday in a has-been hangout was not Ava's idea of a comeback.

But a comeback was precisely what she needed. Otherwise what would she do? Resort to animal preservation, that timeworn fallback of past-it starlets like Tippi Hedren and Bardot herself? She wondered what Saint-Tropez denizen Catherine Deneuve might be up to nowadays. Perhaps making a full-time career of attending fashion shows?

Ava set her jaw. The same determination that had driven her from Houston to Hollywood at age eighteen flooded her spirit anew. Fortunately for her, Jean-Luc Boursault was not her only contact in the European film industry. If she needed to cast her net wider to entrap the prize she sought, then she would do so.

From inside her handbag, her cell phone rang. It had to be either Jean-Luc or Max. "Working on your Saint-Tropez tan?" It was Max.

"Trying not to get one. What's new at home?"

"Same old, same old. Except for one thing. You know that deal I told you about, to acquire premium chardonnay grapes? I negotiated the guy down even further. The price is rock-bottom now."

Porter's gravelly voice reverberated in her memory. *You get what you pay for.* She shook her head. "I don't know, Max. With the economy like it is, how can it be a good time to add a new varietal?"

"What it's time for, Mom, is to take Suncrest to the next level." Now Max was sounding like Will Henley. She wasn't sure if that was good or bad. "Besides," he went on, "chardonnay's a solid performer. We should've added it a long time ago."

Napa's not known for chardonnay, Porter said in her head. *Leave that to Sonoma Valley.*

But how could she squash Max's enthusiasm? Second-guess him at every turn? If she wanted him to run the winery, she had to let him run it, mistakes be damned. It was also a wonderful contrast to his lackadaisical past that he was taking such an active interest. And for all his caution, Porter had made a few early misjudgments that nearly killed Suncrest. Her son deserved the same latitude.

"Well, use your own judgment," she told him, and rang off a minute or so later, having no triumphs of her own to impart. She didn't want to admit that no, she wasn't having the time of her life; no, she wasn't conquering the *cinéma français*; no, she wasn't head over heels for Jean-Luc.

Who by now was most likely waiting for her at the hotel.

Duty forced her from the bench and back up the hill. Gravity and reluctance dragged at her legs. Ahead, atop Saint-Tropez's highest peak, the Hotel Byblos shimmered in all of its stuccoed glory. It echoed the patchwork of colorful shuttered buildings that rose in tiers from the harbor—one sunflower yellow, one terra-cotta red. Yet the bold colors of Provence failed to cheer her.

Nor did Jean-Luc's expression when she pushed open the door to their suite and he turned to face her. Her friend looked old and discouraged, and weary.

Even before she was fully inside the suite, Ava began to plan her flight out.

It was very hard to work when all Gabby could think about was sex.

Midmorning in the vineyards, the foggiest it had been in weeks, and she was doing her rounds. Theoretically she was thinning the crop, which involved yanking the mediocre-looking fruit so the vine could focus its energy on what remained, giving those grapes a deeper, more complex, nuanced flavor. But every time she tossed a cluster of grapes onto the dust, she remembered being there herself.

Her blouse torn open and breasts naked to the air. Her skirt bundled around her waist. Will's body above her. His hands, demanding. His tongue, insistent. The hard rough need of him that had her bucking and moaning . . .

Stop it. Stop it.

She took a ragged breath, forced the image out of her mind. Off came her baseball cap, followed by a rough smoothing back of her hair. Then she smashed the cap back on her head.

What the hell was it about sex? She'd gone without for a year and managed just fine, thank you. Then one reintroduction, and she's as good as in season.

It's not the sex. It's the man.

That was the worrying truth of it. The good news was that Will had blasted Vittorio from her fantasies. The bad was that he'd claimed center stage for himself. And though right now he seemed sent from heaven, she feared that in the end he would prove no more dependable than Vittorio had been.

About a hundred yards away, two men stood amid the vines calling instructions to each other. They were young, Hispanic, male—typical Napa field-workers— but Gabby didn't know them. That was because they were temporary hires, brought in not long after Max had insisted Felix fire several full-timers. Now they were making a meal out of spraying fertilizer, but it was probably the first time they'd done it.

All the arguments she could muster about how it was too close to harvest to get rid of experienced workers meant nothing to Max. He didn't care that she and Felix didn't have the manpower to handle routine tasks, like mowing the grassy ground cover beneath the vines, whose presence increased the fire danger as the season got hotter.

Gabby shook her head. Max could be such a moron. He didn't care about the crop. He didn't care about the workload. He just wanted to cut budget, even though what he saved was paltry compared with what he'd wasted on the rebottling. And all *that* had gotten them was a lower-quality sauvignon blanc.

Disgusted, distracted, she headed for the Jeep, skirting the grape clusters lying on the ground, primed to rot. Talk about throwing money away. But unlike all Max's directives, this more selective yield would actually benefit the wine, which in Gabby's estimation should be everybody's top priority.

Will might not agree with that. She got in the Jeep, got it rolling toward the winery. *But wouldn't he try to understand it? For me?*

He might still buy Suncrest someday. She'd been stunned to hear it. She'd believed the promise she'd badgered out of him—that he would try to keep Suncrest the same—but then again she'd heard promises before. In Italian. And now in English.

She should be more careful what she told him about Suncrest. After all, she had a duty to her employer, and to her coworkers. She shouldn't say anything that might make the winery more vulnerable, or lower its price if it did go on the block. Now she could kick herself for having told him about the rebottling.

It was weird, having to keep basic information from Will. She drove the Jeep through Suncrest's entry gates and up the long drive to the winery. With Vittorio, she'd been able to share everything. But then again, until the end there'd never been any question that they were on the same side.

She bumped to a stop in the employee parking lot and pulled the keys from the ignition. Was she waging a war on all fronts or what? She had to protect herself from Max the Ignoramus and Ava the Absent. And until she heard otherwise, she had to protect Suncrest from Will.

She walked into the winery. "Felix?" Silence. He

wasn't in the break room. He must be out in the fields. She meandered back outside, along the winery's east wall, where they stored vineyard supplies. A few fertilizer barrels were open, presumably the ones the temps were using. She pulled out her walkie-talkie to hail Felix.

It was the smell that stopped her short, the walkie-talkie halfway to her mouth. Warily, she turned to eye the barrels.

It was unmistakable. One look at the labels on the open barrels, one whiff of the contents, confirmed what she already knew.

The temps weren't spraying fertilizer in the fields, where the grapevines were pregnant with the precious grapes that would be harvested in less than a month. They were spraying weed killer.

Max had hired a chauffeured limousine to ferry him and his four companions from Napa Valley to San Francisco and back again. He enjoyed hosting a showy occasion every now and again: it made him feel like the success he knew himself to be. And during the course of the night's festivities, Bucky, Rory, Stella, and Victoria would get an eyeful of just what a canny vintner Maximilian Winsted was morphing into.

A few minutes after eight in the evening, the limo rolled to a halt on an alleylike street in the city's financial district. The hideaway block in the shadow of skyscrapers was lined with pricey restaurants, avant-garde architect's offices, and by-appointment-only antiques shops. By this hour, the daytime worker bees were long gone. Midsummer fog had settled in, giving the streets the look of a Sherlock Holmes movie set. Cigarette in hand, Max exited the limo to survey his quarry.

Cassis was one of those rare restaurants that launches big and never falls to earth. Even after the city's tech bubble burst and tourism flatlined, reservations were as hard to come by as conservative San Francisco politicians. The chef was Belgian, the cuisine French, the owners deep pocketed, and the clientele A-list. The only thing it lacked, in Max's opinion, were Suncrest vintages on its wine list.

Stella Monaco came to stand next to him on the sidewalk. She was looking particularly tasty in a low-cut filmy blue top and the skinniest black skirt Max had ever laid eyes on. Unfortunately she was Bucky's date.

"Cassis has carried our wine from the beginning," she informed Max. "Maybe I should get my father to put in a good word with the sommelier for you."

The thing about Stella was, half the time you couldn't tell if she was being nice or she was being bitchy. Same thing was true of her mother. "Thanks, but I won't need any help," he told her, then tossed his half-smoked cigarette and ground it into the concrete with the toe of his shoe. "Take those inside," he ordered the chauffeur, who appeared beside him laden with the case of Suncrest wine Max had brought for the evening.

"Let me know if you change your mind." She smiled and took Bucky's arm. Max thought the two of them together looked like a Polo Ralph Lauren ad.

"Thanks, but I won't," he told her. He had to be confident. That was everything in this game. Actually, it was everything in life.

He let his friends precede him inside. Cassis's interior reminded him of those long, deep restaurants you find in Manhattan, with soft lighting and small tables close together and everybody looking like they had money. A fiftyish man who looked like he had wads of it approached Max and held out his hand.

"David McDougall." The proprietor, Max knew, he and his wife both Nob Hill big wheels. "Barbara and

I are so pleased to have you dine with us tonight, Max. I've enjoyed having your mother come by on occasion."

Then why haven't you put Suncrest on your list? Max wanted to ask, but restrained himself. "The pleasure's mine. We've brought a variety of vintages and hope you'll sample a few."

McDougall slapped his back. "I certainly will. Let me introduce our sommelier," and Max met Carlos Valvo, the Portugese guy who reigned supreme over Cassis's wine list. He was a bald little man with wire glasses who looked like he might have become a monk if he hadn't gone into the wine trade.

McDougall set up Max's party in a prime booth, as Max had expected. He knew the rules: spend big money and open most of his bottles, so McDougall and Valvo could taste and share with the staff. Max would leave the remaining bottles for later tasting.

And to seal Suncrest's position on the wine list.

He ordered bottled water and a few dozen oysters to get things rolling. Rory's date, Victoria something, immediately dived into the bread basket. She was a redhead Rory had dated on and off since high school, which mystified Max, who thought she was too dowdy and homespun to justify such devotion.

"I'm excited," she declared. "I haven't eaten in the city in a long time."

Stella rolled her eyes and Max wanted to, as well, except that tonight he was being gracious in all ways. Valvo returned with a corkscrew and Suncrest's sauvignon blanc from the year before.

Max decided now was a good time to educate the table, and score a point or two with the friar. "Sauvignon blanc grapes tend to be highly acidic, but that's what gives the wine its bracing quality." He raised his glass, peering at its contents with what he hoped passed for a practiced eye. "The sauvignon blancs

from cooler climates have more herbal flavors, while
Napa's tend to be citrusy, with some tropical fruit
thrown in. Grassy notes, too," he added, as Valvo finished pouring all around.

Everyone tasted. Max kept his eyes on Valvo and
off everybody else. He didn't have to look to see the
hilarity Rory and Bucky were barely containing.

"Agreeable burst of melon and vanilla." Valvo
drank more, ran it through his teeth. "I detect a fig
character, too, in the finish."

Max nodded sagely. "That's exactly my perception,
Carlos, though there's a subtle grapefruit overtone as
well. Provides a wonderful closing zing."

Bucky's face was contorted by the time Valvo left
the table. " 'Closing zing'? You're killing me, Max!"

"Be good, Bucky." Stella lay a hand on Bucky's leg
but leveled her gaze at Max. "We want to do everything we can to make this evening a success for our
friend here."

Max was weighing the sincerity of that remark when
a blonde sashayed past who left even Stella Monaco
in the dust. She was Max's ideal wet-dream fantasy:
skinny legs, skinny arms, and substantial bazooms, and
on the petite side, so comfortably shorter than he was.
Not that he could care less about her clothes but she
was dressed nicely, too.

But even she had to fade into the background as
more wine was poured and more food was ordered.
Max did his best to wow both Valvo and McDougall
but kept an eye out for the blonde. At one point he
saw her respond to the name Barbie—which could not
have fit her better—and concluded that she was on
staff and not a diner.

He threw back more wine, which was going down
nice and easy as the evening progressed. Sometime
before the end of the night, he decided, he'd have to
make Barbie's acquaintance.

* * *

No surprise to anyone at GPG, managing partner Hank Faskewicz—the biggest of the big dogs—resided with his family in a massive stone pile atop Pacific Heights's highest hill. To avoid the Z8 rolling all the way down to the bay, Will set the hand brake before delivering the key to the valet. Faskewicz lived only about six blocks from Will's Victorian, but Will hadn't even considered walking. Somehow this wasn't the sort of house you just strolled up to.

Neoclassical Greco-Roman, he supposed, complete with frieze, columns, and stone lions—all thrown into dramatic relief by carefully orchestrated floodlighting. It was cold and museum-like in Will's opinion, though he would kill for the bay view that could be had on a fogless day: a sweep of the Golden Gate Bridge, Marin Headlands, and Alcatraz Island. This evening, a sonorous horn sounded repeatedly in the distance as fog billowed across the bay. Lighter, more musical notes emanated from the house itself, unmistakable evidence of a party in progress.

Will strode up the walk, buttoned his suit jacket, smoothed his tie. He might have been primed for Faskewicz's annual midsummer revelry if it weren't a command performance, or if he'd been able to bring Gabby along. But he couldn't risk getting out that he was romancing an employee of the company he was trying to acquire. If that gossipy tidbit made its way back to Faskewicz, it would certainly raise questions Will didn't care to answer.

A tuxedoed butler-type answered the door chime but supreme hostess Molly Faskewicz materialized within seconds to greet the new arrival.

"Will, I'm so glad you could join us." She clasped his hands, bussed his cheeks, and enveloped him in a cloud of French perfume. Molly was an attractive brunette of the women's college, sweater-set variety, still reed thin after producing four little Hanks in rapid-fire succession. Rumors were circulating that a fifth was on the way—perhaps at long last a Henrietta—though that wasn't evident from Molly's slim-cut shimmery gold cocktail dress.

She leaned into him confidentially. "It's all people you know, very boring for you, I'm afraid. Hank always wants to keep this an all-GPG party but I'm just *dying* to mix in new blood." She gazed up at him with her big brown eyes, a heavily mascaraed mid-thirties coquette. "Do you know what I mean?"

This time, he had a good answer for her. "Molly, you'll be relieved to hear I'm seeing someone."

The eyes got wider, disbelieving. She peered around him as if he had a woman stashed in his shadow, then gave a stomp of her little high-heeled foot. "Where is she? Are you hiding her from us?"

"She doesn't live in the city. I couldn't get her out here on a weeknight."

"Well," Molly produced a little pout, "sometime soon, I hope."

He was a disappointment to Molly in so many ways, he feared. Will snagged a flute of champagne from a passing waiter and watched her accept a sparkling water. More than once he'd felt compelled to dodge her setup attempts. He could only imagine her armada of candidates: all well educated and good-looking but, he suspected, brittle and high maintenance. Passing them over would win him no points with her or her husband, who at the moment was holding court in a corner of his three-storied marble entrance hall, entertaining an apparently enthralled group of partner wannabes.

Dinner began half an hour later, with GPG's finest arrayed around linen-draped tables for eight set up in the dining and living rooms. Four courses later, over coffee and dessert, their host began and ended the speechifying. The buzz-cutted Faskewicz was as efficient and no-nonsense as ever, declaring that GPG was having a good year despite the tough times, blah blah blah, even better in the future, more blah blah.

Will and his fellow diners clapped in deep appreciation—whether for the firm's financial success or the end of the evening was anybody's guess—then set down their napkins, rose from their chairs, and stretched their legs. Will was calculating that he could get away with an escape when Faskewicz appeared at his side.

"Will, good to see you." No air kissing in this case. An aggressively firm handshake did the trick. "How's everything going in Napa these days?"

"Just fine. Making progress."

Faskewicz glanced across the dining room. He was one of those people who rarely looked at the person to whom he was speaking. "Taking a little more time than you thought it would?"

Will went on red alert. Now Faskewicz was getting impatient about the pace of the Napa deal, too, just like LaRue? But before Will could concoct a response, Faskewicz went on talking. "I ran into an old friend of yours the other day," he said.

"Who's that?"

"Dennis Garnett." Faskewicz waved good-bye to Susan Amos Jones heading out the front door with her consultant husband in tow. "He's running a nonprofit now, here in the city. Some sort of, I don't know, food bank."

No mistaking the disdain in Faskewicz's voice. When Will joined GPG, Dennis Garnett was a junior partner, the same level Will was now. A few years later, he'd been asked to leave. Will had always liked Dennis and knew Faskewicz was bringing him up for a reason. Faskewicz did everything for a reason.

Will tried to keep his voice casual. "I know Dennis

always had a long list of charitable activities he was interested in."

"Well, he certainly wasn't interested in making money." Faskewicz slapped Will on the back. "At least not as far as we could tell." Then, with a nod, he ambled away.

A warning bell shrieked like a banshee in Will's head. *I'm on the outs. The Napa deal's taking too long. And they don't like how I'm handling it.*

In GPG-speak, the reference to Dennis Garnett—following the ostensibly offhand Napa query—was a clear signal. Will knew Simon LaRue had always wanted Will to cast his net more widely rather than focus on Suncrest alone. As Will hadn't yet made a deal happen, no doubt LaRue's disagreement was morphing into dissatisfaction. And now, apparently, Faskewicz was coming around to LaRue's way of thinking.

What LaRue had said in the Monday partners' meeting two weeks back came racing back to Will's mind. *I believe there's fairly significant time pressure here. . . . I'd rather we step up the pace. Once other firms recognize the Napa opportunity, we'll be looking at auctions. And nobody makes money when everybody chases the same deal.*

Funny, Will thought, standing paralyzed in Faskewicz's fancy home while people buzzed around him retrieving shawls, handbags, valet tickets. Given that Will made lots of money, sat in a corner office, and never flew anything but first-class, he was still a long way from calling his own shots. In some ways he was like any working stiff pulling down a salary, one that could be terminated at any time.

Across the marble entrance hall, Will watched Simon LaRue and his redheaded trophy wife in a private chat with Omar El-Farouk. Though he couldn't hear the conversation, he could guess from the body language that the three were planning an addendum to the evening. *Maybe a jazz club?* Will thought. *Or a rousing game of backgammon over sherry and cigars at the LaRues' Presidio Heights mansion?*

In earlier days Will had been invited to join such intimate entertainments. Not tonight.

He watched the three depart, with no halt in their chatter, while blood pounded in his ears. *That Napa deal better happen. And fast.*

Around ten thirty in the evening, with Cassis nearing the conclusion of its second seating, Max poked Victoria in the thigh to get her attention.

"Do you 'member if we opened the other saubignon blanc?" Then he laughed. "Did I say saubignon or sauvignon?" It was hard to make the *v* sound, he realized, it was like his tongue was tied in knots.

Victoria said something, but even though he concentrated on her mouth, he couldn't make out what it was. Her words seemed to come from very far away, even though she was sitting right next to him in the booth.

He leaned closer. "Huh?"

"I don't think so!"

"Don't yell!" He frowned and leaned back. "Maybe we should open it now."

"After all that cabernet?" She shook her head. Back and forth. Back and forth. Max got dizzy watching her.

"But I want them to see my bottle." It was his new bottle, the good French bottle. It was his idea to put the sauvignon blanc in that bottle and he wanted them to see it. Just then, Valvo walked past. "Carlos!" Max motioned him closer. "We'd like to open the other"— he slowed down to ease into it—"sauvignon blanc."

"Certainly." He walked away.

Max turned again to Victoria. "Did he look unhappy to you? He looked unhappy to me." But now she was talking to Rory. Max sighed and settled back against the booth's soft cushions.

It was going well, he decided, very well. For sure Old Carlos would put Suncrest on his wine list, but that would be only the beginning. Max should go to Sacramento next and get Suncrest served at the Governor's Mansion. Hell, he should go to Washington and get it served at the White House!

Max was considering who his date would be should he dine with the president when Valvo returned with fresh glasses and the newest Suncrest Sauvignon Blanc. Max swelled with pride as he gazed at that heavy French bottle. He pointed to it and then to himself. "That was my idea, Carlos. Pretty slick, huh?"

The guy's brows arched. "Excuse me?"

"To use that bottle."

"I imagine it was." That was it. No praise, no nothing. Max might have been a tad disgruntled if he hadn't been in such a good mood. Valvo poured the wine for everyone, including himself, and they all tasted. Then Valvo set down his glass and hoisted the bottle again, eyeing it through those little wire glasses of his.

"This doesn't have quite the character of the prior year's vintage," he said.

"Sure it does!" Max told him. "And when we took it out of those old bottles and put it in these new ones, it got even more character."

"So it's true?" Stella's voice rang out across the table, loud and clear. "Suncrest *did* rebottle?"

Valvo frowned. He leaned down, much closer than Max wanted. "You decanted this vintage?"

"Well . . ." Max set down his wineglass. He was getting befuddled and didn't like Valvo looming over him like it was the Spanish Inquisition or something. "I mean, we had to, to get it in the new bottles."

Valvo stared at him for a second, then walked away. Max watched him go.

Somewhere amid the cobwebs a light flashed on and off. *You shouldn't have told him that,* it said. But then again, he wasn't sure. Who knew and who didn't? It was so hard to keep it all straight.

Maybe it was time to take a leak, before they got in the limo to go home. Max rose from the booth, easier said than done, then made his way to the rear of the restaurant. And—just his luck!—he spied Barbie in the dark little hallway that led to the restrooms and the phones.

"Hello!" He held out his hand to her. "My name is Maximilian Winsted." He had to pause after that, just to catch his breath. Then he leaned confidentially close, closer even than the friar had leaned into him. "I've been watching you all evening."

She laughed, though he noticed she put her hand on his chest. Was she pushing him away? Or was she teasing him? Little vixen!

He laughed. "I find you extremely attractive."

Her eyes got wide. Man, they were really blue. And they got that scared look he kind of enjoyed, fluttering all around like she didn't know what to do next. "David?" she called. Was she talking to him or to somebody behind him in the restaurant?

"No, it's Max," he told her. "My name is Max."

She shook her head. Man, was she built! And she was wearing this tight pink top with a V-neck and he could look down and just see the whole spread. Man, oh man . . .

It was dark in that hallway. It'd been quite some time since he'd copped a good feel. And Miss Barbie here was giving him quite the come-on, what with the hand on his chest. Maybe he should return the favor. Man, was she cute. Very cute.

Max didn't really think about it, he just reached out

and touched her. The next thing he knew he was on the floor, staring not at Barbie's boobs but at dust just inches away from his nose. Or was the scream the next thing he knew? He wasn't sure. Somebody had decked him. Was it Barbie?

He tried to lever himself higher—it was damn hard to do with his head swimming—but he managed to get halfway up. Barbie was standing next to McDougall. In fact McDougall was holding on to her. She was sobbing—now *that* was an overreaction—and McDougall was stroking her hair. They seemed to know each other really well. *Really* well. David and Barbie. David and . . . Did he just call her Barbara? The same name as his wife?

Uh-oh.

Chapter 11

On a Friday evening, as another Napa Valley summer weekend officially kicked off, Gabby stood in her living room, wrapped in Will's arms. It was exactly where she wanted to be and what she'd been waiting for all week. Were it not for the words coming out of his mouth, she would have been blissfully happy.

"Our weekend will officially begin as soon as I'm done with this call," he told her. He pulled back a bit, glanced at his watch. "In fact, I've got to go do it right now."

"I can't believe you've got to do a business call at seven o'clock on Friday night."

"It's not my choice, believe me." His right hand reached out to smooth back her hair. "But I'm close to finalizing a deal. The call has to happen tonight." Then he stopped abruptly, as if he'd planned to tell her more but then thought better of it. "I'm sorry but what can I say? I've told you before I don't have—"

"I know, I know." This time she pulled away, entirely out of his embrace. "A nine-to-five job."

She lifted a pillow from the shabby brown couch, plumped it, then tossed it back into position. *You're sounding like a whiner,* she told herself. *Lay off him. Can't you see he's exhausted?*

In the weak sunlight filtering through the windows, softened by the fog that perched on the mountain like a wool cap, Will truly did look spent. Pale, haggard, as droopy as the collar on his usually crisp dress shirt.

And he had to drive seventy miles to get up here, she reminded herself. *Through Friday-night commuter traffic.*

She took a deep breath. "I'm sorry. I'm a little stressed, too." She walked closer to him, tried to sound as apologetic as she felt. "Work was crazy, and I got home late and dinner's not ready yet anyway. You want a glass of wine?"

"You know what? I'd prefer water. And aspirin."

"Oh, no—on top of everything else you've got a headache?"

He massaged the nape of his neck. "I'm afraid so. It started when I was stopped dead on 29 for half an hour."

"I'll go get you something." Once in the blue-tiled bathroom, she regarded her disappointed face in the old medicine-cabinet mirror, then threw back her head and closed her eyes. *This is really shaping up nicely. My day sucked, it looks like his day sucked, and we can't even talk about it because work is off-limits!*

He had to stay mum about his deals, and no way could she spill anything about the chaos at Suncrest, all of which was generated by Max. Thanks to him, they had a bunch of dead vines from weed killer, a shot reputation at one of San Francisco's best restaurants, and a vintage of sauvignon blanc she was none too proud of.

She reopened her eyes and shook her head. Actually, she had every right to be stressed herself. Will wasn't the only one with a high-pressure job, though at the moment he was sort of acting like it.

She found him in the living room tossing his cell phone back in his briefcase. He straightened to face her. "I forgot I don't get coverage here. Do you mind if I use your land line?"

"Not at all. Maybe you should use the extension in the bedroom since I'll probably be noisy in the kitchen." She watched him shake three aspirin onto his palm. "Should you be taking that many?"

He didn't say anything, just popped the pills down his throat, set down the glass, and bent to pick up his briefcase. "I'll use my calling card," he said, before he disappeared up the stairs to the bedroom.

The house fell silent. She sighed as she turned again toward the kitchen, where a ton of pasta-making awaited her. But no handsome sous-chef to entertain her while she worked.

He closed the door behind him and took a deep breath. *Chill. You'll make the call, you'll move the deal forward. Then you can relax and concentrate on her.*

That was the best he could hope for, he knew. There was still a lot to accomplish on the telecom deal. It was highly unlikely he'd be able to relax. And even if he did, it wouldn't last long, because the Napa situation still hung over him like a storm cloud.

He lay his briefcase on her floral bedspread. The damn thing was, he couldn't *make* the Suncrest acquisition happen. He could bet on it, he could believe in it, but he had to wait for the situation to play itself out. That was the risk he had taken, the gamble he had made.

And on top of that, he'd promised Gabby to try not to change Suncrest if the deal did go through. How stupid was that? That was a promise he could never keep. Not in a million years could he get his partners to agree to a deal that let Suncrest keep operating as a breakeven family heirloom. As Faskewicz had reminded him not long ago, GPG wasn't into funding nonprofits.

Will sucked down another deep breath, let it out slowly. Enough of all that. Time to focus.

From his briefcase he pulled out the tools of his trade. Palm. Blackberry. Laptop. Spiral notebook. Pen. A glance at the bedside clock informed him he was to place the call in precisely two minutes. The future of his telecom deal and a hundred million dollars rode on the conversation he was about to have.

Not to mention that Will Henley Jr. could use a splashy professional success right about now.

He tossed some of the bed pillows onto the floor and used others to prop his back against the pine headboard, then pulled her phone onto his lap from its home on the bedside table. It was a pink princess phone, amazingly enough, which he had thought charming the first time he saw it but which didn't get quite that reaction from him now. On *this* he was supposed to conduct a serious negotiation? It made him feel like Gidget.

He put the call through. It was a complicated business, what with him in California, Ted and Sally in New York, and Marco in Shanghai. Through the floor below him he heard strains of stereo music, fairly muted, and the clattering of pots and pans.

Should I have warned Gabby how long this might take? Probably, but there was no time for that now. He kicked off the proceedings. "Everybody has a copy of the proposed term sheet?" Grunts all around. "All right," he said, "let's start with the post-money cap table. . . ."

Time passed. "I recognize your issue, Marco." Will jotted notes at lightning speed. "But the liquidation preference is completely standard in this type of transaction."

The door opened slowly. Gabby poked her head

into the bedroom, gave a tentative smile. "Dinner's ready," she whispered.

He couldn't even nod, given that he was cradling the Gidget phone between his left ear and his shoulder. Briefly he raised his pen from his note-taking and made an *I heard you* wave. She backed away, closed the door. He glanced at his watch. Eight o'clock already?

He returned his attention to the call. Marco was making outrageous demands, but then again that was his preferred negotiating strategy: start with an insane position to define the terms of the debate and then feign intransigence as everybody else scrambled to save the deal by accommodating him. Will had tried that himself a few times and learned its effectiveness. But it was not entertaining to be on the receiving end.

Time passed. "Sorry, Marco, but the transfer restrictions are necessary. We're putting in over a hundred million dollars, and we want to make sure our interests are completely aligned."

Again the door opened. Again it was Gabby. This time Will looked up to see that there was no smile and no whisper. "The food is done," she said. "It's getting cold."

He couldn't mouth the words that leaped to his mind. *I'm trying to do a major transaction here, Gabby. For Christ's sake, don't bother me about dinner!* But none of that could he say. All he could do in the throes of negotiation was lift his shoulders in a *There's nothing I can do about it now* gesture, which he did. He noted, as she left, that she looked none too happy.

Finally, the call was done. "Okay, then, we're agreed." He capped his pen. "Ted will redraft the term sheet and send it out by e-mail. Marco and his counsel will review it Monday his time, and we'll talk again Sunday night at seven Pacific time. I'll set up the call." Within seconds, everybody hung up. Will rose from the bed to stretch his legs, relieved that the pressure was slightly off, at least until Sunday. He glanced at the clock. 9:18.

Uh-oh. That'd taken two hours.

Gabby would not be pleased. After all, she didn't understand what he did well enough to know that's how long these calls could take.

Nor had he warned her.

He exited the bedroom and stood at the head of the staircase. He didn't hear her, but music was on, a soothing-voiced female vocalist warbling something jazzy. The aroma was terrific—garlic and olive oil and pancetta, was it?—and he realized he was terrifically hungry. But his feet were slow to descend the stairs.

He found Gabby in the kitchen, sitting at the small table. In front of her was an open bag of pretzels, an impressive array of crumbs, and an empty, obviously used wineglass. She looked up at him. "You're done?"

He recognized the tone of voice. It was the *You bastard, how inconsiderate are you?* tone he'd heard from girlfriends past.

Great. Just what he and his stress level needed.

"The call went fine," he told her, aware of a hardness in his voice. "The deal's not done but we're closer," he added, hoping to drive home the point that the call indeed had been important, been worth his time and hers.

She nodded. "After two hours, I would imagine you *would* be closer."

He couldn't help it; the comment annoyed him. "It wasn't my choice it took that long." He watched her, noted no apology in her hazel eyes. "You had a snack?"

"I was hungry." She cocked her head at the stove. "Help yourself to the pasta. You'll probably have to nuke it."

He moved toward the cabinet where he knew the plates were stored. "Can I get you some?"

"No thanks."

"Maybe we should just toss it and do takeout,"

She was on her feet and in front of him in a flash. "We are not tossing that pasta. I made those noodles myself."

He was taken aback. "Okay, then. We'll nuke it."

"You're damn right you'll nuke it." Her hands were on her hips now, her skin starting to flush. "Work was hell today, but somehow I managed to get back here to roll out fresh pasta dough. I know what a hard week you had. I was trying to do something special for you. But apparently you're so self-absorbed you don't appreciate that." She marched to the other side of the kitchen and crossed her arms over her chest. "Go hungry for all I care."

"Whoa!" He threw up his hands in a *Stop right there!* position. "You call *me* self-absorbed? I'm trying to negotiate a multimillion-dollar transaction and all you're worried about is your pasta? I didn't ask you to hand-make something for me. I'd have been happy with takeout. You could've bought something at Dean and DeLuca. But maybe you didn't want to run into your old boyfriend again?"

Her eyes widened. "What the hell are you talking about?"

"Vittorio Mantucci." He felt his control start to slip. It felt good, actually. He didn't do it often enough. "Out to do a Napa Valley acquisition." It had shocked him to find that out. GPG had damn good young associates to do research, and he made damn good use of them. He edged closer to her, and she backed away a step. For a moment, a moment only, he felt bad for giving her a second's physical fear. Then anger and frustration pushed the reluctance away, and he kept right on going. "What did you do, tell your old flame now was a good time to buy in? Thought maybe it'd be a good idea to give GPG some competition?"

"I did no such thing!" She spun away from him, picked up her napkin from beside her empty bowl then threw it down again. "Even though you *should* have competition from somebody like Vittorio, who understands what the wine business is all about. Or should be about."

"Do you have any idea how much I have riding on everything that's going on right now?" By now his control was going, going, gone. "My entire career is on the line. No deals, no job. But all *you* care about is your precious pasta. Or preserving the character of Suncrest, which is on the skids for reasons that have nothing to do with me. Jesus!"

She spun toward him, stance aggressive. "Do not presume to tell me what I should and should not care about. Though clearly I made a huge mistake taking *my* valuable time trying to do something nice for *you*."

"Damn it, Gabby!" His voice shook the rafters. The intensity of it shocked even him. "I have helped you in so many ways! I go with you to the hospital when your father has a heart attack, I help you rebottle the goddamn sauvignon blanc, I even make promises to you that I had no business making about how I might structure Suncrest if I ever acquire it!" His finger pointed in her direction, only inches from her face, while his voice lowered to a menacing growl. "You extracted that promise in bed, Gabby. That was low. No, that was lower than low. You know what that was?" He paused, considered stopping, but didn't. "That was blackmail."

Her face twisted. *Shit, she's gonna cry.* Well, if she did that would be blackmail, too—a woman using tears as a weapon when logic and argument failed.

But she didn't, and as he watched her jaw set and her eyes narrow, he wasn't sure if he was relieved or not. "All you care about is business." Her voice took on a threatening tone, too, as ugly as his own. "Doing deals, making money. The things that should matter to you don't. I guess my first impression of you was right after all."

"Fine." He looked around her kitchen, at its white tiles with their cheery roosters, at the run-down linoleum floor, at the ceramic plates set on stands she'd probably brought home from Tuscany.

He wanted out. He wanted away. Away from her. Away from Napa Valley. Away from all the things that weren't going his way and never might. "You know what, Gabby? I'm not the cause of your problems. But right now you are the cause of mine. I'm out of here." He pounded upstairs to collect his briefcase and everything else that was his from her bedroom, leaving in total disarray the bed where they'd shared so much joy.

He didn't give a damn.

Max sat in his father's old office, at his father's old desk, having a phone conversation his father wouldn't have had in a million years. It was pitch dark outside, but only one light was on, the green-shaded accountant's lamp on the desk. A half-empty bottle of pinot noir—not a Suncrest varietal—loomed over a crystal wineglass. Max was so riled he was smoking a cigarette in plain sight.

"We may very well press charges against you!" David McDougall's voice was loud enough that Max could hold the phone a foot away from his ear and still hear him. "And seek damages. You traumatized my wife, damn you! She can't sleep! She's afraid to go out alone!"

Max stared across the office at the dark-colored tartan sofas against the cherrywood-paneled walls. As though it were yesterday and not a year and a half before, he remembered sitting on one of those sofas while his mother paced a hole in the Oriental carpet.

*The girl's father is threatening to go to the police, Max!
Do you understand how serious this is? What did you
do to her?*

He took another drag from his cigarette and blew
the smoke out of his mouth in little puffs. He hadn't
done a damn thing to that girl that she hadn't wanted
done. And though the details of the soirée at Cassis
were a trifle hazy in Max's memory, he was convinced
the same was true for Mrs. McDougall, regardless
what she was telling her hubby now.

As his mother had done when she'd banished him
to France to let the dust settle, Max would keep an
eye on the bigger picture. He could not risk McDougall pressing charges, criminal or civil. Or, Christ,
both.

He closed his eyes, imagining all the ways his life
would go to hell. Everybody in the valley would think
he was an idiot, or worse. His mother would be on
the next plane home to grab Suncrest back out of his
hands. And that stupid girl from two years ago might
get wind of the whole thing and decide to get on the
Press Charges Against Max Winsted bandwagon. In
short, he'd be royally screwed.

He stubbed out his cigarette and took a deep
breath. "David, as I said before, I am tremendously
sorry for what I did and how much I upset your wife.
If there was any way I could make it up to her, and
to you, I swear I would." He paused, both trying to
gauge if he was getting through and gearing up for
the words he found so very difficult to say. "Please,
I'm asking you not to press charges. I had too much
wine, I behaved like an ass, I made a stupid mistake.
But I'm already paying for it."

McDougall sounded truculent. "How do you figure?"

"Well, of course there's no way Cassis will carry
Suncrest wines now."

"You got that right."

"And I embarrassed myself not only at your restaurant but in front of my friends. My reputation's taken a serious hit."

"If I had anything to say about it, that wouldn't have been the only hit you'd taken."

Max had to stop himself from chuckling. McDougall was fifty if he was a day, but he was threatening to punch out a guy half his age? No wonder the guy was so pissed: he could probably tell that his wife wanted to sample some younger flesh.

But something in that comment gave Max the sense that McDougall might be softening. He shifted the phone to his other ear and prepared to deliver what he considered the most potent weapon in his arsenal. "David, I'm asking you to cut me a break. I've just taken over the helm here at Suncrest, I'm following in my dad's footsteps, and I've got to tell you, it's not easy. You got kids, right?"

"Well, from a prior marriage, yes."

"Then you know what I'm talking about. They've got to make their way in the world in the shadow of a very successful parent. I'm here to tell you, it's not easy!" He let that sink in. Then, "I'm asking you not to press charges, David. Please. I'm begging you. Believe me, I've learned my lesson. I'll never do anything like this again."

Silence. Max waited, barely breathing. His father's brass clock ticked away the seconds of his life while his fate balanced in David McDougall's hands.

Then, "I'll tell you what," McDougall said. "I'll talk about it with Barbara."

Max nearly yelped. He felt as if a life preserver just got tossed in his direction.

"It's up to her to make the decision," McDougall went on, "but I will tell her what you told me."

"Thank you, David. I can't tell you how much I appreciate this."

"Get your act together, Winsted."

"Yes, sir. Thank you, sir." But McDougall missed the final *sir* by hanging up.

"Yes!" Max let out a breath. He'd been that close—*that close!*—to disaster. He paced a bit to let off some steam. Man, he'd dodged a bullet. He sloshed some more pinot noir into his wineglass and threw it back, then poured water into the glass and drank that, too. The French said you didn't get drunk if you downed as much water as you did wine. Max believed them.

He was about to shut the office down for the night—it was already after nine—when the phone rang again. He considered letting the call go to voice mail but then picked up, figuring the Had-His-Act-Together Max Winsted would always take a business call, regardless of the lateness of the hour.

"Hey, glad I caught you, Max. Burning the night oil, huh? Joseph Wagner here."

The *Wine World* writer. Max cringed. Had he heard about the Cassis thing? Max took a deep breath and tried to sound cheery. "How you doin', Joe? Played another round at Cypress Point?"

"I wish. I need friends like you to pull that off. Listen, I got a question for you."

Max steeled himself. "Shoot."

"There's this story I'm hearing and it sounds kinda nuts to me, but I have to follow it up. There's a rumor going around that you guys rebottled this year's sauvignon blanc. Is that true?"

Max laughed, a forced, unpleasant sound. *Shit!* It wasn't what he expected, but it was just as bad. He had a vague notion that that topic had come up at Cassis, too, but he was far from clear on the details. Nor could he ask anybody without raising a boatload of questions.

"Wow!" he said, trying to buy time. "What a wild story! Where'd you hear that?"

"Oh, here and there." Wagner wouldn't spill that,

no surprise. "But it's hard to believe because people are saying there was no problem with the wine, it was just that you guys wanted to switch bottles."

Apparently Joseph Wagner didn't think that was such a hot idea. Gabby DeLuca's voice echoed in Max's head. *If it gets out that we rebottled, everyone will assume there's something wrong with the wine. And why wouldn't they? No winery would decant unless it had to!*

Max's mind worked fast, as it had a tendency to do when he was in trouble. Some people might say that was because it'd had a lot of practice. "So have you tasted our new sauvignon blanc?"

Wagner let rip a huge sigh, something Max was not happy to hear. "I did. And I thought it was pretty good but not really up to Suncrest standards. It seemed a little past its peak to me. I'm going to have trouble scoring it very high. Sorry, Max, but that's where I am right now."

That's the thanks I get for showing you the high life in Pebble Beach? Max stood in the half-dark in his father's office—pissed off, frustrated, and vaguely recalling that Cassis's sommelier hadn't been too keen on this vintage, either.

Man, these wine world people were snobs! One less-than-perfect vintage and they went all judgmental on you.

Well, Max wasn't going to take the fall for that. But he knew somebody who could.

"You know what it is, Joe?" He made his voice sound confiding. "Our winemaker had a heart attack this summer. He's fine now, but his assistant, his daughter, has been filling in for him." Max paused to let Joseph Wagner connect the dots.

Which he did right away. "You mean Gabby DeLuca?"

"Yeah. She's good, don't get me wrong, but, you know, this is her first time taking the lead. There's a learning curve involved, we all understand that."

A smile cracked Max's face. He was proud of himself for so deftly finessing this difficult query. He'd just said something mildly nice about Gabby DeLuca—while burnishing his own reputation for being magnanimous and understanding—and still was wriggling out of that pesky problem of the less-than-stellar sauvignon blanc.

But then Wagner came back at him with a question Max hadn't anticipated. "So are you worried about this year's cabernet sauvignon, too?"

"No!" That came out too loud. Max lowered his voice. "Not at all. Cosimo DeLuca's coming along great, and he'll be back in the saddle by harvest. We're really psyched about the cab grapes this year, actually," he added, though he had no idea how the fruit was ripening. "We think it's going to be a banner vintage."

"So what I'm hearing you say is, you *didn't* rebottle?"

He had to answer. And fast. "No," he heard himself say, "nothing of the kind."

Wagner hung up soon after that. Max wasted no time going into the employee files to look up Gabby DeLuca's address. She had to be warned that this rumor was out and about and that they had to haul ass to bottle it up. No pun intended.

He poured more pinot noir down his throat, and more water, then hightailed it to his mother's Mercedes—at least, *she* thought it was her Mercedes—and made a beeline for Crystal Mountain Road.

Better mad than sad, she decided. Gabby stomped upstairs, stormed inside her bedroom, glared at the mess Will had left behind. Pillows topsy-turvy on the floor. Bedspread half off, bunched and bundled. Window left wide open, as if it weren't forty-five degrees outside.

She began to straighten, plump, restore. *I should have trusted my instincts!* It hugely galled her that Will had all but accused her of two-timing him with Vittorio. What did he take her for? Well, she knew what *he* was. She'd seen the cold capitalist's heart beneath the knight-in-shining-armor veneer. All he cared about were his precious deals. And apparently that was Vittorio's priority number one, too. The two of them deserved each other.

Once the bed was remade, off came the sexy peach-colored camisole—new—she'd worn especially for him, though of course he hadn't noticed. Off came the sleek black trousers that had just enough spandex in them to highlight her curves. With brisk efficiency she removed her lacy bra and panties—also peach, also new—that she'd imagined would be peeled off in quite a different manner, in quite a different mood. On went the floor-length black negligee she'd picked up in anticipation of future seductions. *Might as well wear it,* she thought grimly. *It won't get used any other way.*

Anger propelled her down the stairs and into the kitchen. She pulled open the fridge and yanked the cork out of the chardonnay she'd hoped to share with him, poured herself a second glass. But standing there in that kitchen—empty, fluorescent lit, clinically clean after the furious scrubbing she'd given it—the words he'd roared at her seemed to echo from the white-tiled walls, lashing her heart in a cruel rhythm.

Blackmail. Blackmail. Blackmail.

Did he honestly believe that? Was that how little he understood? Of her, of this valley that she loved and was only trying to protect?

Though it was true that the trouble Suncrest was

in had nothing to do with Will and everything to do
with Max.

You know what, Gabby? Will's voice blared again,
harsh, accusing. *I'm not the cause of your problems.
But right now you are the cause of mine.*

Tears came, prickling behind her eyes, defying her
rage and threatening to turn it into heartache. *Right
now you are the cause of mine. You are the cause
of mine. . . .*

She didn't know how often the buzzer sounded before she heard it and recognized it to be the doorbell.

She stilled, frowned, tried to decide if it was her
imagination. *Bzzzz.*

No, it was real. *He's come back. To apologize.* Her
heart leaped in a jig of relief. Will wasn't really the
jerk he'd acted like before, he couldn't be.

She knew, as she raced to the door, that she'd forgive him. She'd say she was sorry, too. She was. She
hadn't exactly been on her best behavior herself. She
knew that if she weren't so stressed, she wouldn't have
gotten so upset. Normally she'd be able to absorb a
disruption in her dinner plans, maybe even tolerate
cold pasta she'd spent hours making. Next time she
would.

She whipped open the door. Her elation crashed
and burned. "Max."

Down his eyes flickered, then up again. "Hi, Gabby.
Glad you're home. Mind if I come in?"

She peered around him, as though Will would be
standing in his wake, hidden in the shadows. But that
was stupid. Who was she kidding? There was no Will.
He was halfway to the city by now.

Anger—at Will, at Vittorio, at Max, too—flared up
again, stiffening her back, raising her chin. She crossed
her arms beneath her breasts, flimsily covered by the
black silk of her negligee. "What are you doing here?
And at this hour?"

"May I come in?" he repeated.

She wanted to get out of the cold herself but didn't want to let him in. The thin layer of fabric she wore, with nothing beneath, did little to shield her from the mountaintop's foggy night air or from Max's roving eyes. She watched them drop again to her chest, then return to her face. Why had she been such a numskull as to answer the door dressed like this?

Because at ten o'clock on this Friday night, there was only one person she could have imagined standing on her stoop.

Fooled again.

"Max, just say what you have to and then go."

"I will." He laughed, then shouldered past her into the living room. "But I'd kind of like to do it inside, where it's not freezing cold."

She gritted her teeth, slammed the door shut, then pointed a finger at Max's face. "You are not staying long." She grabbed an afghan from the couch and threw it over her shoulders while he halted in the middle of her living room.

"Nice place you got here," he said.

"Save it. What're you here for?" She knew she should take care how she spoke to Max Winsted: he was her employer, after all. But by now her patience was as thin as her peignoir.

His eyebrows flew up. "Somebody's in a bad mood."

She stepped closer, unwilling even to try to mask her anger. "Max, thanks to you, I've had one hell of a day. And Monday's not going to be any better. We've got a vineyard half-ruined by weed killer. We're a laughingstock because of what you did at Cassis. And thanks to that damn rebottling, I've got a vintage of sauvignon blanc that tastes like—"

"All right already!" He frowned. "It's that last thing I want to talk to you about."

"What now?"

He looked away from her, finally, down to the hardwood floor. "Joseph Wagner called to ask if we rebottled. Said there's a rumor going around that we did."

"Oh, shit." She threw back her head. From bad to worse, this night, her life, everything. "How in the world did that get out? Did you say something?"

He hesitated, still staring at the floor. Then, "No."

I'll bet. "What'd Wagner say when you explained?"

"I didn't explain." He met her eyes. What did she see there? Belligerence? Challenge? "I denied it. And so should you. That's our story, and we're sticking to it."

"What if he starts calling around to the companies that lease decanting equipment? If he's any kind of real reporter, that's what he'll do. What then, Max?" She saw a flicker of fear in his eyes before he cocked his chin defiantly in the air. "You didn't think of that, did you?"

She was going to make him angry. She was amazingly good at that tonight. Somehow, after the queer turn the evening had taken, she was even enjoying that ability. It appealed to a base part of her she rarely investigated and didn't much care for.

Max stepped closer. "You think you're so smart."

"I'm smarter than you! I told you not to do that rebottling. I told you it could hurt Suncrest. And it sure as hell looks like I was right!"

"You're always right, aren't you?" He stepped closer still. "Just like my mother."

She didn't like the sound of that. Nor did she like the vein bulging on his neck, the quick beat-beat of the pulse evident even on his skin's surface. She turned away from him, put the couch between them. "Okay, you said your piece. Now go."

"I'm not ready to go." Instead he moved around the back of the couch, too, staring at her, his gaze unwavering. She thought she'd never seen such focus on Max Winsted's face in her entire life. Through her surprise and incredulity she realized that this must be how a rabbit felt being chased by a fox. No, not quite that. She wasn't being chased. She just had the odd, disconcerting sensation that she should get away, now, while she still could. . . .

A beat later she tried to make a dash for the front door—*But what am I going to do? Run down the mountain? Barefoot, in a negligee?*—when the next shock came. Max's hand shot out to clench her arm, viselike, and she found herself twisted entirely around, toward him, against him, his beefy face inches from hers, his breath, which stank of alcohol and nicotine, puffing in her face.

This isn't happening. This isn't happening.

But it was. "Don't give me the innocent act," he was saying. He had her by her upper arms now, squeezing them in a killer grip. "Look what you're wearing." His spittle hit her face. His eyes were dark and wild. "You damn women. You never admit you want it."

"I don't want a damn thing from you, you asshole!" Somehow, even as they wrestled and the afghan she'd thrown over her shoulders tumbled to the floor, she was more angry than scared. She got one arm free of Max's clutch and slapped his face, hard, leaving an angry red stain that buoyed her. He stumbled back a step like a drunken sailor but then lurched toward her, chortling, and grabbed hold of her again, harder this time.

"You like to fight, huh? You like it rough?" Then his mouth came down on hers. She twisted her head away, heard a shriek she realized yowled from her own throat. Then she had a better idea.

She gathered herself—*one, two, three*—then hard as she could, jammed her knee up into his groin.

He yelped and let go of her. She watched, panting, as he stumbled backwards, doubled over. Bewildered, in a sort of stupor that had her thinking at half-speed, she then realized the front door was rattling and a loud male voice was yelling her name.

Will. She flew to the door and wrenched it open.

He burst in and stared at her, his features contorted. Like hers, his breathing was harsh and fast. "Sweetie, are you okay?" Then his eyes turned toward Max, who by now was prone on the floor in the fetal position. "What in the world is going on here?"

How to explain? Gabby's mind raced as Max's moans filled the silent house. Will stared at him for a moment longer, then again turned toward Gabby. "Are you okay?" he repeated.

This time she found her voice. "I'm fine." She said it, maybe she even meant it. She looked down at herself, saw welts rising on her arms, the ugly bruises Max's hands had made. Then, only then, she started to tremble.

"Oh, baby." Will came toward her, gathered her gently, so gently, into his arms. "I didn't know what in hell I was hearing through that door." She felt his breath in her hair, the rapid hammer of his heart against her chest. "Dammit, I'm so glad I came back." He pulled back a bit, held her at arm's length.

For a moment he said nothing, just looked at her with those sky-blue eyes of his, but she swore she could hear words spill from his mouth into the chilly air. *I love you.*

Then his lips moved, and she heard actual words spoken. "I came back to apologize. I was such a jerk. I can't believe the things I said to you. I am really sorry, Gabby. Can you forgive me?"

"Oh, Will." Forgive him? Who was kidding who? "I said such terrible things, too. I am so sorry." She collapsed against him, crying, choking, telling him she'd been so unfair, knowing in her soul that it was oh, so right to trust him.

And hoping she'd never forget that again.

Chapter 12

First thing Monday morning, well before eight o'clock, Gabby did something highly irregular. When she arrived at work, she bypassed the winery and instead went straight to the Winsted residence. Mrs. Finchley greeted her at the front door, as neat and starched as a naval officer in her housekeeper's uniform.

"Sorry to stop by so early," Gabby said, "but I'd like to speak with Max if he's available, please."

The older woman's brows arched. "Is there a problem?"

No, except for the fact that your boss assaulted me Friday night. Gabby made a dismissive wave of the hand. "Oh, it's just something I'd like to fill Max in on before he gets busy at the winery."

"He may not be available just at the moment," Mrs. Finchley said, which Gabby knew was a diplomatic way of saying *He's not up yet.*

She smiled, confident the housekeeper would promptly march upstairs and rouse him. "I'll wait."

Mrs. Finchley set Gabby up in the living room with a mug of coffee and a warm apricot scone, then sailed off. Gabby settled in a cozy upholstered chair beside the white brick fireplace and tried not to drop crumbs on the pristine hardwood floor.

It was a lovely sunlit room, elegant but not fussy, with art books and photographs on the few tables and cheerful blue-and-yellow chairs and sofa. The only decoration was a restful painting of a winter stream hanging over the fireplace, but Gabby supposed that the view through the French doors of garden, pool, pergola, and vineyards provided plenty enough to look at.

She finished her scone, emptied her mug, crossed her legs, and twitched her foot rhythmically in the air. She knew exactly what she was going to say to Max and wanted to get it over with, already. He'd surprised her Friday night. Well, now it was Monday morning and time for *her* to surprise *him*.

When he finally appeared, he looked surprised, all right. And wary.

You should be, you jackass, she thought as she rose to her feet.

He stepped a little farther into the room, moving so tentatively she thought he might turn tail at any moment. She could tell from his damp hair and soapy scent that he was freshly showered. Fortunately he didn't reek of cigarettes and alcohol like the last time she'd seen him.

"Good morning," he said.

She skipped the pleasantries, kept her voice low, and edged closer. "I'll make this fast, Max. There are three things you need to know. One, you don't have a single thing to say about how my father and I handle harvest or any aspect of the winemaking. You got that? Nothing." Out shot another finger. "Number two. You tell Felix to rehire every single field-worker you made him fire. Today. And three, from now on our official story is the truth. Yes, Suncrest did rebottle the sauvignon blanc, because you decided to switch the bottles. Anyone who calls me and asks, that's what I'm going to tell them. I suggest you do the same."

Max stood planted on the floor, mouth agape.

It was precisely the reaction she wanted.

She was nearly out of the room before she spun on her heels and fired her last salvo. "And if ever again you so much as stand too close to either me or my sister, I will personally see to it that your life becomes a living hell. Have a nice day."

Her heart was pounding when she got outside. It was nerves, partly, but also exultation. She could have gone to the police, she knew, but didn't imagine she'd get much satisfaction. All too easily she could imagine what they'd say, see the dubiousness in their expressions, hear the incredulity in their voices. *So you had a fight with your boyfriend? You were drinking wine and wearing your negligee? And at ten o'clock on a Friday night, you don't expect the guy to try something?*

Gabby half jogged down the pebbled path that sloped from the residence to the winery. She might go to the police someday. But just at the moment she was much more in the mood for private justice.

Three days later, Max's life hadn't improved.

You know what? he mumbled to himself, lumbering downstairs from his father's office. *This isn't much fun anymore.*

It was eleven o'clock on Thursday morning, and the top item on his agenda was an appointment with Leo Gordon, the manufacturer's rep for the company that made Suncrest's automated bottling line. Max had spent the last two hours bent over mind-numbing paperwork, and now all he had to look forward to was schmoozing with a balding, middle-aged salesman.

And this counted as a good day. Nothing catastrophic had happened yet. For example, none of the female hired help had bitched at him about what he must and must not do.

He hit the bottom of the stairs and loped past the stainless-steel fermentation tanks, with their spouts and knobs and temperature gauges, then pushed open the heavy oak winery door and emerged into the late July sunshine. The air hit him like a furnace blast. He blinked rapidly as his pupils adjusted to the blinding white light. Out from his rear trouser pocket came his cigarettes. He tamped one against the packet then lit it, tossing the match onto the pebbled path.

He squinted west toward the Silverado Trail, waiting for Gordon's truck to drive through Suncrest's bronze entry gates. Vineyards rolled away from him in fruit-heavy majesty. They were getting close to the big season now—Harvest with a capital *H*. The white grapes would be brought in in a month, then the reds. Everybody around him was getting excited, like crush was the Second Coming.

Could this possibly be all there was for him? Max wondered. Would he be standing here in twenty, thirty, forty years waiting for Leo Gordon's kid to show up? With some woman employee analyzing his every move? The thought felt like a noose around his neck. He could be dragging around this cursed winery until he was dead!

His eye caught the motion of Gordon's truck as it pulled off the Trail and barreled up the drive. It was a massive black flatbed with monstrous wheels, the sort of vehicle that gave Max the willies every time he drove past one in his red Mercedes two-seater. Usually the driver was some heavily sideburned he-man who oozed attitude and testosterone. It was safe to say that Leo Gordon broke the mold.

Gordon careened to a stop, dust billowing behind him, then leaped from the cab and scurried toward

Max, right hand outstretched, thick-framed nerd glasses perched on his nose, mouth pulled tight in his salesman's grin.

"Max, good to see you, good to see you." He pumped Max's hand vigorously.

Max concluded that Gordon must have a severe perspiration problem, judging from the slickness of his palms and the impressive stains in the armpits of his short-sleeved dress shirt. Max slid his hand from Gordon's grasp and tried to be nonchalant as he wiped it on his trouser leg. "Thanks for coming by."

"My pleasure, my pleasure. So you thinking about putting in a second line?"

"Thinking about it. Haven't made any decisions yet."

"Expansion's always good, always good."

Max tossed his cigarette butt and led Gordon inside the winery to the warehouselike space at the rear where the bottling line was located. Gordon pranced around it at high speed, examining, nodding, then finally halted in front of Max as if ready to make a pronouncement.

"You got yourself a good line here. Standard forty-eight feet. Solid, reliable equipment." He raised his right arm and waved expansively, providing a wide and clear view of his stained armpit. "Plenty of room to put in a second line. Always a good idea."

"How much would that run me?"

"We could do it for half a million."

"What?" Max nearly choked. "I thought it'd be a lot less than that!"

Gordon slapped his back and laughed uproariously. "It's a capital investment, my friend! You have to spend money to make money."

Yeah, yeah, Max knew all about that. Problem was he'd been doing lots of the spending lately but the making wasn't happening nearly so fast. "I don't know," he told Gordon. His enthusiasm for doing much of anything these days was pretty shot. "I'm going to have to think about it."

Gordon went on as if he hadn't heard. "Young man like you probably wants the newest thing. Is that right? Have I got that right?"

"I'd say you do."

Gordon lay a hand on Max's shoulder. "Screw cap, my friend."

"What?"

"Screw cap! Real cork is getting harder to find, plus screw cap keeps the wine fresher. It's the new style! And *you*"—he jabbed a finger into Max's chest—"you can be on the cutting edge."

Max shrugged, unmoved. "It's an idea."

"It's a fantastic idea!" Gordon looked astounded that Max wasn't convinced. He pushed his nerd glasses higher on his nose and peered at Max as if at a specimen on a slide. Then he shrugged himself. "You think about it. Let it stew. Young man like you, you'll see the wisdom. After all these years in the business, I know that much. No need to give you the hard sell." He slapped Max on the back and started to walk away. "By the way, sorry I didn't have that corker jaw you people needed July Fourth weekend."

Max stilled. "Refresh my memory?"

"The corker jaw?" Gordon halted and looked back at him. "Your guy told me it slowed you down by a few hours. See?" He pointed at Max with an *I told you so* expression. "You put in a screw-cap line, you won't have that problem. Anyway, sorry I couldn't help. Can't get a corker jaw on a holiday." He waved again then scuttled off.

Max remained standing next to the sleeping bottling line, adding two and two together. His mind ground to one inescapable conclusion: the rebottled sauvignon blanc had gone bad because Gabby DeLuca let it sit for hours while she tried to find some damn part! No wonder it got too much oxygen and went "past its peak," as Joseph Wagner put it. If she hadn't screwed up, he told himself, the rebottling would've worked. *Man.* Max shook his head, filled with disgust. He couldn't be held responsible for that but yet he was, because the buck stopped with him. The rebottling fails? His fault. The field-workers spray the wrong shit? His fault. Some restaurateur's wife won't admit she got hot for a younger guy? His fault again!

Thinking of Barbie McDougall made Max think of Gabby DeLuca. He headed for the stairs, his lips curling in a sneer. Self-satisfied slut! Acts all saintly with him but clearly is putting out for Will Henley. What killed was that he had to be supernice to her now, despite how bossy and arrogant she was. That tirade she went off on? *Man!*

Deep in the recesses of his mind, Max knew that others might perceive a nasty pattern in his behavior: the girl from two years ago whose father made those gnarly accusations, then Barbie McDougall, then Gabby DeLuca . . .

But the only pattern Max saw was women who did one thing and said another, and never once took responsibility for their own actions. He was sick of it. Actually, he was sick of a lot of things.

He opened the door to his father's office, sat down at the big mahogany desk. He looked around him, at this office he'd known all his life, had played in as a kid, with its tartan sofas and cherrywood paneling and sports trophies from the '40s and '50s. It hadn't changed one iota in the two years since his dad had died.

It's still my father's office. The revelation hit Max as clearly as if the sky had opened and God Spoke From Above.

This is my father's life. It's not mine.

The more he thought about it, the more obvious it became. This life had been foisted on him. By his father and by his mother. With its meaningless decisions about what grape varieties to plant and how many worker bees to hire and fire and whether to stop up the bottles with corks or screw caps. And now, thanks to Gabby DeLuca, he was hamstrung in every way. He could barely take a leak without consulting her first.

He sat at his father's desk and pondered. What he needed was something new, something that would allow him to pursue his own ideas. Suncrest sure didn't fit that definition. It was a drag, and it would stay a drag for the rest of his life. If he let it.

I need a way out. But I can't just quit. That would be too embarrassing.

Max's mind clanked and groaned and eventually came around to the conversation he'd had with Will Henley and his mother when he'd just gotten home from France. *We could take Suncrest entirely off your hands,* Henley had said. *Free you up. Provide to you, in cash, the substantial value of your holdings. Thirty million dollars . . .*

Thirty million dollars. That was a nice chunk of change. Max would need cash to launch his next venture, whatever it might be. Thirty million would be enough to do something cutting edge, as that bozo Gordon put it.

Maybe, just maybe, he should call Henley and feel him out. Sure, it'd be weird. The last he'd seen him, Henley had been spitting fire, all riled up because of Max's little touchy-feely with his girlfriend. Max wasn't too keen on the guy, that was for sure. He was a full-of-himself city slicker who had a big job and thought he was smarter than God. But how smart could he be if he wanted to buy Suncrest? The thing was *cursed.*

Yet Henley was so gung-ho, he already had an offer on the table. He was hungry for the deal. Max bet he still would be regardless of the to-do with his girlfriend.

Max chuckled. What a beautiful turnaround to unload Suncrest on Henley. Max would be free, with money in his pocket to do whatever he pleased, and Henley would be stuck holding the bag.

Now *that* would be sweet.

Max decided he didn't have time to preview all this with his mother. If it got serious, he'd just have to bring her on board. Because he had to move fast. There was some nasty shit floating around about Suncrest, and he didn't want Will Henley to hear any of it. At this very moment Gabby DeLuca could be poisoning Henley's mind against him. Who knew what she was telling him, what spin she would put on events?

Max reached for the phone.

Will sat at his GPG partner's desk with telephone calls lined up like aircraft at San Francisco International. On the active runway was Napa insider Jonathan Crosby. And on deck? Will smiled as he glanced at the pink telephone-message slip currently on top of the pile: *Max Winsted*, his assistant Janine had printed in her careful hand. *Please call back ASAP*.

Will would return the call, though his notion of ASAP might differ from Max Winsted's. ASAP would occur once Will had plied his sources for last-minute tidbits of information, any one of which might prove useful in the ensuing conversation.

For he could guess why Max Winsted was calling. The ASAP had given it away.

Will returned his attention to Jonathan Crosby on speakerphone. "How widespread is the rumor at this point?" he asked.

"That Suncrest rebottled? Oh, it's done the circuit."
Jonathan laughed. He owned an outfit that not only
made its own wine but also provided fermentation,
barreling, and bottling facilities for other small to
medium-size producers. Which made him highly plugged
in to everything that happened in Napa Valley. "More
to the point, lots of people believe it. Especially given
everything else that's been going on at Suncrest. I hear
the distributor's starting to have trouble moving the
bottles."

So Suncrest's new sauvignon blanc wasn't selling
well. It was exactly what Gabby had feared. Will felt
another surge of disgust toward Max. What a pathetic
excuse for a human being. He was a loser on every
dimension but still held Gabby's future—and that of
every other Suncrest employee—in his feckless hands.
It was more than time to get rid of him.

"I suppose everybody will blame the winemaker for
the poor quality of the sauvignon blanc?" he asked
Jonathan.

"Most will. Anybody who doesn't see it up close,
doesn't know the DeLucas . . ." Jonathan's voice
trailed off. Then, "You know, they're an old-time family around here. People have a lot of respect for
them."

"The Winsteds have been around awhile, too."

"Yeah, well, that's different." Jonathan paused. "At
least since Porter died."

What Jonathan was too politic to enunciate blared
from the speakerphone. *I knew Porter Winsted. Porter
Winsted was a friend of mine. And let me tell you, Max
is no Porter Winsted. . . .*

Will finished the call a short time later, satisfied that
he'd squeezed Jonathan Crosby for every useful scrap
of information he could provide. Certain that Max was
sitting in his father's old office panting for his call,
Will rose from his desk and strolled toward his floor-

to-nearly-ceiling paned windows to scan the view. The Embarcadero's lunchtime foot traffic was out in force—businesspeople, joggers, knots of tourists. All looked busy, purposeful. Even the tourists, with their maps and their guidebooks.

A smile of profound satisfaction broke wide on Will's face. *I called it. Max is caving, just like I knew he would. He's ready to sell.*

It hadn't taken long, but Will thanked his lucky stars it hadn't taken longer. Now everybody at GPG would have to admit that his strategy, risky though it might have been, had been dead on. In a heartbeat, he'd go from pariah to hero—provided he could do the deal fast and not go above the original offer. Hell, at this point he might even be able to negotiate Max lower, if Max was desperate enough. The ASAP sure sounded desperate.

Yet somewhere in Will's unconscious, a worry lurked. *Gabby. What is she going to think about this? And what is Suncrest going to end up looking like?*

The promise she'd extracted from him dimmed the roar of triumph in his head. Yet still Will had to chuckle as he ambled back to his desk to place the call, deciding to put Max on speakerphone just to have that much more of a psychological advantage. He hoisted his legs atop his desk and crossed his hands in his lap.

The call was answered after the first ring. "Max Winsted."

"Will Henley."

"Thanks for calling back."

"My pleasure." Will nearly choked on those sylla-bles. The last time he'd seen the bastard, he was man-handling Gabby and might have done much worse. Will despised him, but strategy demanded that he bury his antagonism. At least until the deal was done.

"There's a business matter I'd like to discuss with you," Max said.

"Shoot."

Max cleared his throat. "You recall the discussions you've had with my mother and myself about a possible acquisition of Suncrest?"

"I do indeed."

"Well, I want to let you know that my mother and I didn't mean to discourage you with our refusal. We both assumed that your initial lowball offer was just that. But for the right price, I can tell you that we would be interesting in pursuing the matter further."

I'll just bet you would. Though Will seriously doubted that Ava was on board with Max's plan at the moment, or even knew about it. The last he'd heard she was playing movie-star wannabe in Europe.

"I'm pleased to hear it, Max," he said. "I continue to be interested in acquiring Suncrest. As I've said before, it's a unique property."

"Should we talk about a more realistic price than the one you offered before?"

"Now, here's the thing." Will paused to give Max a chance to worry. "My partners agreed to that offer a few months back. There've been a variety of negative developments in the wine industry since then, and at this stage I can't really tell you what their appetite is for that price point."

Silence. Will smiled. He wanted Max to believe that if anything, the price of Suncrest was going down over time, not up. That way Max would be thrilled to nail down a sale at the original, so-called "lowball" offer.

"Well, perhaps the wine business is having some troubles," Max declared, "but Suncrest is doing as well as ever. Even better."

Even better, my ass! Will bit back the guffaw that rose in his throat. Apparently Max was arrogant enough to believe that Will had no idea what was actually going on at the winery. Even if Max knew

Gabby wasn't telling him anything—which she wasn't—he should gather that Will was sufficiently well connected to have other sources of information.

"As I say, Max, I'll have to consult with my partners."

"Tell you what." Will could imagine Max hunched over the phone, his brain cranking into overdrive to try to find a way to make the deal work. "My mother and I would sell at your initial offer if you could do an all-cash transaction."

Will shook his head. This was like taking candy from a baby. No doubt Max Winsted thought he was being very clever but he'd just broken the cardinal rule of negotiating. He'd just told Will exactly what he was willing to do.

I want cash. I want it fast. And I'll give on price to make that happen.

That was all Will needed to know. And those parameters suited him just fine. For him, cash was no problem. Price and speed were his issues.

And Max was truly a fool if he thought he was pulling a fast one by pushing a deal through quickly, before Will got wise about Suncrest's growing roster of difficulties. Will could "discover" all those things he already knew during the due-diligence process, and reduce his offer price even more then.

"So, Max," Will said, "let me make sure I've got this straight. You and your mother would sell Suncrest to GPG for thirty million dollars if we were able to handle an all-cash transaction."

"That's right. If you were able to do it in, say, a month."

Well, that was pretty darn clear. Will smiled. "Max, I'll tell you what I'll do. I'll go back to my partners and lay all this out. I'm not sure on the price, but there's a real possibility we can make something work." He could almost hear Max's sigh of relief. "Then I'll work up a term sheet for you and your mother to take a look at."

Will would generate that document ASAP, complete with a no-shop clause to prevent Max from using GPG's offer to get a better price. Will needed no reminding that he was not the only player in Napa Valley attempting to make an important acquisition.

Max bit at the prospect of a term sheet like a shark chomps on a seal pup. Minutes later Will ended the call, linked his hands behind his head, and sat at his partner's desk for some time, watching the world go by through his big paned windows.

Sunday evening found Gabby standing next to Camella at the kitchen sink of their parents' home. With the barbecue over and the sun just dipping behind the mountains, Cam was rinsing dirty dishes and Gabby was loading them into the dishwasher.

Cam threw back her head and cackled. "I can't believe you went in Max's face and laid down the law!"

"Shh!" Gabby cocked her chin at the half-open window above the sink, beyond which was the patio on which Will was having one last beer with the rest of her family. "Keep it down. He'll hear you."

"So what if he hears me?" Cam's volume didn't drop a notch. "Don't you talk about work with him?"

"No, I don't."

"How weird is that?"

"It's not weird. It's"—she struggled for the right word—"prudent."

Cam scoffed at that notion, though Gabby knew her sister didn't begin to understand why she insisted on keeping the details of her work life secret from Will.

Including the latest. As she'd known he might, Joseph Wagner had called her and asked flat out if Suncrest had rebottled its sauvignon blanc. And she'd done exactly what she'd warned Max she would do: she told him the truth. The big question was whether Wagner believed her explanation. It was very likely he'd think that Suncrest rebottled because she and her father had screwed up the wine. She dreaded every upcoming issue of *Wine World*, knowing that the piece Wagner eventually wrote about Suncrest could wreak havoc on her reputation as a winemaker.

And on her father's.

She sighed and raised her head to eye her father through the window. In the fading light, he stood next to Will, the two of them debating the relative merits of charcoal versus gas grills. Her father was thinner than he had been before the heart attack, a little grayer, maybe a little more fragile looking, though she hoped that was only in her imagination.

One thing was undeniably true, though, and it loosened a bit the perpetual worry knot she had in her stomach these days. Her father and Will looked sweet together, the older man and the younger, chatty, comfortable, relaxed. Will was the first man she'd brought to her family's home since college. Vittorio, damn him, had never made the trip.

Gabby took a bowl from Cam's hands and found a place for it on the dishwasher's bottom tray. "Daddy doesn't know the half of what's been going on at Suncrest," Gabby said, "but I'm going to have to bring him up to speed."

On some things, not others. Certainly not on Max's attempted assault or the ongoing question of whether Will would someday acquire the winery. Gabby had unilaterally decided—with no help from the cardiologists—that her father's heart was in no condition to hear either of those news flashes.

No wonder I'm a basket case. She straightened to stretch the kinks from her back. *I'm keeping secrets from everybody.*

"Do you think Daddy's ready to go back to work?" Cam asked.

"The doctors say he is. It's been seven weeks, and it's only part-time—till harvest anyway." She would keep an eagle eye on him while he was at Suncrest, that was for sure. If he so much as looked winded, she'd make him rest. And as a precaution, she and her mother both had learned CPR, so if something happened to him at home or at the winery, they'd know how to help him.

Gabby lowered her voice and edged closer to her sister. "Now don't you say a thing to Daddy about what Max did to me."

"I won't."

"I mean it. It'd make him really mad, and I'm not sure he could take it."

"You know"—Cam set her hand on her hip—"have you wondered whether maybe we should all just quit?"

Gabby was silent. Of course she had, though even now the idea of Suncrest permanently out of her life was impossible to fathom. "Well, *you* could if you really wanted. But you know Daddy won't quit. And I can't, especially not right before harvest. It'd be too irresponsible. Suncrest could never bring in another winemaker that fast. Plus I promised Mrs. W. It wouldn't be fair to her." Gabby sighed. "It's not her fault her son's such a disaster."

Cam shot out her chin. "It's at least partly her fault. She raised him, didn't she?"

Gabby looked through the window at her own mother. She looked happier than she'd been in weeks, what with her eldest daughter dating someone so eligible and her husband on the mend.

Sofia DeLuca, dutiful Italian wife that she was, had nevertheless complained to her daughters that having their father underfoot was driving her crazy. Taking naps in the middle of the day and never remaking the bed. Leaving dirty dishes in the sink. Redoing her vegetable patch for reasons God alone understood.

Every complaint session ended the same way. "I love him, he is my husband and the father of my children, every night I thank God on my knees that he is still here with us." Then she raised her index finger in the air for the final pronouncement. "But that doesn't mean I'm not ready for him to get out of the house and go back to work."

Gabby got the dishwasher going, then turned toward Cam. "Will Mom kill us if we put candles on Dad's cake?"

Both sisters approached the kitchen table to peer at the *torta angelica* their mother had baked that morning. They knew from delicious experience that it was truly heavenly, a sponge cake soaked with Malvasia dessert wine then topped with blueberries, blackberries, and chilled zabaglione. In deference to their father's new health concerns, Sofia had agreed to vary the standard barbecue menu by grilling chicken instead of beef and using light mayonnaise in the potato salad. But no true DeLuca celebration would ever occur without some sort of homemade *dolci* to mark the occasion.

Cam furrowed her brow. "I think candles are good. How about three? For the past, the present, and the future?"

Who couldn't get behind that idea? But as Gabby watched Cam poke around the miscellaneous drawer, she wondered what that third candle held in store. She'd never been this uneasy, not even in that blighted time when she'd fled Tuscany for Napa, fresh from Vittorio's betrayal. Then she'd had some idea what lay ahead of her. No more.

Holding the cake with its candles lit, Gabby stood poised at the kitchen's screen door as Cam pushed it open and began to sing to the "Happy Birthday To You" tune. "Happy Suncrest to you, happy Suncrest to you . . ."

Everyone joined in. Gabby stepped carefully onto the patio, eyes trained on her father's megawatt grin, for a moment glancing at Will to see the smile that lit his mouth and his eyes, the private gleam meant only for her. Will fit in so well with all of them, it was almost frightening. The old fear about getting too close was always with her these days; she couldn't quite shake it. He seemed so devoted now, but who knew how fleeting that might be. She'd seen devotion die before. What was to say it wouldn't again?

Her father had plenty of breath for three candles. He blew, everyone clapped, Lucia's husband Ricky let out a whoop that rose to the dusky heavens. Then they all stilled, while crickets clicked and mosquitoes flitted about seeking bare flesh. Will moved beside Gabby and draped an arm over her shoulders. Very gently he kissed her forehead as she watched her father gaze at each of them in turn.

"I am blessed," he said. "I knew that even before the heart attack, but I really know it now. And since I'm an old man who's even wiser than he used to be"—he paused while his family noisily disputed the assertion of greater wisdom—"then let me say that this is what life is all about. Having your family around you, living in the place that you love, enjoying as best you can every day that God gives you."

Gabby watched the father she adored turn toward the man she was so close to loving. "And let me thank you, William. I've heard more than once how much you've helped this family when they needed it most. I am very grateful."

"I was glad to do it, sir."

Cosimo DeLuca nodded, giving Will a steady gaze that Gabby was gratified to see he steadily returned.

Her father ended the moment. "Come on." He waved his arm to move everyone toward the cake perched on the patio table. "Let's cut."

A half hour later, with leftovers packed in aluminum foil resting on Gabby's lap, she sat in Will's car as he drove them in the dark toward Crystal Mountain Road. She wasn't sure exactly where on Highway 29 he told her, but knew she would never forget the moment when he suddenly swerved off the road, turned off the ignition, and pivoted in his seat to clasp her hands in his. For the rest of her life, she knew she would remember the flashes of white light on his face as cars hurtled toward them on the opposite side of the narrow highway.

"I want to tell you something, Gabby," he said.

She was almost afraid to ask. "What?"

"I know it hasn't been a long time. Not even two months." He stopped, looked away out the windshield, staring at something she wasn't even sure was visible. She held her breath, willing him to say what she felt in her own heart but didn't yet have the courage to put into words.

Again he met her eyes. And smiled, and ran a finger down the curve of her cheek. "I love you."

"Oh, Will." It was what she wanted, and yet she was going to disappoint him. She watched him wait for her reply and hated to do it but couldn't bring herself to say what no doubt he longed to hear. It wasn't easy for a man to put himself on the line like this, she knew, especially not a proud man like Will. *Like Vittorio, too,* she thought, and hated to include him in this moment. Yet it was because of Vittorio that she couldn't reply in kind to Will. *Not yet, I'm not ready yet,* she tried to say with her eyes and her smile and a squeeze of his hand, *but just give me a little more time, and I know I will be.*

Perhaps somehow he understood, for he leaned forward and kissed her on the lips, a soft kiss with no hint of recrimination. Then he fell back in his seat and took a deep breath. "There's something else I need to tell you, Gabby. Something is happening at Suncrest. Something that matters to both of us."

"What is it?"

"I can't say any more."

She frowned. "You can't tell me more than that?"

He shook his head.

"Because of professional ethics?"

He said nothing.

She twisted back in her seat to stare straight ahead, her left hand still holding his. Really, it was true, he didn't need to say more. She understood him perfectly.

He restarted the car, got back on the road. The valley flew past on both sides of them, the grapevines glinting silver gray in the moonlight.

Now, everything would change. For good or for ill, it had started.

Chapter 13

Ava sat on the sofa in the living room of her leased Paris apartment and watched her son gear up to play the charming persuader. *Really,* she thought, *he wouldn't make a bad actor. Were he ever able to commit to one script long enough to memorize it.*

For she knew Max wanted something from her; she knew he must have some agenda for this supposedly spontaneous trip to the City of Light. Her son wouldn't come so far merely because he longed to see his *chère maman.*

He stood with his back to her at the open doors that led to the walled garden. A weak breeze, the best this steamy August afternoon could produce, fingered the gauzy white draperies. "This place is fabulous! How many bedrooms?"

"Four."

"And a garden, too. In central Paris." He turned toward her and shook his head, as if in great admiration that she'd unearthed such a find. "But why'd you pick this area? I didn't know you liked the Trocadéro."

"Actually, it was the apartment I picked." There were only so many choices for short-term luxury rentals, after all. This one had won Ava over with its garden, its well-appointed rooms, its slightly worn elegance—all of which created the right impression for the dinner parties she'd already started giving. "I'm not too keen on the area."

"Too many ministries and embassies and official residences? It is a little overbearing. And of course you're done with the Eiffel Tower and the Invalides."

"I have been for years." Those were for tourists, whom Ava abhorred. She was a traveler, which was a different thing entirely.

She eyed her son, who now sat beside her on the sofa, hands linked between his knees, easy smile on his lips. She was happy to see that he'd lost weight. He looked healthy, well groomed, clean shaven, despite ten hours on a transoceanic flight. And really, he could be quite charming and insightful.

She sighed. If only those moments weren't so forced and fleeting.

"So you had enough of staying with Jean-Luc?" he asked.

Answering that required some delicacy. Ava gave herself time to think while gazing around the living room, at its cherry-red walls, Italian marble fireplace, and wood-framed mirror above the mantel, in which she and Max were reflected as side-by-side toy figurines of Mother and Son.

"I had the sense he needed his privacy," she lied, "especially now that he's revising his script. You know, he's a writer. He can be moody, and he wants to work all hours. Even though he never said a word, I felt I was getting underfoot."

Max nodded. She had the idea he knew she was lying but was willing to buy in to her story for the sake of politeness. There was some truth to what she said. Jean-Luc was doing a script revision—to what end Ava couldn't guess—and there was no denying his moodiness. But to claim he wanted privacy was like saying Romeo had had enough of Juliet. Ava could no longer abide Jean-Luc's clinging, especially after it became obvious that he wouldn't be able to relaunch her career. She made time for him, certainly, but only when her new social calendar allowed it.

For Ava was doing some revising of her own. And Jean-Luc might or might not end up in her final script.

Max cleared his throat. "Mom, I'd like to talk to you about something."

Ah, the moment of truth has arrived. Ava couldn't resist needling her son a little. "Didn't you come to Paris just to see me?"

"Well, I need to talk to you about Suncrest, too."

So there *was* trouble, and it must be serious if he'd come all this way to tell her about it in person. Ava shook her head. She had so hoped that by now Max would have a grip on managing the winery—both for his sake and for hers. It hardly fit into her plans to have to play a more active role. "What is it?"

He looked her right in the eye. "I've decided that I want to sell it. That I want *us* to sell it. I really think it's the best thing to do, for a number of reasons."

Her son's words hung in the stale, unmoving summer air. Ava was stunned. *My God. He's given up already.*

She rose from the sofa and half stumbled toward the fireplace, reaching out to grasp the cool marble mantel to steady herself. She'd feared from the first that Max would lack the stamina to run Suncrest for long, especially once problems cropped up. She knew only too well how grueling, how taxing, often how *boring* managing that winery could be. But to give up in two months? How would that look? Her son would look ridiculous to everyone in Napa Valley. And as his mother, so would she.

"You're not saying anything." Max's voice came

from behind her. "Are you really surprised? I know you talked about this with Will Henley."

"Quite the contrary. Will Henley talked about this with me. There's a difference."

"You told me you thought he made some compelling arguments."

She spun on her heels. "What I told him was that I would not sell him the winery. And that's what I'm telling you, too."

God, why couldn't this child ever do what she wanted? It was the most perfect thing in the world for Max to take over Suncrest! The father builds a business, and at the appropriate moment the son takes it over. It was a Hollywood story if ever there was one. If only the lead actor wouldn't blow his lines.

"But Mom, I don't want to run it anymore." Max's chin jutted out stubbornly. It was if he had suddenly been thrust back in time to the terrible twos. "I've tried it, and I don't like it."

"But don't you understand that Suncrest is your father's legacy? How can you be so willing to just abandon it?"

"I'm not abandoning it!" His voice rose. "Henley's company will make it better than it's ever been before. I bet if Dad were still alive, he'd want to sell it to them."

Ava shook her head. Porter would just as soon have sold her into white slavery as part with Suncrest. But clearly Max didn't share that view. In this as in everything else, the son was the diametric opposite of the father.

She tried to calm herself, marshal her arguments. "Max, for the last month you've been telling me you're making long-term grape deals, you're planning to add varietals, you want to take Suncrest to the next level. You've been so enthusiastic. Don't you want to make those things a reality?"

Now it was his turn to sigh. "Mom, don't get mad

at me." He rose from the sofa and walked toward her, his voice persuasive, placating. "I know this isn't what you planned, but I really do think it makes sense. For both of us."

"Why? Because you're already in trouble? Because the sauvignon blanc isn't selling like it should?"

He flinched. She had a fleeting memory of walking into the kitchen when he was a toddler to find him teetering on a stool, trying desperately to hoist his chubby body onto the counter so he could sneak one of Mrs. Finchley's gingerbread cookies, cooling on a rack. The look he gave her then—*Oh, no, Mom! You caught me!*—was so like the expression he wore now that she had to stifle the laugh that rose in her throat.

"I know about the rebottling," she told him, and watched his shock grow. "You don't think I have people who tell me things?" The faithful Mrs. Finchley for one, who rivaled Ian Fleming's M when it came to spying. "Don't give me this best-for-both-of-us story, Max. You want to sell Suncrest because you've already made a mess of it and don't want to be stuck cleaning it up."

"I take full responsibility for deciding to do the rebottling. But it's not my fault it didn't work right. Gabby DeLuca—"

"I don't want to hear about Gabby DeLuca!" Ava let her voice rise, like a diva launching into the aria that had made her a household name. "This is exactly what I was afraid of, that you wouldn't be able to manage Suncrest! Max, this is your father's legacy. You can't just sell it the minute running it gets tough."

Her voice bounced off the red walls, poured out into the silent garden. It was exactly what she hated to do—rail, nag, harangue. Yet even after her diatribe, her son said nothing. She watched his shoulders droop, his head hang. He slunk to the sofa, where he slumped onto the cushions and let his head fall into his hands.

Gradually, her anger melted into exhaustion. And guilt. All those doubts about what a haphazard mother she'd been—sometimes there, often not—rose and jostled in her mind as she regarded the dark-haired young man on her leased Paris sofa.

Maybe it's not his fault he is what he is. Maybe it's mine. For he was a spoiled child, Ava knew, a rich child who didn't understand responsibility. Before Suncrest, he'd never really had any.

She remembered the puppy she and Porter had given him when he was nine. She'd feared for that dear creature, too. A sweet yellow Lab, all wet nose and brown eyes and gangly paws the poor thing never had a chance to grow into. How many times had she warned Max not to toss the ball near the drive that led up from the Trail? Did he listen?

Yet, really, whose fault was it? The mother's or the child's?

She joined her son on the sofa, laid her hand on his knee. This time her voice was soft, as she wished it had been more often in the past. "Max, do you realize you'll never succeed in life if you don't give things time? You haven't even been running Suncrest for two months. Do you know what would have happened if I'd left Hollywood after two months? I never would've gotten a single role."

He raised his head. She saw tears on his cheeks, felt their tracks on her own heart. But even at that moment she wondered if perhaps they were just another of Max's manipulations, another wily attempt to push her maternal buttons.

"Mom," he said, "let me ask you this. Whose dream were you pursuing in Hollywood?"

"What?"

"Whose dream? Yours? Or your parents?"

It was so much hers that the question seemed too absurd to answer. She remembered to this day what her upright Methodist parents had called her fledgling modeling and acting career: "a foolish escapade." They'd wanted her to march right back to SMU and make a show of studying while doing the real work of finding a doctor or a lawyer to marry. Not until she became a Breck girl did their objections flag. After she snagged a soap role, their grousing quieted. Her first movie shut them up for good. But she wasn't fully restored to their good graces until Porter's three-carat diamond engagement ring graced her ring finger. And her acting career fell by the wayside.

"You went to Hollywood for yourself," she heard Max say. "That's why you stuck at it for so long. It was you who wanted it, nobody else."

"Don't you want Suncrest?"

"No." He shook his head. "I thought I did, but I don't really. It was what Dad wanted, but not me. Not you either, I bet."

That was so true, she had to turn her eyes away. She stared at the faded Oriental carpet, with its mesmerizing weave of crimson and gray and brown.

She'd wanted to stay in Bel Air. She'd wanted Porter to continue as a developer. She'd wanted their carefree life where she enjoyed wealth and comfort, friends and attention, and didn't have to raise a finger to get them. A new winery in Napa meant work and dirt and trial and error. And in those days, before California wines challenged France's great vintages, not much glamour at all. She'd nearly left Porter over it. But his excitement over what he was building, his passion, had won her over. He was a man nearing fifty who wanted one more stab at building something big and new. Who was she to tell him no?

Now she had a son who wanted exactly the same thing. And once again she was the obstacle.

The truth was, she empathized with Max. Though it made her feel like a traitor to Porter, she didn't want to run Suncrest, either. She didn't mind in the least it being an ocean and a continent away. Her desire to return to Napa diminished with every stroll down the Avenue Foch, every visit to the Musée d'Orsay, every café au lait sipped at a shaded sidewalk table.

She rose from the sofa and walked to the garden door to gaze at the gurgling stone fountain in the shape of a half-shell. Porter wouldn't blame her for how she felt, she told herself. And he wouldn't blame Max, either. He'd been an understanding husband and a patient father, far more tolerant of his family's foibles than she could ever be.

Ava turned to regard her son. "I do think your father would understand your desire to pursue your own goals."

Max's face lit up. It was Christmas all over again, her little boy catching sight of the gifts piled high under the tree. "Yes, Mom, he would understand. He spent his life doing what he wanted, and so should I. Then I'll really be committed."

She didn't even haggle with him over the details of Will Henley's term sheet. Thirty million dollars was a tremendous amount of cash; it would guarantee that she'd never have to think twice about money for the rest of her life. And neither would her son. She would not simply hand it over to Max, of course; trusts would have to be established and rules set down. She would take care of all of that, as her maternal duty demanded.

Ava read the document, then reread it. When finally she poised a pen over the space marked OWNER'S SIGNATURE, she had the oddest sensation of Porter behind the sofa, watching her. Judging. And, she had to admit, condemning. The feeling was so strong she actually turned her head to look, half-afraid of what she might see.

But there was nothing there, of course, only the

empty Paris apartment she had leased for a few months. Which might well have ghosts of its own, but none from her swiftly receding past.

Gabby stood with her father among the stainless-steel fermentation tanks, cleaning them in advance of another year's crush. It was a messy business involving hoses and spray nozzles and chemical solutions, and both father and daughter wore plasticized aprons, rubber gloves, and wading boots.

But this wasn't the only messy business going on at Suncrest, and the other couldn't be protected against by proper gear.

"Will says it's called due diligence, Daddy." Gabby carefully stepped down the last few rungs of the ladder that had allowed her to peer down into a tank, a large silolike contraption. She hit the concrete floor and then turned to face her father. "That's why these people are running around, poking their noses into things, and asking questions. He warned me it would start as soon as Max and Mrs. W signed the term sheet."

"That's the document that lays out the details of the sale?"

Gabby nodded and started pulling off her gloves, finger by sticky finger.

"I can't believe Mrs. Winsted signed it," her father said.

"I couldn't, either." Gabby watched a young brunette rocket past, notebook in hand, looking every pin-striped inch like one of Will's colleagues. Will had a few junior GPG staff helping him out, and while Max was still in France had set himself up in the winery's main office, his folders and documents and laptop on what Gabby still thought of as Mr. Winsted's desk. "But at this point, I think it's the best thing, Daddy." She glanced at her father to see if he agreed with her, though she wasn't even sure she agreed with herself. "Max was killing Suncrest, and it's pretty clear that Mrs. W doesn't want to run it anymore. We need a new owner. I have to believe that Will and his company know what they're doing."

Her father nodded. Gabby knew he was having as much trouble as she had had trying to grasp that Max and Mrs. W were selling Suncrest to Will Henley and GPG. It was such a huge development, and so hard to fathom. Truly the end of one era and the beginning of another.

But the Winsted era had to end, she told herself, *one way or another.* Because if someone didn't buy Suncrest, Max would run it into the ground. Of that Gabby was fully convinced.

"So it's a done deal?" her father asked.

"Mostly. Unless they find something wrong they didn't know about. Either Will's people, or the accountants, or the lawyers." What seemed like armies of them had descended on the winery that morning. They all looked cut from the same mold as the brunette, whether male or female. Gabby realized that if she didn't know Will so well, she'd lump him in as just one more of their corporate number.

She didn't dwell on how little she liked the look of them, how poorly they fit in, how much they unnerved her. They were like visitors from another planet. All wore business suits and moved around at high speed and spoke in hushed tones with their heads close together. That is, unless they were on cell phones, in which case they talked loudly. Sometimes they would smile at her when she walked past, but invariably they stopped speaking, as if they couldn't risk her overhearing their conversation. When she was a few yards away, she could hear them start up again, and words she didn't care for drifted toward her. *Expansion. Brand extension. Mass market.* They'd barely been around a day, and already she was building a healthy resentment.

And a certain fear.

Will's not like them, she told herself. *He understands.* Yet the words he spoke in the darkness of her bedroom the first night they made love rushed back into her mind.

If GPG ever does get to acquire Suncrest, I don't know what the deal will look like. It's not entirely up to me. You understand I'm a junior partner, right? I don't get to decide everything myself.

But you'll try? she'd asked.

I'll try.

She winced. Later he'd called her a blackmailer for extracting that promise from him. Yes, he'd apologized, profusely. But still. Did she really expect he would honor it? Or, given the partners he had to answer to, that he even could?

The brunette intruded on Gabby's thoughts. "May I bother you for a few minutes?" She was smiling, looking kind and helpful. *Like a nurse who's about to jab a needle in your arm,* Gabby thought. *But don't worry. It's for your own good.*

"Your name is Dagney?" her father asked.

Another smile. "Good memory!" She brandished blueprints rolled up into a tube. "I have here a map of the property, and I'd love some help identifying which vineyards produce which grapes, and so forth." She cocked her head, all charm. "Will's spoken so highly of both of you, and I know you're both so knowledgeable."

Gabby watched her father wink at Will's young associate and knew he did it in part for his daughter's benefit. "We try. Do you want to spread those out on that table over there?"

Minutes later, all three were bending their heads

over the blueprints, anchored to the table in four corners with bottles of Suncrest cabernet. In light blue ink on white architect's paper, the prints mapped Suncrest's buildings and acres of vineyards. Dagney pointed at Rosemede, on the valley floor. "What's grown here?"

"Sauvignon blanc." Gabby pointed to the other vineyard that produced that varietal. "And these eight, including Morydale here on the slope, produce cabernet sauvignon grapes."

Dagney's pen flew over a page of her open spiral notebook. "That's everything?"

"We also have a few rows of merlot and pinot verdot here and there," Gabby's father added. "For our cabernet. We sort of paint with those."

Dagney's pen stopped. She lifted her head and arched a brow. "You do what?"

Gabby piped up. "We add complexity to the wine by weaving in the flavors of those other grapes."

Dagney nodded slowly. Then she pointed to an area that didn't delineate a specific vineyard. "What's grown here?"

"We don't use that acreage," Gabby's father said. He pointed to several other blank areas. "We don't use any of that, either."

Dagney frowned. "And why is that?"

"It's substandard soil," he said. "It doesn't have the pH value we look for."

"So you don't think it's good enough." Dagney seemed to consider that while biting the end of her pen. Then, "Okay, let's move on." She consulted a list of typed questions. "What is the yield per acre? Approximately?"

"About three tons per acre," Gabby's father said.

That time Dagney stood straight up, her tone incredulous. "Don't most wineries get more like eight?"

No wineries that we like, Gabby thought. "The rule of thumb is, the lower the yield, the higher the quality of grape. So Suncrest has always been very selective in which grapes make the cut, so to speak."

"So you *could* get a higher yield if you wanted to?" Dagney asked.

"We could," Gabby's father said, "but the quality of the wine would suffer."

"Would it suffer by a lot? I mean, they're Napa grapes, so they're still pretty good, right?"

Gabby and her father looked at each other. Then Gabby spoke. "Maybe the difference in quality wouldn't be apparent to everyone. But it certainly would be to Suncrest customers, who are looking for more complex, nuanced flavors."

Dagney bit her pen and again bent back down over her notebook. Somehow Gabby got the impression that nuance and complexity weren't high on her agenda. She asked a few follow-up questions and then let Gabby and her father go, with protracted thanks for how helpful they were and what valuable "resources" they were proving to be.

"Maybe she'll put gold stars on our foreheads next time," Gabby's father muttered as they ambled back toward the fermentation tanks. But halfway there, he abruptly sat down on top of an overturned plastic crate.

Immediately Gabby crouched down next to him. Her heart started pumping a faster rhythm, but she hoped his hadn't varied by a single beat. "Are you okay?"

"I'm fine."

"Do you need to take a rest? Because I can do everything else myself."

He shook his head and smiled at her, a wan smile that she knew lacked its usual vigor not because of the grim prospect of hosing down the tanks but because of the Q and A they'd just undergone. And what it foretold.

Gabby watched her father rub his forehead and could guess what he was thinking. *Somebody stop this craziness. Make it go back to the way it's always been.*

She edged another crate over and sat next to him. He didn't look at her but stared into the middle distance, as if replaying scenes from the past in his mind.

"You know," he said eventually, "maybe we should tell that young lady that a lot of the vines that Porter and I planted twenty-five years ago are still producing grapes. Just a few years ago they were in their prime, but they're getting past it now." He met his daughter's eyes. "Dagney may want to pull them. Their yield's already way down."

Something about the way he spoke frightened her. "Daddy, we have to give these people some time to get their bearings. Will has our interests at heart, I honestly believe that. He understands how we feel about Suncrest, and he'll try to take care of it. He won't let his people do anything to hurt it."

A little voice chirped in her ear. *Not deliberately. But how much control does he really have? And anyway, maybe his idea of what will hurt it is different from yours. . . .*

Her father patted her knee. "I agree your Will's a good man, honey. It's just"—he shook his head—"all this. It's not what I pictured when I imagined coming back to work. I pictured it the way it used to be, without all these strangers in business suits. Just you and me doing another harvest together. I really looked forward to that." He smiled. "Our second harvest."

"We'll still do that, Daddy," she said, but she could hear the wistfulness, and the hint of desperation, in her own voice. "We still will," she repeated, but it sounded no more convincing the second time around.

Dagney walked past with her male associate, the two in such deep conversation they didn't seem to notice the father and daughter to their left hunkered down on crates. Gabby's father met her eyes. Again he gave her a smile, though it was no more vibrant than his earlier attempt. "I think I'll go in the break room and lie down for a few minutes," he said, then slowly levered himself to his feet and lumbered away.

Gabby watched him go, her heart thudding. Activity buzzed on all around her: people holding meetings, having conversations, taking notes, making phone calls. Normally she was right in the thick of things. Not that day.

She catapulted off the crate and strode toward the stairs to the second floor.

Will sat on one of the tartan sofas in Porter Winsted's office, half his mind following the chatter of his two young associates and half on Porter Winsted. He still thought of the office as Porter's—not as Ava's and not Max's—though he'd had to shove a few of Max's personal possessions aside. That hadn't been hard, especially since Max was still in France and would be gone for a week at least. Will had simply called for a box, made a swiping motion of his right arm across the flat plane of the mahogany desk, and then set the box on the floor outside the door.

Next!

He took much more care with what had belonged to Porter. His respect for the man who had founded Suncrest Vineyards was growing exponentially. He had long admired Porter's keen developer's eye, which early on had recognized the unique value of this particular swath of Napa Valley. But more and more he came to understand how steadily and responsibly Porter had built this business. Will spent fascinating hours poring over the winery files, which went back twenty-five years and described in painstaking detail how Suncrest had matured. This many grapes were harvested, this many bottles produced the first vintage, so many more the next, on and on till an abrupt halt two years before. Someone—no doubt Porter himself—had pasted the bottle labels from every vintage into a scrapbook. Even decades-old correspondence had been kept, along with reviews, print ads, the first check cut to the fledgling winery.

It was like a father's mementos of a beloved child. Will knew this was akin to what his grandfather had felt building Henley Sand and Gravel. He'd spent his entire high-powered career entertaining a mild disdain for family businesses, yet felt a surge of envy that surprised him.

He turned his attention to Dagney, who was sitting beside the other associate, Jacob, her equal in youth and workaholism. The latter was a disease that all qualified GPG employees suffered.

"It seems to me," she was saying, "that we could triple production without a significant decrease in quality."

Jacob looked at Will. "It would take three to five years if we wanted all the grapes to come from Suncrest vineyards. But as I was telling Dagney, we could do it right away if we import grapes from the Central Valley."

Will nodded. "As a matter of fact, Max Winsted just signed a purchase agreement for chardonnay grapes from there. The problem is he signed a five-year deal at way too high a price."

Dagney's brows flew up. "Five years? Can we get out of it?"

"That's one of the things we have to find out." Will had known going into this that Max had made a fine hash of things. He hadn't realized *how* fine.

The good news, which would make Will even more

of a hero at GPG, was that the due diligence had uncovered enough problems to justify lowering the purchase price. It was like buying a house. If during escrow, the buyer found problems, the seller either had to fix them or cut the price in order for the sale to go through.

And Max would cut the price, Will knew. He wanted the cash out of the winery, and fast. He'd put up a fight, but he'd cave. Max excelled at caving.

Dagney giggled. "I just had a funny conversation with the winemakers. The DeLucas?"

"What do you mean funny?" Will kept his tone casual. None of his colleagues knew of his relationship with Gabby. He still considered this a sensitive time and that a sensitive issue.

"Oh"—she shook her head—"they're very sweet. But they were talking about *painting* with some of the grapes. You know, using different varieties to make the cabernet more complex?"

Jacob laughed. "They'll find out soon enough they're going to be painting by number from now on!"

"I don't think they get that," Dagney said.

All three turned their heads at the light rap on the half-open door. "Excuse me," Gabby said. "May I have a few minutes, Will?"

"Sure." He leaped to his feet. *Did she hear any of that? What exactly did Dagney and Jacob say?* Then he berated himself. None of them had said or done anything to be ashamed of. Especially not in discussing how Suncrest could be salvaged from the ruins into which Max Winsted had plunged it.

Once Dagney and Jacob were gone, he shut the door and took Gabby in his arms. Where, he noted, she remained stiff. He dreaded the answer but had to ask the question. "How are you?"

"I'm okay." She pulled away and went to stand at the window, bending slightly to look beneath the half-closed Roman shade which attempted to beat back the midday sun. Then she turned her eyes to his. "Actually, I take that back. I'm trying hard not to get upset."

"Okay." *Here we go. I've been on site barely two days and already we've got problems.* He didn't let himself retreat to Porter's desk chair, though part of him wanted to put some distance between them. "What's upsetting you?"

She took a deep breath. "I'm getting a little concerned about what I'm hearing from Dagney and that other young guy. They keep talking as if there's going to be some huge expansion. And they don't seem to understand the kind of wine we make. What they're talking about is a lot lower-quality than what we do."

"Jacob. The other guy's name is Jacob." Will perched on the corner of Porter's desk, thinking fast. "First of all, Gabby, you need to understand that we're going to be talking about a lot of things in the next few weeks that are never going to happen. We just need to explore every possible avenue before we set a course of action. So I recommend you not take anything too seriously at the moment."

She stared at him. "I'm trying not to. But it's hard."

"I understand that."

"And my father's upset, too. So much so that he had to lie down for a while. I just don't know if he can stand the pressure of all this."

Great. Will rubbed his forehead. What if Cosimo DeLuca had another heart attack? On premises again? Should Will insist he go back on medical leave? Then a more terrifying thought struck him. If Gabby's father did suffer another cardiac arrest, would Will get the blame?

As if he'd spoken the fear aloud, Gabby came close to him and rested her hands on his shoulders. "I don't mean to pester you, and I know you're under a lot of pressure. But I'm worried about my dad." She paused, then, "I'm worried about all of us."

He raised his head. God, he was tired. And this was only the beginning. "Gabby, I don't know what to tell you. This is going to be stressful, whichever way you cut it. It's a big transition."

Apparently that wasn't what she wanted to hear. She turned away, went back to the window. Will watched her, and listened to the loud male voices of the field-workers outside. He knew they were bringing the packing bins out of storage for the upcoming harvest. All day long he'd heard them hammering together the wooden pallets on which the bins would be stacked. He could imagine Porter Winsted in this office listening to those sounds every August for twenty-five years.

Again Gabby turned her face toward his. "So I shouldn't worry about Suncrest expanding in a big way?"

He wanted to throw up his hands. "Gabby, I can't make any promises." *I'm not going to make that mistake again.* "The winery may well have to expand. I'm not sure it can survive if it produces only very expensive wines."

"But it has for twenty-five years."

"But it doesn't make any money. It's breakeven, at best."

She frowned, hesitated. "Is that true?"

"Yes, it is." He watched her take that in. Should he have told her? Probably not. But he wanted her to understand where he was coming from. Because he didn't think she got it.

Not for the first time, he found himself a little resentful of Gabby's fantasy Napa Valley, where family-owned wineries made scads of money producing high-end bottles bought by high-end consumers, both sides applauding themselves for their artistry and highly evolved taste. But all the while, he had to live in the real world, where real people bought Two Buck Chuck and were perfectly happy. And dealing with that reality was a lot less pretty.

She stepped closer. "Why were you so intent on buying Suncrest if it's not profitable?"

He was trying to decide how to answer that question without upsetting her further when she asked a follow-up he didn't much care for either.

"Because you knew you could *make* it profitable? Let's say, by using the brand name to expand down-market?"

It startled him how perfectly she'd phrased that, as if she'd graduated right alongside him from Harvard Business School. And yes, that pretty much had been his strategy. A damn good one it was, too. But at the moment he doubted Gabby would appreciate its wisdom.

A knock sounded on the door. Before Will responded, it opened and Jacob walked in. "Excuse me," he said to Gabby, then approached Will and handed him a file. "I forgot to give you this before. It's a list of Central Valley grape growers, with their varieties and prices. You'll see they're a lot cheaper. And I think they're plenty good enough," he added before he turned and walked out again.

Shit. Will tossed the file on the desk. He didn't look at Gabby but felt her eyes scorch his face.

She came up close to him, cocked her chin at the file Jacob had just brought in. "What about that promise you made to me, Will?"

"Gabby." He stood up, in a little psychological gamesmanship that forced her to raise her head to meet his eyes. "Yes, I did tell you that I would try to keep Suncrest the same. And I will to the extent that I can." By now he was starting to feel that responsibility not just to Gabby, but to Porter Winsted, too. "But it has to change to some degree, because otherwise it can't survive."

Silence. A silence that deafened him with its intensity. Then, "You've known this all along?"

Why did that question make him feel as if his entire relationship with this woman hinged on the answer? He looked into her beautiful, intelligent, demanding hazel eyes and knew what he had known for some time. He loved this woman and would not lie to her. But he wouldn't coddle her, either.

"What I know," he said, "is that one person and one person only moved this winery downmarket. And that is Max Winsted. He did it when he forced you to rebottle the sauvignon blanc. He did it when he got drunk at Cassis. He did it when he lied to Joseph Wagner. Suncrest does not have the reputation it used to, Gabby, and that's a fact. It's not my fault and it's not yours, either. But I'm not going to apologize for trying to salvage what can be salvaged. And," he added, "for trying to keep everybody who has jobs here employed for the long term."

"While making tons of money doing it."

He regarded her steadily. "We should be so lucky."

She turned away. When again she spoke, her voice was so quiet he almost couldn't hear it above the field-workers' hammering outside. "It always comes down to the same thing, doesn't it?"

She was right. It did. "But it doesn't have to, Gabby. I am not your enemy." That was the one thing she never seemed to understand. He grabbed her arm, forced her to face him. "This is business. This is not personal. This is not about you and me."

"Is there a you and me?"

"Of course there is. I love you, Gabby. I said it and I meant it." And there he was saying it again, even though she'd never responded in kind. He knew she was holding herself back for some reason, and it frustrated him. He wasn't her enemy in that, either. "I promise you that I am doing my damnedest to save this winery. I am trying to save your job, and your father's, and Cam's. But don't you see? It can't be the way it always was. Things are different now."

Her eyes shone with tears that didn't fall. "You're right," she told him, then moved away. "I totally agree." Then she walked out, clicking the door shut behind her, and leaving Will to wonder if they'd even been talking about the same thing.

Chapter 14

It all looked just as she remembered.

Then again, Gabby thought, hurtling her tiny rental Fiat south on an *autostrada* that sliced through the heart of Chianti, Italy, didn't change much over centuries. Why in the world would she expect it to change in little more than a year?

Because I'm so different. She pushed her foot down even harder on the accelerator, jerking the red needle on the Fiat's speedometer past 130 kilometers an hour—amazingly, the official speed limit on the Superstrada del Palio. No longer was she the lovesick girl who'd been so head over heels over Vittorio Mantucci that she'd been willing to toss aside country and family to be with him. Nor was she the brokenhearted wretch who'd fled Tuscany for home, cursing the man who'd hurt her, cursing herself for being such a fool as to let him.

Now, a year later, she was stronger, more sure of herself and what she cared about. There was nothing like losing something precious to learn a fast lesson about what really mattered. The older, wiser Gabby knew. Her family. The valley. Suncrest. For her, they were the holy trinity of what was dear.

Yet something else was becoming dear, too. Someone.

When Gabby thought of Will, tears blurred her vision, made the highway lines run together in strips of fuzzy white. *I love you,* he had told her. Would he ever say that to her again, after this?

What a terrible choice she was forced to make. And how very ironic. In the last days she'd come to understand Vittorio better than ever before. Now she grasped what he had gone through, now that she, too, had to choose between her family and her lover. Now she understood the guilt, the anguish, he must have felt.

You could go back. The temptation was always there, needling her. *Turn around and drive back to Florence airport, get on a plane home. You're risking too much. Give up. Give in.*

She shook her head. She couldn't do that, not really. She was the only thing standing between her family and "economic inevitability," or whatever phrase Will might use to try to mask how real people got hurt. People like her father. Now, after the heart attack, he needed the stability of what he was accustomed to. She didn't think he could handle the pressure of a big, corporate winery—which clearly was what Suncrest would turn into.

No one even knew she had engaged in this battle. This trip was secret to everyone but Vittorio. Her family thought she was in San Francisco visiting a girlfriend from college, and Will had no idea where she was. She'd simply found a discount airline ticket in the *Chronicle* classifieds and bought it. Now she was here.

When Will found out what she was doing, he would be enraged. He would think it a massive betrayal. He might even lose his job if the acquisition of Suncrest fell through, and naturally he would blame her. He was always telling her he was only as good as his last deal, and that he'd been in a dry spell.

The horrible truth was, Will would be right. She was betraying him. But her only other choice was to betray her family. For if she didn't fight to protect what they loved and needed, what had been precious to them for twenty-five years, wouldn't that be a betrayal, too? She could only hope that in the fullness of time, Will would understand. And forgive her. Though that might be the most foolish hope of all.

She sped past a highway sign that read SIENA, 7 KM. From Siena it wasn't far to Castelnuovo. Nervousness shivered through her as she realized how close she now was to the task that lay ahead. It was time to dry her tears, shove all doubt aside, and do what she had come to do.

Briefly she considered stopping in Siena—a gorgeous walled medieval city—for a bowl of pasta and a glass of the local wine. What could be more natural? It was past lunchtime, she'd been traveling for twenty hours now, and was exhausted and hungry.

Yet who was kidding whom? Gabby forced herself to ignore the turnoff. She would only be procrastinating, and postponing the inevitable, and Vittorio would be insulted that she'd eaten at a restaurant rather than allow the Mantucci family to feed her. And now was not the time to insult Vittorio. Not with what she wanted him to do for her.

And for himself, too. I'm doing him a favor, giving him an enormous opportunity. Which is far more than he deserves.

Clearly he'd been shocked at her phone call from California. He'd stepped all over himself trying to be gracious, even offering to send a driver to Florence airport to retrieve her. No, of course she must not stay at an inn but at the winery, in her old room. No, of course he could accommodate her visit, even though Chiara was days away from giving birth to his first child.

Gabby knew Vittorio would keep his former lover and his pregnant wife far, far apart. She knew she would not see his parents. She knew that his hospitality would not extend beyond the perimeters of the winery. Yet all that was appropriate, and just as well.

Minutes later, she turned onto a country road that twined through the mountains and valleys that separated the historic rival cities of Florence and Siena. Dark green cypresses on both sides of the narrow asphalt pierced the perfect blue sky. Ahead lay Castelnuovo Berardenga, the sunbaked land that gave birth to so many of Chianti's premier wines. As the Fiat chugged up one slope and hastened down another, she caught a glimpse of an old church, a grove of olive trees, a small vineyard. Centuries-old villas hid behind low stone walls, their residents the descendants of Siena's rich banking and wool families. She drove past one village, then another—barely more than a few farmhouses grouped together, sharing a *trattoria*, maybe an *ufficio postale*. Here and there a door was open, revealing a cool dark interior. An old woman wearing a kerchief swept a stoop; an old man eyed her passing car as he puffed on his pipe. It was all as heart-stoppingly beautiful as she remembered, and as timeless.

Her heart thudded as she turned onto the private lane she knew so well, every bend and dip, every puff of dust from its age-old surface. As she ascended a gentle slope, trees eventually gave way to vineyards, well tended as ever and heavy with the sangiovese grapes the region was famous for. Ahead atop the hill, where it had stood since the Crusades, perched the Mantucci family winery, Castello di Corvo. Shimmering in the sun as if plucked from a fairy tale, it rose from the ground in wheat-colored stone, with the ravens it was named for swooping and cawing above its crenellated battlements.

Gabby brought the Fiat to a halt on a dirt-packed courtyard in front of the winery. She stood to stretch her legs and collect herself, the sun baking her shoulders, the midday quiet broken by distant church bells. Then a motion caught her eye, and she turned to see Vittorio rushing toward her, smiling, both hands outstretched in greeting.

Tuesday morning, as Max trotted past the foyer table on his way from the kitchen to the pool, he noticed in the pile of mail that Mrs. Finchley had brought in that the latest issue of *Wine World* had arrived. There it lay among bills and glossy magazines and junk-mail flyers.

He stared at it, then stubbed out his cigarette on the table's ashtray. A cold sweat broke out on his back. With nervous fingers, he picked it up and continued outside, his bare feet padding on the hardwood.

He shed his white terry-cloth robe in a heap on the grass and took up a poolside position on a chaise longue. Then he picked up *Wine World*, a weekly newsprint periodical the size and shape of the *New York Post*. That was about where the similarities ended. Max doubted the *Post* had ever seen fit to print words like *viticulture* or *meniscus* or *viscosity*, many of which he only half understood himself.

Joseph Wagner's chatty column was easy to find. Max took a deep breath, then scanned it quickly looking for the word *Suncrest*.

Damn. There it was, in bold type. Two whole paragraphs followed.

He took a second, deeper breath, and started reading.

*What's truth and what's fiction? Depends on who
you ask. Suncrest Vineyards owner and general
manager Max Winsted denies that the esteemed
winery founded by his father rebottled its 2003
sauvignon blanc. But other insiders say otherwise,
as do an assortment of usually reliable Napa Valley folks in the know.*

*What makes this story an even greater mystery
is that apparently the decanting wasn't due to a
problem with the wine but a change of heart with
regard to the bottle. Seems that Mr. Winsted's
taste for all things French lingered even after his
return to California from* cette belle patrie.

*Problem is that as appealing as I, too, find this
vintage's heavy French bottle, the wine itself
leaves a bit to be desired, particularly at thirty
bucks a pop retail. And I'm not the only one
turning up my nose. Sources tell me that sales are
sluggish, a real turnaround for a winery whose
offerings typically fly off the shelves. . . .*

Fuming, Max threw the paper aside, where soon the
breeze carried the pages all around the pool and pergola area, some on the grass, some against the low
mesh fence that separated the residence from the vineyards, some even into the pool itself.

That's where the whole damn thing deserves to be!
Man, it would be none too soon that he unloaded this
albatross his mother kept insisting on calling a legacy.
And bidding adieu to traitor employees like Gabby
DeLuca, who clearly was the "insider" Wagner re-
ferred to. She'd threatened to spill the beans, and by
God, she had! And the bitch probably considered her-
self loyal.

Max shook his head in disgust. Women. But thinking
of women made him think of his mother, and that made
him smile. The signature he'd wrested out of her would

make a thirty-million-dollar payoff possible. He relaxed his head against the chaise and closed his eyes, enjoying the hot sun as it beat against his skin. Did he play her like Menuhin played a Stradivarius or what? His performance in Paris had been nothing shy of sublime.

Someone loomed over him, cutting off the sun. "Good morning, Max. I take it you've read Joseph Wagner's column?"

Max's eyes fluttered open. It was Henley, sounding and looking mildly amused.

Arrogant prick.

Max levered himself into a sitting position, wishing the strewn pages of *Wine World* didn't make it look like the column had sparked a hissy fit. "I glanced at it," he said.

Henley helped himself to an adjoining chaise, on which he sat his trim, tall, well-dressed body. "Sorry to disturb you at home, but there's something we need to discuss." He glanced at his watch—pointedly, it seemed to Max. "I wasn't sure when you'd find time to make it down to the winery."

Another dig. Max wouldn't miss this Henley guy once their business was concluded. But until that happy day, he had to be nice. "What can I do for you?" he asked.

"Well, as you know, we've been going through the due-diligence process."

"And how has that been progressing?"

"Just fine. But new facts have emerged that have a bearing on the acquisition price that we discussed."

Max sat up straighter on the chaise. "We didn't just discuss a price. We agreed to one."

"True. But that price is contingent upon certain assumptions I made about Suncrest's financial health. And some of those are proving to be unfounded."

Max didn't like the sound of that. He narrowed his eyes at Henley. "A deal's a deal."

"So it is. Max, don't get me wrong!" Henley chuckled and raised his hands in the air. "I very much want to acquire Suncrest, that hasn't changed. But given what we've learned through the due-diligence process, it's obvious that I can't do it at the price we discussed. Let me tell you why. . . ."

And Henley embarked on a dissertation about how the sauvignon blanc wasn't selling and how by now everyone knew it was rebottled and how they might have to write the whole vintage off and who knew how much collateral damage would be done to sales of the cabernet sauvignon, which accounted for 80 percent of revenues.

Max listened to all of this with his heart pounding and sweat starting to run from his armpits down into the too-tight waistband of his trunks. Just when he thought this damn deal was done, Henley was trying to retrade it! By how much? It sounded like mucho millions! How was Max supposed to get his mother to agree to *that*?

Henley finally wrapped up. "As far as I'm concerned, we should just withdraw the sauvignon blanc from the market. Admit that it's ruined and write it off entirely."

"That's ridiculous!" Max rose from the chaise and stared at the pool. "It may not be totally perfect but it's still great wine."

"That may well be, Max," Henley's voice said behind him. "I'm not the connoisseur you are."

Max shook his head. Even when Henley delivered a compliment, it sounded patronizing.

"But the fact remains that it's not selling," Henley went on. "And that it'll be years before it sells as well as it has in the past. And there's no doubt that sales of the cabernet will be affected. And that accounts for—"

"I know, I know. Eighty percent of revenues."

Henley came to stand next to him. Both of them stared at the pool, on whose cheerful blue surface floated two sodden pages of *Wine World*. Henley kept his voice low. "Max, if I go back and tell my partners all this, we may not have a deal at all. I have just *got* to cut the price to make it happen."

Screw you, Max thought. But the fact remained that he wanted a deal, too. And he wanted it now, and in cash. And that meant Henley was his man.

He steeled himself. "How much?"

"Ten percent. We can do it at twenty-seven million."

Max felt an enormous surge of relief. He'd been worried it might be a lot bigger than that. Ten percent he could finesse with his mother, especially if he waited for just the right moment to tell her about it. "Would we have to do a new term sheet?" he asked.

"No, we'd just put the new number in the final documents."

Max nodded, and Henley slapped his back. "Good doing business with you." Then he was gone.

It wasn't until Max was back on the chaise that it occurred to him that he probably should have negotiated with Henley before kissing off three million bucks. But he'd felt such huge relief, he hadn't even thought about it.

He frowned, suddenly wondering whether Henley might have been playing a little violin himself.

Gabby's alarm roused her at five o'clock in the afternoon. Waking in that tidy, familiar room—with its whitewashed walls, stone floor, lacy curtains billowing at the lone window—disconcerted her at first, threw her back in time to years before. It took her jet-lagged brain a moment or two to remember exactly why she was back in Castelnuovo, and what she hoped to achieve there.

She stretched like a cat in the narrow single bed, its snow-white starched linens scratchy against her bare skin. The greeting part of her trip was over, and had been more comfortable than she'd expected. Vittorio had held lunch for her, as she'd known he would. Together they ate at the long refectory table in the winery's old kitchen, feasting on hearty *ribollita* vegetable soup and Tuscany's famous coal-charred steak, *bistecca alla fiorentina*. All was washed down, of course, with the winery's own Chianti. After such a meal, and so much travel, she'd been only too happy to take Vittorio's suggestion that she nap the rest of the afternoon. Now, fed and rested like a proper Tuscan, she was ready for espresso and business.

She hoped Vittorio was, too.

She bathed quickly in the aged tub, dressed in simple blouse and slacks, applied a light makeup, then forced herself from this sheltered oasis down the stairs to the main part of the winery. She found Vittorio in his office, at his desk, his dark head bent over an enormous ledger.

She took the chance to spy on him from his half-open door. The office had the white walls and stone floor of her room upstairs, and looked as if it didn't change much as it passed from one generation to the next. It boasted several pieces of heavy dark furniture and a huge, faded, woven rug, thin from centuries of use. Dust mites danced energetically in the shaft of sunlight that fell across Vittorio's shoulders. He seemed all concentration as his right hand rapidly made entries on the ledger's huge lined pages. He looked Roman and aristocratic, and no one could doubt how seriously he took the responsibility of running his family's business. In a flash of insight, Gabby recognized just how much tradition he came from and what it must mean to him. And the chasm it had created between him and the American girl who'd once been his love.

Finally he raised his eyes, saw her, started, and smiled. "You slept well?"

"Like a baby."

He rose from his chair. "Let me call for coffee."

They settled on a sofa with their espressos on a low table in front of them. Ever polite, Vittorio waited for Gabby to speak.

She set her tiny white cup down in its saucer. "I have a proposition for you, Vittorio. One I believe could be very beneficial to both our families."

"A business proposition, you said on the phone." He smiled. "Gabriella, don't tell me you're giving up winemaking to get behind a desk?"

"No, never. In fact, it's because I want to keep making wine the way I always have that I'm coming to you with this."

He frowned. "I don't understand."

She took a deep breath. "The owners of Suncrest Vineyards, the Winsted family, want to sell the winery. They've received an offer from a San Francisco investment firm. And though I'm sure the investors mean well," she was careful to add, "I know a little about how they work. I have an idea what they're planning to do. And I'm very concerned that they'll take Suncrest in the wrong direction, turn it into a big corporation that makes mediocre wine. And use the Suncrest brand name to do it."

Vittorio's eyes didn't waver from her face. "I know you would not like to work for such a winery."

"No, I wouldn't. And neither would my father."

"But Gabriella, if this sale comes to pass and things go as you fear, why don't you simply take a job at another winery? Surely in Napa Valley there are many smaller, more traditional wineries that would suit you."

Of course she'd thought of that. But it wasn't as if winemaker jobs at elite wineries grew on trees. And anyway, what about her father? "I hope it doesn't come to that, Vittorio. Right now what I'm trying to do is keep Suncrest the way it's always been. And that's where you come in."

He shook his head. "I'm sorry, I still don't understand. What can I do?"

She gathered herself. Guilt seared through her, and fear, and a horrible foreboding. Yet it was for this moment that she had traveled six thousand miles. "You can consider buying Suncrest yourself," she heard herself say. "Have Castello di Corvo make an offer."

Silence. Vittorio's dark eyes widened in obvious shock. Outside the castle's thick stone walls ravens cawed, their shrill cries as familiar to this sun-drenched hilltop as grapevines. Gabby stared at Vittorio, willing him to take her proposition seriously.

Vittorio jerked his thumb at his own chest. "*Me* make an offer? For Suncrest?"

"Why not? I know you've been exploring possible acquisitions in Napa Valley." It was ironic. When Gabby had first heard that, she'd been infuriated. She'd felt as if Vittorio were invading her own private territory. But by this point, she'd like nothing better than to see him lay claim to Suncrest. "It's a highly desirable property. That's why these investors want it. It's in the Rutherford Bench, which is the best part of the valley. Property there almost never comes available. You couldn't do better," she added, convinced that was true despite all the damage Max had done in recent months.

Vittorio frowned, rose from the couch, and walked to a large window cut into the thick stone wall. She watched the afternoon sun play on his even features,

accentuate the lines in his brow as he furrowed it in
thought.

Eventually he spoke. "I agree with you that Suncrest is very valuable, Gabriella." He turned his head
to meet her eyes. "I have been keeping track of it."

He didn't need to say why. She cleared her throat.
"Then you understand what a rare opportunity this
could be for Castello di Corvo."

He shook his head. "The problem is, it is a much
bigger acquisition than we could handle. We're looking at wineries in the ten-million-dollar range. Do you
know what the offer price is that this buyout firm
has made?"

"No." Will certainly hadn't made her privy to that
kind of information.

"I would guess it's at least three times the size we're
looking at." He rubbed his chin. "Do you have any
idea when the Winsted family plans to respond to
this offer?"

She grimaced. "They already have. They've already
accepted it."

He threw out his hands. "Then Gabriella—"

"But it's not a done deal yet!" She shot up from
the sofa and approached him. "The Winsteds have
signed a term sheet but not the final documents. Those
aren't even written up." *At least they weren't when I
left California.* "Isn't it true that nothing's set in stone
until those final documents are signed?"

"Yes, but—"

"So it's not too late."

"But it may very well be, Gabriella!" There was
frustration in his voice. "I'm sure the Winsted family
has agreed not to talk to other potential buyers. A
'no-shop clause,' it's called. The investors don't want
them to get a better offer."

Gabby knew that no-shop clause or not, Max

Winsted would jump at the chance to improve his take. "But the Winsteds don't have to know that you know about this other offer. As far as they're concerned, you're just interested in buying Suncrest."

He stared at her. "I don't remember you being this conniving."

"We have a saying in English, Vittorio. 'Desperate times call for desperate measures.'"

"I don't know." He shook his head, leaned his weight on his hands, resting on the wide stone sill beneath the window. "Why do you even think we'd be any better at running Suncrest than these investors you're telling me about?"

"Because the Mantuccis have run a family winery for centuries. You've survived war and strife and God knows what, Vittorio, and still you make wine the old-fashioned way. That you've survived this long proves that there's a niche for the kind of winery that takes care of its workers, that understands how important it is to preserve the land and the values for the next generation. It's not all about the money for you."

"We're not so idealistic as all that, Gabriella," he said, then looked away and sighed.

He thinks I'm crazy, that I've gone off the deep end. She twisted away from him, a sob rising in her throat. *Maybe I have. This is lunatic. But don't I have to try? What do I have to lose?*

Actually, a great deal.

She felt Vittorio's hand on her arm. His voice was soft. "Gabriella, you coming all this way to ask me this, it does have the smell of desperation."

She hung her head and stared at the stone floor, uneven, warped by centuries. "I know."

"You don't even own Suncrest. Why do you care so much?"

"Because I've known it all my life, Vittorio, I grew up in those vineyards. They're home to me." By now a tear was tracing a slow track down her cheek. "Because apart from here, it's the most beautiful place I've ever seen. I want to protect it, for me and for my family. And for all those people who've been buying Suncrest wines all these years.

"And it's not just Suncrest, it's the whole valley." She threw out her hands, tried to explain. "It's changing in ways that everyone in my family hates and I want to try to protect it in what little way I can." She hesitated, then, "I love it, Vittorio, I always will. It's that simple."

Gently, he laid his hand on her cheek and wiped the tear with his thumb. "Love is never simple, Gabriella. You and I know that."

They had learned that lesson together. But emerged on the other side still able to talk. Still, she realized, friends.

She raised her eyes to his. "I know I'm asking a lot. But I also know this could be a huge opportunity for you and your family."

"It could be. But it's very awkward. I just don't see how I can manage it."

"Will you try?" Once those words were out of her mouth, she understood their great irony. Here she was again, asking another man—another lover—for another promise. It was very likely she'd get the same answer.

And she did. "I'll try, Gabriella. But let me warn you, it won't be easy. I will need to investigate, to find a partner. And it will have to happen very fast."

"You can be fast." She put a tease in her voice. "Pretend you're on the *superstrada*."

He chuckled. "Giving the car an Italian tune-up?"

"Now you can give Suncrest an Italian tune-up."

He shook his head, but she saw the fondness in his eyes. And heard the affection in his voice. He took her hands. "I always told myself that if I ever had the chance to do something for you, I would."

"If you could do this for me, I would appreciate it for the rest of my life."

Slowly, he nodded. In that silent stone room, they stared at one another. The sun shone in the Chianti sky as it always did, the church bells pealed, the ravens cawed. But Gabby knew something had changed for both her and Vittorio.

Yet that was appropriate. And just as well.

Chapter 15

Will saw harvest begin on a sunshiny Monday morning in August. Driving past Suncrest's Rosemede vineyard on his way to the winery, he spied the lemon-yellow bins that appeared each year for crush, piled high with sauvignon blanc grapes. Pickers moved rapidly down the rows, tugging on grape clusters with one hand and slicing them off with the other. They were paid by the bin, so they worked fast.

Will squinted through his dust-streaked windshield as he moved past, searching for a woman's slim figure, or for strands of honey-gold hair poking out from underneath a baseball cap. But all he saw were men—dark-haired, hunched-over men. More than a little surprised—*Is it possible Gabby's still not back at work? Even though now harvest has started?*—he arrived at the winery to find Felix driving a tractor past the employee parking lot. "So crush has started?" he called, proud of himself for using the right lingo.

Felix nodded. "We been at it five hours already."

"You started at three in the morning?"

Felix laughed at the shock in his voice. "Better for the grapes. They're cooler. So are we." And he laughed again, waved and continued on, leaving Will no chance to ask the question he really wanted answered: *Hey! Where's Gabby?*

The last time he'd seen her had been nearly a week before. They hadn't fought *exactly*, but she'd walked away from him in tears, then just disappeared. She'd sent an oddly short and impersonal e-mail telling him she was going away for a few days. Just like that. Nothing since.

Will stared after Felix's disappearing tractor, and despite the heat already beginning to rise from the asphalt parking lot, felt a cold shiver along his spine. *Gabby's got to be around here somewhere*, he told himself. *She wouldn't have quit.* No matter how angry she was with him, how much she feared the changes at Suncrest, the last thing she would do was abandon the winery. Certainly not during crush, which to a winemaker was the busiest, most critical time of the year.

He let himself into the main winery building— empty because everyone was in the vineyards—and sprinted upstairs to Porter Winsted's old office, thinking maybe she'd left a note for him there before she went out into the vineyards. He opened the door, to which no note was taped, then strode inside to inspect the mahogany surface of the desk. Nothing there either. He looked around. Nothing anywhere.

Damn. He let his briefcase drop onto the Oriental carpet. A fresh new week had started—more to the point, *harvest* had started—and still she was radio silent. There was no question that the acquisition was coming between them, exactly as he had feared it might. Of course she thought he was betraying her, breaking his promise. Sometimes when he pondered where Suncrest might be headed, he feared she was right.

Just to be sure she hadn't decided to cut her losses, he opened the drawer where the employee files were kept, pulled out DELUCA, GABRIELLA, and flipped it open. No resignation letter lay inside. Mildly reassured, he returned the file to its place, knocked the drawer shut with his knee. What now?

Go find her, you idiot. You won't be able to get a lick of work done till you see her anyway.

That was so true. Even if the news was bad, even if she wanted no part of him anymore, he had to hear it. He had to get out of this limbo where he didn't know if the woman he loved was throwing him over. Ironically, because she didn't trust him to do right by her. Will Henley—Boy Scout, doer of good deeds— was suspected of being a lout. That was a lifetime first.

So was the niggling worry that the accusation carried a kernel of truth.

He hitched a ride back to the Rosemede vineyard on a tractor driven by a Spanish-speaking field-worker he didn't know, who'd come back to the winery to offload bins of grapes for the mechanized destemmer. Once at the vineyard, Will leaped off the tractor and walked up to the first picker he saw. "Is Gabby here? Do you know where she is?"

The man nodded, sweat running down his brown lined face, and pointed north up a row of vines. Will thanked him and headed in that direction, the sun already intense enough at 8:30 in the morning to bake the nape of his neck.

Never had he felt so like a fish out of water. While all the pickers wore jeans and T-shirts, he was in a dress shirt and tie, gabardine trousers and leather shoes, which were literally biting the dust at the moment and would figuratively do so at the end of the day. The difference in garb made him feel like the bourgeois capitalist boss come to check up on the proletarian workers. It was also hot as hell, and he would have much preferred to be wearing less clothing. But when all was said and done it was worth it, because after a few minutes of plodding through the dirt, he spied Gabby ahead of him, in profile, hand on her hip, speaking into her walkie-talkie.

His heart slid a little in his chest, out of both relief and worry. He stopped to catch his breath and watch her. She wore khaki shorts with a tiny enough inseam to spark his imagination, a short-sleeved bright orange T-shirt, little white tennis socks, and running shoes. She looked adorable—fit and tanned and healthy and outdoorsy.

It couldn't be his imagination, what he felt for this woman. There was some kind of primeval pull that wrenched at his soul every time he was with her. He just wanted to be near, wanted to be close, wanted to be connected.

Seeing her in the flesh, he decided he would act as if everything were normal, as if she hadn't gone AWOL for a week, as if he didn't fear she was going to dump him right then and there, like a cluster of grapes not quite up to snuff. After a quick glance around to make sure no one was looking, he grabbed her from behind and nuzzled her neck, his nostrils filling with the summer-happy scent of Coppertone. "Morning."

She spun around. Behind the light-purple lenses of her sunglasses, her eyes widened and—he was thrilled to see—her mouth instantly broke into a smile. "Will!"

"You look glad to see me."

"I am!"

"I was a little worried."

The smile faded a bit. "I know." She paused, then, "I'm sorry."

Was that guilt he saw in her eyes? Or his imagination, because of the guilt he was feeling himself? Then Felix's voice blared over her walkie-talkie. "Row sixteen or seventeen next?"

She put her walkie-talkie to her mouth. "Seventeen, Felix. I'll be there soon. Over."

"So you're pretty busy," he said. But seeing her smile, knowing he couldn't possibly be misreading the delight on her face, filled him with enormous relief. "How's it going?"

"So far so good, but I don't like this heat spike." She shoved the walkie-talkie into the waistband of her shorts. "I'm worried the grapes are going to shut down."

"Shut down?"

"Stop ripening. And for sure the cab needs more hang time." She set both hands on her hips. A light sheen of sweat glistened on the curve of her chest revealed by the U-neck of her T-shirt. "I wish we'd get some fog."

"We haven't had any in a week. It's been sweltering."

She looked away and said nothing, leading him to believe she had no idea what the local weather had been like. Curiosity urged him on.

"So . . . you were out of town?"

She nodded, still looking away.

"Where'd you go?"

She returned her eyes to his and wrinkled her nose. "Would you mind if we didn't talk about it?"

"Well, it's just kind of mysterious." He stopped, waited. She said nothing, so he continued. "I mean, did you have some kind of surgery you don't want to tell me about?" In her absence, wild scenarios had spun in his mind. One was that she was suffering from some nameless female ailment she'd been too embarrassed to tell him about. "Or do you have some other boyfriend somewhere you went to go see?"

Her eyes flew open in what seemed genuine astonishment. "Why would you ask that?"

"I don't know. You go AWOL suddenly, right before harvest—it doesn't seem like you. It doesn't make sense. It makes me wonder." That sounded a little hostile. He tried again. "I missed you."

Their gazes locked. A picker moved past, thankfully deciding not to work in that particular area right at that moment. Then, "I missed you, too," she said. She edged closer, reached up to smooth the collar of his dress shirt, then left her hand on his shoulder. She kept her voice low. "I didn't have surgery. And I certainly don't have some other boyfriend. Though I have to say I like the idea that you'd be jealous."

"I'd be insanely jealous." He'd been jealous thinking about Vittorio, who'd been history before Will had even appeared on the scene. "So you're not furious with me about Suncrest?"

She shrugged. "I guess I realized that we're going to have to agree to disagree about Suncrest. I know you're just doing what you have to do. Maybe now I understand that." She paused, then, "You'd feel the same if the situation were reversed, right?"

He was so taken aback by how calm she was on the topic that he responded instantly. "Of course." He regarded her, blithely smoothing the front of his shirt. Maybe the week away had been a good thing after all, given her new perspective. Maybe Suncrest wouldn't end up being such a huge problem between them.

He felt a weight lift from his chest, as if he'd been holding his breath underwater and now was free to grab great gulps of sweet, saving air. He glanced around, saw no one looking in their direction. He put his hands on her hips, pulled her even closer, and smothered her lips in a kiss.

She tasted sweet, started a low burning in his groin. "So . . . just how busy are you, Ms. DeLuca?"

She laughed softly. "Very busy, Mr. Henley."

"Because I'm experiencing a bit of a heat spike myself."

"I can tell. But we can't exactly do anything about it right here."

"Vineyards have worked nicely for us in the past."

"*Private* vineyards."

"Hm. Good point." He clutched her hand, pulled her after him. "But I can think of someplace else private."

"Will . . ." But she didn't really resist, which only heightened his ardor. By the time they'd hitched another tractor back to the winery, he was a man very much on a mission. Her eyes flew open when they got upstairs and he slammed the door on Porter Winsted's office, turned the lock, and spun toward her, whipping off her baseball cap and pulling her T-shirt up over her head in two swift surprising motions. Her bra flew in an arc that landed next to the tartan sofa. His mouth was on her breasts in seconds.

"Oh, my God . . ." she breathed, her hands clutching his head.

He was possessed. His own clothes came off in a rush, his desire to be inside her rampant. Off came her shorts, or at least mostly off, because he had no time to fuss with little white socks and running shoes.

On the Oriental carpet with the woman of his dreams beneath him, his mouth leaving wet trails on her sweat-salty skin. She tasted like Coppertone and the cutest girl in the senior class and the best of summer's hot stolen moments. He cut off her moans with his mouth—"Shhh, someone could hear us . . ."—bringing her to climax with a sticky finger that he then sucked on with his own mouth.

He had never felt harder, more potent, more in need. It wasn't a sweet lingering love they shared that morning, but it rocked him to the bottom of his soul.

Afterwards they clung together, a tangled mass of damp limbs, breathing fast, listening to Felix's voice outside the office windows as a tractor came and went. Silence again descended.

She giggled and nipped at his ear. "And I thought you were such a straitlaced businessman."

"Just goes to show how wrong a person can be."

"I guess." Her head fell back on the carpet, her honey-gold hair a tangle on the weave of crimson and blue. He watched her look at him, and something in her face changed, in a way he couldn't quite put a name to. "But I don't really think I'm wrong about you," she said.

He was almost afraid to ask. "No?"

She was silent for some time. Then those lovely hazel eyes of hers filled with tears, which surprised him. "Don't cry, sweetie." He wiped one errant tear with his finger, kissed another away. "Why are you crying?"

She looked away. "Sometimes I cry when I'm happy."

"Is that why you're crying now?"

She said nothing. Another tear slipped from her eye, cascaded down her cheek. Then, "I guess I'm crying because underneath that capitalist pig exterior, you're a wonderful man, Will Henley."

He chuckled then waited, sensing there was more to come. Knowing what he wanted it to be. He got what he wanted.

"I love you," she said.

His hand was very tender as it smoothed the hair back from her face, from which her tears were running like soft rain. He stared into the eyes he'd been looking for all of his life. "I love you, too, Gabby."

On a late August Tuesday afternoon, a week after Suncrest winemakers had begun their harvest, Max sat on the shaded terrace of Napa Valley's Meadowood

Resort, anxiously awaiting his lunch guest. At long last he spied the tall, dark-haired stranger who'd crossed a continent and an ocean to meet him. After yet another quick glance around the terrace restaurant to make sure no one who knew him was present, Max half rose from his chair, reached out his hand, and plastered a smile on his face. "So we meet at last, Vittorio. It's a pleasure."

Mantucci smiled, shook Max's hand, then sat. "The pleasure's mine. After all those phone conversations, it's wonderful to put a face to a name."

Max resumed his seat, more pleased with life than he'd been in some time.

Mantucci had thrown his hat in the ring at just the right moment. If another week had passed, it might have been too late. By then Max and his mother might have signed the final documents selling Suncrest to GPG. But now—hey! As far as Max was concerned, the window of opportunity for a better deal was still wide open.

And to hell with the so-called "no-shop clause." If Henley had really expected him not to consider other offers, he shouldn't have knocked down the purchase price by 10 percent. So fair was fair.

Though Max sure hoped he could conclude this transaction on the QT. That's why he couldn't risk having Mantucci come to Suncrest. For if Henley did get wind that Max was talking to another potential buyer, the deal with GPG could vaporize. Then Max would *have* to make it work with the Italian stallion— who hadn't actually made a formal offer yet—or run the damn winery himself.

The waiter who'd led Mantucci to Max's table cleared his throat. "We have a bottle of this gentleman's sauvignon blanc chilling in the back," he told Mantucci. "Before you order lunch, shall I bring it out for you?"

"Vittorio? Would that suit you?" Max proffered a warm smile, waved a gracious hand. *What would you like, my new friend? Anything, anything at all!*

"On this hot day, that would be perfect." Mantucci smiled in return. Max nodded at the waiter to signal his own assent, then took a long look at the guy on whom he might be able to unload Suncrest. A little slick, maybe, a little too good-looking, but you could say the same thing about Henley. And this guy was straight out of the Old Country, so could probably be led around by the nose easier than Henley could.

Mantucci leaned his elbows on the table and squinted at the expansive lawns that rolled away from the terrace, on which people dressed entirely in white meandered around in small groups. "I didn't know Americans like to play croquet."

Max restrained himself from declaring his honest opinion on that subject. "It's very popular at Meadowood," he said instead. "I'm sure you'd be familiar with another sport that people around here are playing more and more. Bocce."

Mantucci laughed. "Is that so?"

"There are a few leagues here in the valley." None of which Max had joined, of course. He considered bocce only slightly less of a pansy European sport than croquet.

The waiter returned and made the usual show of opening and pouring the wine. Max raised his glass in Mantucci's direction. "To successful ventures."

"Hear, hear," Mantucci murmured, and both sipped. They chitchatted for a while, ordered their meals. It wasn't until their entrées had been served that Mantucci seemed ready to get down to serious business.

Make an offer, Max begged silently. *And make it bigger than Henley's.* For that would be the true coup. Not only would Max get to walk away with more moola, he'd get to screw Henley, as well. And Gabby DeLuca by extension.

Mantucci dabbed at his mouth with his napkin. "Of course, over the phone you and I have talked in great detail about Suncrest, Max. And my own people have done quite a bit of research."

Though chewing on his steak sandwich, Max tried to put an encouraging expression on his face.

"It is a very attractive property in so many ways," Mantucci went on. "Brand name, location . . ."

Max chewed and nodded and listened to Mantucci proceed with the transaction foreplay, all of which he'd gotten before from Henley in the same mind-numbing detail. What he wanted was an offer, and a time frame, and a promise of cash—lovely, spendable, U.S. dollars.

"I am very interested in Suncrest," Mantucci finally said. "There is a strong likelihood that I will make a formal offer to acquire it. But given its high value, and the fact that you are seeking an all-cash transaction, I need to secure a financial partner in order to do so."

What? Max stopped chewing, steak and French bread clumped in a soggy mess in his mouth.

"I have obtained some real interest from the first parties I have approached on this," Mantucci went on, "but nothing has yet been nailed down. Still, I came to California to make clear to you how serious I am in pursuing this matter."

He stopped, clearly waiting for Max to say something positive in return. But Max could not, for he could not speak. Because he was transfixed by a man staring straight at him over the back of Mantucci's head.

For not only did Vittorio Mantucci *not* make an offer to take Suncrest off Max's hands, the man who *had* was standing twenty yards away. Looking bug-eyed and red-faced and like he might just explode at any moment.

Oh . . . my . . . God. Does Henley know what's going on here?

Because it certainly looked like he did.

Only once before in his life had Max felt like this. It was when he'd been in a car accident. He'd gone through an intersection after the light had turned red, thinking he could just squeak through. Just a second too late, he realized he couldn't, that a white Honda was going to get him. He remembered time switching into slow motion. He remembered watching the Honda approach, seeing his own car move forward but not fast enough, waiting for the impact, wondering just how bad it was going to be.

Right now, he felt exactly like that all over again. But this time the approaching Honda was Will Henley, who was actually more like a Mack truck when it came to how much damage he could do.

Henley came over to their table and looked first at Mantucci, who was rising from his chair to shake Henley's hand.

"Vittorio," Henley said, "welcome back to the valley." Now Henley looked as friendly as friendly could be, and he wore a smile wide enough to crack his face. "How nice to run into you again. Are you here on business? Perhaps toying with a possible acquisition?"

The blood in Max's veins turned as cold as the white wine he'd been downing. *Henley knows Mantucci. And he knows what he's here for. I am so royally hosed.* He gulped, trying—but failing—to dream up an escape hatch from this situation.

Mantucci laughed, shrugged. "It seems I can't keep away from this beautiful valley. Business or"—he laughed again and indicated Max with a wave of the hand—"no business."

Henley laughed, too. Ha ha ha! He gave Max a

smile that could melt ice cream. "And how are you, Max?" He slapped Max on the back, hard enough that Max had to struggle to remain upright. "Enjoying your lunch?"

Max felt like he just might regurgitate his lunch. "What brings you to Meadowood?" he managed to croak.

Henley's eyes gleamed. "Funny coincidence, isn't it?" He cocked his head at the two young guns he worked with, who were standing inside the restaurant, watching the whole thing. "My colleagues and I had some extra time today, thought we might enjoy watching the croquet over lunch. You play?" he asked Max.

"Uh, no."

"Not much for games, huh?" He smiled like the devil himself, then nodded and backed away, apologizing for disturbing their meal.

Max wanted to crawl under the table. But it was too late to do any good.

Tuesday afternoon Gabby was alone in the Calhoun vineyard, painstakingly filling baggies with sauvignon blanc grapes, when Will came to find her. Each baggie contained fruit from a particular row of grapevines. Her plan, before Will threw it into severe disarray, was to take the baggies back to the winery to test the grapes' sugar levels, to decide which rows, if any, were ripe for picking the next day. It was a crush ritual, one of many, that was keeping her busy every day from three in the morning until five in the afternoon, after which she'd drive home bleary-eyed to bathe, eat, and collapse into bed.

If only that day were like every other.

She wondered later how she knew Will was upset when he was still a hundred paces distant. Some lover's instinct, perhaps, like the wife who clutches at her heart the very instant her soldier husband is killed half a world away. Gabby rose from her crouch and watched Will approach, her left hand clamped on a half-empty baggie and her right shading her eyes, as the bill on her baseball cap wasn't big enough to shield them from the sun's glare. Was it just her guilty conscience, or was there some hint of disaster in his long-legged stride, some clue that her world was about to shatter in the way he swung his arms, set his jaw, tilted his proud blond head?

When he got closer, she could identify the difference, and gooseflesh rose on her skin. He wouldn't look at her. He'd look anywhere but right at her, as if he'd already reached the point where he could no longer stand the sight of her.

This is it. He knows. She'd had a vague plan of confessing if things progressed far enough between Vittorio and Max that she needed to. A coward's way out, she knew, but she couldn't bring herself to risk Will if she didn't absolutely have to. That Will had already found out the truth was unnerving. Hadn't Vittorio told her it was just this very day that he was meeting with Max? And the assignation certainly wasn't happening at Suncrest. How did Will find out so fast? She was reminded yet again that she was dealing with a highly intelligent man, one she couldn't fool if she tried.

Not that she had any intention of trying. Though she was terrified that her actions would cost her this man she had come to love, she also knew she'd only done what she had to do to try to save what was dear to her and her family. *Pray God he'll understand.*

He came to within a few yards of her. No kiss, naturally, no hug—no vestige at all of the man who'd held her in his arms and told her he loved her. But he did meet her eyes, and her soul shriveled at the ice-cold fire in their blue depths.

"I've just come from seeing Max with Vittorio Mantucci," he told her. "They're having lunch at Meadowood. Can you explain that to me?"

"Yes." Her heart pummeled her rib cage like a boxer's fists on a punching bag. "I asked Vittorio to consider making an offer for Suncrest."

"You asked Vittorio to consider making an offer for Suncrest." He nodded and turned away. She watched his profile, a study in self-control. A muscle twitched in his jaw. His hands clenched and unclenched, fists formed and unformed. A silent battle seemed to rage as much within him as between them. He didn't look at her when he spoke again. "Is that where you were last week? When you"—his voice reeked of sarcasm—" 'went away for a few days?' You were in Italy?"

"Yes."

"So you're not going to deny it?"

"No. I did what I had to do. And if you'll let me, I'll explain why."

"You did what you had to do." He threw back his head and let out a whoop of laughter, obscenely loud in the silent, sun-baked vineyard. "That is rich, Gabby! That is truly rich!"

She tried to slow her breathing, but it was like trying not to pant in the middle of a marathon. "I had to try to save Suncrest. I—"

"From me." He jabbed at his chest, his features twisted. "You had to try to save it from me."

"Yes. Because I knew that try as you might, you are going to kill the very heart of the winery. I hear what the lawyers say, and the accountants, and the people you work with. I know what's up and I also know you may not be able to stop it. So I had to try. I love Suncrest." She struggled to speak through the uncontrollable trembling of her lips. "So does my father. My whole family. I had to do whatever I could to protect it."

He shook his head, over and over. "You've got some nerve telling me about love, lady."

He turned away from her and strode a few paces

down the row of grapevines, staring at the ground, shaking his head, muttering, his hands on his trousered hips. Part of her wanted to run to him, to touch him, but she was afraid. It was like getting too close to the bars of the cage behind which the lions and tigers paced. One wrong move—*whoosh!*—and you could find yourself scarred for life.

"Will?" She spoke to his back, tried to steady her voice. "Will, I do love you. It wasn't easy for me to do what I did. It killed me. And I feel so guilty because I know how much you want Suncrest. But at the same time I have to know that you care about what matters to me. I'm not asking you to agree with all of it, but I do have to know that you respect it."

"Nice speech." Again he faced her, and her heart caught in her throat. Had she ever seen his features so cold, so set? "Does that go both ways, by any chance? Because as far as I can tell, I'm supposed to kowtow to everything you want while you get to stand back and pass judgment on me. Somehow"—he raised his voice above her protests—"somehow, what's getting lost in all of this is that *I* am the one in the trenches, trying to salvage what is left of this damn winery!" His voice resounded through the vineyard, seemed to hammer the very earth and sky. "It's going down the tubes, Gabby, get it? If it weren't for me, Suncrest would be auctioned off to the highest bidder. Maybe not this week, maybe not this month, but someday soon. And I can assure you that the new owners wouldn't give a rat's ass what *you* think about how they should run their business!" He came closer, jabbed his finger at her face. "They certainly wouldn't care about your job, or your father's, or Cam's. Is that what you want?"

She met his eyes. "You know it's not. What I want is to keep Suncrest as a winery that cares about quality, that takes care of its employees, that tries to preserve the land for future generations." He scoffed and turned away. She raised her voice. "There is a niche for that kind of winery, Will. And it's what the valley needs more of. I'm trying to preserve a way of life here."

He shook his head. "Honestly, Gabby, I *really* hate when you get on your moral high horse. And I also find it damned hypocritical. Especially right at the moment, with this knife sticking in my back."

He stalked farther away, flung back his head. "Goddammit!" he shouted at the empty sky. Her hands flew to her mouth, hovered there, as the oath shuddered in the air, dispersed a flock of curious birds that had been watching them from the overhead wires. They took flight in an agitated disruption of fluttering wings, shrieking across the empty vineyard, seeking escape.

"I'm sorry. But I had to do it." Her voice sounded weak, tremulous. It didn't help that tears had started falling, that her heart was having trouble beating its normal rhythm when it was breaking once again in two. "I hoped you'd understand. This is just one deal for you. But for me and my family, it's our whole lives."

He closed his eyes, let his head fall back. "There are so many things I don't understand, Gabby. One of them is why you had to go to Vittorio. Of all people." His voice was quiet now, as if his strength had been sapped. He raised his head and looked at her. She thought she'd never seen such weariness on a man's face in her life. "Then again, you couldn't go to Mondavi or Gallo or Beringer or any of the other usual suspects. They're all big bad capitalists like me."

"I knew Vittorio would listen to me."

"And you were right." Will paused. "Is he in love with you?"

"No," she said immediately, though to be honest, she couldn't say she knew for sure.

"Are you in love with him?"

"No." That question she could answer, though she doubted whether Will would believe her. Or believe what she was about to tell him next. "I love *you*."

"Right." He looked away. "So you keep saying."

She watched him. It was as bad as she had feared it would be. Yet she clung to the fact that he hadn't walked away yet. That gave her a scintilla of hope. Until he walked away, she had a chance. To explain. To make him understand. But what was the right tack to take? To cry? Beg for forgiveness? Use logic and reason?

"Will, I know you try to do the right thing. I want you to understand that's what I feel I've done here. I know the valley can't stay the same forever—I'm not Tinkerbell. But it kills me to see people from outside coming in, paving it over, making their money, then leaving. I can't apologize for trying to stop that."

"What breaks my heart, Gabby, is that you think I'm one of those people."

I don't want you to be! she wanted to scream at him, *I want to believe you're just like me!* But how could she, seeing him so cold and unrelenting, not giving an inch. Not, from what she could tell, trying in the least to understand her. Simply ready, as Vittorio had been, to cast her aside if she didn't fall in with his master plan.

Will got to fire the final salvo. Because she was too spent to manage it.

"What you don't seem to understand, Gabby, is that you extract a promise from me, you make me the bad guy if I don't live up to it, then you take advantage of what I've told you, in trust, and call yourself an angel and me a sinner. Well, if that's your idea of doing the right thing, I'd say we don't have much to talk about."

She lost him then. He turned and walked away through the vines as she had feared he would from the beginning. She had too much pride to call after him. She was too wise to keep trying at that moment to explain. And for the life of her, she couldn't tell if there was really any point.

Chapter 16

A day and a half after his vineyard battle with Gabby, Will sat at an umbrella-shaded table in front of Taylor's Refresher, a longtime St. Helena burger-and-fries hangout. While waiting for Max to join him, he nursed an old-fashioned milk shake and watched traffic crawl along two-lane Main Street, clogged with locals and late-August tourists. It was another scorcher. Heat blistered from the pavement and an unpleasant, gusty north wind snapped at the Stars and Stripes hanging high on a nearby flagpole.

Yet what seethed in Will was an ice-cold anger. Toward Max Winsted, in part. But the far greater share was directed at Gabby.

She had betrayed him. That she could be so disloyal, so untrustworthy—he never would have guessed it of her. He couldn't trust her again—that much was sure. What she had done was so counter to what she knew he wanted, what he'd been working so hard for. She'd accused him of betrayal in the past, but she was so much more the guilty party now.

He still couldn't believe that she would go to her old lover to try to unravel the deal on which she knew he had so much riding. And on the basis of what? Ill-conceived, barely thought-out views about business and its many abuses. The fact that she didn't really understand what Will did, didn't really care to learn about it, didn't stop her for a minute. As far as she was concerned, she was right and he was wrong and that was the end of it. She was so quick to condemn him!—and yet had the nerve to spout off about love and loyalty.

His heart pounded just thinking about it. The only salvation, the *only* one, was that all was not lost where Suncrest was concerned. Despite Gabby's outrageous behavior, Will still believed that he had the upper hand when it came to the winery. Chances were very good that he could still back Max into a corner and get the deal done.

His attention was drawn by Max's shiny red two-seater convertible—top down, of course—screeching to a halt in the parking lot. Will watched Max get out of the car, shake his legs to get the creases out of his khaki trousers, then smooth back his dark hair. Once, then again. Then he took a deep breath. During all these ministrations, he remained within a foot of his Mercedes, clearly reluctant to face the man waiting for him.

Will shook his head. *You should be nervous to see me, you sneaky moron.*

Max Winsted was nothing if not easy to read. Once Will got over the initial shock of seeing him with Vittorio Mantucci, he'd immediately understood why in recent weeks Max had started dragging his feet on GPG's acquisition of Suncrest. All of a sudden Max was throwing up roadblocks. This was a problem, and that, too. Then other staff stepped onto the work-slowdown bandwagon. Suncrest's lawyer took a day to answer a question when it should have taken her only a few hours. Same with the accountant. And all the winery-wide stalling was for one reason and one reason only, Will knew: Max was waiting for an offer from Vittorio Mantucci.

And such an offer was possible. But Will's experience told him it would never trump GPG's. There was no way it would be larger. And all cash. And, most crucial of all, that it would come together quickly enough to be a real threat.

And even if it did, Will still had an ace in the hole: the no-shop clause. If Max tried to accept another offer, Will could sue him until his eyes blurred. And pending lawsuits would sure give Vittorio Mantucci something to think about.

Will watched his prey abandon the safety of the parking lot and manfully approach the fenced-in front patio of the restaurant. He lumbered over to Will, who didn't bother to get up.

"Didn't know you liked this place," Max mumbled, taking a seat.

"You can get a good steak sandwich here," Will said. "Probably'll cost you only a third what it does at Meadowood." Max blanched. "Shall we go order?" Will asked.

Max agreed. Will beat him to the screened-in window and chuckled again at the menu. This was the Napa Valley equivalent of fast food, with gourmet options and of course a wine list. "I'll take an ahi tuna burger and another White Pistachio shake," he told the order-taker, then pivoted toward Max. "What can I get you? My treat."

Max seemed surprised by even this low-level generosity. "I'll take a Miss Kentucky," he said, which turned out to be a chicken-breast sandwich with mountains of jack cheese, mushrooms, and onions.

Once they resumed their seats, Will dipped his chilled extra-long spoon into his second shake and cocked his chin at Max's meal. "I guess both of us are living large today. Then again, we do have something to celebrate."

Max frowned and set down his sandwich, ranch dressing dripping between his thick fingers. "What do we have to celebrate?"

"The definitive documents. They're done." Will reached down beside his chair to pull a sheaf of papers from his briefcase. "Here they are, ready to go." He set them on the table, then leaned forward. "I was thinking we'd hold the signing ceremony tomorrow at ten a.m. I'll bring all my people over to the winery. How would that work for you?"

"Uh, can't make that." Max shook his head. "Anyway, how can the final documents be done? There are still outstanding issues."

"No." Will kept his tone light. "Everything's been resolved."

"But my mom's not here to sign. I don't know when she'll get back from Paris."

"We don't need her to sign. She gave you a limited power-of-attorney, remember?" Will smiled at Max's stricken expression. "To do the deal as defined in the term sheet. Our lawyers spoke with yours about that. It's done."

Max started sputtering. "But she hasn't agreed to the cut in the offer price. And there's still some fine print I have to go over with her."

Will laughed. "Honestly, Max, if I didn't know any better, I'd say you've come down with amnesia! We handled the new price with your mother two weeks ago. As I said before, every single detail has been dealt with." Will deliberately fell silent so he could enjoy the spectacle of watching Maximilian Winsted squirm. Then he snapped his fingers, making Max jump. "You know, Max, maybe you *do* have amnesia. Because you *also* forgot that the term sheet you signed has a legally binding no-shop clause."

Max literally choked and had to suck down some Coke. Will watched him, half hoping he would expire right then and there. "You know, Max, when I saw you the other day at Meadowood with Vittorio Mantucci, I knew what was going on. I have to say, it doesn't make me happy to know I'm doing business with somebody who's not on the up-and-up."

Max sounded truculent. "I haven't done anything wrong."

Will sat back in his chair, folded his hands in his lap. "That would be something for the lawyers to decide, wouldn't it? That is, if we were ever to involve them by filing suit. After all, GPG's already invested hundreds of thousands of dollars in the due diligence, and we'd hate to think we spent all that money for nothing. And you wouldn't want the added financial burden of a suit, would you, Max? Or the negative publicity?"

He paused to let that sink in. Then, "I think you've got a lot more common sense than that, Max. I find it very hard to believe that you'd walk away from twenty-seven million in cash on the slim hope that you'll get more out of some European dealmakers who don't know you from Adam. Who haven't done step one of their due diligence. Jeez, who haven't even made an offer yet!"

Will didn't really know if that was true but kept his eyes on Max's face to gauge if he got it right. Judging from Max's somberness and uncharacteristic silence, Will guessed that he did. And was damned relieved.

"So I'll see you tomorrow at ten," Will said. "And let me be perfectly clear. Tomorrow is it. The end. Do we understand one another?"

Max stared down into his sandwich. "Yeah." He looked and sounded like a rebellious overgrown teenager.

Will rose from his chair, pulled out his wallet, and threw a five-dollar tip next to his nearly untouched tuna burger. "And if you bring up some new bullshit issue to try to stall, GPG will walk and the deal will be off. And I guess you won't get that twenty-seven million after all."

Then Will strode across the patio toward his car, one thought skipping through his mind. *Not even Max Winsted is stupid enough to let this bird-in-the-hand deal slip away.*

Friday morning shortly before nine, Max was in the convertible, driving as fast as he could in the hope that it would clear his mind, free his thoughts, provide him clarity.

So far it wasn't working.

He barreled along the Silverado Trail, which had less traffic and so allowed him to go faster than Highway 29. He'd already driven north all the way to Calistoga and now was looping back in a southerly direction. There was no fog anywhere—again. It was hot as blazes, and the north wind was blowing and neither was helping his ability to make a decision.

When he made it back to Suncrest, he might just turn around and do the same loop over again. How else was he going to figure out what to do? To sign or not to sign—that was the question. And the signing ceremony was in an hour. Should he just do the deal with GPG and get it over with? Or stall somehow so Mantucci could come up with an offer?

At least this was his own decision. His mother had given him power-of-attorney to handle the deal, though it was humiliatingly narrow.

He careened past the entrance to Meadowood, which brought back in skin-crawling detail the unexpected face-to-face with Will Henley. That guy was sure full of surprises. Max would've bet his mother that after seeing him with Mantucci, Henley would call off the deal, call in his lawyers, and sue Max's ass to kingdom come.

But no. And why not? Max knew damn well why not: Henley wanted Suncrest so bad he could taste it.

Max thought that was a pretty good argument for not signing. Because if Max gave Mantucci time to make an offer, Henley would counter it. Max knew that in the marrow of his bones. And then Max would be the beneficiary of a good old-fashioned auction, and not have to settle for this fire-sale price of twenty-seven million.

But Henley's cocky voice resounded in his memory. *I find it very hard to believe that you'd walk away from twenty-seven million in cash on the slim hope that you'll get more out of some European dealmakers who don't know you from Adam. Who haven't done step one of their due diligence. Jeez, who haven't even made an offer yet!*

All true, unfortunately. But Max just wasn't sure. Wouldn't he be a fool not to wait and see if an offer from Mantucci panned out, and if so, how big it would be? Naturally Henley wanted to make it sound beyond stupid for Max not to sell immediately to GPG. But Max found it very hard to believe that even if he didn't sign today, Henley would walk away. For whatever reason, Henley really wanted Suncrest.

Fine, Max thought. *Then let him pay for it.*

Max made a sudden right onto a narrow, tree-lined residential road that would lead him to Main Street in St. Helena. Maybe he'd pick up a coffee, see if after he got more caffeine in his system he'd still feel the same way.

He left the car in a back alley off Main Street and was on his way toward his favorite bakery when he spied a tiny storefront he hadn't seen before. Or maybe he just hadn't noticed it. On its window, behind which hung dark curtains that hid the interior, were pasted big red letters in a half-circle: MADAM NATALIA. And below that, straight across: PSYCHIC READER AND

ADVISOR. The door was open and the inside lights—
what there were of them—were on.

Max paused. He'd never consulted such a person
before, never even thought of it. He suspected most
of them were charlatans whose only "gift" was getting
hold of people's credit-card numbers. But then again,
mysteries did abound in the universe. And right at
the moment he had a pretty serious need for some
inspired counsel.

He glanced both ways down the sidewalk, saw no
one he knew, and ducked inside, his footfall setting
off a singsong chime. Inside a dimly lit anteroom was
a small round table draped with dark heavy fabric and
set with two rickety chairs. Atop it and the few other
tables that filled the space were an assortment of candles and crystals and framed drawings of unknown
seers, who peered at Max with narrowed eyes.

He cleared his throat. "Hello?"

From the rear a woman pushed through a narrow
arched passage hung with beads. "What can I do for
you?" she asked. She looked like a frowsy housewife
on the wrong side of fifty but had a handshake like a
stevedore. And a subtle accent he couldn't identify.
Armenian, maybe?

"Uh, I'm wondering if it would be possible to get
some sort of reading."

"Of course. Tarot card, palm, or psychic reading,
the best is the package of all three for seventy-five
dollars." Her mud-colored eyes never wavered from
his face.

"How long would that take?"

"Anywhere from twenty minutes to an hour. It depends on the complications in your life."

He snorted. "Then it might take a while."

"Here." She waved him toward a chair at the round
table. "Sit. I'll be right back," and she shut the front
door, flipped the sign to ADVISING—COME BACK LATER,

and bustled off through the narrow passage with another clattering of beads.

He claimed a wobbly chair, relieved the place was air-conditioned and didn't reek of incense. Instead he sniffed unidentifiable cooking smells and wondered if he'd interrupted his psychic's breakfast. He picked up a business card from a stand and noted that Madam Natalia had three wine-country outposts.

He stuffed the card in his pocket. She might be more successful in business than he was. Maybe one of his next ventures should be to back *her*.

Madam reappeared, balanced her substantial rump on the other chair, and slapped a stack of tarot cards down in front of him. "Cut twice, toward you."

He obeyed. She collected the cards and proceeded to lay them faceup in long overlapping rows. Max tried to tell if light, happy cards or dark, foreboding cards were turning up in important positions and had no idea.

"Give me something of yours to hold," she said, "so I can pick up your energy. Something you've owned for more than a year."

He removed his watch, handed it to her. "That's a Rolex."

No reaction from Madam Natalia, who simply clutched his watch in her left hand, shut her eyes, and swayed briefly in a trancelike manner. Then she glanced at the tarot cards and frowned. "Let me see your palms."

Shit. She's seen something horrible. He held out both palms, afraid she'd touch him and find out how damp they were. But she only leaned forward to look, then fell back in her chair. "One thing is very clear. You are at a significant crossroads in your life."

He felt a rush of cold that didn't come from the air conditioning. "That's true."

"You have an important decision to make."

"Yes."

"And you worry you will do the wrong thing."

"Yes."

She nodded, leaned forward again to peer at the cards. She shook her head, her brow furrowed. "Have you had some sort of accident or mishap lately? A fire, perhaps?"

"No." Now she was off on a weird tangent. He tried to rein her back in. "What can you tell me about this decision?"

"It's not a love decision. It has to do with the success and money part of your chart, is that correct?" Her laser gaze was on him again.

"Yes."

She rubbed the face of his watch, pursed her lips. "I sense a separation of some type. Perhaps the loss of a great deal of money. Is that possible?"

You're damn right it's possible, he thought. *If I sign with Henley and then get a better offer from Mantucci, too late to do anything about it.* But to Madam Natalia he only nodded.

She looked again at the cards, fingered one. "There is a great deal of pressure around this decision. Perhaps you are being bullied. I see in your chart that you have been thwarted before in what you seek to do. Is that correct?"

Max was starting to build real faith in Madam Natalia's gift. "It sure is," he told her.

She nodded. "I see that you are an old soul who has fought this battle in prior lives. You have come to this life to learn to act on the courage of your convictions." She paused to meet his eyes. "I would love to do a past-life regression for you. I believe it would provide a great deal of illumination. It requires three days of my preparation and costs"—she glanced at the watch—"two hundred and fifty dollars."

Seeing his watch reminded Max that he didn't have

much time to play with. "I might be interested in that down the line, but for now I just need to know what to do."

She arched her brows. "But I have already advised you. To achieve your goals, you must not be bullied, you must not be pressured, but you must do what your heart and your soul tell you is right. You must act on your own convictions." She waved a hand over the cards. "That is very clear from all of this." She stood up. "Thank you. That will be seventy-five dollars."

That's the best seventy-five bucks I ever spent in my life. For Madam Natalia had told Max exactly what he wanted to hear. He rose, dug out his credit card, and reattached his Rolex to his wrist. It was ten to ten. He was still hyped but on some level calmer than he'd been in weeks.

He exited Madam Natalia's into the garish bright light of a Napa Valley summer day. On the way to his car, he used his cell phone to call Suncrest's lawyer and declare that no, he would not attend the signing ceremony. Simple as that. He listened to a minute or so of her protests, then said he was going to hang up. He did, then shut off his cell. He had no desire to hear how Will Henley might react to this latest turn of events.

To revel in his newfound confidence—and also to avoid running into Henley and his lawyers—Max didn't drive straight back to Suncrest. Instead he headed for his favorite overlook, where he'd taken his mother the day he bought her the Mercedes, up a little-traveled road that wound into the Howell Mountains on the east side of the valley. At a dirt-packed clearing, he parked and went to stand at the low guardrail, beyond which the ground, dense with oak trees, dropped off steeply. He gazed at the vista of forest and meadows and vineyards, a panorama of gold and green and brown. Some of Suncrest's vineyards were down the hill, so close that if he craned his neck he could see pickers moving along the rows, harvesting the cabernet sauvignon grapes.

The view was stunning, but conditions weren't great. At ten in the morning it was already close to ninety degrees and the north wind was annoying—swirly and gusty and constantly blowing dust in his eyes. Max leaned against the car and lit a cigarette.

Man. He chuckled. *Henley must be apeshit right about now.* But Henley was too arrogant; that was his problem. He thought that with his snooty investment firm and his fancy title and his big pot of money that he could always get what he wanted, when he wanted it. Well, guess again. He might still get Suncrest someday, but he'd have to wait for it. *And* shell out more cash.

Max flicked his cigarette butt. He watched it roll a few inches along the dirt and was about to lever himself away from the car to go stomp it out when the wind suddenly got hold of it and whisked it under the guardrail and into the grass and trees below.

Shit! Max scuttled over to the guardrail and peered down the hill, searching for the butt. He didn't see it. Thankfully nothing was happening. Eventually he started breathing again and ambled back to the car to relax against the chassis. He let his head fall back and closed his eyes, listening to birdcalls and a distant chopper and the rare whoosh of a passing car. It was a fine thing, having nothing to do. And nothing to worry about.

Minutes passed. The sun baked Max's face; the wind gusted around his body. Then he took a deep breath, and frowned. Did he smell . . . smoke? He raised his head, opened his eyes, and stared. *Oh, my God, I do smell smoke.* Because there was a fire crackling right in front of him, mere yards away, just beyond the guardrail.

Max bolted upright. He didn't entirely trust what he was seeing. He blinked, shook his head, but there it still was, right in front of him. Flames, spreading fast, consuming like a greedy beast the dry, sun-baked grass that hadn't felt any cool, damp fog in weeks. Before he knew it some leaves on the oaks were alight. The fire seemed to skitter from one place to another, carried by the wind. Some area wouldn't be lit and then seconds later it would be.

Max backed away from the fire, started to pant. He looked around wildly, for what he didn't know. A fire extinguisher? A jacket or blanket or something smothering he could throw on top of it? But there was nothing around, and the fire was already too big anyway; it was feeding on the grass and the trees amazingly fast. That damn wind! It was making the fire way too monstrous and hot and scary for Max to do anything about.

All he knew was that he wanted to be gone. In desperation, he threw himself back in the convertible, made a screeching U-turn, and sped down the mountain road as fast as the car would take him. Once he passed a Smokey Bear signpost declaring FIRE DANGER: HIGH, and once he went by a fire department call box. But he ignored it. Because if he called in, they'd figure out it was him who'd been up there on the overlook. They'd think it was *his* cigarette that had started the blaze.

He jammed his foot down even harder on the accelerator.

At 10:30, Will stood in the hallway outside Porter Winsted's office and tried Max's cell phone one more time. Instantly voice mail responded. The phone was turned off. He flipped his own phone shut and returned it to his trouser pocket.

"Damn." He muttered the word, paced a few times,

raked his hand through his short blond hair. *I can't believe it.*

Believe it. The devil on his shoulder cackled, then threw back his head and outright roared. *And you thought Max wasn't stupid enough to walk away!*

Apparently he was, though stupidity might not provide the whole explanation. Cockiness also played into it. Bravado.

Will set his hands on his hips and stood at the head of the stairs, staring down to the first floor, where a male worker in wading boots was hosing down the concrete floor near the fermentation tanks, several of them now full of the sauvignon blanc crush.

Max thinks he's still got me in his pocket. Even after this. He thinks he'll get an offer from Mantucci and I'll counter it. Will threw back his head, gazed at the hundred-year-old beams that crisscrossed the winery's coved ceiling. *And he might be right.*

But he only *might* be. Because Will highly doubted that Mantucci would come up with an offer. Suncrest was too big an acquisition for Mantucci to swing. If Max was counting on that, he was dreaming. And for Will to make another offer, he'd have to have his partners' consent. But he already knew what they'd say. *This Winsted guy's an idiot. And he can't be trusted. It makes no sense to spend more time on him.*

True, all true. Will shook his head in disgust. So much for his resuscitation at GPG. With the blowup of this deal, he'd go from success to failure, just like that. He wouldn't get fired the minute he got back to the office but he'd have an enormous blot on him. And his partners weren't too keen on blots.

This is happening because of Gabby, his devil reminded him. *Max would never have even heard of Vittorio Mantucci if Gabby hadn't forced the introduction.*

And what would she get out of her little Italian jaunt? A big fat zero. Mantucci would not ride in on his white horse. Now, most likely, Suncrest would get auctioned off to the highest bidder, or sold off in pieces.

She'll get what she deserves, Will's devil said. And Will—angry, hurt, thwarted—agreed.

Porter Winsted's door opened, and Dagney walked out into the hall. Before she closed the door behind her, he caught a glimpse of his two male lawyers and Suncrest's one female on the tartan couches, still waiting, not quite giving up yet.

But he had. Unless something truly bizarre happened, this game was over.

Dagney joined him at the head of the stairs. "What do you want to do?"

"Go back to the city."

"I'm really surprised by all this." She seemed genuinely perplexed, her demeanor somber, her brow furrowed. He realized this was the moment for him, as the senior member of the team, to dispense wisdom and perspective.

He took a deep breath. "Some deals just fall through, Dagney. Often at the eleventh hour. Emotions play a big role, and people do unexpected things. In this business, it's really true that it's never over till it's over. That's why it's so important always to have several possibilities in play." Right now he could kick himself for not following his own advice. "Come on, let's get going. We've got work to do."

She nodded, seemed mildly cheered, and followed him as he said his good-byes and collected his paperwork. They exited the winery together and halted in unison as they stepped onto the pebbled path. "Wow," she said. "Something's burning."

"The smell is really strong, isn't it?" Will half jogged down the drive that led to Suncrest's entry gate, twisting his head around to look behind him. Then he saw it, to the southeast of the winery, up on the forested ridge: flames consuming the oak trees and gray smoke mushrooming into the perfect blue sky.

Dagney jogged up next to him, nearly out of breath. "It's a wildfire."

It certainly was. Already claiming a good chunk of the slope, seeming to move very fast. Will knew a fair amount about such fires, having grown up in Denver where during the hot summer months enormous blazes regularly broke out in the local mountains. He knew conditions were ripe for such a conflagration: weeks of scorching weather without a whisper of fog, and today this erratic wind. Combine that with acres of grassland that had grown long in previous rainy seasons, which provided plenty of fuel to light the oak trees, which seemed as if they were made for burning. . . .

For a second Will couldn't speak, as if he were close enough to the flames that his own lungs were sucking in the noxious fumes. His mind raced when he realized just how close the fire might be to some of Suncrest's vineyards, those that lay just below the easternmost slopes of the Howell Mountains.

And Gabby's there.

Gabby stood in Suncrest's Morydale vineyard with her arm around her father, both with their backs to the wall of fire not far up the hill. A cough stalled in her throat like a boil. Tears squeezed from her smoke-seared eyes. *It's a nightmare. I've died and gone to hell. And the flames prove it.*

She had to yell above them. At this short distance they were amazingly loud. "Daddy, there's nothing we can do. We've got to get out of here. Fast."

He couldn't speak, either, at least not in words. The horror in his dark eyes told her all she needed to know. For what more could befall Suncrest? Why had the gods turned so cruel?

This vineyard that nestled up close to the forest, that she and her father had tended with such care, would be devastated. In an ugly irony, the grapes that were so close to harvest would be destroyed right at the peak of their perfection. And not only would the fruit be lost: the vines would burn, too. For the vineyard was covered with grasses grown long over the past months and now tinder dry, gone to nature when Max fired the field-workers that would have kept them mowed. And once the grasses caught, they would incinerate every grapevine they passed. The entire vineyard would be lost, and years in the remaking.

"Come on, Daddy." She moved him forward down a row of grapevines. There was no time to waste; already the fire was licking at the vineyard's edge. Field-workers streamed around them, running toward the tractor while balancing on their heads the yellow bins that held what grapes they'd been able to harvest, what grapes they might be able to save.

Her father clutched her arm. "I have to stop."

She wouldn't let him. "Not yet," she shouted in his ear. "Let's go a little farther."

Oh, God, don't let him have another attack. The panic, the smoke, was a danger to all of them but particularly to her father, given the fragility of his heart. She urged him forward, turning her head to look behind her as they continued to move. So much of the forest was engulfed now, so many of those mighty oaks were writhing in their death throes. Somewhere in her scientist's brain she understood that fire was a natural, cleansing part of nature's cycle. But still she hated it, the ruthless power of it, the indiscretion, the haphazard destruction of everything in its path. Including so much of what she loved, what she'd fought for.

If she believed in signs from above, this would be

one. *Give up on Suncrest,* this fire was telling her. *You've lost that battle.*

With that realization, it was Gabby who stopped short. Her father turned to look at her, surprise in his eyes. This time it was he who forced the pair onward, he who suddenly waved his arm above his head in what Gabby realized was a greeting.

It was for Will. He was running toward them, Will in his business suit with his crimson tie flapping over his shoulder, with worry creasing his brow and something she couldn't read in his expression. He came up close to them and met her eyes. "I thought you'd be in one of these vineyards. I've been trying to find you. Are you all right?"

She nodded, seriously doubting that he much cared. She knew it made no sense to blame him for this fire, but she couldn't help but tie him to all that had gone wrong at Suncrest. Certainly so much of it was caused by Max but some of it was due to Will, too—Will with his unrelenting competitiveness, his heartless calculation of what made business sense and what didn't, the people who were affected just so much collateral damage. Now Suncrest would be reduced to a shell of itself. But knowing Will, he'd probably see it as an opportunity.

He gazed at her a moment longer, then took her father's other arm, and together they made it faster to the edge of the vineyard, where her dusty Jeep was waiting. She and Will were helping her father into the passenger seat when she heard a roar overhead. She stopped to watch. Her father did, too, half in and half out of the car.

It was a white firefighting tanker plane skimming low over the woods. They watched it glide just above the leaping flames, then release a cloud of retardant over the trees. It fell like a mantle of red dust.

All three lingered at the vineyard's edge to watch as two other tankers joined the aerial performance. One made a pass over the vineyard, a good part of which was now engulfed, the fire consuming the grasses and torching the vines with appalling speed.

Gabby slumped onto the oven-hot seat of the Jeep. That was that, then. The fire would destroy both the grapes and the vines—some of the latter as old as she was. For them, as for her, it was the end of the line.

Chapter 17

Max learned one thing from the fire: he wouldn't be a good actor. Because it was making him a nervous wreck to have to go around pretending he had no idea how the conflagration started.

Early Saturday, on the proverbial morning after, he stood with Gabby and Cosimo on the charred wasteland that used to be Suncrest's Morydale vineyard. Now, though it was way too late to do any good, the fog had come back, the wind had disappeared, and the temperature had dropped twenty degrees.

In this as in everything else, he was a victim of bad timing.

"So how bad is it?" Max asked Gabby.

She shook her head. Even in disaster, she looked good—little shorts, fleece pullover, nice wave to the hair. "Bad. As far as the crop goes, we took a huge hit. But the bigger disaster really is the vines."

"Tell me about the crop first."

"Most of the damage is limited to two vineyards. We'd only just begun harvesting in those, so basically we lost the whole crop."

Her father piped up. "All told, about a quarter of our cabernet sauvignon grapes were destroyed."

That was not good. Suncrest made most of its money from the cab. But now they wouldn't be able to produce nearly so much of it. And it wasn't like they could make up the lost revenues with the sauvignon blanc. Thanks to the rebottling debacle, that wasn't exactly selling well.

Max kicked at the nearest vine, a gnarled, blackened thing he almost didn't recognize as something that would grow grapes. It was so brittle and dried out, a whole branch dropped to the ground from his foot's impact. "And what about the vines?"

"They're gone," Gabby said. "They're dead. We'll have to yank them and start over."

That was even worse than not good. It took at least three years to get usable grapes off a vine, sometimes five, and a buttload of cash to pay for it. You had to plant the vines and nurture them and in the meanwhile buy grapes from someplace else. Mantucci wasn't going to like that, and Henley wouldn't, either. If he even cared. Maybe Mantucci wouldn't care, either.

Max felt sick to his stomach. Earlier, he'd called Mantucci—he hadn't been able to stop himself. But had Mantucci finally made an offer? No. Had he heard about the fire? Yes. Apparently the news of this bizarre vineyard blaze had traveled all over the wine world—like wildfire! And while Mantucci had been really sympathetic, and nice as could be, and swore he'd call back later, Max had gotten a bad feeling. A very bad feeling.

Max turned from Gabby and Cosimo and walked a few yards away, rubbing his forehead. The only good thing was that he didn't have to pretend not to be upset. Everybody expected that a winery owner whose vineyards got incinerated would be upset. But nobody could know that was only part of it. That what *really* killed was that Max knew he'd done this to himself—

accidentally, of course. And that he'd made a catastrophic error by not cashing in on the damn winery
when he had the chance.

In fact, he realized, if he'd been at the signing ceremony, he wouldn't have been at the overlook smoking. And someday very soon, he'd have twenty-seven
million dollars cash in the bank. And Suncrest and its
problems would be a thing of the past.

He trundled back to Gabby and her father. Cosimo
he had no problem with, but Gabby had caused him
a lot of grief. He narrowed his eyes at her. "If you'd
started harvesting earlier, we'd have more of the crop
already back at the winery."

Gabby shot back. "If you hadn't canned the field-
workers, we would've had enough manpower to keep
the ground grasses mowed. Like we have every other
year. Then the vineyard wouldn't have lit up like a
bonfire."

Cosimo raised his hands between the two of them,
as if he were stopping a fight. "All right, all right.
What's done is done. What we need to do is deal with
the situation at hand."

Max threw out his hands. "Which is what exactly?"

"What do you care?" Gabby said. "It's not your
problem anymore, anyway. It's GPG's."

Whoa! Max reeled backwards but kept himself from
saying a word. Either there was trouble in paradise
and Henley wasn't telling Gabby a damn thing, or
he'd told her he was still buying Suncrest.

Max felt a rush of hope. Was that possible? Maybe
it wasn't over. Maybe even after Max bailed on the
signing ceremony, maybe even after the fire, Henley
still wanted Suncrest.

"Gabriella," Cosimo said—pretty sternly, Max
thought—"what we need to focus on is salvaging what
we've got." That seemed to simmer her down. Then
Cosimo turned to Max. "We'll continue with our har-

vest plan, and we'll increase the yield from the vineyards that haven't been affected."

"That'll make up some of the loss," Gabby said, "but won't have a substantial impact on the quality of the wine. Which we can't afford," she added, but Max had had about as much of her opinions as he could take.

"Fine. Do what you have to do." He started back toward his convertible, which he'd left on the side road. "I'll talk to you later." He had e-mails to return, calls to make, business to conduct. Maybe now was the time to call Henley back. Feel him out.

Mrs. Finchley emerged from the kitchen the minute Max got back to the house. She handed him a slip of paper. "A Vittorio Mantucci called while you were out. He asked you to please return the call."

Max returned the call from the extension in his bedroom. *"Buona sera,"* Mantucci said.

"How are you, Vittorio?"

"Very well. And please let me repeat what I told you earlier, how sorry I am about the catastrophe that has befallen your winery in California."

"I appreciate that." *Get on with it already,* Max thought. He could barely take the suspense anymore.

Mantucci took a deep breath. Max cringed in anticipation. "I'm afraid I have bad news," Mantucci said. *Shit.*

"It pains me to say that I will not be able to make an offer for Suncrest."

I knew it.

"Even before this terrible fire, this was a very difficult arrangement for me to make. As you know, I have to line up a partner. But now"—he let his voice trail off—"now, with this bad news that has made its way to Italy and all around the world, I'm afraid none of my potential partners is willing to make the commitment."

Suncrest is cursed. Now everybody knows it.

"This is a great disappointment to me, Max. I am very sorry."

Mantucci didn't know the first thing about disappointment. Max didn't want to sound desperate, but he had to say something. "Suncrest is still very valuable, you know. It's not like the fire *ruined* it."

"Of course not, I completely understand. But you see . . ." He sounded pained. "The fire, may I say, is the culmination of events. I know you have had difficulties with your sauvignon blanc this year, and there have been other matters."

Max harrumphed. Mantucci might live in Italy, but he was surprisingly plugged in to valley gossip.

"Again, I am sorry," Mantucci repeated, and at that point Max gave up. He ended the call a little later and flopped down on his bed, staring at the ceiling. Then came a knock on his door. "Come in," he muttered.

It was Mrs. Finchley. "I thought you should know that your mother will be coming home tonight."

"What?" He bolted upright. "Why tonight?"

Mrs. Finchley's brows arched. "Why, because of the fire, of course."

"*She* knows about the fire?"

"Of course she does." Mrs. Finchley backed out into the hall, looking as prim and self-righteous as ever. "I called her." The door clicked shut.

Max closed his eyes. Just what he needed.

Ava behaved uncharacteristically on her first morning home in Napa. She slept late, well past ten, then instead of going down to the kitchen asked Mrs. Finchley to bring tea and toast to the master suite, where, still in her robe, she breakfasted off a tray in the sitting area overlooking the pool.

Part of her lassitude was caused by fatigue. Her

flight from Paris had been delayed, and the long limo ride north to the valley from the airport had seemed endless. It wasn't until after midnight that she'd collapsed into bed, even forgoing a bath. Then, courtesy of jet lag, she'd awoken at three and suffered through a few sleepless hours.

But it wasn't exhaustion alone that kept her in seclusion. Ava sipped tepid tea from her china cup, gazing without joy at the magnificent view. She dreaded seeing Max, whose actions she found more inexplicable than ever. She dreaded assessing the fire damage with her own eyes. And she dreaded dealing with Suncrest's future, which looked uncertain indeed. She'd thought that by this weekend she'd be free of the winery, for once she'd agreed to sell it she was impatient to have it done. But no. Like everything else that involved her son, something had gone wrong.

She was mystified as to why Max had failed to sign the final documents selling Suncrest to GPG. Why he'd balked at the eleventh hour, when he'd been so terrifically intent before, she had no idea. Neither did her attorney, who'd informed her that her son had left Will Henley and numerous attorneys waiting in Porter's office while he was off God knew where doing God knew what. Then the fire began. Minutes later.

Ava shivered, though on this Sunday morning the sun had already burned through the fog and the breeze through the open French doors was balmy. She was not a churchgoer: one of her youthful rebellions had been to turn her back on her parents' Methodist faith. Though her own views on the Almighty were murky and unresolved, she couldn't help but think of the fire as some sort of celestial sign. If it wasn't from God, then perhaps it was from Porter, who'd sent a thunderbolt down from the heavens to show how mightily he disapproved of the way his beloved Suncrest was being managed.

She hung her head. Porter would be colossally disappointed, she knew. And not only in Max.

Ava wished she had managed Suncrest better, and raised Max with more care. Yet he'd always been such a handful. She shouldn't resent her own child, but sometimes she couldn't help it. And now nothing was going as it ought, and when had that started? The day Max returned home from France.

She forced herself to throw her napkin aside and rise from her breakfast. Perhaps it was just as well that this morass had dragged her back to California. She'd been shirking her duty, and it wasn't as if her European pursuits were flourishing, anyway.

Ava showered and dressed quickly so as to be ready for her first visitors of the day. It was time to find Max and face reality. She exited the master suite to hear the noise of a televised sporting event blaring from the family room. Could it be football season already?

Max hoisted himself off the sofa to hug her. "Hey, Mom, welcome back." He gave her a tight squeeze before he released her. "How are you? I guess the flight got in really late last night."

"There was a mechanical problem. A five-hour delay."

He winced. "Ouch."

She eyed him. He might be lounging in front of the television on a bright weekend morning but he had taken some care with his appearance, in deference to her return, no doubt. He'd showered and shaved, and wore pressed khakis and a polo shirt. She even caught a whiff of cologne. "You seem to be holding up well," she said.

A wariness came into his eyes. "You mean . . . after the fire?"

"And also the—" She didn't know what to call it. "—end of the sale to GPG."

He dropped his gaze. "Yeah, we need to talk about that."

"I should say so." The doorbell rang. "Ah, they're here. I want you with me for this."

He followed her into the foyer. "Who is it?"

She pulled the door open and stepped aside. "Gentlemen, please come in." Ava turned toward Max to include him in the introductions of the two uniformed men from the Napa County Fire Department, but was startled to see an expression of raw panic take over his face.

He stammered. "What are they doing here?"

"I asked them here." She frowned as she watched her son back away a few clumsy steps and bump into the narrow foyer table, making the dendrobium orchid atop it dance. *Why in the world is he acting so oddly?* She smiled at her guests to try to dispel the awkwardness. "I wanted a report on the fire and these gentlemen were kind enough to come here to the house to provide it." Though Ava considered the housecall less a kindness than a duty. After all, she was a major taxpayer in this county.

One of the men held out his hand to Max. "Fire Captain Ralph Dunphy." He pivoted to indicate the man behind him. "And this is Fire Captain Jimmy Marcino."

Max nodded, shook hands with both of them. "Good to meet you," he said. Ava ushered everyone into the living room, where seats were taken and throats cleared. Max didn't sit, though, she noticed; he stood at the open French doors as if ready to flee at any moment.

Dunphy took the lead. "Mrs. Winsted, my colleague and I would like to extend our sympathies on the losses you've suffered to your vineyards. It is a terrible thing."

She bowed her head. "Thank you." She'd find out just how terrible when she met later with Cosimo and Gabriella. "I gather a great deal of forestland was burned, as well?"

"Thirty-two acres." Marcino consulted a small notebook. "We fought the blaze for about three and a half hours, deployed one chopper and three tankers on it, and of course stayed on it overnight. In case of flare-ups."

"I appreciate that."

"We considered it a significant blaze," Dunphy said.

Yes, Ava thought, *particularly to us.* "Do you have any idea how it started?"

Marcino spoke. "We know exactly how it started, ma'am."

"And how was that?"

He held up a baggie with a small object inside it. "This, ma'am."

Ava squinted at it. "Is that a cigarette butt?"

"Yes," Dunphy said. "Most common cause of this sort of thing."

"We consider this type of incident accidental," Marcino said. "Caused by carelessness. Negligence."

"But," Ava said, "might it not be arson?"

"It might be," Dunphy said, "but we have no way to prove it. And so there are no real ramifications even if we could trace it to an individual. Especially if that individual has no prior convictions."

"I see." She paused, considered. "But since you know how the fire started, I gather you know where it originated, as well?"

"Yes, we do," Marcino said. "Just west of overlook number four on Drysdale Mountain Road. We suspect an individual tossed the cigarette over the guardrail and into the ground brush, which caught instantly."

"The north wind exacerbated matters," Dunphy

added. Then he shook his head. "We think it was probably a foreign tourist who started this fire, Mrs. Winsted. It's a strange brand of cigarette. French."

Marcino consulted his notebook. "It's something called a Gauloises," he said.

Marcino massacred the pronunciation, but Ava immediately understood. She froze. *That's Max's brand. And he goes to an overlook on that road. In fact, at his suggestion we went there the day he bought me the Mercedes.*

She was afraid to look at her son, who remained as still as marble, staring out at the pergola. She struggled not to let any emotion show on her face. *Is that why Max seems so petrified? Because he started this fire?* It was a terrible thought, a preposterous notion. Her son might be many things, but he certainly wasn't an . . . No, she wouldn't even think the word.

Still. It wouldn't surprise her that he was still smoking. And a Gauloises cigarette? That overlook? And now, this bizarre behavior?

By now she had one thought and one thought only. *Get these men out of here.* For whatever Max had or had not done, he was still a Winsted, and her and Porter's son, and it was her duty to protect him. She rose from her chair and struggled to keep her voice steady. "Mr. Dunphy, Mr. Marcino, I so appreciate your time today."

They both stood. Dunphy spoke as she led them back to the foyer and held open the front door. "I'm sorry we couldn't give you more satisfaction, Mrs. Winsted. I know that in a situation like this, you want to be able to bring the guilty party to justice."

"Quite right. Very perceptive, Mr. Dunphy. Thank you again." Then, after the requisite good-byes, she closed the door and her visitors were gone.

She returned to the living room. "Not so fast, Max." He was halfway across the lawn to the pergola, but she waylaid him. "Did you start that fire?" She couldn't believe she was asking that question, but yes, she was. It hung between mother and son, the latter taking far too long to say no. "You did, didn't you?"

"Of course I didn't." He sounded belligerent. Some part of her admired him for at least putting on some show. "I would never do something like that."

"Not intentionally."

"Not any other way, either."

"It's very odd. That the fire was started by a Gauloises? And the timing, too."

He crossed his arms over his chest. "What's weird about the timing?"

"It started right after what should have been the signing ceremony with Will Henley. And the location is highly coincidental. I know you like that overlook."

Max had nothing to say to that. He turned away and jutted out his chin.

"I can just imagine you being upset, going up the hill to have a smoke, and tossing the cigarette away. That sounds like something you would do."

His mouth twisted. "You *would* think that, wouldn't you?" He sounded surly as a teenager whose curfew had just been lengthened by another week. "I thought mothers were supposed to give their kids the benefit of the doubt. Wrong again."

"I have given you the benefit of the doubt a thousand times. This is a thousand and one." She grabbed his arm and forced him to look at her. "You are going to sit down and tell me exactly what happened Friday. What you could possibly have been thinking when you failed to sign those sale documents. Then *I* will decide what to do."

"You mean about Suncrest?"

She didn't answer her son, just led him back inside the house to begin his long overdue reckoning. *I mean about everything.*

* * *

Tuesday afternoon, the last day of August, Will sat at his GPG desk and pushed his intercom button. "Yes, Janine?"

"Ava Winsted is here for your four o'clock."

"Please show her in."

He rose, lifted the suit jacket from the back of his chair, slipped it on. *I'm either a glutton for punishment*, he told himself, *or the luckiest man alive.* For when Ava Winsted had called and asked for a meeting, he'd only been too happy to oblige. That old hope had leaped anew in his heart. He'd known that nothing but a bizarre incident could salvage the Suncrest deal for him. But then he got one.

He still wanted Suncrest, even after the fire had rendered it an even paler reflection of its formerly grand self. By now people in the wine world were clucking their tongues: could more catastrophes possibly strike one winery? Its brand name was shot. Its value had plummeted to a new low. From the partial loss of the cabernet sauvignon crop and vineyards, its revenues would be down for years. It had been barely breakeven before, but now would require major cash to keep operating.

But that was the time to buy!—when times were the worst. That's when the price was right, when the best deals could be made. And Suncrest still had that precious, heaven-sent, underutilized land—so perfectly situated, so primed for grape-growing, so difficult to acquire. And the land would recover. It always did.

Ava appeared at his office door, looking lovely and elegant in the way of classic older actresses. It was as if, even thirty years out of Hollywood, she still utilized daily stylists for hair, makeup, and wardrobe, as if every outing were An Appearance. This afternoon she was dressed for business in a turquoise suit cut of such fine silk no actual businesswoman would find it remotely practical.

He greeted her with hands outstretched. "Ava, it's good to see you. It's been too long." How true was that? For if he'd been dealing with her on the deal instead of her son, no doubt Suncrest would be his already.

She smiled as if she hadn't a care in the world. "Thank you for agreeing to see me, Will. And on such short notice."

"Of course." He swept her toward his leather sofa. "May I offer you tea or coffee?"

"Coffee would be lovely."

So she wanted to stay awhile, another cheering sign. Will buzzed Janine, then took a seat on the opposite end of the sofa. "I am so sorry about the fire, Ava. You may not know that I actually witnessed a bit of it."

He shook his head, the image of those flames screaming down the rows of grapevines part of his memory bank forever. As soon as they had gotten away from the worst of it, he'd watched Gabby regain control, directing the firemen to the other endangered vineyard, shouting orders to the field-workers desperately trying to quench the flames with a few ineffectual hoses. He didn't think she noticed him slip away to call his partners, and they hadn't seen each other since. But he would never forget her face as the inferno raged—frightened, disbelieving, tortured. He pushed that recollection aside.

"The blaze moved amazingly fast, Ava," he went on. "The only good thing is that Napa's firefighters are so well trained. Otherwise the damage would have been even greater."

"Yes." She looked down into her lap. "I can hardly bear to see the burnt area. Porter would have been devastated."

Will eyed his guest. Ava Winsted might be chilly, she might be theatrical, but it seemed she had loved her husband, and she was nobody's fool. He doubted Porter would have married her otherwise. True, her son exhibited a distinct lack of character. Was that her fault? Perhaps in part, but Will wasn't inclined to blame the parents for the sins of the children, particularly not the adult children.

Janine appeared with coffee, served quickly, and departed.

"How was your stay in France?" Will asked.

"Enjoyable." Again Ava smiled. "But I'm glad to be home."

He was wondering just how true that was when she shifted position on the couch as if to signal her readiness to get down to the business at hand. "I know that Max did not participate in the signing ceremony," she said.

How delicately she'd phrased that. A more accurate construction might be *Max blew it off* or *Max really screwed GPG, didn't he?* But Will wouldn't challenge Ava, or embarrass her, or demand an explanation. His goal was Suncrest, and to get it he'd better let its owner save face. "No, he didn't," he agreed mildly.

"Despite that, I remain very interested in selling the winery to GPG. If you care to pursue the matter further, I would love to hear a new offer."

He kept his face expressionless as conclusions spun out in his mind. *So Mantucci didn't make an offer. As I predicted. And Ava doesn't want to run Suncrest any more now than she ever did. She certainly won't let Max run it now, even if he wants to.* This was what Will wanted, this was *so* what he wanted, but he was hemmed in by his partners, as always. He needed to wring concessions out of Ava—gently, of course—to convince the GPG brass to go another round.

Carefully he set down his porcelain cup and saucer.

"Ava, as you know, we had a deal with you and your son. You also know that he backed out at the last minute. We invested a great deal of time and money in the due diligence. I can tell you that my partners feel poorly used by what transpired. And now, given the fire"—he spread his hands—"I can only say that any price I might offer would be significantly lower than the one we agreed to before."

She nodded. "Let me assure you, Will, that from now on you will be dealing only with me." *Translation: My idiot son is out of the picture.* "I have been advised by my counsel that the final documents are fine and need no revision. I'm prepared to do a transaction here and now, if you and I can agree on a price."

So far, so good. "I should also warn you that any agreement you and I reach is contingent on my partners' approval."

"Fine."

This could not be going more smoothly. Will cast his mind back to the price he had calculated earlier, should his conversation with Ava move in this direction. The old price, from the prior Friday, was twenty-seven million dollars. "I can offer nineteen million dollars," he said.

She hesitated only a second. Then, "Twenty-two."

She just wants this done. A thrill pulsed through him as he realized that he was about to get what he wanted. He shoved aside the image of Gabby that rose in his mind. She was wrong about him, she was wrong about Suncrest, and he wouldn't let her resentment spoil this moment. "Twenty million," he said to Ava, knowing this would be it. He would get his victory, his ultimate vindication. He would win at last.

Ava held out her hand, her gaze steady and clear. "Done."

*   *   *

Dispense the fledgling wine from the fermentation tank, roll it in the mouth, judge the flavor, spit it in the drain gulley that runs the length of the concrete floor, go on to the next tank. Motions one after the next, repetitive, pointless, bereft of their usual joy and satisfaction. *Meaningless*, Gabby thought, *like everything else.*

It was Friday, late in the day, evening really. Gabby was alone in the old winery building, everyone, including her father, gone to get a jump start on Labor Day weekend. Yet she wanted to be alone, and she wanted to be working. Right now she was good for little else. She had no plans for the weekend and no ability to be social. She felt amazingly similar to the way she had a year before—raw, wounded, shell-shocked.

She moved on to the next tank, placed her wineglass beneath the spout. Out flowed an ounce or so of the thin crimson liquid that over time would become a complex, nuanced, multifaceted cabernet sauvignon. Not only would it carry a prized Napa Valley appellation, but it would also be an estate wine, as all the grapes used to make it had been grown on Suncrest property.

Gabby held it up to the light, assessed its color, viscosity. It was the last of a dead breed. Suncrest would never make another vintage like it. That era was over.

She ran the wine through her teeth, calculated how far the fermentation had progressed, then bent over the gulley and spit it out. The ceaseless mechanical whir of the tanks hummed in her ears; the vinegary smell of grapes fermenting assailed her nostrils. Another week and the baby cab would go from tanks to barrels, to age for two years more. In the end, because of the peculiarities of the soil and the climate and the sunshine and the rain and the exact moment she had chosen for harvest, it would have a flavor distinct from any other cab she had ever made or ever would make. That was the wonder of it, and the beauty.

She abandoned her wineglass and walked outside to stand on the pebbled path. Here it was quiet, save for a stray birdcall, and the air was sweet. The sun teased the jagged crest of the Mayacamas; soon it would disappear behind the mountains and roll across the Pacific. Its last rays caressed the grapevines that covered the slope down to the Trail, the grapevines that had every excuse to rest not just for the night but for the season. Their fruit had been taken, and their labor was done.

She was back inside the winery doing the last of the closing-down for the night when she heard footsteps behind her on the concrete floor. She turned, surprised, then caught her breath, more profoundly shaken. "Will."

He stepped closer. "I thought I'd find you here." He wore gray suit trousers and a white dress shirt open at the neck. "Sorry if I startled you."

"No," she said instantly, though he had. She hadn't been sure she would ever see him again, except in some businesslike setting where she was getting the corporate word along with every other Suncrest employee. And even though this was Friday night and they were alone, this was pretty much along those lines. The tone of Will's voice, the planes of his face, were cool and hard. By now she could barely remember seeing them any other way. "How are you?" she asked.

"Fine," he said, though to her he looked exhausted. Then again, that was typical for him late on a weekday. "And yourself?"

"Fine. My father, too," she added, to forestall the polite inquiry she knew Will would make.

Silence fell between them. The tanks chugged relentlessly, their task never done. Gabby busied herself

making a useless notation in her notebook, something
she'd just have to cross out once Will was gone.
Though in some ways he already was. The man she'd
known had disappeared behind a mask of distrust
and formality.

"I've come to tell you something," he said.

She didn't look up from her notebook. All the horrible possibilities of what that something might be
zigged and zagged in her mind. Very likely of course
was that this was the formal breakup announcement,
though by this point that wasn't really necessary. Then
again, Will was the type who liked to dot his i's and
cross his t's.

He spoke again. "Ava just signed the final documents selling Suncrest to GPG."

She caught her breath. "So you own it now."

"Well, GPG owns it."

"Congratulations." How trite and false that sounded,
echoing off the walls of the tank room. She didn't say
You won, though it occurred to her. But she didn't
want to sound petty, didn't want to add that to the
list of damning adjectives that Will no doubt used
these days to describe her.

She turned away. *It's over.* Here it was, the moment
she'd been dreading. Yet she felt oddly detached. It
was as if she'd already begun, some time back, to separate from Suncrest. *To give up on it,* she corrected
herself, which made tears prick hot behind her eyes.
It was like the feeling she'd had when her Grandma
Laura died, when Gabby knew that her nonna was
going in one direction and she was going in the other,
and that as much as they loved one another, neither
could share the other's path.

Will's voice interrupted her thoughts. "I'll be going
then," she heard him say. "I just wanted to let you
know."

And to rub her face in it, at least a little. That didn't

really seem like Will, but apparently she'd read him wrong. A mistake she'd made before, with another man. In another country, in another life.

Something, perhaps a last frantic bid to keep him from leaving, possessed her to call after him. "I gather Vittorio didn't make an offer for Suncrest?"

Will halted, half turned. "No. He didn't."

"But you still can't forgive me. Or understand why I did what I did."

At that his eyes, as cold a blue as the frigid North Atlantic, rose to hers. She had a moment's thrill thinking he might actually pick up the bait, get down in the muck with her and yell and scream and shout, which would be so much preferable to this chilly interchange. But he only shook his head, minutely, and she knew she'd lost again. He wouldn't bother. Only people who cared about each other fought. People who were walking out of each other's lives didn't go to the trouble.

"I understand everything I need to," he said, then turned again to go.

Hollow tomorrows stretched out in front of her, gray and without definition. Rainbow colors gone, everything dull and faded. Nothing as it ought to be.

And Will was lying. Supposedly honest, trustworthy Will. He said he understood but he didn't. He wasn't even trying.

She watched him walk away for good, heels clacking in efficient rhythm on the concrete floor he now owned, the floor he'd won, the floor of her undoing.

The big oak door closed behind him. Somewhere the winery building groaned in an unseen settling of its old bones.

She told herself, as the tears came, that this was how it must be. For after the debacle with Vittorio, she had to be with a man she understood, and who understood her. Didn't she? Otherwise what did she have, really? Something impermanent. Something throw-away. When what she needed was something that could last.

It still eluded her. And might always.

Chapter 18

Late afternoon on Labor Day, when most valley residents were firing up their barbecues while chugging down a cold one, Max got home from a weekend trip to find himself getting grilled. Not surprisingly, by his mother.

She was sitting at the antique desk in the living room writing something, wearing her typical laze-about outfit—white pants, white top, white headband, white sandals. She'd worn that sort of thing all his life. The incredible thing was, he'd never once seen a stain on her. "Did you have a nice time?" she asked him.

He dumped his duffel on the floor, slumped onto a chair. "It was fine."

She kept her eyes on her writing. "How was the surfing?"

"Fine."

"The water wasn't too cold?"

"Mom, it was *Malibu*."

"Hm, I suppose you're right." She looked up, then over at him. "How are Rory and Bucky?"

He took a deep breath. "Fine." It'd been sort of fun to get away with them, but he was ready for them to leave Napa Valley already. Seeing them sort of made him feel like a failure. Though he wouldn't be for long. Not once he got away from Suncrest. And pocketed his cash.

"Bucky flew you down?"

"Yeah." That was another annoying thing in a growing list. Not only did every female on the planet think Bucky was hot, he was in med school, so everybody took him for a brainiac. And then he went and got himself a pilot's license, so now he was flying around this hot-shit Cessna he rented out of Angwin airport. If that wasn't a babe magnet, Max didn't know what was.

Max kicked at his duffel, which skidded a few feet along the whitewashed hardwood. Bucky had it so easy. Rory, too. Unlike him, they weren't plagued with life's big questions, like what the hell to do with the years that stretched ahead of him like the runway for a 747. *I must be more complex than they are,* Max told himself. *That's why I've got all these challenges.*

His mother was talking to him again. "Did you tell me Rory is joining a law firm?"

"Yeah."

She waited. Then, "Care to tell me where it is?"

"D.C."

"What sort of work will he do?"

"Corporate."

She sighed. He was irritating her, he knew, but he was too hot and tired to be a scintillating conversationalist. Then, when he was about to hoist himself off the chair to go in search of a beer, she spoke up. "Since it's fairly clear I can't get anything out of you but monosyllabic replies, perhaps I should do the talking. There's something I need to discuss with you, anyway."

That sounded portentous enough to stop him. "What's up?"

"I've decided how to disburse the cash from Suncrest."

He frowned. He got no more joy out of talking about Suncrest now than he ever had. At first he'd been pretty impressed that his mother had pulled off a deal with Henley, and so fast, too. Then he'd found out for how much and knew it was no wonder Henley had bitten. It ate Max alive that the price was so pathetically low, but there wasn't a damn thing he could do about it. "What do you mean, *disburse* the cash? You get your half, and I get mine."

She arched her brows. "You think you're entitled to half?"

"Isn't that what Dad always intended?"

She looked down at the desktop. "Your father intended a lot of things that will never come to pass."

Max rolled his eyes. He hated when she started delivering melodramatic lines that sounded like they came right out of a B-movie script. "So what *am* I gonna get?"

She said nothing for a while. And when she finally did speak she didn't look at him. "I'm giving you a million dollars."

His immediate reaction was to laugh. Then to think for sure he'd heard wrong. "What? What did you say?"

Her face turned toward his, and the expression on it freaked him. Because it was so damn serious. "I said I'm giving you a million dollars."

"But . . ." This was weird, in fact, so *beyond* weird that he wasn't really worried. It couldn't possibly be true. "But you sold the winery to Henley for twenty million."

"Which I know you think is absurdly low. I don't care to get into that with you again."

They'd had a battle royal about it. "No kidding!

You sold my legacy out from under me for a pittance!"

She shook her head but he got the feeling she wouldn't get mad at him again. She was too tired or fed up or . . . something. "I find it curious that Suncrest is your legacy when you want the cash from it and that it's your burden when you don't care to exert yourself to run it. But be that as it may"—she raised her hand and her voice both when he started to object—"the fact is that the deal is done and the proceeds are twenty million dollars. That will not change."

No, it wouldn't. Amazing.

He took a deep breath, struggled to control himself. "Okay. So you sold it for twenty million. That's still ten for you and ten for me. The way Dad intended."

She tapped her pen against the table. *Tap. Tap. Tap.* "The way I see it is this. When you took over the winery, Will Henley offered us thirty million dollars for it. That figure decreased by a third directly because of your actions." She looked at him then, and he was surprised that her expression didn't seem so much angry as sad. That gave him a little worry knot in his stomach, like maybe she wasn't just trying to scare him. "You cost this family ten million dollars, Max."

He shuffled his feet. "That's sort of a harsh way to look at it."

"I've thought about this a great deal." She turned away from him. "And it's quite painful for me. But the truth is that I see no reason why I should suffer any more because of your actions. I also believe this presents an opportunity for you to learn some long-overdue lessons."

"Okay. Okay." He didn't like the sound of any of this. He felt himself start to hyperventilate. "So you want fifteen." That was hard to swallow, but maybe he could get used to it if he absolutely had to. "But that still leaves five for me. So where do you come up with one?"

"Well, a portion will go to taxes, of course." She shuffled around some of the papers on her desk. "And a few million will go to a nature-conservancy charity. To make up, in some small way, for the destruction you caused. And to teach you that actions have consequences. It'll still leave you with a million dollars, an amount most people would be extremely grateful for. I certainly would have been at your age."

At that moment it struck Max that she was completely serious. All of a sudden his head was spinning. He reached for the chair he'd just vacated and fell into it. "But . . . but I didn't start that fire." Somehow it didn't sound very convincing when he was stammering. "And I don't want to give millions of dollars to charity."

"We'll make the donation in your name." She just kept going. She wore a faraway expression, as if she was talking to herself and he wasn't even there. Max, panting, thought *I hate her. I actually hate my own mother.* "Of course, we won't tell anyone that you yourself started the fire that destroyed your own vineyards. I'm certainly not going to put myself, or you, through that ridicule." She turned her eyes on him again. "People will say you're very generous and sensitive. You don't care nearly enough how people think of you. But I do. And that's the impression I'd rather they have."

She was crazy. There was no other explanation.

"It's very difficult to be a parent," she went on. "It's very hard to know what is the right thing to do. I know I've made many mistakes where you're concerned. I've coddled you far too often. But I'm hoping this will finally force you to grow up."

She'd gone certifiably nuts. But maybe he could still

reason with her. "Mom, remember when we were in Paris and we talked about how important it is for me to do my own thing in life? Like you did when you became an actress?" He watched her. She seemed to be listening. "Well, if you go ahead and do this, that'll be impossible for me."

She actually had the nerve to chuckle. "Max, most people don't have a penny to help them make their own way. You'll have a million dollars."

"But why not give me a leg up? It's really competitive out there, you know."

"If it weren't for the fire, perhaps I'd agree with you. But that was the last straw. You still won't admit the truth, Max. You still insist on lying. I'm sorry but"—she threw out her hands—"this is my final decision."

He stood up and started to pace. He wasn't shocked anymore. He was pissed. *Man!* Money really showed what people were made of, didn't it? Even his own mother. He pointed at her from across the living room. "You just want the fifteen million! And you're willing to screw your own son to get it. That's what this is *really* all about."

She rose from the desk. "I knew you'd be angry. Perhaps someday you'll understand. When you're a parent yourself."

"So what the hell am I supposed to do in the meanwhile?" he yelled at her as she walked past him. "You're the one with all the answers. You tell me that!"

"I suppose you'll have to get a job."

"A *job*?" He was incredulous. "But what am I trained for?"

"That," his mother said as she exited the living room, "is a very good question."

On Friday afternoon, at the end of the shortened

work week that had begun with Labor Day, Will was attending a meeting held in the living room of one Hannah Harper, the crack CEO he'd just hired to run Suncrest. She owned a stunningly decorated home in Sonoma Valley, another gorgeous swath of wine country just west of Napa. Will was trying hard, without much success, to pay attention to what was going on around him, and attributed his distraction to the fact that he spent too much of his life in meetings. More than half, for sure. As much as two thirds? He did a quick mental calculation. Possibly.

He didn't like that idea. It raised a life-passing-him-by issue of some type or other. But he was too busy preparing for meetings, attending meetings, or doing the follow-up to meetings to have time to figure it out.

From the country-casual upholstered chair to his left, Hannah spoke. She was a late-thirties brunette, razor sharp and city slick. "It seems to me we have two immediate concerns. First, we need to cut costs to get them in line with the reduced revenues Suncrest will generate. Second, we need to minimize the revenue loss by seeking alternative sources of grapes."

Will watched Dagney and Jacob nod solemnly. Both were clearly cowed by Ms. Harper, and it was no surprise. She was a business supernova who until recently had been running the wine division of a major beverage company. Will wooed her with a can't-refuse offer and her first CEO title. He suspected she was already picturing her face on the cover of *Forbes* or *Fortune*.

"Suncrest's revenues will take a hit for some time," Hannah continued, "but we're in a good position to build a platform for the future."

"Speaking of which," Dagney piped up from the couch across the room, "here is the worksheet Jacob and I drew up analyzing some other wineries we might acquire and merge into Suncrest." She handed around a thin sheaf of papers.

"About a third of them are in Napa," Jacob said, "but there are some here in Sonoma Valley and also a number of options in Mendocino and Santa Barbara counties."

Will glanced briefly at the worksheet, which he'd seen before. A few times. He let it drop onto his lap and again his mind wandered. It was funny. His plan, conceived months before, was unfolding before his eyes, and yet he wasn't nearly so jazzed as he would have expected to be. As he had envisioned, Suncrest Vineyards was becoming the linchpin of a much larger winemaking enterprise. Its brand, though battered, was still valuable; and its land, burned or not, remained underutilized. Over time, several less well-known labels would be subsumed under the Suncrest umbrella, and volume would be ramped up. Profits would soar. His partners would be positively delighted. As had become his habit of late, Will didn't allow himself to think about those people who would have quite the opposite reaction.

He looked past Jacob's head out the front window of Hannah's six-thousand-square-foot "cottage," to the designer-perfect porch complete with pristine white railing, wicker rocking chair, and side table laid with a vase of summer blooms and an apparently untouched paperback. The scene looked posed, but then again the house did, too: its furnishings too coordinated, its casualness too contrived for real life. It was as if the prior owners had staged the property for sale, and Hannah hadn't bothered to move her own things in after taking possession.

He eyed Hannah, who was leading Dagney and Jacob in a detailed discussion of how appropriate grapes might be acquired. They were spellbound, clearly hoping she'd drop nuggets of wisdom they could parlay into their own business success. She was an impressive woman, Will agreed, and attractive, too—if you glossed over the fact that she might eat her young to get ahead.

Will guessed that quite a number of attractive women would have to cross his path before he would be willing to plunge again into romance. His current modus operandi was to pretend that such a thing didn't exist, at least not for him. His life was focused on work and on working out, and he was doing both with grim gusto. Some days he put himself through his rowing-machine regimen twice, in the morning and evening both. Paired with a fourteen-hour workday, it allowed him to drop into bed exhausted. It allowed him to shorten that dangerous interval in the dark when his thoughts might drift to Gabby, to where she might be and what she might be doing and whether she was thinking of him.

He thought of her constantly, was forced at all hours to push thoughts of her away. Even still, treacherous ideas would dip their toes into his mind. *Maybe she's right that you didn't even try to understand her. Maybe it's true that she did what she did for her family. Maybe her motives are more pure than you're giving her credit for.*

But he drowned those ideas under waves of resentment. *No, she betrayed me. She used her old lover to do it. She betrayed me. She knew how much I needed Suncrest; she knew how much I needed that deal. She cares only about herself and her naïve business ideas. She betrayed me.*

He couldn't get past it. And, he told himself, there was no reason to. The last thing he needed was a woman he couldn't trust. The right thing to do was cut her out now, like an impacted tooth. And it would help that Hannah Harper was on board at Suncrest. She would free him up, allow him to spend less time at the winery. Then he wouldn't keep running into Gabby. The less he saw her, the less he had those rebellious thoughts.

He turned his attention back to Hannah. "There's no question there's fat at Suncrest," she was saying. "It's been run loosely, like so many family wineries. It needs a shake-up."

That concept should be music to Will's ears, but it disconcerted him. "Along what lines, Hannah?" he asked.

"Well, first of all I want to make sure we have the right people in place. Not everybody there is totally motivated. But there are some people I've worked with in the past that I think are terrific and want to bring in."

He nodded. It was true that Hannah's wine-industry contacts were part of the reason he'd hired her. And as CEO, she certainly had primary say over staff. Still, he had his own opinions. And as the representative of Suncrest's owner, he had say, too.

"For example," Hannah said, "there's a vineyard manager I'm very excited about hiring. And a winemaker I've worked with before has just come available. The timing couldn't be more perfect."

Will sat up straighter. "In terms of the winemaking," he heard himself say, "it's important that we maintain continuity. We don't want to make too radical a shift."

Hannah turned her gaze on Will's face. "I understand that Cosimo DeLuca has been at Suncrest for a long time. And I'm sure he's very good at what he does. But—"

"Not just a long time," Will said. "Twenty-five years. From the founding of the winery. And his judgment and skill are the reasons Suncrest has had so many award-winning wines, Hannah."

She paused, regarding him. Then, "I don't mean

to downplay his contribution, Will, which I'm sure is substantial. But the person I'm thinking of is truly exceptional. He's one of the top talents in the valley. And unlike Mr. DeLuca, he's accustomed to a larger operation."

"Perhaps down the road," Will said, "it would make sense—"

"He won't be available down the road."

This had become a pissing match, Will realized, one Dagney and Jacob were finding both instructive and entertaining. It was time for him, as Hannah's boss, to end it.

"That's a risk we'll have to take," he said, finality in his voice. "We need to satisfy Suncrest's longtime customer base. And to do that we have to keep the two main varieties of wine that Suncrest has always made as unchanged as possible. That necessitates retaining the current winemakers."

After that, the discussion veered onto less controversial territory. Will told himself that his forcefulness on the winemaker issue was entirely a function of good business sense.

That's what he told himself.

The breakfast of champions, Gabby thought, standing beside a fermentation tank swishing baby cabernet in her mouth. She bent and spit it out, rose to check the tank's digital-red temperature reading, then carefully wrote *81* in her notebook, alongside the tank number, the date, and the hour. The digits took their place in neat, steadily lengthening columns, little numeric soldiers goose-stepping down the page.

As they had most of her life, the winemaking rituals gave Gabby comfort. They allowed her to move through her day without giving much thought to anything: first do this, then do that, then do the next thing. She would intersperse these automatic tasks with simple pleasures, things she knew would soothe her soul in small ways, massage around the edges of the big ache. She made a point of taking her mug of morning coffee outside the house for the sheer joy of feeling dawn's cool air on her face. She treated herself to a daily pastry from Dean and DeLuca's, and didn't lament long if she failed to balance it with a workout. She loaded up on escapist novels and in the evenings disappeared into fictional lives, where she could feel confident that everyone's problems would handily work themselves out by *The End*.

She had no idea how her own difficulties would find solutions. Time, she supposed, would do most of the trick. Time, enough of it, would scab over the loss of Will, though the hole would always be there. Time would sever her official ties with Suncrest, though exactly how it would happen remained a mystery. She knew she wouldn't leave before her father did, because she refused to abandon him to all the changes the winery would undergo, most of which he would hate. When he was ready to walk away, she'd follow. But not before.

She was hosing down the floor around the tanks when her father came to find her. "It's Hannah," he said without preamble. "She wants to see us in Mr. Winsted's office."

Gabby turned off the hose, tossed it aside. "What about?"

Her father shook his head. Gabby knew he wasn't overly fond of the new CEO, either. To them, the fact that Hannah Harper had presided over a jug winemaking operation was hardly a recommendation. Yet, apparently it was to Will.

She trailed after her father as he trod slowly up the stairs. He looked tired these days, and did things he never had before. Like count the hours until five o'clock, when in the past no one in the family could get him away from the winery. On weekends he wouldn't go in unless he had to. His heart wasn't in it anymore, Gabby knew. Neither was hers.

Hannah waved them inside Mr. Winsted's office. "Come in, come in. Sit down." Her smile flared, then evaporated just as fast. Hannah struck Gabby as an older, less charming version of Dagney. Her efforts to be winning were even more cursory, but maybe her elevated position on the corporate ladder required less.

When they were all arrayed on the tartan sofas, Hannah leaned forward with an earnest expression. "I want to reassure the two of you about your futures here at Suncrest. I value your work very highly and look forward to a long and productive work relationship with both of you."

She stopped, gazed at them with brows raised expectantly. *She thinks we're thrilled,* Gabby thought. *She expects us to gush with gratitude. If she only knew.*

"Well, Hannah," Gabby's father said, "I appreciate that, and I know my daughter does, as well." He patted Gabby's knee as if to preclude any ill-advised remarks. Gabby remained dutifully silent, though she practically had to bite her tongue to manage it.

Hannah bestowed another fleeting smile. "So many exciting things are going to happen here at Suncrest. I know you'll enjoy being a part of them." She cleared her throat. "Cosimo, there is one matter I would appreciate your handling for me."

"And what is that?"

"We'll be bringing in a new vineyard manager, someone I've worked with a great deal in the past and think very highly of. What I would—"

"You're demoting Felix?" Gabby heard herself say.

Again Hannah's brows shot up. She seemed affronted that one of her new employees had the temerity to interrupt her. "Actually, we're letting him go."

No. This time Gabby's father spoke, his tone disbelieving. "Excuse me, Hannah, you're *firing* Felix?"

"I'd rather not use that word." *Of course not,* Gabby thought, *you want to use some euphemism.* No wonder Will had hired this woman. She was just like him. "Cosimo," Hannah went on, "I know you've worked with Felix for many years, you have an enduring personal relationship. I believe the news would be better coming from you than from me."

Silence. Gabby couldn't bear to look at her father's face. *Felix. This bitch is firing Felix.* Even worse. She wanted Gabby's father to fire him so she wouldn't have to do the dirty work herself.

Gabby found her voice. "Felix has been here for twenty-five years. Ever since Mr. Winsted founded Suncrest. Just like my father, he's a good part of the reason this winery has been so successful, and that it now presents such an opportunity for *you.*" Gabby paused to take a breath, noted the fierce light in Hannah's dark eyes, but did not let it stop her. "There is not a single vineyard manager in this valley who is better at his job, or more devoted to it, than Felix Rodríguez. It is absolutely unconscionable of you to fire him."

Hannah looked as if she might spit fire, but her voice was ice cold. "I applaud your defense of your coworker, Gabriella. It is laudable. But the fact remains that this decision has been made. It has been made," she repeated, raising her voice over Gabby's objection. "And I have done you and your father a courtesy by giving you the option of informing Felix yourself. If you would rather pass on that opportunity—"

"We have no intention—" Gabby started to say, but her father interrupted her.

"No, Gabby," he said. "I will tell Felix."

She was stunned. "Daddy . . ."

"No, Gabriella." He lay a restraining hand on her knee. She couldn't stand the stoicism on his face, in his voice, when she knew that his heart was breaking. "I think it *is* better that Felix hear this from me."

I'll call Will, she thought suddenly. *I'll make him stop this.* "All right," she told her father, and nodded at the despicable Hannah, whom she would dearly love to grind into Napa's dust with the wheels of her Jeep. "Then let's go," and she stood to leave.

When they hit the bottom of the stairs, she whipped out her cell phone. She wished she didn't, but she still knew the number by heart. "I'm calling Will," she told her father. "He's Hannah's boss, and he can tell her where to shove this idea of hers."

They went out to the pebbled path so Gabby could put the call through. But according to Will's secretary, he was unavailable. That worried her. *Maybe he's just dodging me,* she thought. *Maybe he knows about this Felix thing and that it's happening today and that I might try to get him to stop it.* "Janine," she said into the phone, "can you pull him out of his meeting? This is important."

"Gabby, I can't." She sounded apologetic. "It's the Monday partners meeting. I really can't. But it shouldn't last much longer."

"Please have him call me." She repeated her cell number on the chance that Will had burned it from his memory. Then she snapped her phone shut. "We're not doing anything till I talk to Will," she told her father. "I'm sure I can get him to stop this," she added, though she wasn't sure in the least. But there was no pride involved here. She would beg if she had to.

The sun traveled west across the sky, and still Will did not call. Gabby tried again, only to be informed by Janine that the partners meeting was over but that now Will was tied up on an international conference call. *Are you sure he knows I'm trying to reach him?* Yes, Janine was quite sure.

Shortly before five o'clock, Gabby saw Hannah corner her father. Afterwards he came to find Gabby in the barrel-aging room, looking older than she'd ever seen him. "I can't put it off," he told her. "Otherwise Hannah's going to do it. I can't let that happen. I have to talk to him, Gabby."

She couldn't stop him. She watched him hail Felix as he came in on the tractor, watched him lead the other man down the long sloped drive that led to the Trail, where they might have something like privacy.

With dread in her heart, Gabby stayed in the dark cocoon of the barrel-aging room, and through the open door spied on their two figures. She watched her father put an arm around Felix's shoulder, watched Felix pull a handkerchief out of his shirt pocket and swipe at his face. All the while she cursed Will and the troubles he had wrought, wished she could turn back time, make life go differently, just a change here and there that would keep the people she loved safe and sound and happy.

Her phone didn't ring.

She was returning it to her pocket after checking its battery one more time when she happened to look up. She frowned when she realized the picture before her had changed. Now Felix was running up the drive toward the winery. Alone. His face twisted. She looked beyond him and let out a gasp. Her father was lying crumpled on the drive, nearly at the bronze gate where the two men had been standing, but now he was in a heap, unmoving.

She raced out the door. Felix caught her halfway down the drive. He was panting, with tears on his cheeks. "He collapsed. He was telling me about my job, and then he said he felt light-headed and he collapsed. He just collapsed."

Out came her cell again as she raced with Felix toward her father, punching in the emergency digits as her feet pounded the ground. *No,* with every step, *no, no, no.*

With a plea to 911 to please hurry, she reached her father. She dropped to her knees beside his inert body and struggled to reconstruct the CPR lessons she and her mother had taken after his heart attack. Jumbled instructions crowded her mind. *Listen for his breath.* Not a whisper. *Is there any movement in his chest?* Nothing. *Feel for his pulse.* None.

Oh, my God. Gabby jerked upright. *His heart's stopped.*

At that moment her very world ceased spinning. The heart of the man who had given her life was still.

No. She clenched her jaw and stared down at him, battling to maintain some kind of grip on herself. *Give him mouth to mouth,* her training reminded her, *then do the chest compressions.* With Felix kneeling beside her, she did what she could, relieved to have something she could try. Her movements felt jerky and awkward; thoughts swooped around her brain in a delirium of fear and crazy hope. *Lay one palm on the bottom of his sternum, the other crossways on top.* One push every second. She counted off fifteen, then remembered to give him two breaths before continuing on.

The ambulance came quickly, in a jarring blur of light and sound and motion. Curious eyes watched from cars slowing on the Trail as the paramedics bent over her father, yelled questions about what had happened, ripped his shirt open and lay paddles on his chest. They gave him the electric shock, shouting at everyone to stay clear, once, twice, then again, his body arching off the ground each time with a horrible shudder.

Her cell rang. Fear, frustration, a desperate prayer to God to save her father one more time gathered in Gabby's chest as her clumsy fingers answered the call.

It was Will. She didn't wait past the first word from him but shrieked into the phone, watching the paramedics lift her father's stretcher into the ambulance. "My father's having another attack! Hannah made him fire Felix, and now he's having another attack." She couldn't stop herself from heaving the accusation that flew to her lips. "His heart stopped, and it's because of you! It's because of you," she yelled. She slammed the phone shut and scrambled inside the ambulance after her father.

As the ambulance sped toward the hospital, Gabby wedged herself into a tiny space behind the paramedics and willed her father to find the strength to survive. This was the worst possible thing that could have happened, the thing she'd been trying most to prevent. But still it had sneaked up, attacked her father like a mugger on the street.

And, oh God, what she had just said to Will. She shut her eyes. It tore at her soul, how extremely cruel she'd been to him. Somewhere in her soul she knew Will wasn't to blame for her father's condition. He'd practically saved his life once, when they were only strangers. But anger and pain and desperate hurt had made her lash out at him, the very man who meant the most to her after her father.

Out the ambulance window, the vineyards that Gabby loved rushed past in a blur of brown and green and gold.

Chapter 19

"Dammit!" Will slammed an open palm against his steering wheel. The car in front of him rolled to a stop at a yellow light, forcing Will to halt behind. All he could think as he sat pinned in Napa Valley's rush-hour traffic, stymied and nerve-racked, was that his fellow drivers on Highway 29 were conspiring to keep him from his goal. Which was Gabby and St. Helena Hospital.

And, possibly, relief. How he longed to hear that Cosimo DeLuca was all right. But relief might not come, he knew. He might well get the opposite. Tragic news. Blame. Recrimination. A lengthening, deepening of the nightmare.

After everything that had happened, now this. Another attack, Gabby had called it. But the words that had followed tore at his soul, fanned the flames of the guilt he couldn't quench. *His heart stopped, and it's because of you. It's because of you. . . .*

Was it? Will's head said no but his heart didn't allow so clear-cut an answer. Certainly the doctors would attribute this cardiac episode to Cosimo's prior condition. But Will knew better. He knew the poor man's heart was broken. Will wasn't sure where he had gone wrong anymore. He just knew that he had and that he wasn't the only one paying for it. But he couldn't go back; none of them could. What was done was truly done.

The light turned green. The white sedan ahead of him inched forward as if its tires were filled with lead. Will crawled along behind, nearly pushing into the infuriating car's bumper, willing the traffic to part in front of him.

He hadn't thought for a moment about not going to the hospital. Though he dreaded what he might find when he arrived, he'd flown out of his office as if the devil were on his heels. A few times he'd called patient information from his car phone, but all he could get out of the on-duty nurse was that Cosimo DeLuca had been admitted to urgent care. Was Will a family member? No. Even in emergencies, he had a hard time lying. And the nurse wouldn't divulge much to a man who could only claim the ill-defined role of friend of the family.

Will grimaced thinking of the phrase. In its own way, it was a lie. What kind of friend was Will to the DeLucas, really? True, he mouthed platitudes and sent flowers. But in the clutch, did he come through for them?

I protected their jobs, he told himself. But how much did that count for now? It barely registered on the cosmic scale. It would go unremarked, unrewarded, while the sin of hiring Hannah Harper, who had put Cosimo DeLuca in an untenably stressful position, would be added to the litany of his transgressions.

Maybe it deserved to be. Maybe it was unfair. Who knew anymore? And who cared? Not him. He no longer gave a flyer who got blamed for this or who got points for that. Keeping a balance sheet of good versus evil doings, which he'd spent a lot of time updating in recent weeks, was a small-minded, mean-spirited enterprise, beneath the man he tried to be. But lately he couldn't get past nursing a malevolent grudge. And for what? Did it make him happy? Did it give him intellectual satisfaction? Did it get him what he wanted? He couldn't even find an equation to weigh the importance of what he wanted against what he'd been focused on for so long.

An opening appeared in the lane to Will's left. He veered into it and sped past the stop-at-every-yellow-light sedan. Finally, finally, he was making real headway. He glanced at the digital clock on the dashboard. 6:34. Cosimo DeLuca had been at the hospital about an hour. A lot could happen in that time.

Will took a deep breath, maneuvered around another vehicle that had the gall to clog the roads by moving at the official speed limit. Gabby's voice screeched in his head. *His heart stopped. Because of you.* The accusation cut at him, chipped at his beliefs about himself. He'd felt so much pain walking away from her, yet also a sort of soothing righteousness. She'd betrayed him; therefore, he was right to leave her. He'd taken a macabre satisfaction in the cool logic of it. He'd hardened his heart and shoved aside everything that didn't fit his own neat analysis of what had transpired. Including every single word that Gabby told him.

Maybe she really had felt caught between him and her family. Maybe going to Vittorio really had been an agonizing choice. Surely if he knew one thing about this woman, it was that she was devoted to her family. Maybe she, unlike him, actually did the tough things her family needed. Maybe she, unlike him, didn't always choose for herself. Maybe she sacrificed for them, something Will had never even considered, let alone put into practice. He'd pushed her aside for reasons that now seemed so obviously wrongheaded. Yet that damage, too, might never be undone.

A few turns more, and the hospital appeared in front of him. It looked like every other such institution he'd ever seen, its sterile facade masking the turmoil within, the joys, the hopes, the dashed dreams of so many. Will screeched the car into a space and ran through the sliding front doors, doing a deal with God. He wasn't a praying man, but he was a dealmaker. If ever there was a *You give me this, I'll give you that* moment, this was it. Yet as he raced inside and headed without directions for cardiac urgent care, he knew there was only one kind of deal he was willing to strike: the kind that had no losers. Will wanted Cosimo DeLuca alive and well and Gabby willing to forgive, willing to love him again. Those were long shots, and Will didn't have much to bargain with. All he could count on were the good heart of a man he had come to admire, and the good heart of a woman he had never stopped loving.

He spied the DeLucas back where he'd seen them three long months before. They stood in a knot beside the nurse's station, Gabby, her mother, Cam, Lucia. They were deep in conversation, their heads bent close together. As he pounded toward them down the long, fluorescent-lit corridor, Gabby turned, and their eyes met. Her whole family pivoted toward him as a unit, but he could see only her face.

Which crumpled into tears as he neared her. *God, oh God, don't tell me this.* She broke away from her family and stumbled into his arms. "You came."

He almost couldn't breathe. "I had to." He searched her face. "How is he?"

"Oh, Will." She let out a choked gasp. "He's alive." Her head fell against his chest, sobs racked her. "It's amazing, I can't believe it, but he's going to be okay. The doctors say he suffered sudden death. His heart stopped. But I gave him CPR. . . ."

Will clutched Gabby as if he held salvation in his

arms. He only half processed the tale she told him. That in another time and place, her father would not have survived. Were it not for the CPR, the speed of the paramedics, the well-equipped facilities, the alignment of the stars, Cosimo DeLuca would not have been spared. But in this, he had been blessed by the fates. And by a daughter who would stop at nothing to save him.

"He's awake. We all spoke to him. There's a lot he can't remember, he may never remember." Gabby raised her brimming eyes to Will's. "Maybe that's better."

"Oh, Gabby." After this, what man couldn't hope for his own miracle? "I am so sorry," he started to say, but she shook her head and lay a trembling finger on his lips.

"So am I. But that's for later. I need to be with my family now."

She was right. More important, he understood. And he was beyond content just to hold her. Later would come; he was blessed to get it. Will shut his eyes and pulled Gabby tighter against him as the world of the hospital flowed around them, some people's dreams over, and others just beginning.

Ava led Paul Erskine, head of the moving company that bore his name, to her foyer. He paused to clasp her hand and deliver his final reassurances. "We will see to everything, Mrs. Winsted." His tone was stentorian, as befitted a man whose mission in life was to transport the irreplaceable possessions of affluent families. "My crew will be here the morning of the twentieth at eight o'clock."

"Thank you, Paul." Then he was gone, off to climb in his Mercedes-Benz, and Ava was once again alone in the home she no longer owned, but had sold along with Suncrest to GPG.

One week more she would live in this house. She strolled to the French doors in the living room, open to admit the September evening. The day's hot air was softening as the hour melted toward twilight. The sky above the rolling crest of the Mayacamas glowed pink as a peony, while close at hand the grapevines beyond the mesh fence huddled in endless, undulating rows. Here and there an olive tree punctuated the horizon like nature's exclamation point.

Ava was not a sentimental woman, but still tears gathered in her eyes. If Porter had lived, this glorious valley would have remained the stage of her life. But Porter had not lived. Her role as his wife was over. And it was long past time for her to find a new script to memorize.

She went to the kitchen to pour a glass of sauvignon blanc, then repaired to a white wicker chair on the flagstone terrace between the residence and the pool. She would miss Napa Valley. It amazed her that it had been her home for thirty years. How accidental life was, how it could turn on a chance meeting, a haphazard introduction, a stray idea. If she had married a man other than Porter, she might have made her home in Minneapolis or Houston or New York or London. And if Porter hadn't been possessed by the urge to found a winery, she never would have found herself uprooted from Southern California and transplanted here.

Yet life flowed in a circle, too, didn't it? For now she would return to Bel Air, where she had history and friends and a precedent for starting over. True, she'd been much younger the first time she went to Los Angeles to seek her fame and fortune. But thanks to Porter, the latter half of her quest had already been most tidily achieved.

Ava watched a leaf from a nearby oak tree flutter into the pool, setting off a ripple soft as a baby's breath across the water's surface. She owed so much to Porter. That was another reason she couldn't bear to stay in the valley. Though she couldn't even fathom how wounded he would be to see how Suncrest was changing, she felt the pain of it herself. She knew how her husband had strived for excellence, perfection even. What the new owners would do, she didn't know, but was sure Porter's lofty goals were not on their agenda.

Still, she told herself, she couldn't live her life fulfilling the dreams Porter had run out of time for. She had her own life to live.

The phrase brought a wan smile to Ava's face. She had received a call a few days earlier from one of the Hollywood contacts she'd assiduously maintained over the years—under the guise of friendship, of course. Once the conversation had wound its way through the pleasantries, he had asked if she would consider a role in daytime television. Apparently a long-running soap had an opening for a woman of her age, as the love interest of a beloved male character who had been widowed. Ava thought the role had potential, as she happened to know that the body of the character's wife had been found, identified, and duly buried, precluding her shocking reappearance in a ratings-grabber a few months down the road.

Why, yes, Ava had said, *I am interested.* She'd been so delighted by the prospect of call times and rehearsals and wardrobe fittings and the sheer joy of being once again under the klieg lights that she chose to ignore how much of a comedown a soap role would be from her former career. Pragmatic Ava knew that beggars could not be choosers, particularly at her age and particularly in Hollywood.

She wondered if her son would ever learn any part of that lesson. There was no question that Max had a sense of entitlement. She couldn't help but think she must have given it to him. He was so flawed, it amazed and sometimes revolted her. But still he was her son, and she loved him. She was proud of herself for not having succumbed to his importunings for more cash. For once she had stood firm, not let guilt over her bad mothering drive her. Certainly she had felt his rage and frustration, but she knew he would get past it. She also knew he recognized that they were the only two Winsteds left in the world. That would mean something to him.

Ultimately, she would protect him, of course. In the end he would inherit quite a bit from her, because much as she liked to live well, Ava's native caution kept her from excess.

She sighed, sipped from her wineglass. It was true that some lessons were very difficult for a mother to teach. She had to stand by and watch, pained and helpless, as her baby either flew or stumbled. And pray that should it be the latter, he would fall neither too hard nor too far.

Mrs. Finchley appeared beside Ava's chair. "You have a call, madam, from Mr. Boursault."

"Jean-Luc? At this hour?" It was past four in the morning in Paris. More than a little curious, Ava followed Mrs. Finchley inside. Ava had been relieved to learn that the faithful housekeeper had been unfazed at the notion of accompanying her employer to Bel Air. Ava thought that if she had asked Mrs. Finchley to move to Timbuktu, the woman would have procured a pith helmet and shown up ready to decamp at the appointed hour.

Ava took the call in the kitchen while Mrs. Finchley discreetly busied herself in another part of the house. "Jean-Luc? *Comment ça va?*"

"*Ça va très bien.*" Then he made a point of adding, "Thank you for taking my call, Ava."

A touch of sarcasm there, she noted. "Isn't this an odd time for you to be on the telephone?" She frowned. Was that a horn she heard in the background? Could he be driving at this hour?

"Well, actually, I'm in Los Angeles. So it is not so very late."

"Ah." How odd that he had come to California and not bothered to alert her. Ava, who had delivered her share of slights over the years, recognized a definite snub. "Is this trip business or pleasure?" she asked, rhetorically, because she knew it had to be the latter. Jean-Luc knew no one in L.A.

"Business," he said. Her brows flew up. "I have come to finalize my movie deal. In fact, we inked the contracts today. The script is revised, and I have found producers with ready cash all set to go forward. So you see, the film will be made. I believe that you will read about it in the trades."

Ava could not have been more stunned if Jean-Luc had declared that he had been elected president of France. "Well! Congratulations." She couldn't think what to say next, for she had a strong inkling that her role in this resuscitated endeavor had evaporated like the bubbles in uncorked champagne. "I'm so happy for you, Jean-Luc. And I am not in the least surprised that you have succeeded in this endeavor."

He chuckled as if he didn't quite believe that last sentiment. "Well, Ava, perhaps if you were not so busy with other projects, we might have worked together again. But alas. Ah, please excuse me for a moment." Then he broke away from the call to speak to someone. He was giving directions to a driver, she realized. The likelihood that Jean-Luc was being ferried about Hollywood in a limousine only added to her sense of insult.

He came back on the line. "Ava, I'm sorry, but I

must go. *Au revoir*," and before she could utter a
word, he had hung up, leaving her fit to be tied holding a dead receiver in her hand.

Ava replaced it without a slam, never one to let
anger or any other emotion carry her—unless the role
demanded it. With an effort, she calmed down, refusing to think how humiliating it was that she would be
performing a small role in a soap opera while Jean-
Luc was directing his cinematic chef d'oeuvre. But by
the time she returned to her wicker chair and her
wineglass, she was once again sanguine.

No matter, she told herself. *If that is the sort of
friend Jean-Luc is, it is better that I find out now, rather
than waste another fifteen years of friendship on him.*
She sniffed, and set all thought of the Frenchman
aside. She hadn't intended to include him in her new
life, anyway.

In the dim light of a nighttime ward, Gabby lingered
at her father's bedside, the rest of the family gone
home for the night. He dozed while she held his hand
and halfheartedly watched the television mounted to
the wall across from his bed. The eleven-o'clock news
was on, the usual recitation of tragedies followed by
sports and weather. Even with the volume so low she
could barely hear it, she had a pretty good idea what
was going on. Nothing earth-shattering in the great
wide world, though the headlines in her own personal
universe were four inches tall. FATHER SURVIVES.
LOVER BEGS FORGIVENESS. WOMAN GETS NEW LEASE
ON LIFE.

Her father stirred, emitted a little snort, settled back
into slumber. Gabby smiled to herself, squeezed his
hand. He was attached by various tubes to equipment
that beeped and gurgled and read out an astonishing
digital array of numbers and charts, but apart from
that he looked very close to normal. His color was

good; his breathing was regular. Even more amazing, his heart—the very heart that had stopped beating—once again pounded a steady rhythm.

Sudden cardiac arrest, they called it, or more frighteningly, *sudden death*. Not a heart attack, but the most feared complication of the one he had suffered three months before. If she hadn't performed CPR, if the paramedics hadn't been so fast . . . She hated even to think about it. But thank heavens she didn't need to.

The next day the doctors would give him a defibrillator, in what they described as minor surgery. Most likely he could go home the day after. Simple as that. She was sure he'd have a list of shoulds and should nots, but there was every reason to believe the long-term effects from this harrowing event would be minimal.

She punched the power button on the remote control, and the room slipped deeper into shadow. Two nurses in soft shoes and pink cotton uniforms padded down the corridor past the half-open door, giggling to each other and weaving around a wizened old woman in a frayed robe laboriously pushing a walker. Somewhere a call button buzzed; a male patient hollered for a nurse.

The hospital was as Will had described it months before: a world unto itself that you didn't think about until it was your world, and then it was all-encompassing. It held your dreams and your hopes; you could barely function outside until the life-and-death questions it held within its institutional walls were answered.

Had she gotten a different answer from Will that day? *I had to come,* he told her. *I am so sorry.* She believed him. She'd seen the genuineness of the apology in his eyes; she'd felt it in the way he held her. Was that enough? She knew she loved him—that had never stopped. She also knew she had betrayed him when she went to Vittorio. She had faulted him not for being angry with her, not even for not understanding, but for not *trying* to. Was he trying now? And would that be enough to bridge the differences between them?

That question, too, would be answered soon. She had put off their own moment of truth-telling, but like any hour of reckoning, it was approaching.

Her father fidgeted, drew her back into the present. "Daddy?" She rose from her seat, bent over him. "Are you awake?"

His eyes fluttered open, focused on her face. "Gabby." His voice was hoarse.

"Are you thirsty?" She was already handing him a little cup of water. He sipped, fell back against the pillows. "How are you feeling?"

He seemed to think about that. "Groggy. Not too bad." He frowned. "Shouldn't you be at home in bed? What time is it?"

"Almost midnight. I just wanted to make sure . . ." Her voice left her at the same moment that he found his.

He took her hand and squeezed it. "I'll be fine, Gabby. I'm in good hands here. You should get some sleep. Your mornings start early."

At dawn, but so did his. That was the winemaker's life. "I'll go home soon. Let me just sit for a while."

She returned to her plastic bedside chair. The big round white-faced clock on the wall, the kind found in high school gyms and community centers, ticked away the seconds of the night. Around their private cocoon of father and daughter, other people slept, and still others held vigil.

After a time he spoke. "I can't remember what happened today."

She remembered all too well. "Let's talk about that another time."

"Did something bad happen at work?" He gave a

weak laugh. "Something else bad?" When she said nothing, he spoke again. "Gabby, I think I might want to leave Suncrest."

She turned to look at his face. It was funny how often truths came out at night. Maybe weariness and shadows made some realities easier to face. "Really?"

"Would that upset you? What with Will there . . ." His voice trailed off. "I don't want to leave you, or him, in a lurch."

"Oh, Daddy." What a fine heart her father had, despite all its troubles. "You wouldn't be doing that. And besides, you need to do what would be best for you."

He nodded. "I hate to say it, but I think leaving would be best for me."

She watched him, heard the regret in his voice, saw the sadness in his eyes. All those years he'd spent at Suncrest, and now it had come to this. But maybe sometimes it was wise to walk away. Maybe it wasn't always surrender.

"I've been thinking about it, even before today." He grimaced as he resettled himself on the thin hospital mattress. Her heart ached to imagine how much pain he must be in, despite his "not too bad" demurral. "Part of what's been keeping me there is Porter. Of course, the rest of it is you and Felix and Cam and everybody else. But Porter . . ." He shook his head. "I hate to see what's happening to what he built. He loved that winery, Gabby."

"I know, Daddy. But there's nothing we can do about it anymore." In fact, she hadn't been able to do much even when she'd tried.

"Porter Winsted was about my age when he founded Suncrest," he said. "Maybe a few years younger. I always envied him that."

Gabby was surprised. "I never knew you wanted to start your own label."

"It was always a pipe dream of mine." His eyes moved to hers. "A label for the DeLucas. A fantasy, you'd have to call it."

What a fantasy. To craft a wine just as you wanted it, to make your own decisions about the grapes with no interference from anyone else, the almost unimaginable pride of seeing your own name on the label. Yet it was an extremely expensive fantasy, which is why Gabby had never allowed herself to nurture it. "How do you feel about going to work for somebody else?"

He shrugged, then smiled. "I don't have much choice, Gabby. I can't retire yet. It won't be easy, though, to convince a winery to take on an old man with a heart problem."

"That is not true." She said that louder than she'd intended, maybe to convince herself as well as him. She lowered her voice back to a half-whisper. "People in the valley know you're a terrific winemaker. And you have lots of friends. And despite all this"—she waved her arm to take in the expanse of the bed and high-tech cardiac equipment—"you're still okay."

He arched his brows as if to remark that even that analysis was an overstatement. Then his eyes fluttered partway shut, and Gabby realized she should take her leave, let him sleep.

"Good night, Daddy." She bent forward, kissed his brow, tears rushing anew to her eyes, though now it was joy she cried for. How lucky she was, how very lucky. She would always love the valley, she would always have a place in her heart for Suncrest, but it wasn't flesh and blood and bone, in the end it wasn't what really mattered.

She exited the hospital into the cool, cloudless Napa Valley night, where love and home were, and always would be.

Chapter 20

Will hadn't slept well. Now, on a Saturday morning before dawn, he stood in the kitchen of his Pacific Heights Victorian spooning ground coffee into a drip coffeemaker and mentally replaying the scene from the night before.

As if they were frames in a reel of film, images rose in his mind. Beth, standing in his living room after a hell-bent flight from Denver. Trying not to cry, not always succeeding. Her words the last ones Will wanted to hear. *Bob's taken a job in Philadelphia. He's already there. He wants us to join him as soon as we can.*

Will had hated himself for what he'd wished for. How selfish could a brother be? Did he ever put anybody but himself front and center? *What are you going to do?* he'd asked her, knowing the answer he wanted to hear even as he despised himself for it.

We're going, she'd said. *Bzzz!* the wrong-answer buzzer sounded in Will's brain. *You mean you're not going,* he wanted to say. *You can't go because you have to stay in Denver to run Henley Sand and Gravel.*

And why? Because big important Harvard Business School graduate and GPG partner Will Henley didn't want to take on the task. And he was the only other heir. He'd had some nerve criticizing Max Winsted for not appreciating the incredible legacy he'd been handed. Because for years Will had been doing the exact same thing.

He paced the hardwood floor between the center island and the counter. Lights switching on in the Victorian next door caught his attention, prompted him to look out his window into his neighbor's kitchen, one floor down and perhaps fifteen yards away across their shared alley. He could eye the goings-on through both sets of rectangular glass, an easy-to-see tableau in the blackness of this predawn hour. A man was making coffee, like Will was, a man a few years older and equally bedraggled. A boy, maybe ten, the man's son no doubt, spun into the kitchen fully outfitted in a Little League baseball uniform, the cap on, the shoes laced. He was tossing the hardball repeatedly into his mitt as if to warm up.

Will smiled. The boy looked excited, fully awake, ready to go—*Come on, Dad! We're gonna be late!* Probably he had an out-of-town game several hours' drive away and was counting on Dad to get him there. The boy's father nodded, produced a sleepy smile, concentrated on making the coffee Will knew he hoped would wake him up.

As clearly as if there were a cartoon bubble over the man's head spelling out his thoughts, Will could guess what he was thinking. *Christ, I wish I could sleep in. I killed myself at work this week. Now I've got to do three hours out and three hours back and five hours of kiddie baseball in between.*

But it was equally clear that the father would make the trip. He'd slap water on his face and pull on his jeans and grab some to-go coffee and get in the SUV and drive. And why? Because it was his son, and families did things for each other, whether they always wanted to or not. That was how it worked. That was the trade. Sometimes one person made the sacrifice and sometimes the other did, and it pretty much evened out in the end. Or it evened out close enough, because Will had learned lately it was a bad idea to try to keep a balance sheet.

Will tried to think how often he saw his father. Twice a year? On visits that ended too fast and were too falsely separated from "real" life. Will couldn't fault his brother-in-law, Bob, not really, for wanting to be near his family in Philly again after so many years of living half a continent away. His parents were getting older, and he was worried there wasn't that much time left. There was a lot of sense to what Bob was doing. There was a lot of sense to what Beth was doing, too. Which was more than Will could always say about his own life.

His sister came into the kitchen just as the coffee finished coming down. "Did you sleep okay?" he asked her.

She rolled her eyes, accepted a mug.

"I slept all right. How about you?"

"I spent a lot of time staring at the ceiling."

She shook her head. "I'm sorry about all this."

"No." He touched her arm. "You have nothing to be sorry for. I understand what you're doing, and it's the right thing," he added, giving himself a few points for being—even briefly and belatedly—magnanimous. "And besides, you've been running Henley S and G for years now. I don't know why this is so hard for me. It really shouldn't be."

"Well." She moved to sit on one of the two bar stools at the end of the center island. As Will went to join her, he noticed that the father next door swung into his kitchen, dressed and combed, to grab his car keys and switch off the lights. "It's your whole life, Will. It's leaving your job *and* San Francisco."

And Gabby, too. Beth didn't even know that part.

"It's also running Henley S and G," she went on, "which you've never wanted to do."

"It's not that I never wanted to," he said, then stopped.

But knowing him too well, his sister chuckled and picked up where he'd left off. "Okay, you didn't want to once you realized how humdrum it is."

He drank from his mug, set it down. "I had an idea last night."

"What's that?"

"There may be a way to use GPG to make Henley S and G a bigger enterprise. I could imagine them making an investment, ramping the company up, giving it a bigger platform. Expanding beyond the mountain states, taking on some of the larger players that the company's never really challenged before."

Will saw Beth's face light up. He was reminded, once again, how relieved Beth would be if he took over. She could feel confident that she was leaving the family company in good hands, and could move with a clear conscience to Philadelphia.

"You love this stuff, don't you?" she asked him. "Taking businesses and growing them. You actually like it a lot more than I do."

"A lot I do like. A lot I don't. The politics. The dog eat dog."

"There must be a lot of that at GPG."

"You don't know the half of it." Ironically, this would be a good time for Will to quit. He'd leave on a high, after having just scored a deal that everyone judged a big winner. Who knew when that would happen next, if ever? "Funny enough, I've been thinking lately about running my own show. I did a deal in the wine country, bought a family business, and learned a lot about the man who founded it. I don't know." He shook his head. "It gave me something to think about."

They were silent for a time. Shapes began to emerge from the shadows outside the windows. Will heard the stray birdcall. Slowly, gently, the day was dawning.

Beth spoke. "Wasn't there a woman in the wine country?"

Will shut his eyes. Yes, there was a woman. He hadn't known her long, not really, but she loomed large in every part of his life, his past, his present, his future.

"Are you serious about her?" Beth asked.

It took him a while to answer. "Very serious. But I couldn't ask her to leave Napa Valley."

"Why not?"

"Well, she's a winemaker for one thing. There's no winemaking in Denver."

"She could come up with something else to do. I'll have to."

He shook his head. "You can't begin to understand how much she loves it there, Beth. She's lived there all her life. Her family's there."

"So what? I've lived in Denver my whole life and my family's there and now I'm moving to Philadelphia."

It wasn't as simple as that. Now Gabby's father had serious heart problems. She wouldn't leave him. And Napa dirt flowed in her veins. If ever there was a woman tied to a place, it was Gabby to Napa Valley. It was Tara to her, Eden, the soil of her birth and the dust of her death. There was no taking Gabby out of Napa. Will understood that, even if his sister didn't.

Briefly, he shut his eyes. It was Gabby who had taught him about loyalty to family, Gabby who showed him how high the cost of that loyalty might be. If it weren't for her, he wouldn't have learned his lesson nearly so well.

Beth sighed. "I know I said it before, but I'm really sorry I'm putting you in this position, Will. I just wish there were an easy way out."

That brought a wry smile to Will's face. If only.

A job, a job, a job. Max exited the salon where he'd just had a massage and paused on the sun-baked sidewalk to put on his shades. Muscles relaxed, pleasantly drowsy, he raked a hand through his hair, damp after his shower, then meandered north in the direction of the restaurant where he was meeting Claudia Landower for lunch.

A job, a job, a job. Problem One was that he didn't know what he wanted to do. Problem Two was that he didn't really want to do anything. It had occurred to him that maybe, when he'd been running Suncrest, he hadn't fully appreciated the benefits of being his own boss. Not having anyone to report to, not having to show up or leave at an appointed hour, not having to keep somebody else happy to retain his employment. All of those struck him as fairly major pains in the ass. And they would all become regular irritants unless he came up with an inventive way to make money on his own.

That is, if he really had to. On some level, he still wasn't convinced he did. He had to think there was a good chance that his mother would cave, throw another five mil at him. He just could not believe that when it came right down to it, she'd out-and-out screw him. So, to the end of winning her over, he'd reinstated his charming-as-can-be strategy. Hey, it'd worked before.

Max ambled on, glancing at an oil landscape in the window of an art gallery, one of the many that could be found even here in the northernmost reaches of Napa Valley. Calistoga was a lot less chichi than St. Helena—it had more the look of a Western frontier town—but still it had its share of upscale establishments selling art, clothes, jewelry, and food. It had a few good restaurants, too, and the Wappo Grill, where he was meeting Claudia Landower, was one of them.

His mother was making him do this lunch, though he was already bored to tears and it hadn't even started yet. It had come about because of his forced donation to a nature-conservancy group. Apparently the one his mom had picked was a favorite of the Landower Foundation, and it was just his luck that a family member involved in the charity stuff happened to be in Northern California and wanted to thank him personally.

Great. He could just picture Claudia Landower— some blue-hair who'd be as entertaining as fruitcake. The Landowers were as rich as the Rockefellers, but that didn't mean they were interesting. So he'd opted for lunch over dinner, figuring it was less likely to drag out. And there was no way he was picking up the bill.

Man. He hated having to think about money, but now it was on his mind constantly. He'd started paying rent for a bungalow in St. Helena, since in two days he had to vacate the house. The bungalow was nice and all, but it didn't have a pool or a Mrs. Finchley. For sure he'd have to hire someone. He certainly wasn't going to clean, or do laundry, or cook, or shlep around his dry cleaning.

The Wappo Grill was housed in a bungalow, too, of the yellow clapboard type. On a day like this, people were eating in the redbrick courtyard, sitting around the fountain at little tables draped with blue-and-white gingham tablecloths. A trellis shaded the whole area so the diners wouldn't pass out from heat stroke.

"Your guest is already here," the waitress informed Max, and led him to a table occupied by a woman about a third of the age he'd been expecting.

She didn't stand, but her scrubbed, preppy face lit up as she held out her hand. "Max, I'm so delighted to meet you!"

Max shook her hand. "Hello, Claudia. The pleasure is mine." Then he sat down, trying to remember why he'd been so sure that Claudia Landower would be a geriatric patient. No good reason, he realized, just an assumption that the younger members of the family wouldn't bother themselves with the foundation.

"It's *such* good luck that I happened to be in San Francisco when I heard about your donation." This was one cheerful woman. She didn't stop smiling. She was wearing khakis and a pink polo shirt and had a ribbon tying back her long blond hair. She seemed no-nonsense and outdoorsy. "It's so generous of you, and quite sensitive," she added, "after the fire at your own vineyards."

"Oh. Well." Max tried to look modest, never his strong suit. Funny, wasn't that exactly what his mother had predicted people would say? He remembered something else she'd told him: *You don't care nearly enough how people think of you.* Well, maybe he'd take a page from his mother's book and try to give Claudia here a positive impression of him.

He set his elbows on the gingham and leaned closer to her. "My family has always been deeply interested in conservation," he said. "In fact, had we not sold Suncrest, I was considering a move toward organic farming in our vineyards."

"Were you *really*? I am *such* a believer in organic agriculture." She leaned closer, too. "Any chance you're into animal husbandry, too?"

Animal husbandry. He had no idea even what that was. "Yes," he heard himself say, "I love animals. The bigger, the better."

"I love animals, too. Horses and dogs and sheep and goats and . . . Do you ride?"

"Yes," he declared, "yes, I do. Love to ride."

"What other sports do you like?"

He tried to think what would be the right sports to like. "Golf," he managed, "sailing, lacrosse"—which he'd toyed with in college, without much success— "and tennis, of course."

"Skiing?" she demanded. "Downhill or cross-country?"

"Both?" he wondered aloud.

She smiled. Apparently he'd passed muster. "Shall we order?"

Obediently he picked up his menu. Claudia was clearly a take-charge kind of gal. One other thing was for sure: she didn't just believe in sports and organic agriculture, she believed in food. He didn't know how long he'd kept her waiting, but she'd put an impressive dent in the bread basket and sucked down all of a large iced tea. Then she confirmed his opinion of a healthy appetite by ordering a steak sandwich.

Over the meal, he asked a million and one questions about the foundation, what she did there, what she liked and didn't, blah blah blah. She was a bit of a Plain Jane, but she was easy to talk to.

"So, Max." She swiped her last french fry through the puddle of ketchup on her plate. "Now that your family has sold its winery, have you decided what you're going to do next?"

He hadn't the foggiest idea but guessed his companion would disapprove of a lack of direction in life. "Well, I'm considering a number of options." He assumed a solemn expression. "I do know that I'd like to give something back. I've been so blessed, and surely there is nothing as rewarding as what you're doing, Claudia. Helping others less fortunate than yourself."

"That is *so, so* true." She fell back in her chair and stared at him. Then, "You know, Max, it just so happens that we're looking to expand the leadership team at the Landower Foundation. Have you ever considered a career in philanthropy?"

It was safe to say he had not. Max set down his fork, as if a matter of such gravitas could not be discussed while eating. He had to think philanthropy was one of the most boring occupations out there. But then again, compared with other jobs, it might not be half bad. He couldn't imagine it would be too strenuous to hand out money, and it probably would involve lots of being wined and dined by all the people who wanted a handout. And he'd be a personage of some importance, because anybody who had millions of dollars to give away automatically was.

"It's a fascinating idea," he told Claudia.

Her face lit up. "Next time you're in Chicago, you'll have to come riding with me at our family farm on the North Shore."

A farm on the North Shore. Max knew there were some serious mansions there, but he'd never heard of a farm. "I'd love to," he told her, knowing he'd have to take lessons first so he wouldn't fall off the damn horse.

"We have stables there, and I've been riding since I was three. I go every weekend I can get away. I love my apartment in the city. . . . Did I tell you I have a penthouse on Lake Shore Drive, near the foundation offices? But I still like to get out to the country as often as possible."

Max nodded encouragingly, beginning to take a new interest in Claudia's chatter.

"It's got just wonderful views, the penthouse, I mean," she went on. "And of course I always ride whenever I can get down to the ranch in Kentucky. We breed thoroughbreds there, you know."

No, Max hadn't known. But now he was glad he did. He was getting quite a picture of Claudia Landower, with her stables and her farm and her penthouse and her ranch. He did a quick assessment of her face and figure and judged her to be in her early thirties. And still with no ornamentation on that all-important left-hand ring finger.

He cleared his throat, pretended to be casual. "And does your husband like to ride, too?"

She looked away. "Actually, I'm not married."

He feigned surprise, then arched his brows as if this revelation were of profound interest to him. Actually, it was. "Well." He smiled at her. "That's hard to believe. But interesting to know."

She smiled back. Then the moment passed, and they began to chat about ordering dessert, busying themselves with a topic that had nothing to do with the one each was secretly mulling.

For his part, Max was trying to imagine life with this woman and an assortment of large farm animals. And big-boned, athletic children with names like Biff and Muffy.

There were worse fates, he told himself. He could imagine weekdays in the city, weekends in the country, Landowers gathering for black-tie foundation dinners and cross-country ski trips and barbecues and pickup football games, sort of like the Kennedys. He would be a son-in-law, a secure, enviable position, particularly once he sired a few members of the next generation. And he had nothing against the Midwest; he could get used to the cold. Plus, it wasn't like he'd have to *shovel*.

He gave Claudia a conspiratorial wink when he caught her glancing at him. She blushed slightly, looked away. She wasn't bad. Attractive enough. A nice girl. Easy to talk to, relaxing to be with. Older than him, so likely to be grateful. He could do what had to be done. Plus, after a few kids, she probably wouldn't want to anymore anyway.

He could do what British women were told to do in Victorian times: *Close your eyes, and think of England.*

Max could manage that. He'd just think of his bank account.

On Saturday evening, Gabby was alone in the old winery building hosing down the floor around the fermentation tanks, when she looked up and saw Will watching her. She'd had no warning that he would come by and hadn't heard his footsteps over the noise of the jetting water. He suddenly appeared, not smiling, not frowning, just watching.

"Hi," he said.

"Hi." She turned off the hose and listened to the water gurgle into the drain gulley that ran the length of the concrete floor. She was keenly aware of what a sorry spectacle she must make in her shorts and wading boots, her T-shirt speckled with baby cab stains and her hair in a sloppy knot on top of her head. Will wore jeans and a casual shirt with the sleeves rolled up, and looked clean and healthy and strong. *Maybe tired*, she thought, assessing him, her heart clenching as it always did when she saw him after an absence.

"Saturday night and here you are." He smiled. "Do you work constantly?"

"Now *there's* the pot calling the kettle black." She busied herself with arranging the hose in a neatish circular pile. *Is it my imagination or are we awkward with each other?* Maybe that wasn't so odd. So much had happened; they'd each been so angry and so hurt. There was bound to be tension.

Especially now at our moment of reckoning. For that was what this was, and they both knew it.

Gabby ran out of things to do with the hose and so was forced to look at him again. She noticed he was holding a wine bottle and cocked her chin at it. "What's that?"

He glanced at the label. "Suncrest's 1987 Cabernet Sauvignon. Ava gave it to me. She told me it was Porter's favorite vintage."

"That was nice of her." Gabby knew there weren't many of those bottles left.

Will held it out in Gabby's direction. "I'd like you to have it."

Her arm failed to reach out. She didn't want to take it. Somehow it seemed too much like a parting gift. But there he was holding the bottle toward her, and what else could she do? She moved forward and relieved him of it and then stepped back again, looking at everything but his face. But she couldn't make her ears stop hearing what he next had to say.

"We should talk, Gabby."

There it was again, the unmistakable, hollow ring of finality. "We should," she heard herself agree, though deep in her soul she wished she could turn this scenario on its head and make it unfold in the way she had hoped for. She had dreamily imagined something quite different from this odd scene with its disconcerting last-time quality.

"Is there a place here at the winery you particularly like?" he asked.

That surprised her, too. "You don't want to talk here?"

He hesitated, then, "Not really."

Too many bad memories maybe, of misunderstandings and bruised feelings. They'd had a lot of those. *Maybe too many.* She tried to think. "There's the barrel-aging room. That's always been a favorite of mine."

"Is that where dinner was served the night of the homecoming party?"

She nodded. *The night we met.* She read the same recollection in his eyes and had the fleeting idea that they were moving in a circle.

He took her hand, and they walked there in silence, claiming two moth-eaten director's chairs. In the semi-darkness, surrounded by the two-hundred-year-old sandstone walls and dozens of French oak barrels, they sat and stilled, held in that pregnant quiet that only very old buildings can produce, as if some essence of all those who had passed through before lingered in the air.

He cleared his throat. "I want to apologize to you, Gabby. I've been really unfair. I accused you of betraying me, but the fact is that I wasn't always straight with you. I knew I was going after Suncrest, but I let you believe I wasn't. I didn't out-and-out lie, but I might as well have. I was just so intent on getting Suncrest. Then I went a long time refusing to take you at your word. I know now that you were telling me the truth about why you went to Vittorio." He shook his head. "Maybe back then I couldn't recognize the truth."

"Oh, Will." She touched his arm, but he didn't look at her. "I feel like I did betray you when I went to Vittorio. I don't blame you for being angry with me. But it seemed there was nothing else I could do."

Their eyes met. She gazed into the ocean-blue depths of his and found not a shred of the bastard in them.

"I understand now that you were only doing what you had to do," he told her. "I wish I'd understood it earlier, your love for this place. And what it's always meant to your family."

She forgave him everything. She cared not one whit about the mistakes they'd made, his and hers both, the real and supposed betrayals. She knew that at heart he was a good man, and she loved him, and now she cared only for what they might do right if they had the chance.

Yet something was off. This was the time for him to take her in his arms, for all to be made right again. But instead he looked away, rose abruptly.

She frowned, staring at this back. "What's wrong?"

Time swelled, lengthened into an eternity while she spun nightmarish scenarios in her mind. Still he faced away from her. Still he said nothing.

Then, "There's something I need to tell you," and he began to relate a story that transported her back to a slice of her history she would rather forget, her history with another man, in another country, and another life. *I can't marry you, Gabriella*, that other man had said. *I have to do what's right for my family. I'm sorry, so sorry, so sorry. . . .*

Now words she could never have imagined she would hear again came spewing out of Will's mouth, stories of his family's company and what they wanted him to do and how for years he had worried he'd shirked his responsibilities to them. How his sister had flown out from Denver to talk to him about it. How the timing was so uncanny, because he'd been thinking lately about doing something on his own. Gabby knew it was Napa Valley outside the old sandstone walls but it might as well have been Tuscany. One land exchanged for the other but still the same sad tale.

She couldn't look at him anymore. She felt sick. She had to get away. He was still speaking to her, but she couldn't bear to hear anymore. She rose and made for the door.

"Gabby."

She was nearly out of the barrel-aging room when he grabbed on to her arm, held her back. "You don't understand."

"I understand only too well."

"I don't think so." He turned her around, grasped

her by both shoulders. "I'm not going to do what Vittorio did."

"You don't even know what Vittorio did."

"I can guess." His eyes bored into hers. "I'm not going to Denver, Gabby. I'll find somebody else to run the company." He gave a little laugh. "After all these years with GPG, that's something I'm good at."

She was confused. "But what about your family? What did I just hear you say?"

"You heard me say I feel an obligation to them. And I'll fulfill it, in my own way. But I won't put that obligation over you, Gabby. And I don't feel it's right to ask you to move to Denver, to give up your whole life here. I won't do it."

She shook her head. "But you talked about doing something on your own."

"Not quite on my own." He led her back to the ratty director's chairs, made her sit again. "With you. Let's start a winery."

She couldn't speak. That was so far from her craziest imaginings, she hadn't a thing to say to him.

"Why not?" He laughed again. "I know you don't want to stay at Suncrest. I'm sure your father doesn't. One thing I have from GPG is my own capital to invest. Yes, we'd need to start small, smaller than Suncrest was at the beginning. But we could do it."

Her father's words stampeded into her brain. *It was always a pipe dream of mine. A label for the DeLucas. A fantasy, you'd have to call it.* She looked into Will's eyes, as true and blue as Napa's sky. "You'd give up GPG for this? A little fledgling winery?"

"Well, I'm hoping it wouldn't be fledgling forever." He laughed. "And as far as GPG goes, I'd miss some of the excitement, sure. But I've thought a lot lately about where I'd like my life to go, and I know I don't want to work for somebody else forever. Porter

Winsted made me think about that." His eyes grew more serious. "You, too."

"But how could we be business partners? There's so much we disagree about."

"There's a lot we agree on, too. We'd have to figure out in the beginning just what kind of winery we were shooting for, but I think if we both moved a bit from where we are now, we'd find common ground."

She thought about that. "I'd like my father to be in, too, though he probably wouldn't want to be full-time." This might be perfect for him, she realized. He would enjoy part ownership and yet have the flexibility no other winery would give him.

She took a deep breath. What a responsibility this would be, as well as a joy. To be not just an employee but an employer, as well, with all the burdens that entailed. To take full ownership of the wine she made, the good vintages and the less good.

"I hope your father will join us. I'd want his expertise." Will crossed his arms over his chest. "You have to know, Gabby, that if we did this, it would be serious business. Neither one of us would be satisfied with a two-bit operation. I'd want to grow it, make it something important. You make the wine, with your dad if you want to, and I handle the business end. I think we could make it work."

Maybe they could bring in Felix, too. If they bought land, they'd need a manager for the vineyards. Her mind was reeling. "It's so much to think about. . . ." She stood up. "I have to let it sink in. I have to think it through."

He rose as well, and bundled her into his arms. He whispered into her hair. "I missed you, Gabby. I don't want to be apart from you again. That was the worst mistake I made." His lips slashed against her cheek and found her mouth, and the kiss he gave her was gentle and urgent both. Then he pulled away, and on the uneven dirt floor stained with centuries of wine, he got down on one knee.

Gabby's hands flew to her face, her heart leaping in a dance she'd never once practiced. Now the picture truly changed. She'd never before seen these frames of film. It was a sad movie no longer, but still it brought tears to her eyes.

"I love you, Gabby. Marry me."

He pulled a little black velvet box out of his jeans pocket. She could have hit him for hiding it from her so cunningly, but so he had. Maybe he was a magician, her Will, appearing at just the right moment to make dreams come true.

The diamond inside the little box sparkled bright, like the sun in Napa mornings and the light in a baby's eyes.

"Say yes."

There was a new light in Will's eyes, too, born of truth and promise and so many of the good things she'd once stopped hoping for. Love wasn't free. She had paid for this moment with the pain of the past. She had paid with Vittorio. She had paid with Suncrest. Yet she would do it all again.

Her answer came without volition, from an unscarred place in her heart that had always been waiting for just this man and just this moment. "I would love to marry you, Will Henley."

He laughed and rose again to his full height and wrapped her in his arms. They clung together in an age-old room that had seen lovers before, had heard their stories, all in their own way blessed and cursed, all with their own zigzag road to travel. And this was the way it was meant to be, when love came down from the heavens and shone its light into the shadows and took its lucky lovers on a blessed flight.

The .ring slipped on her finger, like the circle she

had traveled. Vittorio had wished her a man who loved her with all his heart, who could do better than he had. And now, in Will, she had found him.

Crazy, crazy love. It hits pell-mell, and those struck are helpless against the blows. What a sweet fight.

It was a gentle autumn night under Napa's stars, and kind enough to take a long time to become morning.

ACKNOWLEDGMENTS

Napa Valley is a gorgeous spot, and it's easy labor to research a novel there. Between the stunning vistas and the fabulous food and wine, it was hard not to spend *all* my time researching.

Several people very generously shared their time and expertise, and I could not have written this novel without them: Cathy Corison of Corison Wines, Dawnine Dyer of Dyer Vineyard, Sarah Gott of Quintessa and Joel Gott Wines, and Michael Honig of Honig Vineyard and Winery. Great thanks as well to Kim Getto of the Napa Valley Vintners Association, Jon Lovie of the California Department of Forestry and Fire Prevention, Lance Miceli of the Napa Wine Company, Healdsburg resident Joyce Chang, Napa resident Richard Chen, and San Francisco residents Ginny Hoover and Andrea Rockers.

Dr. Paul Robiolio of the Heart Health Center in St. Louis, Missouri, came through yet again! And a big thank-you to title-meister Bill Meehan, whose name would be on this book's jacket if it had one.

My critique partners were brilliant: winery-namer Tracie Donnell, Bill Fuller, Sarah Manyika, and Ciji Ware. Many special thanks to Jen Jahner and Audrey

LaFehr, and to my wonderful agent, Maureen Walters. And I am very appreciative of the support and insight of my editor, Claire Zion, and everyone at New American Library who helped make this book a reality.

And, as ever, my deepest gratitude, and my heart, belong to Jed.

San Francisco, California
October 2003

Diana Dempsey

Catch the Moon

"A real page-turner! Swift, smart, romantic, and wonderfully satisfying."
–Mary Jo Putney

Thirty-something beauty Alicia Maldonado has become Monterey County's star prosecuter. But now her career has stalled—and her alleged love life is in dire need of resuscitation. When a local millionaire is found murdered, Alicia won't let anything jeopardize the case—not even the distractingly handsome news reporter whose interest in her investigation is more than professional.

"Fun and feisty." –Jane Heller

0-451-20945-1

Available wherever books are sold or to order call 1-800-788-6262

Diana Dempsey

FALLING
STAR

"Clever and glamorous." —Jayne Ann Krentz

Meet anchorwoman Natalie Daniels. the
prime-time anchor for KXLA who is on the
verge of her fortieth birthday.

Meet, Tony Scoppio, her boss, who is focusing
on Natalie's sizeable salary and is scheming to
replace her. To make matters worse, her
husband just dumped her and now she's
hopelessly in love with a man who's
engaged to another.

What's a woman like Natalie to do—especially
in Los Angeles, a city already known for shaky
foundations? How about teaching them all a
lesson in success and revenge?

0-451-41035-1

Available wherever books are sold, or
to order call: 1-800-788-6262